# The Crystal Blades

# ASSASSINS

Chris Oliva and Laura Oliva

An Original Publication From Valshan Creations


The Crystal Blades: Assassins
Written and published by Chris Oliva & Laura Oliva
Formatted by Frostbite Publishing
Copyright © 2016 by Chris Oliva & Laura Oliva
All rights reserved.


\*\*\*

\*\*\*


ISBN-13: 978-1537527291
ISBN-10: 1537527290

*To my wife for never calling me Mad as a Hatter for wanting to do this. For my friends who have helped me along the way. It would take a book to name you all.*

*To Laura for pulling me along when I started to waiver and for being the drill sergeant when necessary.*

-Chris Oliva

*In memory of my brother Adam, who had such faith in me that he shared my work with his buddies overseas. I wish you were here to share this with me now.*

*My thanks to my family who put up with this insanity all these years, to Erskine for helping me see it to completion, and to my nephew Chris for sharing his world, making this possible.*

-Laura Ann Oliva

# The Crystal Blades

# ASSASSINS

# Chapter One
## Assassins

*Why?* It was a deceptively simple question. Artearis Berain shoved his appointment book back across the desk and leaned back in his chair. *By Ashlemar, why could so many people want others dead?* He was an assassin, and he didn't understand it. *Why had fate cursed him to be born into an assassin's life?*

He leaned forward over the desk and pulled the book closer. Scanning the page, he realized just how busy tomorrow would be. *It was a good thing that the human race was able to multiply as fast as it did; otherwise, the only humans that would be around would be the Assassins Guild.* He flipped the page back to today's date and found only one noteworthy appointment. The considerable Duke of

Sitar, Jekan Geylas, demanded an audience. Everything else was routine: inspect the initiates, observe the circles, check the supply levels, etc.

Artearis's eyes went to one of the ornate display cases that partially obstructed the path to his massive desk. Inside was a particularly striking silver medallion in the likeness of a raised dragon. One of his ancestors had received it as payment from another Duke of Sitar ages ago. Most of what adorned this room was payment for services rendered by the Assassins Guild. Artearis was particularly fond of the tapestry that covered the left wall in front of him, a cleverly woven scene of the sea that glittered and changed with the flickering of the candles that covered his study.

He liked the room best when his servant was late changing the candles and the third part burned out, creating an artificial sunset for the tapestry. As the light in the room began to fade, it seemed the tapestry came alive. Only then could he clearly see the city glistening on the distant hills of a large snake-shaped island. If enough candles died out, he could even see the path the sun would burn on the water, and if he was daring enough, he could follow that path into those hills before darkness smothered the way.

Artearis wasn't sure which troubled him more, the deception of darkness or the tyranny of light. He had to put up with that tyranny every day, for this room held enough candles to brighten a king's banquet hall. Candlelight couldn't be helped because the room lacked windows. He would have preferred a window view to observe the comings and goings of the people of Ionen, but Artearis was forced to agree with one of those distant ancestors who decided against having the head of the guild living anywhere other than the center of the complex, above the ground floor, away from exterior walls.

Windows did only one thing for people in this profession — allow the next member of the family to be promoted. While no windows did provide a measure of safety for those in this "exalted" position, it also made the room damn near unbearable. Cleverly concealed ventilation failed to relieve the stuffiness or get rid of the heat, and day or night, an escape from the light rarely presented itself. And the firefern wood. Nearly everything in the study was made of the costly dark auburn wood because firefern didn't burn.

Besides the tapestry, not much in the crowded study earned his attention. The gold leaf books lining the outer wall were useful for training only. Few members of the family had taken an interest in any subjects but thievery and combat. Richly carved chests of inlaid jewels and gold etchings sat against the wall bearing the door — not to mention the small chest weighing down the corner of his desk. All this wealth was supposed to overawe clients. Only one door provided access — one entrance to keep an eye on. Unfortunately for Artearis, he couldn't maintain his view of the door while he actively admired the one collection in his prison that made inhabiting it bearable — a wall case display of finely crafted weapons. He wanted to fling open the case and run his fingers lovingly down the ivory-bladed swords that hung mid-center.

The blades had belonged to the Master Bladespinner, Darethan Berain. Instead of gems, fine tracings of silver and gold laced up and down the handles to allow a solid, balanced grip. Darethan had supposedly possessed an even finer set of blades. Artearis sighed. The Crystal Blades were only a legend, an elusive myth, like so many other myths that floated around Corellith. It was also said that Darethan possessed a fine sense of honor — that he had not been an assassin. Another myth?

Artearis knew there had to be something special about the Master Bladespinner and his swords. He had dared to take the blades out of the case once — before his father's death. The handles had fit his hands perfectly, and the blades possessed an unnatural balance and something else. A strange but noble sensation had passed from each handle to his hands, something beyond his reach to explain.

Rising from his chair, he sighed again. Most of what he wanted out of life was beyond his reach. Artearis stepped in front of the full-length mirror hanging next to the weapon case. It would not do to look like a vagabond when he met his "esteemed" guest later. Artearis grimaced at the sight of his washed out complexion. If it weren't for the intensity of his blue eyes, he could pass for one of the corpses the Guild smuggled out of here. He missed that brief time in his life when his high cheekbones and aristocratic nose sported a glorious tan. Had it really been eleven summers since the sun had bleached his shoulder length hair nearly white? He should have run away with the circus that spring before he turned fifteen, but he would never have been able to run away from the mark on his hand.

Artearis smoothed his hand down the functional yet elegant uniform reflected in the mirror. Black trousers were tucked neatly into calf length soft leather boots — boots almost as good as those made by elves. The gray shirt might be skin-tight, but it stretched with his movements and fit well under the blood red trimmed outer vest. As with all other things associated with the Assassins Guild, this tunic held a few surprises. He had paid handsomely to have smuggled mithril chain mail woven between the layers of fabric. Several of his tunics, created this way, made it easier to get around without being conspicuous, a small price to pay for his life.

He wanted to scream. *Of all the places and families why did I have to be born into this one? Had I really done that much wrong in a prior life?*

Artearis threaded his way through the strategically

scattered opulence to the display case. "We must have started out a good family, now look at us — assassins to the depths of our souls," he muttered under his breath, condemned because of a stupid fight between his narcissistic, mage talented namesake and that pompous bastard from the Ashrick family. Artearis rubbed the mark embedded in the back of his hand. During the transition of puberty, every male Berain developed the mark — a sword and dagger, the Berain coat of arms, hovering over the Ashrick dove in flight, with a circle forming around both. The curse would not be lifted until the spelled circle was complete, signifying that only one bloodline remained. Until then no Berain would be free to choose his own destiny. *How could someone mercilessly condemn his entire line for over 500 years?*

Generations had been at the task of eliminating Ashricks. Artearis examined the ring. A fractional gap still existed. His father had been one of the most ruthless, ferreting out and destroying the last family tree — but not the last one.

Artearis slammed the flat of his hand against the glass case. "I've destroyed all but one," his father had snarled from his deathbed. "I expect you to take care of the last. Kill the infant that was spirited away by magic. Finish this!"

*Right, father. Find a female two years my junior who has no apparent family, no known description, no whisper of existence, no clue at all except a birthmark, a closed rose.*

14

*A birthmark, father, placed so high on her upper right thigh that I'll never be able to see it unless I sneak into every bath house in Corellith — IF I can manage to be there when she is. Guild training can only take me so far, father. How can I do what you couldn't?*

Artearis shook himself loose from the specter. He had work to do. Steeling his face into an emotionless mask, he stepped into the hallway. He couldn't put off training inspection any longer. Since taking over the Guild from his father, he had felt compelled to take a personal interest in the training of new recruits. Why, he had no clue. Maybe, he felt more responsibility for others than that bastard who placed this damn curse on the family or the barbarians who designed this ungodly training regime.

Material gain smothered Artearis as he walked through the upper hallway — its walls lined with expensive paintings and pedestals of exquisite sculpture. The Guild itself had only been around for about 350 years. One of his ancestors, an opportunist, had figured out how to turn curse into profit. So the Berains stopped hunting only the one family and started taking on other jobs, training non-family members in death. After that the Guild became very successful. And all that success came back to the Berain family. The Guild's training was cruel at best but extremely effective. It hadn't taken the family long to become strong enough to intimidate the most established nobles.

Even worse than the opulence surrounding Artearis was the constant presence of the two guards who had saluted then flanked him when he exited his office. Artearis's fingers crept to the sickly green jewel he wore around his neck. If they knew the truth would they be so obedient? He would prefer not to test that supposed link of loyalty with Haydrim. The black-haired guard flanking his right had been a soldier until he'd been caught standing over his commander's body — his hand still on the sword piercing the officer's chest. Haydrim had killed two other soldiers while fleeing, breaking one man's neck and stabbing the other in the abdomen with a dagger. The man had come to the Guild to disappear. Haydrim had not nor would ever have been Artearis's choice for a bodyguard. The pretend noble was too full of himself to be a trustworthy companion. Artearis felt the only protection he had against Haydrim turning on him was the soul-link that bound his blood guards.

Artearis briefly studied the reflections of the three in the tall mirror hanging at the end of the corridor. Haydrim swaggered as he strode down the hall, his face an expression of contempt; contempt toward Artearis wouldn't surprise him. The cruel and vindictive streak Cresten Berain possessed was unleashed mercilessly on the son that had failed to measure up to his heartless expectations. Haydrim made the sort of bodyguard his father knew Artearis would abhor, unlike Daric.

The well-built guard flanking his left matched Artearis's stride in true military discipline even though the blood guard had never served. Daric fit well an assassin's profile. Brown hair and brown eyes made Daric look commonplace — able to blend easily in most settings. Well-muscled as all laborers were with the deeply tanned and weathered skin of an outdoors man added to Daric's appeal as an assassin, unlike Haydrim's sallow complexion that easily branded him as such, yet Daric possessed a finesse that could be mistaken for breeding and one other quality rarely found in the guild. In assassin's garb, Daric looked like any other assassin. Only a select few knew Daric was a woman.

Daric had come to the Guild to avenge the deaths of her merchant parents and brothers, murdered by a rival merchant while she had been away selling her father's wares. Artearis suspected that unresolved justice brought Daric to the Guild just as he could sense that Daric possessed exceptional intelligence and honor — two qualities his father would never have intentionally allowed in a Berain blood guard. Daric's skill must have impressed his father greatly to be selected, especially with only a year of active service to her credit before being selected. Yes, Daric was a bodyguard Artearis sensed he could trust with his life — possibly his father's only mistake beside not killing his eldest son.

# Chapter Two
## Initiations

Haydrim watched as their *leader* inspected the isolation rooms. His right hand flexed repeatedly around the hilt of his sword. He wanted desperately to run his blade through these social rejects. So what if they didn't like the life destined to them. Not one possessed the real streak of blood thirst essential for a *true* assassin. To Haydrim's mind the six occupied cells represented wasted resources, time, and space. The only potential success should *never* have been allowed entry to begin with. Women might make adequate fronts or instructors, but they were worthless as assassins.

Digging his fist into the side of his leg in anger, Haydrim wondered how the Guild had fallen so far. More undesirables petitioned each year, and unlike Artearis's father who had dismissed most out of hand, Artearis gave serious consideration to them all. Artearis had even rejected some very worthy, bloodthirsty candidates in favor of those like the failures in the cells. Was the imbecile trying to destroy the Guild from the inside? How could its leadership have fallen into the hands of a fool — no, not just a fool but a fool and a cheat? So what if he had brutally murdered that family on his first guild assignment. Cresten Berain should have cut down the boy as soon as it was clear he had been sneaking out of his cell during initiation.

Haydrim vividly remembered the anger of the old guild master, Artearis's father. "Someone must be helping the boy sneak out of his cell. No one can make it through three years of isolation without breaking down at least once." Who had the boy bribed to smuggle him out of his cell? Cresten had doubled the watch on Artearis. He'd even toyed with the idea of adding another year to Artearis's initiation. Without proof, however, even the guild master would have had a hard time selling that idea. Any hint of imperfection or weakness could damage the Guild's position, especially when it reflected on the future guild leader. If Haydrim had been in charge, he would have quietly dispatched Artearis — end of problem.

Haydrim peered through the magical one-way window. He knew from personal experience that the cell occupant had no way of knowing he was being watched. The four walls of the ten-by-ten cell looked blank from the inside. Excrement littered the entire cell, Haydrim noted with disgust. Food trays had piled up except near the slot. At least the server had had enough sense to remove the ones in reach before leaving a new tray.

"This one's gone," he heard Artearis say. "Order the cleanup detail to dispose of the body and prepare the cell for a new initiate. Send it to the current graveyard."

It took Haydrim a few moments to locate the pathetic wreck who had wasted three and a half years of cell space. The wretch had stripped himself bare, dead body covered with old bruises and unhealed teeth marks. It even looked like he had tried to chew off his left wrist. Good riddance to that candidate.

Haydrim shuffled behind Artearis to the next occupied cell. His grip tightened around the hilt of his sword until the knuckles turned white. The cell held a too tall woman with too bright red hair and a way too muscular body. He caught a glimpse of admiration flash across Artearis's face when Haydrim turned his head. The woman probably wouldn't even make a good courtesan. Oh, she was more than attractive enough. She was just that type who never knew her place and would want to dominate the affair. That she was here, where women didn't belong, proved his point. If he had been guild leader, he would have killed any woman who had come to the Guild looking for work. He wouldn't care how skilled she appeared to be or how many extended push-ups she could do. Haydrim glanced at the chart on the wall — three moons left. Too bad she was likely to survive initiation. He took one last look as they started moving away. Her almond-shaped green eyes seemed to stare into his black ones. The sensation sent a chill along his spine. Haydrim definitely didn't trust that one.

As they came up to the last occupied cell, he looked over Artearis's shoulder at the wretch in that room. The thing appeared to be begging and pleading to be let out. More wasted space and time. Why didn't Artearis do something sensible and get rid of him now?

Frustrated, Haydrim said, "Sir, aren't you going to do something about him?"

Artearis didn't even turn. "Like what? Break training? Hold his hand? Drug him and send him to an asylum? Add another unexplainable body to an overly full dumping ground without seeing if the man will recover from the breakdown? Should we have ended your assassin's career when you went over the edge, Haydrim?"

Haydrim's hands tightened reflexively on the hilts of his blades. For a moment he saw nothing but a red film in front of his eyes. In that moment he wanted to run his blade through his *master*. He clenched his teeth together. *How could the guild master even compare this nobody with himself? How could he **spare** this pathetic thing?! What a* *fool! Why not just hack up the body and throw it out with the garbage? It would eliminate the waste and solve the graveyard problem. If not for this cursed soul-link....*

Two servants holding trays approached the inspection party.

"Excuse us, master. It's time to feed *this* initiate."

Haydrim remained as he was with hands on weapons while Daric backed down the corridor a few steps. Artearis shifted his footing enough to allow the servant to push the tray through the hinged door. The tray had almost disappeared into the room when it was jerked out of the servant's hand and shoved back into the hallway, catching Artearis off guard. He recovered instantly but not before Haydrim had slammed his palm on the door release button and jumped into the room, blades drawn. A slash of Haydrim's dagger to the throat and a sword thrust to the stomach ended any possible threat from the deranged initiate. Haydrim reveled in the blood that splashed over him.

"What in the hells?" Artearis shouted.

A surprised Haydrim turned toward his master. Emotion? Haydrim's eyes sought the jewel around Artearis's neck. It glowed a sickly green. Haydrim watched as Artearis reflexively brought his right hand up to enclose the jewel. The sickly green light began to pulse. Suddenly, Haydrim's stomach began to churn. The light pulsed faster. Haydrim dropped his weapons as he doubled over and began to wretch furiously.

"No one dies without my approval, Haydrim."

No shred of emotion touched those words.

"Daric, help Haydrim up. I have the circles to inspect yet."

Haydrim shakily stood up and collected his weapons. The green jewel had a sickly glow but remained steady. If it weren't for that soul-link, Haydrim would gladly kill this man.

The feel of death broke Sharaya's concentration. She knew she had been watched a short time ago. She could feel it just as she would if someone pinched her. She knew who watched her, too. Guard Daric always confounded her readings, but Haydrim's feelings of hatred screamed into her consciousness. He was in a dangerous mood today — and careless. Haydrim had let his heightened anger drive him to recklessness. He had killed. His emotions swirled through anger and hatred and fear and surprise. They were so strong Sharaya had a hard time focusing on the object of interest to both.

Sharaya did her best to shut out Haydrim's storm and concentrated on the feeling of dread of her appointed assignment. The council had left her in place when they realized Artearis was different from his predecessors. Somehow, Artearis had gone through the fifth circle of assassin training and retained some level of emotion — not the sham that previous Berains presented to the world. Even as proficient a thought sensor as Sharaya could not define for the council the depth of Artearis's emotions. If he had full use of them, he also had considerable control. That control must have slipped, for Sharaya knew the object of most of Haydrim's torment was the guild master.

Sharaya, herself, could feel the pulse of dread lightly beating beneath Artearis's conscious thought. At first, she believed the source of the dread was Haydrim. As Sharaya searched that part of his mind accessible to thought sensors, she realized the source came from an entirely different perception — the dread of killing children. Coming from an assassin, the sensation puzzled Sharaya. She needed to understand the implications. She needed to stretch her senses to observe the rest of his activities today. It would have been easier if she had already finished her initiation phase.

Still, the council and her uncle would need to know. Events were moving in the world. Serastus would be striking soon. They needed to find the heir to the blades, and Artearis was the only Berain alive to have finished his training who had mastered the blade spinning skill. Time was slipping away.

Daric watched as Haydrim's face alternated from a stony expression to one of absolute contempt for Artearis. She knew who Haydrim was. Daric had heard of the man just after he had been indoctrinated into the Guild and had made a point of investigating him. Changing the name hadn't changed the description of the wanted man or what he was capable of doing. Daric watched the two men as Artearis inspected the cells. No matter what else happened, Daric had to make sure that Artearis lived. Fedoral was going to need him, and very soon.

# Chapter Three
## The Circles

The trio exited the stairs into the true heart of the school. Artearis inwardly raged at Haydrim's uncontrollable behavior. He'd have seen the man put into the same dumping ground as his victim if Haydrim hadn't been necessary to hide the deception Artearis performed during the fifth circle. Artearis could feel that the victim had almost reached his turning point. That one would have been able to piece himself back together.

Artearis inwardly shuddered at the memory of his own four years in the initiation cell. He had come so close to losing his identity. Sometimes when he inspected the initiates, he felt like he had cheated to survive the initiation process. Born into the Berain family, Artearis learned at a young age what he would have to endure, and he had prepared. Thankfully, people like Marte, had been willing to help him, although no guild member had been able to save him from the monstrosity of the fifth circle. To save his soul from the curse's spell, Artearis had been forced to discover his own solution.

The mage might have been a bumbling fool, but he had possessed true power. Artearis could vaguely feel the fear creep through his veins as he remembered sneaking out of the guild compound that lightless night and carefully breaking into the mage's home. The mage was gone, but the feel of magic had made Artearis sweat. Even now he could feel his hand flinch away from the power radiating from the spell book he needed to read. The spell seemed simple enough — a light spell to put a glow into the jewel his father would give him. He had heard the mage utter the thing at a merchant's stand one day and saw the gem the mage held glow dimly, almost sickly. The mage had frowned in frustration and uttered another spell to remove the inner light. The sing-song rhythm of the spell stayed with Artearis, but the words had eluded him. That was why he broke into the house — to learn the words. For months after, he bought or stole cheap gems and practiced applying the spell to each.

The effort convinced Artearis he was never meant to be a magic user. It took weeks to get the first gem to show a candle wisp of light. Even after weeks of practice, he had not been able to create a glow strong enough to be believable. And to add to the problem, Artearis could not dispel the weak glow from the gems, so he had to find a way to destroy them to hide the evidence. He refused to give up, however. The rest of his life depended on his ability to cast that spell believably. He was not going to walk out of that fifth circle a hate machine. He only regretted that he couldn't save his brother from the same fate, but the Zotearis that survived the initiation phase of assassin training possessed a dark aura and a ruthless face — not someone with whom Artearis felt he could share such a deadly secret.

Morgan's shrill aristocratic voice intruded on Artearis's reverie. The first circle instructor's tone carried more authority than usual, today. Artearis entered the circular training room door and stopped immediately. Someone had erected a scaffolding platform between the back wall and the center of the circle. The benches that weren't actually carved from the walls were arranged about the platform. One table and pair of benches sat in front of the scaffolding. Four students sat at the judgment table — two on each side of an empty chair. Artearis raised his left eyebrow. One fledgling, standing at the far end of the platform, wore a hood. Two others flanked a third at the base of the stairs leading up to the top of the scaffolding. Holding a piece of parchment, Morgan mounted the scaffolding. The rest stood around as if they were a milling crowd. Artearis looked closer at the young man being escorted up the erected staircase. Beads of sweat glistened from the harsh glare of the oil lamps placed every ten feet along the walls. Their flickering tongues cast a surreal pattern along the floor and scaffolding base.

Artearis stepped farther into the room.

"Mikal, bring the sign you made to the charge stand," Morgan instructed. The trainee lugged a large wooden board to a tripod fixture in front of the platform. He grabbed it firmly by both sides and set it in place. The words "CONVICTED ASSASSAN" were painted in huge red letters.

"Mikal, you spelled assassin wrong. Two weeks extra writing duty."

Morgan turned to the three students waiting at the base of the stairs. In a voice that sounded suspiciously like glee to Artearis, he said, "Bring up the prisoner."

Artearis watched the two escorts shove their companion up the stairs and to the center of the platform.

"Callum, drop the rope." The hooded student shuffled to a lever running through the flooring and pulled it forward. "Place the noose around the criminal's neck." Morgan watched as Callum yanked the rope down more and set the noose. Callum returned to his place beside the lever.

"Yes, that is it precisely," Morgan said as he left the platform for the waiting chair. He handed the parchment to the female student to his right. "Catherine, read the charges."

With those words, two spectators picked up drums from the floor and began to beat on them slowly.

Catherine cleared her throat and began to read. "Be it known. After due deliberation, this tribunal finds Perkin Slazin guilty of being an assassin. In accordance with kingdom law, the punishment for anyone caught practicing the terrible deed of assassination shall be hung by the neck until dead. Then his body dismembered and posted as a warning to all. There is no reprieve, no last words."

Morgan nodded his head in approval and swiftly, almost savagely, banged the gavel down onto the table.

Artearis watched as Callum snapped the lever in the opposite direction. This time the rope lifted upward with a rush, then a jerk, as it caught the weight of Perkin's body. Whoever had designed the construction had done so efficiently. Before the prisoner had time to complete a gasp of disbelief, the rope had yanked him off the flooring and broken the poor soul's neck.

"Callum, escorts, finish the sentence."

Artearis watched the three stand there hesitantly, still stunned by the results of the little drama.

"One hundred lashes to anyone who doesn't help finish the sentence," Morgan growled, his voice impatient.

No one moved.

Artearis watched as Morgan's face began to turn red.

Suddenly a bench crashed to the ground, and

Catherine marched around the table and up the stairs, drawing a sword. Artearis finally noticed that all of the students except Perkin had swords. Why had Morgan broken protocol?

The young woman walked up to the swinging body, looked the corpse in the eye, and hacked off his swinging left hand. In an unladylike manner that belied her cultured appearance, Catherine then spit on the fallen hand and said, "that's what happens to liars and cheats within the Guild."

Artearis could not help notice that some of the students looked his way before following Catherine's example, drawing their swords as they mounted the stairs then hacking off pieces of the unfortunate student. Morgan, himself, hacked the body from the head and watched in satisfaction as both crashed to the bloody platform.

"This is what failure looks like," Morgan announced to his class.

Callum pulled off his hood, threw it down beside the body, jumped off the platform, and brushed past Artearis into the tunnel. His face had a sickened expression that matched the disgust Artearis felt. Unfortunately, Morgan's statement was all too true. Failure out in Ionen, and even Torenium, could easily end as Perkin Slazin had.

At twelve, Artearis had watched a similar proceeding in the market square of Ionen. The man, dressed as a baker, was dragged to a permanent scaffold, hanged, and relieved of his hands. His butcher had held up the left hand to display to the crowd the assassin's mark burned into it. That day Artearis had realized how truly he had been boxed into the life of an assassin.

The knowledge didn't stop the disgust Artearis felt for Morgan's drama. Guild policy was swift and silent removal of failed candidates not open execution. Still, to confront Morgan here could undermine the instructor's authority, and even though Artearis would personally love to make Morgan's life miserable, it would hurt the Guild, and the Guild was Artearis's responsibility. Artearis took one last look at the bloodshed before moving to the door.

Throughout the whole disgusting drama, Daric kept her face expressionless. Morgan had taken the lesson much farther than necessary. Artearis, however, had been right to leave without confronting the first circle instructor. A worthy leader never undermined his subordinates unless the situation was untenable. Morgan's lesson, although extreme, mirrored reality. Daric had heard Morgan tell Artearis weeks before that Slazin wasn't guild material — that he would have to be disposed of soon. Morgan's patience must have run out. Daric wondered how much patience Artearis had left for Morgan.

As Haydrim passed her to take up his position beside Artearis, Daric noticed how unhappy Haydrim was with the drama, or was it with Artearis's lack of response? Daric watched Haydrim open his mouth to speak to the guild master before Artearis turned to exit the room. She saw how quickly Haydrim snapped his jaw shut when Artearis moved his hand up to the green jewel at his neck. *Interesting — what had happened back at the initiate's cell to cause Haydrim to puke like that?*

Daric wanted to let herself gloat just a fraction but knew she couldn't afford the luxury. Haydrim had no business being a blood guard. Haydrim had no business being alive at all. He had disobeyed orders that got a lot of good soldiers killed, and he had the nerve to put a sword through his commanding officer for insisting on accountability. The man deserved a fate worse than that kid on the platform. Yet, Daric couldn't touch him, not here, not now. Daric realized she couldn't extract justice ever, not if the action would backlash through the soul-link to Artearis. The young guild master was too important to the cause.

As they approached the second circle, Daric could hear the distant sound of Leyana's voice instructing her students in the art of stealth. Guild training difficulty escalated dramatically in this circle. Stealth took patience and practice — two things most raw recruits lacked. From the empty circle, Daric knew today Leyana had her pupils practicing in the halls of hell; at least, that's what Daric's class of trainees called them. The task was simple. Enter the tunnels at point A and exit them at point B. They only needed to avoid the traps set to ward off intruders, the surprises Leyana personally set, and each other. Survival took quick wits and intelligence — again two things most trainees seemed to lack. The benefit was that the one who took down the most competitors AND made it out gained special privileges until the next session in hell. In the extreme cases of failure, even the bloody mess of poor Slazin didn't exist, as a student two years before never had a chance to learn. Leyana had lightened up on her traps just a bit after the unfortunate incident. Daric didn't envy Leyana's cadets.

Artearis approached the group crowded into the southern tunnel, watching them observe Leyana's deft movements. Daric had to admit the second circle instructor easily turned a male eye. She pitied anyone who only saw Leyana's looks. Out of curiosity, Daric glanced at her counterpart. The light from the circular room illuminated Haydrim's face enough for Daric to see the contempt on it. Oh, what she would have given to have had Haydrim train under the newest guild instructor. Daric could just see Haydrim haughtily stalking through the tunnels during his trial, wooden blade in hand. Overconfident of his ability against a female instructor, Haydrim would have ended everyone's headaches by being skewered on the blade of this deadly thief turned teacher. Oh well, Daric could fantasize.

Artearis observed long enough to watch three candidates fail to execute the movements to Leyana's satisfaction before continuing on to the third circle. Normally, Artearis walked an indirect route to acrobat training, but not today. Daric followed Artearis past the students, through the first intersection, and right at the next, before heading left into the huge circular training ground controlled by Marte.

Daric had to admit that of all the instructors she had trained under, no one had been as unmerciful or as deserving of respect as the instructor of the third circle. Marte WAS the third circle of acrobatic training, even if he was no assassin. The former circus performer knew how to refine the body's ability to move gracefully, effortlessly, in unexpected and incomprehensible ways — lessons his current students were feeling with force if the grunts and groans about the room indicated anything. The sounds of human bodies slapping against rock brought shadows of aches to Daric's own backside.

She might be military trained, but Daric had to admit, she only survived the test of the third circle through brute force and intellect. To face down the five hired thugs for the twenty-minute assessment period, Daric had used a "divide and conquer" strategy, physically disabling each isolated man. Daric was sincerely sorry for breaking Lorr's arm. She hadn't meant to use that much pressure when she struck the young thug. The attack on Revlin was another matter. The bastard had already removed an ear from one tester and two fingers from another — casualties of war — once removed he would back out of reach of his opponent, dangling the severed parts in the air. He'd laugh and point to the trophy then hold it over his head and drop it in his mouth and start chewing.

Revlin still had one of those fingers when Daric began her test. Lorr went down quickly with a vicious kick to his arm. Patiently, Daric worked the remaining opponents over to the bottleneck between the ring bands and the vaults, tripping one into the tangle of rope and gear piled to the side of the rings and catching another fully in the groin as he tried a roll and sideswipe maneuver. Daric slid along one vault horse, running her hand along the base until she could feel a break. She lifted both hands to the horse, pushing her body up and over the padded back and swinging her legs around to slam Revlin square in the chest. Daric stayed with the motion to land on her feet; then she reached down, grabbed the finger from Revlin's shirt pocket, and rammed the bloody thing down his miserable throat. Daric didn't have a chance to watch Revlin struggle for breath. Another thug jumped from the ring mount to try the same kind of maneuver on her. Daric clotheslined the thug in midair then darted past the vault horse to the center of the room, drawing her last opponent to ground of her choosing.

Marte wore the same impassive look on his face when Daric finished her test as he did today. The wiry old man beckoned to Artearis. When Haydrim and Daric began to follow him toward Marte, Artearis waved them off. Daric could see Marte pointing at two different students as he said something to the guild master in a quiet voice. Artearis arched his left eyebrow, but said nothing. Daric could see Marte make several more gestures with his hands. This brought a shake of the head from Artearis. Marte looked Artearis up and down thoughtfully then turned away. Artearis turned back to his blood guards.

The trio left through the west entrance at a quick pace. They hadn't covered half the distance to the fourth circle before Daric could hear the clang of steel on steel. The clashes came too close together for Creegen to be instructing in pole arms. It had to be Jastis with the sword and dagger. Then Daric heard the whirring sound. That could only mean Zotearis. Daric refrained from shaking her head at the thought. All third circle graduates trained against multiple fighting styles, including sword and dagger, but only Berains trained against their own weapon style. Ages before, the kingdoms had outlawed bladespinning in an attempt to destroy the Guild. The three kings had commanded all instructors of the bladespinning technique to stop teaching it or die. Excellent teachers who refused to give up the deadly art fell to superior numbers or ambushes or treachery until the practice of one-handed curved blade and curved dagger faded from upper Corellith. Only here, in the guild built by the Berains, the bearers of Darethan Berain's legacy, was the ultimate fighting style perpetuated, and only Jastis was competent in instructing in the use of and defense against it.

Of the six instructors that drilled into their pupils, lesson upon lesson, on how to use and counter weapon styles, only Jastis taught multiple fighting styles: for Berains — bladespinning, for everyone else — sword, sword and dagger, two-handed sword, and sword and shield. If Marte was merciless, the long-time veteran assassin turned teacher, Jastis, was his equal in ruthlessness.

Daric, a warrior of weapons, admired the sword and dagger style greatly, but had never become comfortable in its use. *Was it her military training that confounded her hands when she practiced the technique? Was it because sword and dagger was too close to bladespinning, making her feel she was on the border of breaking her sworn duty? Or because, despite her gender, her true preference ran to axe and shield?*

The only students Jastis feared, if you could call prudence fear, were the Berains. Jastis enjoyed his prestige too much to allow a careless tongue to retire him — permanently. Too bad his latest class could jeopardize that security. Artearis's brother had all the fourth circle instructors treading with extreme care, including Jastis.

# Chapter Four
## Basics

Artearis approached the fourth circle with a lighter step. His blood thrilled at the sound of steel sparking against steel. Only here, in this circle where muscle and steel became one, was Artearis able to shake the sense of doom that haunted his days and nights. Many candidates fell to the skill and experience of the weapons masters of this circle, cutting the number of possible graduates sometimes in half. Even a few Berains had failed to hold their own in the ultimate test of bladespinner against bladespinner. Artearis had bested both champions during his final test to become a true guild member and earn his unwanted place of future guild leader.

His step faltered slightly at the memory. His surviving classmates had gone on to the ceremony where they would be branded an assassin and welcomed into the Guild, even if under supervision, he had been directly marched to the fifth circle — the circle of true hell. His hand rose involuntarily to the jewel at his throat before he could consciously stop it.

Artearis slowed his progress even more as an angry voice echoed along the passageway. He wanted to sigh in frustration. *Why couldn't Zotearis accept being a student instead of constantly pulling rank because of his family? How are we going to keep the respect of our members if we don't prove we can take our own training?* Yet, his brother stood defiantly, disrespecting his trainer because HE was born privy to Berain training style. HE was already worthy of guild status.

*Brother, what are you thinking? You build a strong foundation on the basics. You destroy predictability by learning new moves, new ways. You push your skills toward perfection through constant practice.*

Deep inside, Artearis knew these were the traits that set apart a master warrior. These were the traits possessed by Darethan Berain, Master Bladespinner.

"This is a stupid, pointless drill. I am not some *LOWBORN* wannabe fighter who couldn't even tell you the difference between a sword and a morningstar. I'm a Berain. Bred to combat and stealth. I slit my first throat at ten, you halfwit. What do I need basics for? I learned my skill from the best, my father. Your job is to train me for the next level *MASTER!!!*"

Artearis suppressed a gasp of surprise. He only remembered a bright, light-hearted boy with black hair tagging around after him on their adventures in Ionen. *Where had this killer come from?* Then it struck Artearis that this was his father's voice all over again. Stepping into the full brightness of the immense weapons salon, it finally struck Artearis how much his brother looked like their father. Any pleasure Artearis had felt from this sanctuary died — killed by the hate-filled eyes of his worst nightmare. By the gods, why couldn't he escape his father or shed the family's past?

He studied the confrontation before him. Jastis stood facing Zotearis, his left side toward the three men standing at the southern entrance. He held a curved dagger in his left hand, his arm extending to the floor in a relaxed position. The matching sword would be in Jastis's other hand. Zotearis had squared off his stance, his weapons still sheathed. His face was flushed, but the look of hate and loathing in his over bright eyes confirmed Artearis's first impression. Zotearis wanted control of the situation — just like their father.

Artearis was beginning to suspect that Zotearis would continue his terror until he controlled the entire guild or someone put him in his place. Few guild members had the skill to cross swords with a Berain, even a partially indoctrinated one. Even fewer were willing to risk their positions, and so Jastis was backing down. As guild master, Artearis knew he had to put a stop to Zotearis's insubordination before it infected other trainees.

*But, I'm not ready for this. How can I face down my father?* No, not his father Artearis reminded himself as he approached the two men.

"You break training, student Zotearis. No guild candidate is permitted to refuse instruction, regardless of status."

Zotearis snorted, "I know more than these outcast, lowborn wretches you call instructors do."

Artearis arched his left eyebrow. "You do now?"

Zotearis nearly spit. "We are TRUE assassins. We are Berains, not some wannabe lackeys. We were trained by the best — our father."

"And that proves what? That we know everything there is to know about combat?"

Zotearis's eyes narrowed. "You might have failed in your lessons, brother, but I didn't." He drew his blades from their sheaths, shifting to combat stance against Artearis.

Daric began to draw her own sword.

Artearis bit back a sigh. *This is my responsibility.* He caught Daric's arm and looked his blood guard in the eyes.

Daric nodded in understanding and slid the sword back into its scabbard.

Artearis looked at Haydrim still standing in a casual position. He turned away immediately, carefully schooling his face from showing the disgust he felt. The light in his gem began to pulse rapidly. Artearis felt more satisfaction than surprise this time when he heard Haydrim's retching from behind him.

It took all of his will, but Artearis managed to stare into his brother's malignant gaze. "You do know the penalty for drawing your blades outside of instruction?"

Zotearis laughed haughtily. "Weren't you just instructing me — brother?"

Artearis kept his face clear of emotion as he squared off against Zotearis and drew his own weapons. He stood his ground but kept his blades at an easy readiness.

"Come brother," Zotearis goaded. "Instruct me. Show me my imperfections."

Artearis remained at ease, watching the anger inside Zotearis build.

Seconds ticked by, heightening the rage within Zotearis.

"You coward," he screamed. "Give me my birthright." Zotearis attacked, pouring the raging hate into action. He feinted with his sword, following the move with a thrust to

Artearis's eyes with his dagger.

Artearis expected the rash move. He slashed down with his sword — the move Zotearis expected — then leaned back enough to avoid the dagger to the eyes. The combination was a favorite of his father's and prone to off balancing the attacker. It was a childish move Zotearis should not repeat. Artearis spun to the right, raising his sword to intercept a violent slash from his brother's blade. Zotearis continued through the move, feinting an attack with his dagger as he spun around to get behind Artearis. When Zotearis came out of his spin all he found was five feet of air between him and his brother.

Artearis shifted to the offensive. As Zotearis came forward to engage again, Artearis met him with a continual crisscross sweep of blades. The move, when properly executed, confused the eye, making it look as if he used more than two blades. Artearis darted forward and past Zotearis, using his own spin to come at Zotearis from behind while his blades worked what seemed to be a random pattern.

The maneuver set Zotearis off balance. Artearis moved in with dagger low and sword high, hoping to finish the conflict. He let down his caution too soon. Zotearis parried left then dove into a spin out roll. Snapping to his feet directly behind Artearis, he struck.

The move only briefly caught Artearis off guard. No sooner had Zotearis reached his feet than Artearis spun halfway around, sending his sword in a sweep downward to catch his brother's blades. His sword rang loudly against the oncoming weapon but missed deflecting the dagger. Artearis barely managed to use the momentum of his block to spin out of reach. The sound of the dagger point ripping the material of his sleeve broke his concentration.

Zotearis smiled. He sent his own blades spinning, pressing Artearis — his eyes shining with success, his tongue licking his lips in anticipation of the win.

As Artearis circled back around for another series of blows, he saw the unholy glee on his brother's face. His pulse, already pounding with exertion, beat faster still. His brother wanted blood — his blood. Not in a power struggle after he had made rank in the fifth circle, but here, now — where Artearis's death would prove beyond dispute that Zotearis was the true heir of the Guild.

Zotearis used Artearis's hesitation to increase the pressure of his attack, pushing Artearis firmly on the defensive. Zotearis pressed his brother backward two steps then leaped forward, striking down with his sword.

The angle of the oncoming weapon forced Artearis to pull both blades into a high X to catch the blade before it had a chance to slide down one or the other of his blades and disable an arm. Artearis let the momentum push him down, allowing himself to drop into a backward roll then quickly rise to a crouch and thrust his blade into Zotearis's oncoming chest. It was a basic, non-spin thrust to the heart, and it caught Zotearis completely off guard. He stumbled backward to avoid the blow. Again, Artearis used his momentum to propel himself forward and slam his right leg into Zotearis's exposed chest, sending his brother crashing to the stone floor.

Before Zotearis could rise or raise his sword, Artearis stepped on the blade and rested the point of his own sword against the rapidly beating pulse at his brother's neck. Zotearis was forced to yield.

"A rough-necked swordsman's basic move, STUDENT Zotearis," Artearis said, while sheathing his weapons.

He turned to the fourth circle instructor and the audience of students standing behind Jastis in amazement. "Carry on, Jastis. My lesson is over."

Despite the gnawing fear in his stomach, Artearis's voice held the full authority of a commander. He was one of the best swordsmen to graduate the fourth circle in decades. He knew it was not because of pride or arrogance but because he had put his heart into learning sword work. He worried that his passion blinded him to his own imperfections.

Artearis didn't bother to examine his brother's expression. He already knew that belligerent wrath would be there. He motioned to his blood guards and exited through the north passageway. Inspection was over.

Haydrim followed the fight with whetted anticipation. He wanted Artearis dead, and Zotearis looked to be the one to give him his desire. Haydrim caught a flash of green as Artearis spun out of his brother's reach. Everything was perfect except for that one annoying problem. Haydrim wasn't ready to die.

His eyes followed Zotearis's onslaught. THAT was the brother to whom his soul should have been linked. THAT ruthless execution of will should be leading this guild. Cold, pitiless Zotearis was the true future of the Assassins Guild. Haydrim wished for the favor of some god to sever him from this accursed bond and free him to follow a true leader.

# Chapter Five
## Assignments

The carriage jerked upward, throwing Jekan Geylas against the door. He cursed the driver; then for good measure he cursed the Assassins Guild for not maintaining the road. Then he uttered a third curse because he was forced to leave his amply occupied luxurious bed to be here. A grin crossed his face. Mistress Miriem certainly knew how to keep her patrons satisfied. Maybe he should consider enticing the good proprietress to open an inn in Sitar. He stretched his bulk, remembering the satin sheets and silken hair waiting for him. Damn this meddlesome problem.

Everything would have been much easier if he'd had a son more like himself than the boy's mother. His lack of foresight was just another reason Jekan hated the Assassins

Guild. Cresten Berain always planned a failsafe. He had made that royal bitch give him two sons before he had disposed of her — certain that at least one would suit his needs. Jekan had barely been able to stomach bedding his royal burden for one son. Because she was so much younger than him, Jekan considered whether he could get another son out of her still. He shuddered at the thought. Damn this problem.

The carriage tossed him about as it pulled to a stop. "Driver!"

A well-muscled man in footman's livery opened the door. Another one waited on the other side of the opening. Both men turned to follow the Duke once he had shifted his bulk out of the seat. Jekan stretched his back and took a deep breath of fresh air. The ride had put a large crease in his deep blue tunic. Wrinkles ran up and down the matching trousers. He hated this material. He hated closed coaches. They were so smelly and stuffy. He hated being in Ionen. He hated just about everything this afternoon.

Jekan waited by the carriage for someone to announce his presence. He noticed a man lounging in front of the guild door. Jekan began to tap his foot. The man continued to ignore him. Jekan's foot beat faster. The man took something out of his pocket and began to move his arm back and forth.

"What the ...," Jekan exploded. He waved his hand in the direction of his anger. "Go fetch that man."

Jekan watched impatiently while his escort approached the door. The two talked animatedly for a few moments. The man looked over at the Duke and shrugged. The bodyguard spoke again. The Duke thought he saw a look of bother cross the man's face as he turned to open the door. Jekan could vaguely hear voices. His guard's face shifted into a frown. The voices continued, while Jekan stood in the alley with the sun beating down on him. When a bead of sweat rolled down his forehead and into his eye, Jekan exploded again, this time grabbing the carriage door and slamming it shut before propelling his huge girth toward the entrance. "Berain! Berain! Get your bloody self out here, now!"

The voices on the other side of the door continued in the same tone as before.

"Berain!"

A leathered, wiry man with hard eyes stepped through the door. Behind him came four thug-types wielding weapons. Jekan's bodyguard waited warily.

Perspiration seeped from Jekan's armpits as he maneuvered himself to the door.

"Inspection," said the newcomer.

"What?!" Jekan couldn't believe this.

"You want in, you pass inspection. Cutter, pat him down."

One of the thugs stepped forward. He looked like a meat wagon. "Glad to, boss."

Cutter shoved the guard out of his way as if the guard were a toy soldier. The giant thug began rubbing his hands together as he came up to the Duke. "Nice meat you got there," he said, his face grinning. Cutter grabbed the Duke's shoulders and started working his hands down the bulk of muscle turned to flab. "Nothing up his sleeve, boss."

Jekan heard laughter from inside. His fingers began to flex.

"Nuh uh, old boy," Cutter said. With a laugh, he grabbed up the Duke's hands and held them like he was courting a new love. The first man Jekan had seen began to chuckle. The blood drained from the Duke's face. Cutter dropped the hands almost as fast as he had gathered them up then reached out and clutched the Duke's chest before spreading his hands out as if searching for something hidden beneath the tunic. "Hey, boss. This one's almost got enough there to be a good poke." The first man began to titter, but a look from the old assassin silenced him.

Moving his hands down Jekan's sides, Cutter brought out the dagger from its sheath. Cutter handed the mithril-edged blade to the doorman and continued his search. Sliding his hand down to Jekan's crotch, Cutter gave a squeeze. "Hiding anything here? Ooh, guess so," Cutter sniggered as Jekan's trousers began to tighten. "Even got a decent enough package to do the poking. I like him."

This time Jekan heard peals of laughter from the

other side of the door. An unknown voice said "Does he rent out his services?"

"Yea, Cutter. You've been looking for a flame with substance," another rough voice laughed.

Cutter's grin widened. "I have at that." He looked Jekan in the eye. "You sure you don't have something else I can search for? Something that'd require a strip search? No?"

Jekan felt the blood rush into his face.

"Guess he's clean, boss."

The wiry old man stepped back from the entrance.

"Pass, Duke of Sitar."

Jekan's blood pounded in his veins. They knew who he was and still treated him like this? What an outrage! To calm himself, he carefully straightened his tunic and trousers. The movement prompted Cutter to smack his lips together. As Jekan passed Cutter he growled, "Be careful what toys you decide to play with, boy. Sturdy toys can break sturdy boys." He stepped through the doorway.

Cutter dropped his cupped hand to his thigh. "But old toys are broken easy enough, mate."

Jekan's guard put his foot on the sill to follow.

Cutter stepped in front of him. "Not you, mate. Only one dove in this roost at a time." The men in front of Jekan laughed harder — all except one. A brown-haired man dressed in uniform pushed a path through the onlookers and carefully took the Duke's arm, escorting him out of the foyer and down a long hallway.

Jekan wasn't about to thank the well-built thug for saving him from that mob of embarrassment. This guild had grown too full of itself. Give him one legitimate reason and he'd level this place.

Laughter followed Jekan down the hall. Before the sounds died away, a final voice carried the distance — "A good poke if you like rock slugs" — then more laughter and finally silence.

His rescuer's back stiffened, but the man remained silent.

By all the gods, he was one of the most powerful men in Corellith. That bastard of an assassin should have come to him, he inwardly raged, not let his men subject him to such humiliation. Jekan should have forced the guild leader to come to him. *No, Jekan,* he told himself. *This delicate matter requires surprise and secrecy. A Berain in Sitar would raise even more questions than him being in Ionen.*

Jekan followed the guard up a small flight of stairs, down another series of halls, and up another flight of stairs before he felt the first stitch in his side. He stopped, pretending to admire the expensive sculpture strategically placed in the luxurious hall. His escort stopped several paces ahead and waited. Jekan breathed deeply; while his eyes examined the winged mount's delicate feathers. The artist had painstakingly drawn out the tips to give realism to the work. A part of Jekan wanted to "accidentally" bump into the piece of art to make it topple to the ground; the more refined part of him detested the destruction of this beautiful piece. He took another breath and started moving along the hall again.

His rescuer must have caught the sounds of his footfalls, because he proceeded ahead of Jekan, this time at a slower pace. They traversed another set of stairs and another series of hallways before the man stopped in front of an identically dressed assassin with black hair, standing guard at an elegantly paneled door. The second guard marched up to Jekan and began to pat him down.

"Absolutely not again," Jekan bellowed.

His rescuer came to Jekan's aid yet again. "He's been inspected, Haydrim. Let him pass."

Haydrim flashed Daric an angry look that the guard ignored. Daric stepped up to the door and rapped softly.

"Come in, Daric."

Daric opened the door. In a soft yet strong voice, Daric announced, "The Duke has arrived, Sir."

"Send him in."


Daric stepped out of the way to allow the Duke to enter the sanctum.

Artearis leaned forward in his chair. "Yes, Lord

Geylas?"

"Are we alone?"

Artearis waited until the door clicked shut. He waved his hand at the chair in front of him. "What trouble has brought you to Ionen? To my guild? It's not to seek the blessing of the three kings, who I'm certain have no idea you've come to visit."

Lord Jekan Geylas, Duke of Sitar, heaved a sigh of relief as he sank his quivering mass into the chair in front of the assassin's desk. "I'll get right to the point."

"Please do."

Jekan scowled at the interruption. "I am here for a delicate matter that requires immediate, yet discrete, resolution. I know you are aware that the line of succession for the Human crown was broken when Astinus lost his last son in that border skirmish several moons ago. With no direct successor from the King, the crown must designate a royal heir from the extended royal family." Jekan bent forward, his eyes capturing Artearis's. "Of the two ELIGIBLE families that share blood with the royal family, mine is obviously the most acceptable choice to rule."

"However," continued the Duke, "my cousin has used considerable political muscle to enhance the prestige of his family with King Astinus's advisers, and he has used his connections to grow his young son's popularity."

Jekan slammed his meaty fist down on the desk. "I

will not have my son upstaged by my cousin's flimflam tactics."

Artearis continued to hold the Duke's stare. "What," he paused, "does this matter to me?"

Jekan's pale eyes flashed with hatred. "I want you to kill my cousin's son, guild master." Jekan reached out and captured Artearis's forearm resting on the desk. "You, personally!" Jekan could feel Artearis's pulse increase under his hand.

Artearis removed his arm from under Jekan's grip. In a steady voice, Artearis answered, "And what price is worth the life of a child or the future of your son?"

The Duke of Sitar sat back in the chair. "Three thousand gold royals for the speedy end to this problem, Berain. That should be more than enough to satisfy the greed in your blood."

Artearis stared at Jekan, a thoughtful expression on his face. "Yes, my lord Duke, the offer is quite generous — generous enough to ensure a timely solution."

"Good," Jekan responded with pleasure. "Now, how would you ..."

"However," Artearis interrupted, "there is the matter of retaliation against the Guild."

"Five-thousand gold royals. Just do the job quickly and quietly. I need a clear field when I present my son at court on the next festival day. With my son as king, I can assure the Guild silent patronage from the crown."

"That gives me little time to collect information on the boy's location and set up a clean hit."

Jekan began to grow angry again. "My cousin resides in Gessin at that time of year as I'm sure you know. Now, enough of this game. I depart for Sitar in two days. I shall conveniently forget a small chest with half of your payment inside. You can make arrangements with the proprietress, Miriem, to collect it. When I receive confirmation of the boy's death, I will arrange a second chest to be delivered to Miriem. This is not negotiable, Assassin."

Artearis sat back in his chair — his eyes studying Jekan, his right thumb stroking the green gem hanging from his throat — the infamous Berain gem. Jekan Geylas could almost grow to like this cool bastard who had cheated his way out of initiation hell. Almost but not quite. He was still the son of Jekan's hated nemesis — the son of that whore, the stolen betrothed who would have vaulted his issue to kingship without question.

"Know this, Assassin." The Duke's eyes grew hard. "Should our little discussion reach the ears of my cousin or the King OR my son travel to the Capitol to discover he is not the sole candidate in the succession, I will obliterate every member of your guild."

Artearis sat forward. "Remember who you are talking to, Duke. Ask an Ashrick how well the Berains have mastered the art of extermination. IF, you can find one to ask."

"Be careful, Assassin. When your father expressed that same sentiment, I didn't have the base to contest him. Today, I have the funds and the power to track down every one of your cold-blooded killers and have the lot of you hanged and quartered for the murderers you are."

Jekan rose from the chair. "I'll see myself out."

The man disgusted Artearis — made him itch to run both blades through that rubbery hide. The entire political circus disgusted Artearis. To have a rival killed to ensure political victory was abhorrent enough. To target a nine-year-old boy who hadn't even had time to make real friends let alone enemies was barbaric. And for what?

Something this tragic could shatter the peace that the joint rule of elven, dwarven, and human kings had maintained for the better part of two hundred years. Only Novus had declined the joint rulership, but the barbarians kept to themselves and were no threat. This had the feel of a greater plot than to seat a new king, and Jekan had deliberately ensnared the Guild within the conflict. To what end?

The doom that had haunted his footsteps throughout the day confronted Artearis. Declining the job meant undermining the Guild's prestige — a death sentence in itself. To complete the task effectively sealed off any hope he nurtured of escaping an assassin's life.

But how could Artearis do this horrifying deed? How could he kill a child? Only the grisliest of luck had saved his soul from eternal damnation two years ago. Luck would not save him again. He could run, at the cost of his honor, yet the Guild, no his brother, would tear apart Corellith to find him. Killing himself would be even worse. Artearis shuddered at the idea of roaming the planet forever as a wraith. Trapped — trapped in the curse of his family. The hopelessness of his situation seeped deeper into his bones. Would not some god somewhere take pity on him?

# Chapter Six
## Memories

Silence — the crying that had gone on while he waited in the tree no longer disturbed the night air. In its place was the whisper of death. The baby's naked and brutalized body lay on the floor in the center of the room, blood spread out in a pool. Her dead eyes stared up at him. The bright red rattle he had watched her shake earlier in the day was drenched in her blood, as if it were an offering to Kaylei, Goddess of Hate. His gaze was fixed on that little piece of joy turned into a nightmare. The color dissipated from Artearis's face as he remembered thinking it was cruel to let a baby cry so much and how relieved he was when the crying stopped. Now, he wished the crying had never ceased. *No, that wasn't true because the poor thing would still be suffering.* He wished he had investigated the crying himself. *What kind of monster would do this to children?*

Artearis jerked upright. He couldn't move, couldn't breathe. His lungs tried to expel the scream of rage, but some deeper force refused to let it out. He strained his ears. Silence. No feet pounded down the hall in response to a disturbance. He sat on the edge of his bed — his head pounding in his hands. The image of the bloody red rattle hovered before his tired eyes — always there — the child's uncomprehending stare — always accusing him of not rescuing her from her torment. Was the pain in his chest from a scream or from the horror of that night?

Shaking himself, Artearis strained his ears to listen for any sign that he had betrayed his emotions. More than two years had passed, and still, he couldn't escape — no, he had to find a way to purge himself of this nightmare. He pulled on his trousers then reached for his sword and dagger. He had to move — had to DO something. He twisted the handle of the door, paused, listened. The sound of Haydrim snoring faded as the past reached out to him.

No sounds reached his ears — no snoring, no settling noises, no insects, or animals. The silence had an eerie feel to it. He edged the door open and slipped into the hallway, easing the door shut behind him to prevent the window's light from spilling into the hallway. He stopped again to listen — no breathing, no bed creaking from someone turning in his sleep. Artearis ran the floor plan through his head one more time. Lord Fenris's younger brother had the room next to the servant's. The twelve-year-old boy was on the other side of the stairs between the two rooms. The sad little girl's room was across the hall from her brother. The master bedroom was sandwiched between hers and the nursery directly across from Artearis. From where he stood it looked like all the doors were closed. Trap?

Artearis approached the brother's room. He pressed his ear against the door and placed his hands on the wood — no sounds, not even breathing, and no sense of life. He freed his dagger from its scabbard and inched open the door, sliding into the room just to the side of the doorway. The absolute stillness of the man lying on the bed stopped Artearis from completely shutting the door. He moved to the bed. A pool of congealed blood soaked the upper part of the bed clothes. The man's face was rigid. His shoulders, arms, and hands locked by his side. Someone had slit the man's throat from shoulder to shoulder in an efficient stroke that had severed the vocal chords. He had drowned in his own blood as his life spilled out onto the bed. By the state of the body and blood, this man had died a couple of hours past dusk; while Artearis had been biding his time in the tree.

*But how?* From early afternoon onward, he had kept

watch on the house. No one but the family had left and entered again. The guards hadn't even approached the house. Artearis tightened his hand around the dagger hilt. *Had his father lost so much faith in him that he felt the need to send another assassin?*

Artearis shook himself out of the memory. When he had come back from that house, he had not told anyone what had happened there apart from the contract was fulfilled. The family was dead. Word quickly reached the Guild of the condition of the victims. From that time forward, fear met his eyes from other guild members. Only his father had not been surprised. Artearis quickened his pace along the hall to the training area.

"You've done your family proud, son," his father had said. Artearis shuddered as the damning compliment echoed in his head. The Guild's status had reached a new level from that act of barbarism.

The dim light in the hallway barely illuminated the door to the guild training grounds. He stepped through the portal, trying to escape the images of the past. They pulled him back to that night, to that house.

Artearis backed away from the corpse and slipped through the door, leaving the room undisturbed. He turned to the door behind him and put his hand on the knob. A stab of fear entered his mind. *What waited behind this door?* He turned the handle and gently pushed the door inward. Artearis lifted his eyes from the rotating knob to the bed in full view. His hand contracted around the dagger hilt. The bed covers lay in a heap on the floor. On top of them were the shredded remains of the woman's night clothes. The smell of old blood could not mask another familiar odor, but the smell eluded Artearis.

Someone had neatly plunged a knife or dagger into the spot between her breasts and pulled it downward, slicing through breast cartilage, stomach, and abdomen, but stopped just before reaching her womb. The woman's lower abdomen had a slight rise to it as if she had been pregnant. Someone had wiped the blood away from the small mound. He could see traces of spatters the killer had missed. Below the womb, the same knife or dagger had been plunged over and over, creating a bloody pulpy mess of hair and tissue.

Trying not to lose the contents of his stomach, Artearis raised his eyes to the woman's head. Her eyes stared upward in horror. Blood stained her mouth and chin. Her hands were bound to the posts of the bed. Stretched out on the sheet beside her left arm was her tongue. *By the gods, this wasn't an assassination; it was an abomination.* Artearis looked around the room for Fenris's body — no sign of the monster that had done this. His heart raced, the force of it slamming him back to the present.

His feet began to run at the pace of his pulse. He had to run — had to try to out run the nightmare. His feet led the way to the fourth training circle — the weapons room. In front of him was the training rack. He couldn't think. He didn't want to think. His hands chose to do it for him. They grabbed a pair of axe handles. The small axes were used to help a student build wrist and upper body strength and to teach control. He needed control right now. His arms began to slice away at the wooden training log. Curled strips of wood rained down on the floor but couldn't wash away the rage building inside of him, rage that sucked him back to that house.

Artearis detected no sign of the lord of the house, but the door leading to the nursery was wide open. Dread followed Artearis's silent steps. He closed his eyes at the sight before him then quickly reopened them as he realized that he had not seen the killer leave the house. The smell of blood and that other scent were fresher here. The bodies of the four-year-old and the baby were still limp and the deeper pools of blood not yet dried. Each child had had the night clothes ripped to shreds and discarded on the floor. The boy lay on his stomach in the bed. Purple welts laced his back.

As Artearis moved closer, he could see that the killer must have raised the boy's head up and sliced his throat in the same manner as the brother was killed. *But why do it from the back?* The only blood on the bed was near the head and the buttocks of the boy. Artearis couldn't detect any other signs of mutilation, but he wasn't about to turn the body over to find out.

The sob he had been unable to utter that night broke free from his throat now. In frustration, Artearis threw down the axes. Ignoring the clatter as they hit the floor, he stumbled back to the weapon's rack and yanked a two-handed sword from its place. It only took a few swings for him to adjust to the weight and balance of the massive weapon. He brought the sword down on a wooden dummy, shattering the arm. Reversing his swing, he brought the weapon upward, removing the other arm. "How could anyone commit such cruelty?" he raged inwardly.

Rotating the sword to a horizontal position, he drove the blade into the body of the dummy. His arms ached from the shock. With a vicious kick, he tried to dislodge the unyielding sword. His second kick unbalanced him. He hit the ground hard. Artearis fought to control himself, but his mind would only acknowledge the paneled door of the oldest son's room in that house.

Uncaring of the noise it would make, Artearis kicked open the door. He, too, was stripped and laying on his stomach, but the body was almost as stiff as the master's brother. It was likely that he was the second victim. Artearis turned to the last door on the third floor. From behind it he heard sobbing, then a gurgling sigh. Cold rage burned in him at that death sound.

Past and present blurred as a scream built up inside him. Artearis released his hold on sanity. Death — the sadist deserved death. He reached for his own blades and stalked to the center combat ring.

Or was it the door to the girl's bedroom. The butcher was here — Artearis could feel him — and he was going to die — brutally.

Shock — shock immobilized Artearis as he stared in disbelief at the calm man standing next to the bed straightening his pants and shirt. Leaning against the bed was a bloodied sword. Across the coverlet, quickly being enveloped by a puddle of blood was the weapon that had done so much butchering tonight, a mithril-laced dagger with a crimson-studded hilt. Its last victim's eyes shone wide with fear — her clothes hung from her young body in tatters, her throat deeply slashed. The pungent smell of blood and, yes, that was it, semen burned Artearis's lungs. His hands gripped the hilts of his blades so hard that had a normal craftsman made them he may well have snapped them in two.

The master of the house reached for his sword, smearing the handle with the child's blood. Fenris's eyes blazed with fury. "I knew you would come, Assassin. He warned me what he would do if I failed to pay. No one tells me what to do. No one takes from me what is mine. Not him. Not you."

The rage engulfing Artearis cooled into a sheet of ice. He loosened his grip on his blades, relaxed the tension in his arms.

Fenris waved his free hand in the direction of the other rooms. "I am lord here."

Artearis shifted the weight on his legs.

Fenris clenched his jaw in anger. "Because of you, I have lost everything here. Because of you, I will have to start over in some faraway place. Because of you, I will become ... the tragic father who couldn't save his family but managed to kill their ruthless attacker." Fenris charged forward, sword arcing to intersect Artearis's neck.

Artearis easily sidestepped the blow, bringing his sword up high and his dagger down low. He stilled his blades just long enough to register his attacker's next move then shifted his stance slightly to prepare for a downward stroke.

Red rage burst onto the lord's face. "I am the Lord Fenris. I decide who lives and dies in this house. And, you must die!" Fenris pivoted, slashing at Artearis's face.

Artearis parried the blow and locked their blades together. His blue eyes shone metallic in the flickering lamp light.

"They were mine.... My property," Fenris growled. "I can destroy my property if I like." Fenris set up a series of blows in an effort to force Artearis off balance.

Artearis blocked the thrust and spun to the side, bringing his sword down into a block to his abdomen. Sparks flew as their blades clashed. He brought his dagger upward — a feint to the lord's eyes.

Fenris backed away.

The mistake was the opening Artearis had waited for. He spun around, bringing his sword high and his dagger low.

Fenris blocked sword to sword — confident the dagger couldn't reach him.

Artearis immediately changed his momentum and stepped to the left, slicing the dagger across the butcher's ribs.

The injured man stumbled — a grimace of pain covered his face. His hand instinctively gripped his side, leaving his sword hand unprotected.

Artearis neatly brought his own sword down on the exposed wrist. Instantly, he recovered his stance and spun around, sword high. The blow was swift and accurate. Artearis came to rest in the guard position — low crouch, sword up, and dagger down — his eyes fixed on the head coming to a rest under the window. Artearis had fulfilled at least that much of the contract.

# Chapter Seven
## Sanity

Treadon let out a nervous sigh as he let himself into the house. Two weeks gone and the master had given no guidance on how Treadon was supposed to eliminate the threat. Time was running out. Artearis leaves for Gessin about mid-morning tomorrow — then he would be too far for Treadon to reach.

The hiss of shadows made Treadon jump.

A dry voice rasped, "You worry too much, beast. Time cannot help the assassin. Time belongs to me — among other things. You do remember other things, my beast?"

Treadon cleared his throat. Nothing. He tried again, and his throat constricted. He tried to breathe. The air couldn't move past his throat. Treadon nodded his head while praying silently for relief.

"Remember what I say, beast, or lack of air will no longer trouble you. On the floor away from the fire is a sack. Take the sack with you to work in the morning. When Artearis's saddlebags have been prepared, empty the contents of the sack into one of them. Be quick at the task. Be accurate. Do not leave the sack near warmth. Are you clear?"

Treadon could feel consciousness beginning to leave him. He tried to swallow. He tried to take in enough air to say yes. His throat constricted even more. Treadon, his head beginning to pound, nodded again.

"We shall see, beast."

The shadows darkened briefly; then Treadon felt the air rush into his aching lungs. His tormentor had gone.

Only a fraction of Marte's attention was on the hot water he poured into the thick cups holding the cook's special Elim tea. His forehead knotted. The young man slouched across the wooden table, his head collapsed into his shaking hands. Artearis had troubled Marte from the moment he had been born into this twisted circus.

Marte sensed the turmoil playing out inside Artearis's brain. That cursed mage contract two years before nearly destroyed everything. It tormented the boy — no, the young man — and had come close to costing him his secret on multiple occasions. Marte had to get Artearis to talk about it, to get him to release the demons to the light where they belonged. Marte picked up the cups of tea before he failed to control the urge to smash his hand down on the side board and spill the comforting drink. No one could know that the boy never completed the ritual of the fifth circle. If anyone found out, if any guild member had witnessed Artearis's loss of control tonight, it would be the end of hope.

Marte carried the tea across the room, approaching Artearis from the side. Carefully, he set the tea down halfway between Artearis and the bench across from him. The quiet thud of tea mugs landing on wood brought no reaction from Artearis. Marte clasped the young man's left shoulder. "You went back to that house again, didn't you, boy." Marte's fingers tightened briefly. "You need to let it go before it gets you killed."

Artearis groaned into his hands. "Would it be such a bad thing — one less killer in the world?"

Marte's voice took on the tone of the teacher. "It would IF you were a killer, Artearis. But you aren't. Something your enemies don't need to know. Something they are going to find out if you don't learn control."

Artearis raged. "Control?! How can I control this nightmare pounding through my head? How can I make the horror go away? Do you have any idea what he did — the monster who handed me that reputation?"

Marte flexed his fingers into Artearis's shoulder, but he kept his voice quiet and firm. "Tell me, boy. Tell me about the monster."

"She was so hurt by her brother's words, sitting there at the base of the shirem tree crying. The harder her shoulders shook from the tears, the more I wanted to climb down from the branches and comfort that girl, the more I wanted to punish the boy who was turning into a clone of his father."

"Why was she crying, Artearis?"

"The family almost looked like a normal family when they came back from the market that evening. The mother was holding her infant daughter in her arms — the baby shaking a bright red rattle someone must have gotten her while they were out. But the girl, the older one, looked so pale and sad. Her father had his arm draped over her shoulder with his hand resting on her chest. I should have guessed then. I should have seen, but I didn't. I was too wrapped up in my own anguish."

"See what, Artearis?"

"Why do grown men use children as their shields? What honor is in that, Marte? Fenris had used the little girl as a shield that night while he was confronting his own guards." He had pressed her so tightly against him that

Artearis could see her foot jerk forward to keep herself from falling. He could hear words exchanged but couldn't make them out. When silence did fall among them, the father put both hands on his daughter's shoulders and steered her toward the house. Within a quarter of an hour, the guards left their post, closing the heavy iron gates behind them as they left the estate. The act set off warning bells, but when Artearis searched the perimeter and the outside of the house, he couldn't find any surprises. He was forced to rely on the supposition that the master believed he was safe behind the magical barriers originally placed by the mage who had hired the Guild. The mage assured his father that he had tweaked the spell to allow Artearis entry. That had been his father's excuse for Artearis completing the blood oath to the mage — so that he would have the means to alter the spell.

The assurance hadn't made Artearis feel any more secure while he sat there pressed against the grainy wood, breathing in the smell of summer blooms Lord Fenris paid workers good gold to cultivate. The almost too sweet smell from the garden had sickened his senses the way the assignment sickened his heart. It bothered him that he couldn't figure out the Lord's strange behavior. Every grain of intuition warned him something was terribly wrong. Why hadn't he paid attention?

"How can you trust a man who sacrifices his own dog — or his own son for that matter?" Artearis shivered at the memory of Fenris's huge dog. Patrolling the grounds like the previous night, suddenly it began to whine and paw at its head. It struggled to complete its circuit of the grounds, but its pace slowed to a stop near the garden. To Artearis's astonishment, the huge brute toppled over. He hadn't been able to shake the feeling that someone was setting him up. Was his father that desperate to be rid of him? Had fate been offering him a way out, but he was too stupid to grab it? The questions still haunted him.

"Speak, boy. Let it out." Marte took the seat opposite Artearis and reached for his tea.

"He brutalized them — all of them, especially the females — even the baby girl. And he was proud of it!" The red rattle hovered before his vision, drenched in blood that innocent offering to Kaylei.

"'No one tells me what to do,' he said. 'No one takes from me what is mine. Not him. Not you.'"

"I couldn't get my mind around it. I'm an assassin. I know what men are capable of; yet, I couldn't bring myself to understand. Then he waved his free hand in the direction of the other rooms and said, 'I am lord here. My family is mine to do with as I please — when I please.'"

Marte let him continue.

"His grin was malicious — malicious and well satisfied. 'And I have pleased myself greatly tonight,' he said."

Artearis shuddered again, remembering how the man brought his free hand down to the body lying on the bed, running his fingers along the limp leg and sighing, "'She was just becoming obediently enjoyable. Look how beautifully she has painted her lips with my juices. So tight. So compliant. Not like that old cow in the other room — only good for providing me with more diversions. Now, I will have to produce a new brood to satisfy me.'"

"They were so young, so fragile. He destroyed that."

"Who destroyed them, Artearis?"

Marte watched a single drop of liquid dash itself against the wood.

Artearis shuddered. The contract to kill Lord Fenris was his initiation into the guild proper — initiation of body and soul into the very life he reviled. Betrayal of the blood pact would damn him as an oath breaker to the Guild and curse him in the afterlife. Damn that mage! Damn Fenris for crossing the mage! Damn his heartless father, and damn fate for not giving him a better way out! Now Jekan Geylas wanted the merciless assassin to destroy the innocent again. Artearis choked on a sob. He couldn't do it.

Daric puzzled over Artearis's words. Why do men use children as shields? Jekan Geylas! Daric needed to get word to the protectors.

*Sssizzle. Crracck. Pop.* The flames shot upward, throwing a streak of light toward the table and the doorway where Daric listened. She shifted a little deeper into the darkness, bringing the other door more fully into her view. The reflection of firelight on the well-worn wooden door disappeared. Daric peered closer. Treadon carried a box of supplies into the room and set it just inside the doorway. Daric watched him turn around and shift a second box into the room. Treadon reached into the second box, pulled out a leather sack, and stood up, facing the direction of the table.

A witness. Marte warned Artearis about having a witness. Daric eased her throwing knife out of her armband and pulled her arm back.

Treadon's face filled with surprise then excitement. He shifted the bottom of the bag to his right hand and shook the opening loose with his left, launching the contents of the sack toward Marte and Artearis.

Daric followed the objects with her eyes, shifting her arm to meet this new threat. She heard the angry hissing of snakes only a moment before one reared up and spread its hood. Daric sent the knife pounding into the center of the hood. She had just enough time to see Marte dart his hand toward a multi-colored snake before movement from Treadon drew her attention. Treadon fled the room. Daric dashed out of the doorway. She had to get Treadon.

The chaos jolted Artearis from his torment in time to see Marte crush a crystal snake. A third snake, a sky blue snake, wriggled across the stone floor toward Marte's right side. Artearis lunged across the table, ripping his sword from its scabbard in an upward motion. The instant the blade hit the arc Artearis brought it straight down into the space between the snake and Marte. The snake was quicker. It snapped its fangs into Marte then reared back for a second strike as the sword descended upon its neck.

Marte staggered against the table. "Learn control, Artearis. Learn it or everyone dies ...." He fell to the floor.

"Noooo!!!"

# Chapter Eight
## Departure

Daric followed Treadon through the streets of Ionen. Treadon was careful. He continued to wind through the streets long after most people dropped their caution. The house Treadon approached was not unusual except for its seclusion and the chill. Shadows enveloped it, making it hard to see inside. Daric watched Treadon nervously open the door. What made the man so jumpy?

A dry, raspy voice floated from the doorway. "You disappoint me, beast. The assassin still breathes."

"Master ...."

"I have no more time to waste on you."

Daric shivered. The temperature had dropped dramatically. She stared hard, trying to see through the darkness. Treadon backed into the street.

"Master, no!"

Treadon stiffened. His hand clawed at his neck. "Masss ...."

The shadow laughed. "Die, beast."

Treadon fell to his knees — both hands clasped around his throat.

Daric could almost see him trying to gasp out words, but no sound came out.

The air grew even colder.

Treadon crumpled to the street.

Harsh laughter reached Daric's ears then silence. The air grew warmer. The house became easier to see. Treadon lay dead. This was NOT good.

"Control is not the absence of emotion but the channeling of it to strengthen your position," Marte had told Artearis many times. Marte was right; if he couldn't pull himself together, the Guild was going to learn his secret. Artearis toyed with the idea. If the Guild disposed of him, it wouldn't be suicide. He'd be free. *But the child would die.* Assassin and honor didn't go together. Artearis knew he couldn't let that boy die. He had to warn the Duke even if it meant sacrificing his life to do it.

Artearis shuffled to the wardrobe and pulled out one of his few treasured possessions, a bag of holding. He rummaged through the items inside it, adding clothes to the bag before quietly opening the door to his room. He turned to examine the place he had occupied for the last eleven years. The remnants of death suffocated the very air. Nothing else in the room was worth taking. He closed the door as quietly as he had opened it and headed for his office.

The Guild owned little that Artearis cared about, but he would even sacrifice his soul to prevent his brother from possessing Darethan's blades. Zotearis was not going to get the chance to dishonor them.

He unlocked the case and, with utmost care, withdrew the blades from their positions and placed them in the sheaths resting on the bottom shelf. He placed the weapons in the bag then put his own accursed weapons in their places, closed the case and locked it.

The key in his hand felt dirty. He went to the desk and dropped it on the appointment book. Let his brother have the rest. His eyes shifted to the small chest. He sighed. He would need funds to get to Gessin.

Artearis opened the chest. Inside rested several stacks of coins, a heap of precious and semi-precious stones, and lying on a small crystal pedestal, his mother's ring. The band was made of mithril fashioned into a ring of leaves. Embedded into three leaves slightly larger than the rest were a sapphire, a diamond, and a ruby. The outer two were cut in a smooth circular pattern, but the diamond glowed brilliantly with the life of a star.

No, Zotearis wasn't going to get the chance to touch their mother's ring either. Artearis retrieved a velvet-lined bag from a drawer and carefully placed the ring in the jeweler's bag before adding it and the chest to his bag of holding.

Artearis scanned the room. He would miss the tapestry. His soul longed to follow the dying light to the shores of that island. He sighed. Picking up his bag of holding, he began to thread his way through the maze of cases. His eyes fell on the silver dragon medallion. Yes, he would take that, too.

If only Artearis had some way to bring Geylas down. With him dead, the boy would be safe. But the Duke had been right about his power. He might possibly have the resources to bring down the Guild. The thought of Geylas destroying the Guild for Artearis's treachery appealed to him. With the Duke eliminating Artearis and destroying the Guild, and with luck, Zotearis, this accursed bloodline would end, and the Ashrick girl could live in peace. The bloodshed would be over. Artearis smiled a grim smile. It was another reason to die for.

Artearis walked from the room, closing and locking the door behind him. He handed the key to the off-shift guard. "Give this key to Daric when ..." Artearis barely managed to suck in the 'sh' sound, "he comes on duty." The guard nodded and accepted the key. Artearis continued down the hallway, retracing the Duke's steps to the exit. It was time to end this.

Daric worked her way back to the guild compound. The image of Treadon writhing on the ground still had her shivering. She turned into the alley leading to the merchant entrance of guild headquarters and froze. Someone was quietly exiting the building. Daric backed into the deeper shadows of the alley, taking care not to disturb the garbage piled against the walls. The shadow moved too slowly to be a delivery person. Had Treadon's killer come here to finish the task? Daric waited as the figure approached the guild end of the alley.

When the figure slowed, Daric edged toward the corner. The potential threat turned his head back toward the guild door. Daric relaxed. She'd know that profile anywhere. Artearis was leaving earlier than expected. Before Daric had a chance to ponder if she should tell Artearis about the merchant Treadon, Artearis hefted a bag under his arm and headed down the street toward the outskirts of Ionen.

Daric backed out of the alley. Blades she could handle.

Magic ... magic she had to risk contacting the Captain's agent directly. Daric headed to the guild stable and saddled up.

The sound of a horse approaching the Ionen safe house stopped Artearis in mid-preparation. Standard guild practice dictated all travel rations be picked up and dropped off at the safe house to avoid overt attention to headquarters. Every trained field operative knew this. So did Zotearis.

Artearis placed the sack of meat rations into the saddle bag then stood up and walked to the center of the room, drawing both weapons as he faced the door. Guild protocol may state that he remains visible as a courtesy to prevent accidental bloodshed, but Artearis wasn't taking any unnecessary chances after the kitchen incident.

Damn but he wished he knew whether his brother or Jekan Geylas had sent the man. Hell! He needed to know who, regardless — and why.

The door swung open without hesitation.

Artearis slid his blades back in place. That golden shell earring could only belong to one black-hearted assassin, Gregory.

"You still shine like a lighthouse beacon."

Gregory stopped on the threshold.

"I thought you were canvassing the waterfront along the northern and western borders."

"Hey, boss. What'r ya doin' outa yer hidey hole?"

Artearis waved Gregory inside and signaled the man to shut the door.

"High level assignment, you wharf rat, but don't change the subject."

"Hisanth, Cap'n. Trouble's a brewin' there. Norland an' Garad."

Artearis settled back against the bar and crossed his arms.

"I mosied inta Hisanth ta supply up. I'd no soona walked inta the safe house an' a bounca tried ta toss me out. There wa' gamblin' tables eva'where. I jangled me pouch, an' he let me in."

Artearis frowned.

"A talkie gambla named the runners Norland an' Garland. They wa' deep in talk wit' a clucka. Wantin' some mark iced by tha sound. No warrant came up tha pipe. Least not when me contact updated me. Blessed or no, them two's drawin' lots a legal notice. Bad business there."

Artearis shifted his leg, banging it against the base of the bar. The hollow ring it made set his mind turning. He grilled his unofficial second-in-command for nearly an hour. The longer Gregory talked, the deeper Artearis's fingernails dug into his arms. He finally dropped them to his side — bad business indeed.

Artearis moved around to the back side of the bar.

"Listen, Gregory. As you like to put it, trouble is

brewing, and not just in Hisanth — here in Ionen, too."

Artearis shifted a panel to reveal a money box. Unlocking the miniature safe, he pushed aside two empty money belts and several partially depleted ones. Even this safe house wasn't being kept up to standard. Withdrawing a full belt, he handed it to Gregory.

Before Gregory could speak, Artearis said, "Be prepared. That's what you keep telling me. This time I think I should listen."

Gregory's mouth dropped open; he quickly shut it and frowned.

Artearis clasped his hand over Gregory's outstretched forearm. "Take the belt. Head to the chapter house at Kentor — the one near Solyndra's Breach. Repair it. Restock it. Reinforce it. Expand the underground system if you need to. You know OUR numbers. If all this goes south, I want an alternate base available."

"Alert HQ?"

Artearis shook his head. "Keep this quiet. You know who we can and can't trust. If you don't know, don't trust."

Gregory nodded. "Tha signal?"

"Keep your ship lines tight. You'll feel the wind change if it comes."

Gregory clasped his empty hand over Artearis's.

"When tha rats come outa the hidey holes, it's time to abandon ship." He grinned. "Ship but na cap'n."

Artearis found it hard not to crack a smile. He released his grip. Turning his attention back to the money box, Artearis dug around for a second full belt. Cash drew less attention than stones. "I think it's time we both abandoned this ship." He grabbed up one of the saddlebags he'd been filling and chucked it toward Gregory. "BUY what you need."

"Don't give the bloody cluckas a wake to follow, you mean."

Artearis nodded.

# Chapter Nine
## Road to Damnation

Artearis didn't like the feel of any of this. Jekan Geylas decides now is the time to eliminate the competition to the throne by hiring the Assassins Guild. Zotearis chooses to push his status as Berain into the faces of key guild personnel before he even passes the fifth circle. Guild chapters are conducting private deals under the protection of the Guild's reputation. Not to mention the attack in the kitchen yesterday morning. The players might not be connected, but the Guild was the center — like a spider web with all threads leading to the Assassins Guild or to him — but why and why now?

Even this road felt off. The breeze out of the west was warm, yet he felt a disturbing chill, and the air had a rancid smell like unwashed flesh — an odor that grew stronger the closer he came to the thick stand of trees skirting the southern edge of the road. With the steep decline along the northern edge and the setting sun glaring into his eyes, this was an ideal place for an ambush — as if he needed any more tests to prove his inadequacies.

After his near failure against Zotearis and his inability to save Marte, Artearis had serious doubts that his skill with the sword matched his perception of his skill. Perhaps he truly wasn't worthy to carry Darethan Berain's blades, no matter how right they had felt to hold. Darethan Berain would not have let the blood lust blazing in Zotearis' eyes distract him. Darethan Berain would have found another way out of this dilemma besides dying.

The bay underneath Artearis whinnied and began sidling side-to-side. He reined in his troubling thoughts. Horse and rider had almost reached the stretch of trees. Guild horses had been trained to be as perceptive as their riders. Someone was out there. Artearis stopped the horse. The rancid smell came from up ahead. This was definitely an ambush, but by whom? Was he the intended victim or a random mark? His intuition was setting off alarms.

If he traveled farther, he could have opponents ahead and behind him. He needed more time to assess the situation — and possibly draw his attackers out of hiding. He knew it was more than one attacker. The smells were too diverse to come from one man, particularly that unfamiliar scent. Artearis dismounted and reached into the saddlebag for a hoof pick. Keeping the horse's bulk between himself and the trees, he casually leaned down to pinch the back of the right front forelock and raised the hoof as if to inspect it. The view from under the horse gave him a different perspective of the shadows along the tree line. He could see that the shadow of a bush that had grown close to the road was shifting against the wind — one attacker. The snap of a twig deeper into the trees warned him of the second attacker's position. The strong smell coming yet farther down wind warned him that at least three amateurs were playing robbers.

*Let's see just what kind of amateurs.* He scraped the hoof for a few more seconds and released it, standing up to replace the hoof pick. Using the horse to shield his actions, Artearis dropped the reins to ground tether his mount, loosening both blades from their sheaths.

His attackers apparently didn't care for his horse welfare check. A man slightly taller than Artearis stomped out of the trees about fifty feet ahead of him. Artearis had to squint to get a clear view of the stocky man wielding a knife. The breeze picked up, bombarding Artearis with the stench of sweat, urine, and beer. The man shuffled closer.

After advancing about ten feet, the second attacker emerged from the trees carrying a stout tree branch. He lumbered to the north side of the road as slowly as the ox he resembled. By his girth and ragged clothes, Artearis assumed he must be a farm hand turned brigand.

When the two reached the bush that had first caught Artearis's attention, the third attacker stood up. He, too, was carrying a thick tree branch, one too heavy for his skinny frame.

The first man, the apparent leader, gestured for Artearis to move away from his horse.

"Listen up, rich boy, or yer a dead rich boy."

The skinny man chuckled.

Artearis shifted his eyes slowly upward. The sun was still a problem. He needed to buy five or six more minutes or shift his position enough to get the sun out of his direct line of sight.

"Ya hearin' me, boy?"

Artearis finally nodded.

"Move away from yer hoss."

Artearis stroked the horse's mane, signaling it to stay still.

"I said, move away from yer hoss, boy. Are ya deaf or jus' slow like Jake here?"

With deliberate slowness, Artearis moved closer to the three while keeping to the northern side of the road.

"I'm a thinkin' this one's not too bright, men. He don't know when he's out powered."

The heavyset man, Jake, snorted.

"Lemme see yer blade, boy. Don't need ya tryin' to stick me when I go 'bout collectin' the road tax."

Artearis composed his face into a bored, rich man's frown.

"Road tax?" he finally said.

"See, men, not bright 't all. Ya want to go west, ya pay us fer keepin' the road free o' baduns. Now drop yer blade and toss me yer purse, purdy boy. Or I'll let Jake here have you."

Jake grinned and reached his right hand down to his crotch and rubbed it. The other two burst out laughing.

The annoying sound grated against Artearis's patience. Still keeping his movements slow, he pushed his cloak away from Darethan's blades. Even more slowly, he drew out the blades.

The skinny man grabbed the leader's arm. "Bill, them blades are ... are ...."

Bill stared hard. He looked down at the weapons then up at Artearis's face then down at the weapons.

"Sure are, Skinny. Guess ya really are touched like Jake here. Them's 'llegal 'round here, boy. Them's as ... as ... um ... killer's weapons."

Artearis scrunched his face into a frown.

"Really? I'm holding assassin's blades? Are you sure?"

All three nodded vigorously.

"Doesn't it make you wonder how I got them?"

Bill laughed. "Paid fer 'em 'o course. Yer too purdy to be one o' dem Black Killers."

Bill's cohorts laughed at that.

Skinny said, "Ain't there a re-ward for any o' dem that's got killer's blades, Bill?"

Bill grinned. "Shore is, Skinny. I think we could use a re-ward."

Jake tugged on Bill's sleeve.

"Boss, kin I 'ave 'em furst? They's jus' gonna kill 'em anywho."

"If in you git him, Jake, me an' Skinny git your share o' his stuff. 'Greed?"

Jake frowned and rubbed his groin some more. "He's got some purdy stuff, Bill."

Ya want purdy stuff or purdy him? Ya can't have both."

"He's gawd awful sweet lookin', an' he even has his own mountin' post." Jake pointed at the saddle.

Bill laughed harder. "Yes'sin, he does, Jake. Deal?"

Jake squeezed himself harder. "Kin I have that purdy, shiny rock hangin' down, too? It shines jus like the sun only green?"

Bill looked over Artearis and his horse. "A rock and a Rock fer you and the rest for me an' Skinny. Deal!"

Jake's frown deepened. "Only if we don' turn 'im in 'til I'm all the way dun. You made me stop early wit the stable kid."

"Take ther' whole blame night. Just 'gree, so we can git to it."

Jake nodded.

"Time to pay up, purdy boy."

The three moved forward.

Artearis casually studied the three. They made horrible brigands. Instead of separating to come at him from multiple sides, all three rushed straight on. To make matters worse, they were so close together that Jake's lumbering stride kept rocking the tree branch perched on his shoulder side-to-side. It banged the leader in the back of the head. Bill let out a howl.

"Watch it, Jake, or I'll stick ya."

Bill pulled back his knife in a threatening gesture and cut Skinny across the forearm. Skinny screamed. His heavy club slammed down onto Bill's foot.

Artearis wanted to burst out laughing. The only way these three could rob anyone was by surprise and a ton of luck. They needed to see just how dangerous being a brigand could be. Maybe he should encourage them to find more "dependable" work.

He let them come nearer. Slow Jake was the closest. Artearis launched a kick to his groin. Jake doubled over in a protective reflex, giving Artearis the chance to slam down the hilt of his sword into the back of Jake's head. The huge man tumbled over unconscious. Using the momentum his previous action had created, Artearis swept his sword up above Bill, who had crouched down to protect himself from a similar attack, and into the heavy tree branch Skinny had stuck straight up into the air. Skinny lost his club and his balance, tumbling backward onto his rear and hands.

Artearis turned to Bill. The man didn't know whether to crouch or stand. Bill backed up a few paces and brought his knife mid-chest in front of him. Artearis advanced. Skinny tried to scramble out of the way. Artearis smacked Skinny on the back of his head with the hilt of the dagger before engaging Bill. He used the flat of his sword to knuckle-slap the hand holding the knife. It clattered to the ground as Bill cried out. Quickly Artearis reversed the sword hilt into Bill's knee, dropping him to the ground. Bill curled up, clutching his smarting hand over his throbbing knee while his good hand tried to ward off an attack.

"Perhaps you fellows need to find new work if a pretty boy like me can stop you."

Artearis turned to the trees studying the shadows, listening for movement. That unfamiliar scent drifted closer.

Bill muttered, "Ya really are one o' dem Black Killers." Bill's voice grew louder. "We's seen ya an' the law'll give us coin for tellin'."

Artearis was only half listening to Bill. Something still wasn't right. He could feel it.

"We's gonna tell 'em all. Have 'em all hunt ya down, purdy boy!"

"Who's going to believe you, Bill?" Artearis walked along the stretch of trees, searching.

"Huh?"


"Who's going to believe you and your friends fought with an assassin and lived to tell about it? Thank whatever god you pray to that you're still alive. Assassins never leave survivors, ever." Standing in the shadows, Artearis noticed a green glow. He looked down. Slow Jake was right. His pendant was glowing like the sun. Something definitely wasn't right. The gem had never glowed on its own before. Then Artearis realized how quiet it was.

"No, they don't."

Artearis turned around. Blood pools were forming under the three bodies.

"My master told me your kind was something to be feared. Seeing this," the stranger waved his hand over the scene, "I think he has put entirely too much confidence in your abilities."

Artearis cursed himself. He assumed any other surprises would come from ahead not behind. Now, the stranger had the advantage he had been stalling for earlier. The gloom of twilight made it hard for Artearis to make out details of this new threat, but he knew this was no common robber or an assassin loyal to Zotearis. One of the Duke's men?

"And your master would be?"

"My master? You are unworthy to know my master's name."

Artearis could barely make out the man wiping his blades on Bill's dead body. The strokes were short, like from cleaning daggers.

The man stood up.

"Perhaps if you die well, I will gift you with his name."

The man raked one blade edge against the other, producing a loud, painful screeching sound. Artearis winced.

"Perhaps I will not."

Artearis carefully observed the man as he advanced. This new opponent walked on balanced feet and kept his arms loose. The two daggers he held were not the balanced blades of throwing weapons, so when the man pumped his arm back to throw, Artearis knew it was a ruse and shifted his feet in preparation.

The follow through of the "throw" provided the momentum to propel the attacker forward. Artearis quickly spun to his left, bringing his sword down in a sweeping arc meant to disable his opponent at the shoulder.

The man was good. Just as quickly, he blocked the blow. Shifting his grip on the dagger in his right hand, the man tried his own spin to come behind Artearis for a back blow.

It was a rookie assassin's move. Artearis brought his own dagger into an underhand cut, opening a gash in the wrist blocking his sword. Artearis continued his forward motion, spinning past his opponent and putting distance between the two. This man was well-trained. Although not a killing blow, the cut was in a sensitive area, yet the man neither flinched nor cried out. Without treatment the man would bleed out.

Artearis held his ground, waiting to see how his opponent would react.

"So, you are better than I first perceived. No matter. My master desires you dead, Artearis Berain, and dead you shall be. At first, he thought you would be of use. Now ... now he tires of your interference with his plans and wishes no further disruptions."

This man not only knew he was an assassin, but he also knew Artearis's name! Geylas expected Artearis to go to Gessin not Hisanth. Only Gregory and he knew Artearis was headed there, and Artearis trusted Gregory explicitly. So who was this man and his master?

The attacker had no plans to run. He came at Artearis with his left hand across his body and the right straight down. Artearis knew exactly what the man intended. He headed directly for his opponent, bringing his sword up in a preemptive block of the other man's slicing cut and his dagger down in an arc to sweep aside the dagger thrust to Artearis's stomach. Spinning off to the right, Artearis used his opponent's imbalance to slice a huge gash from right shoulder to hip with his sword.

This time the man screamed. Adrenalin filled him. The attacker backhanded a swipe at Artearis's waist. Before he realized his mistake, Artearis slashed downward. Both men watched the hand bounce upon the road.

Training took over. Artearis sent the next sword thrust through the man's heart. The man stiffened for a moment then sighed as he fell to the ground. The stranger was good, better than most professionals, but no match for a fully trained bladespinner.

Artearis was tired and sore and left with two major problems. He had an unknown, and certainly dangerous, person wanting him dead, and he had a road full of bodies he needed to get rid of or risk someone coming along and asking questions he didn't want answered. For the next half hour, Artearis cleaned up, dragging the corpses deep into the undergrowth and using all of his water to rinse the hard packed road as best he could.

A rider approached as he was finishing the unwanted task. The man looked at the wet ground.

"Hey, you. What're you up to."

The rider dismounted and approached the wet stains.

"I don't know you. Who gave you writ to work this stretch? Not Norland and Garad, or I'd know."

The rider drew his sword.

"You'd best come with me and explain yourself to the bosses. This is their turf."

Artearis had had enough. He yanked out his sword and skewered the newcomer with it.

"They think this is their turf?"

Artearis gathered up the reins of the man's horse before returning to his own horse patiently waiting. After tying the reins to his pommel, Artearis mounted up. This time, he left the body in the road — as a warning.

# Chapter Ten
## Hostile Takeover

As Zotearis spoke the last passage, a thread of sickly green light reached out from the pedestal to the gem swaying in front of his chest. When he began the next verse, two more threads spun through empty air and attached themselves to the two men standing just outside the doorway. Upon reciting the third verse, voices intruded into his mind, seeking. Seeking what Zotearis couldn't tell. As he uttered the last words of the fourth and final verse, the men outside collapsed into unconsciousness; while the voices in his head deepened as if grabbing onto something then retreated. Zotearis felt an unsettling pull on his mind, then stillness.

He knew his efforts were successful when the results of the spell elicited no reaction to the wrenching sensation inside his mind, just as his father had told him. Emotions, like morals, had no place in an assassin's world.

Only the appearance of emotion was useful. As a child, Zotearis instinctively understood that. At ten, he used that instinct to lure his first prey. The beggar child had pleaded for a coin to feed his sick father. The boy believed Zotearis when he said his father was a doctor, trusted him enough to take him home, and was horrified to discover the lifeless body of his father after returning with the bowl Zotearis had requested. Zotearis had relished the look of betrayal as much as he had the feel of running his blade through the heart of that piece of refuse.

Even Artearis had been blind to Zotearis's skill and ambition as a child. His brother was weak. Despite performing the ceremony, their last encounter revealed that Artearis possessed emotions. Surprise is not a trait worthy of the leader of the Assassins Guild. Neither is fear. The time has come to return a true Berain assassin to control the Guild.

Zotearis stepped over the bodies of his newly bonded blood guard. Walking through the training ground, he remembered the intense pleasure he had felt in killing the second circle recruit with the practice blades — the hatred toward Artearis and Leyana for dressing him down in front of the rest of the trainees for the deed. He studied the artwork lining the hall of his ancestors. He had been proud of those accomplishments positioned elegantly along the corridor, had wanted to be the one to fill it with more than any before, including his father. Now, they were merely markers of the Guild's status. Zotearis pondered if he would miss those emotions. No matter, he was finally the perfect weapon.

"Sir, here is the key you requested."

Zotearis snapped out of his thoughts. Garton, the family's spell bonded servant, waited at the entrance to Artearis's, correction HIS, office.

Garton extended his hand, key resting in the palm.

"A guard possessed it."

Zotearis raised his eyebrow.

"He has been ... um ... thoroughly reprimanded, Sir."

Zotearis studied the look of satisfaction Garton tried to mask. Apparently, the old man had not lost his taste for the work after all. Zotearis nodded. He waved to Garton to open the door. He reached out his hand for the key.

"What secrets were you hiding in here, big brother?"

"Sir?"

"The news of my brother?"

"He was commissioned by the Duke of Sitar to personally eliminate the son of the Duke of Saron. It appears he left the day before you entered the fifth circle. He is not expected to return until after the upcoming festival."

"So my brother actually dared to play assassin. And my men?"

Garton shuffled his feet. "In place, Sir. Everyone is waiting for your orders. One question has come up though, Sir."

Zotearis noted the shift in Garton's tone from his fierceness toward everyone to the cringing doubt of question.

"Someone wishes to question me?" Zotearis was impressed. Garton didn't even flinch.

"The initiates in the isolation cells, Sir, what's to be done with them?"

The spell truly was thorough. Before, Zotearis would have said slaughter them all. Now, he saw with clarity, saw the wisdom in the practice his brother rigidly adhered to.

"Leave them for the present. You have work enough to do today. The word is the ninth hour of dark."

Garton bowed before turning to leave.

"And, Garton."

Garton stopped.

"Sir?"

"Fetch my brother's blood guard."

Leyana grimaced at the amount of dirt and refuse that seemed to accumulate during a day of training. For a guild that required invisibility, and the Assassins Guild was adamant about leaving no trace behind, her students failed miserably every day. Perhaps she needed to crack down on this weakness. She would think about it but not now. The sweet sound of silence called to her.

While her circle did require stealth, her students had not mastered the art of silence. The noise grated on her nerves: too much noise, too many footsteps vibrating through the floor, too much breath stirring the air, too many swishes of fabric echoing through the halls, making Leyana feel on edge. Let her have quiet just for a few moments. The soles of her shoes barely touched the surface of the stone as she made her way to their sleeping quarters. Soon the bell announcing the ninth hour would ring, signaling the end of the day and lights out.

When the sound had quieted to an echo, Leyana's stomach tightened. The sound of footsteps was growing closer. The rasping noise of wood being drawn across metal set off more internal alarms. The dagger, always at her waist when she wasn't training students, slipped into her hand, as she backed into the deeper shadows. Her room wasn't far from the students. She headed there for the gear she had dropped off after training earlier that day. From farther down the hall, one of Zotearis's henchmen crept toward her quarters. She let him reach the door, leaving his back exposed, and struck. Leyana slipped her blade into the man's lung before he had a chance to realize she was gone. Carefully, she eased him to the floor.

Sound from the weapon masters' rooms drew her in that direction. Cutter had slipped into that section of the sleeping rooms from the other side. A crash wrenched Leyana's gaze behind Cutter, taking her attention from the man who used the sound to catch Jastis by surprise, knifing him in the back before the door to Lorr's room opened.

"Betrayal," Leyana hissed loud enough for Lorr to hear before she darted into her room. When Leyana darted back out with her gear and a traveling bag, she nodded in satisfaction at Lorr's handiwork.

He nodded in return. "Get them out," he mouthed to her.

Again, Leyana nodded. She slipped back into the corridor connecting the student quarters. It was time.

Zotearis pushed the ledger away and sat back. The number of jobs posted in the ledger only covered about sixty percent of the appointments listed in the book. The jobs that were accepted had amounts twenty to forty percent higher than normal. Zotearis noticed that not one job was for the assassination of a highly placed political target, yet two appointments with key political players had lucrative amounts written in the notations.

Zotearis picked up the sheet of paper listing the figures he had copied down. Guild income had neither increased nor decreased more than five percent for the last three years despite the rise in fees and the increase in scheduled appointments. Was his brother siphoning off money to build up his own personal army? Zotearis thoroughly searched the desk. Nothing indicated any kind of private dealings for goods or manpower. Zotearis hunted through the shelves, looking for a camouflaged ledger. The shelves held training manuals nothing more. Behind the tapestry? He searched for a hidden safe. Nothing.

Leaning against the shelving, Zotearis studied the display cases. All the cases were made of glass with thin firefern frames — too thin to hide paperwork. He studied the floor for unusual wear patterns. Perhaps this room had more than one exit. The only distinguishable wear pattern Zotearis could see was a path from the desk to the weapons display. What did you find so fascinating in here, brother? Zotearis studied the case. Ah, yes. So, big brother, you fancy yourself a hero instead of an assassin. Well, let us see if hero trumps assassin.

Zotearis heard a knock as he returned to the desk. Before answering, he swept the appointment book and money ledger into the top right-hand drawer. He wanted time to consider the most effective way to use this ammunition against his brother. He settled back in his chair and bid the person to enter.


Garton slid into the room.

"Sir, one of your brother's blood guard waits outside. The other is not within the compound."

"Where is he?"

"Missing, Sir. No one knows where, not even the blood guard outside. Could he have gone with your brother, Sir? They both vanished the same night."

An interesting question. Could his brother have sunk so low that he would recruit help for a simple child assassination? Even if Artearis hadn't, Zotearis could still spin it that way — as long as no one could prove otherwise. This was the perfect weapon to undermine Artearis's standing as guild leader.

"Send in the blood guard."

Garton beckoned for Haydrim to enter.

Zotearis recognized the man who had wanted his brother's blood spilled almost as much as he had during that last confrontation. Perfect.

Although Zotearis knew who every person was in the Guild, he said, "You are?"

The man looked at Zotearis with questioning eyes.

"Haydrim."

"And your missing counterpart?"

"You mean that sniveling, straight-laced rat, Daric?"

Zotearis almost wished he could savor the hatred in that reply.

"The deserter couldn't be found by the off-shift guard or anyone two mornings back."

Zotearis looked at Garton.

"The matter we discussed earlier, Sir."

"Ah." Zotearis studied Haydrim until he began to squirm. This man was a brawler not an assassin. Why was he initiated into the Guild? This was the refuse Zotearis planned to shed, and he knew how.

"Daric's unauthorized absence cannot be tolerated. I am tasking you to make an example of him. Make sure the result strikes fear everywhere. Make sure the result is worthy of guild praise. In exchange, I will have you released from your unwanted bond. Understood?"

Haydrim's eyes lit up.

"Really? You can do that? Uh ... yes, Sir. Can I ...?"

Zotearis waved both men away. Before Garton could close the door, Zotearis said, "Haydrim, do not fail."

Zotearis sat back in his chair. The goddess of Death was surely blessing his endeavor. With both blood guard gone, Artearis would be one man against the entire Guild. Zotearis noted the time. A guild that was finally completely loyal to Zotearis.

"Your reign is over, big brother."

# Chapter Eleven
## Hisanth

The noon hour was upon him as Artearis approached the stone entrance of the eastern city gate into Hisanth. Gregory had warned him that the merchant area had recently been put under the "protection" of Norland and Garad. All guild prescribed locations were likewise compromised.

"Business in Hisanth?"

Artearis looked around. "Excuse me?"

The guard waiting at the entrance frowned. "What's your business in Hisanth?"

Artearis shook himself. "Sorry, been travelin' hard for the better part of a week. I'm hopin' to catch a few days of rest before moving on to the festival at Saron."

"So it's pleasure then."

Artearis grinned. "It will be pleasure if I can find me a game or two while I'm here."

The guard snorted. "Regular games are held nightly at the Cold Comfort Inn. Games go on down at the docks when ships come in, but they aren't sanctioned, so don't go crying to the authorities if you get rolled gaming there. Street gaming is prohibited with penalties ranging from a night in jail to conscription. Attempting to fleece military personnel carries the penalty of hanging. Enjoy your stay."

The guard's straightforward attitude caught Artearis by surprise. He mumbled a hasty "Thanks" and hurried through the gate. Inside the city, the salty air of the sea was unmistakable. Its bracing wind revived Artearis enough to start thinking instead of reacting. Gregory had mentioned that Norland's and Garad's attempts to take over the docks had met with failure, so Artearis decided to try his luck by the sea.

Holding his cloak tightly to prevent the wind from ripping it away, he walked past half a dozen places before settling on the "Gusty Wind." The name seemed familiar. The innkeeper was a surly old salt who demanded three nights up front.

"Can't trust you gamblin' types," he muttered. "You lose your stash or get yourself killed or sneak out to avoid bein' shipped out. So it's pay first or find another berth. And I don't take on horses. You want it tended, you do it yourself.

And if'n you bring down trouble with them soldiers, I'll toss your gear out quicker 'en Natty cuts wind. I ain't losin' sailors 'cause some tricksee sharp thought them soldiers made easy marks," he grumbled as he shambled toward the kitchen. At the door he barked, "Another mouth for supper, Natty."

Artearis tightened his jaw to keep it shut. Horse or gear? He looked at the horse blocking the entrance.

"And move that huge varmint outta the doorway. It's blockin' customers," the innkeeper shouted from the kitchen.

Guess it was the horse if he didn't want to draw attention to himself. Artearis led the tired beast to the rickety lean-to built onto the side of the inn. He thought to disguise his mount with carefully placed makeup before realizing two things: one, he didn't' have any camouflage supplies, and two, he didn't need to. The horse was exhausted, ragged, and thin. Maybe he should have kept the guild rider's horse and turned this one loose back at that farmstead.

Done was done. He had more pressing concerns. Patting his horse on its rump and tossing his saddlebags over his shoulder, Artearis made his way up to his room. The bed was narrow and as rickety looking as his horse's shelter. Still, it looked inviting. Artearis sighed. He had a ton of work to do and only a few days to do it. He splashed some water on his face in front of the mirror. No wonder the innkeeper hadn't given him two thoughts. He looked like hell. He grabbed a clean shirt from the saddlebag before it dawned on him that his ragged appearance would fit in better at the docks.

Tossing the shirt onto the bed, he headed back downstairs. As he hitched down them, his sword sheath bumped into his thigh. Damn! He had walked past the guardsman and all the way through town to the docks wearing his sword and dagger. He was lucky the wind was strong, forcing him to keep his cloak wrapped tightly around him. *May the Winds of Fortune ever protect thoughtless assassins from their foolish oversights. But could he remedy the problem without risking his weapons?* Artearis looked around the room. The plain, sparse common area wouldn't do. He thought about his room upstairs — smooth walls, single bed, and panel-less wash stand — then dismissed it as well. He headed to the lean-to, pretending to check on his horse. A couple of possibilities existed.

Deciding that the sword would be out of place in town, Artearis unbuckled the sheath then carefully wrapped it in the horse blanket. Wedging it between the rafters and the bearing wall in the darkened corner of the lean-to, he prayed it would be safe. The horse pawed the ground in agitation. *Crap!* He dug out a brush and groomed it before he hunted for something to feed the animal. Finally, he went to fetch it some water.

Before leaving the shed, he carefully went over his appearance one more time. Even without its counterpart, the dagger stood out. "Forgive me, Darethan," he whispered as he grabbed a handful of muck.

The wind remained strong all afternoon, making it difficult for anyone to speak in low voices. Even so, the dock hands and sailors had talked enough to understand that although they didn't care much for the soldiers coming to Hisanth for recreation, they appreciated the change in fortune the military arm had brought. Before the fort had been fully manned, a ship, sometimes two, a week had sunk or vanished. Since the change, they could sail nearly the entire northwestern coast without losing cargo. So when soldiers started turning up dead, the dockers had started digging around.

"'Twas them bloody assassins at that fancy card house causin' the grief," one dock worker said bitterly. Another dock hand and a sailor nodded in agreement. "So we gave 'em what for an' ran 'em off the docks when they tried to set up shop here. Ol' Greg'ry hitched up that one hisself afore hauling anchor," the man said, pointing at the grisly decoration hanging from a nearby ship's yardarm.

The sailor grunted. "The cap'n's gonna leave it sway 'til it rots off."

The other dock hand looked grim. "Ol' Gregory better watch himself he comes back around. Those bastards have the law paid for."

The sailor grunted again. "The law maybe. But not that lieutenant over at the fort — Fedoral. That one knows what's playin' out here, an' if the law ain't careful, they're gonna be playin' to a military tune."

His afternoon at the docks gave Artearis as much to chew on as Natty's hard bread. The well-weathered woman had gladly served up his food early, so she needn't be bothered when the dock workers came round for their end of day meal.

Natty came in to collect his dishes.

"Ya know, there's a shop just up Hadley Lane that can mend that cloak pretty reasonable. Jillian's fast, too." Natty waved her thin hand in front of her nose. "A bit o' a wash wouldn't hurt ya either, young'un. There's a wash house along the way. Can't miss the sign. Least ya wouldn't look like one o' them trouble-making hooligans like now" she yammered on as she crossed the room back to her kitchen. "The law's bound ta mess with ya looking thata way, 'specially with that expensive sticker at yar side."

Artearis had to admit he felt more like himself after the bath, even if he did feel half-dressed without his sword and dagger, but Natty was right about that, too. Even with mud on them, Darethan's blades didn't fit in with a gambler's guise. He had to settle for the dirk he'd won off one of the sailors at the docks. He wrapped his dirty linen inside his cloak. Guess he'd better stash that, too, before deciding his next move. Artearis wasn't about to lose a set of his protection from chance.

It didn't take him long to hide his belongings — and check on Darethan's weapons — and find the seamstress shop Natty had recommended. Jillian's place was located at the intersection that bordered the wealthy part of the city. The outside was plain but larger than most craft shops, being two rooms wide instead of the normal one, and had a second floor, although the staircase along the side suggested that the second floor might not be strictly part of the shop. The tinkle of a bell announced his arrival.

"Just a minute," came from the second front-facing room.

Artearis looked around. Five quality dressmaker dummies were posed near the front window. Three were clothed with women's apparel, one with men's, and one with a cloak and hat. He examined the cloak. The material was nothing impressive, but the cut and stitching were quite elegant.

A woman's voice said, "It's not my best work, but the style is popular these days, and the cloth is affordable." She paused as if in thought, then asked, "Who have you come to see?"

"Who?"

"Daphne, Katie, or me?"

Artearis continued to look around the room.

"Are you here for catering, shampooing, or dressmaking?"

"That's an interesting combination of services, Jillian?"

Jillian shrugged. "It pays the rent while maximizing shop space."

Artearis removed his cloak. "I'm here to see about getting this ...."

A buxom blonde girl burst into the room from the next one babbling "is it for me? Has another customer heard about my talent and come to have me turn them into ...? Oh, man."

"I believe it's for me, Katie, sorry." Jillian held out her hand. "May I see it?"

"Yes, I'd love to see it, too," Katie burst out while Artearis was passing his cloak to Jillian.

Artearis arched his eyebrow. "How long do you think it will take?"

"Yes, how long," Katie echoed.

Jillian looked over the cloak. "To fully repair it, a few hours maybe, but I can have it serviceable in about one if you don't mind a patch or two."

"One hour will ...."

Katie clapped excitedly. "... will be perfect." She grabbed hold of Artearis's extended arm, tugging it in the direction of the next room.

Artearis frowned, but Jillian smiled. "She's mostly harmless, really. She only has two thoughts in her head, but the most active one is how to remake people over into her image of them. She started with herself — didn't care for her red hair."

Katie screwed her face into a pout. "Red just doesn't work for me. I'm not like Daphne."

Jillian laughed. "No one is like Daphne."

Katie tugged harder on Artearis's arm. To prevent it from being dislocated, Artearis took a step toward Katie.

Jillian misunderstood his intention. "I'd think twice about agreeing to anything she says unless you really want a new you."

Katie tugged harder. "Sure he does. Look at that hair all straight and dull blond not bright and shiny blonde like me. Don't worry. I don't do permanent the first time around."

When she continued to feel resistance to her tugging, Katie said, "Come on. This'll be fun. I'll do you up just like one of those glory boys over at the Cold Comfort Inn. They all seem to like my handiwork."

Jillian snorted. "More like Daphne's handiwork."

"Whatever."

Hum ... the solution to his disguise problem? Artearis let Katie lead him into a room with a large mirror, several chairs — one positioned in front of the mirror — and tables with everything from combs and scissors to basins and pitchers to what looked like dyes and pine cones?

Katie shoved him into a chair next to a table with a basin and pitcher on it and placed a towel around his shoulders.

Artearis used the mirror to watch in fascination as Katie adjusted the back of his chair to a forty-five-degree angle before moving the table with the basin directly behind the reclined back.

"Lay back, please," she said, picking up a pitcher.

That hour had to be one of the strangest of his life. While Katie was busy "remaking" him, she rambled on to Jillian about person after person and rumor after rumor. Her talk wasn't limited to strangers either. Apparently, Daphne was a vital part of her information.

"Daphne said that the soldier wouldn't let her come near him until he'd taken off his uniform and stuffed it clean under the middle of the mattress. She said he mumbled something about new penalties if any more uniforms turned up damaged or missing. Well, Daphne said he looked so yummy standing there at attention that she promised him she'd take extra special care of him if he treated her goods the same."

"Did he?"

"Did he! He must have been one appreciative bloke cause the way Daphne went on she must have spread out everything, and I mean EVERYTHING for him. Said he nearly made her fall in love."

"Really! Daphne even dished out ...."

"Yep. Two helpings. She was near to tears when I told her I heard they were rotating out the common soldiers. Some kind of security breach whatever that is. The first batch is shipping out day after tomorrow, so if you got one you fancy ...." Katie broke off and gave Artearis a smile when she realized he was engrossed in her story.

Thank the gods he hadn't said more than a few dozen words while he was there. He was sure those few dozen were going to be broadcast to every one of her clients. The unintended risk had been worth it, however. Now he knew how the assassins were going to strike and their window of opportunity.

Later that evening Artearis settled himself in his perch atop the warehouse roof across from the Cold Comfort Inn's kitchen door. His foray into the inn had been moderately successful, thanks more to Jillian than Katie. Jillian's impressive handiwork had made his own cloak unusable. To patch the longer tears she had devised a geometric pattern out of pieces of cloth embroidered with reflective thread. The kaleidoscopic effect was sensational, and memorable, unlike the cloak on display, so Artearis had parted with a bit more money for the set. When he had counted eight other patrons wearing the same cloak and hat inside the Cold Comfort Inn during his surveillance, Artearis had deemed it money well spent.

Artearis stretched his legs to avoid cramping. In the inn, he'd seen three men huddled at the far end of the bar: the bartender, one light haired man and a darker haired one. The bartender said something Artearis couldn't hear. From the way the light haired man jerked upright, it wasn't good news. The other man started talking, but before he got more than a few words out, his partner barked, "Not now Norland" before dropping his voice.

Although obviously paranoid the way each scanned the inn while conversing with the bartender, Norland and Garad relaxed enough to have an intense exchange with the man. If Artearis had to bet, he'd gamble the two men had just been informed of the unscheduled change in personnel at the fort. Garad had grown fidgety, but Norland shrugged his shoulders, said something to the two men, and laughed. The bartender shook his head as he went back to his stool behind the bar. Norland went into the kitchen where Artearis saw him descending into the cellar. Garad headed in his direction. Artearis had picked up the dice to take his throw, hoping to prevent drawing attention to himself when a warm hand pushed itself inside his shirt. He froze at her touch just as a chuckling Garad passed his table.

"Make us rich, Silky," Garad had told the woman behind Artearis before walking into the high stakes gambling room.

"Let's have some fun," Silky's seductive voice suggested, as her hand caressed his chest.

The warm hand made his abdomen contract and his hand shake. The dice fell to the table: snake eyes. The other men laughed. As Silky's hand explored further, the player on his right scooped up the dice. Silky leaned closer, letting her other hand trail along the inside of the collar of his shirt. This was nothing like he had envisioned while locked away in isolation. The sweetness of her breath as it caressed his cheek paralyzed him. This was not the control he had believed he had achieved from his ordeal. Her lips nibbled at his jaw and along his neck to where his pulse was beating a staccato rhythm.

Artearis let himself become lost in the sensations she created until her hand slid around the green stone he wore under his shirt. The absence of contact with the stone disoriented him — sent a part of his mind into a panic. That part jolted him back to who he was, a trained assassin. He reached up his hand to wrap around the one holding the stone. Managing a smile that did not tremble, he drew her hand out and kissed it. Tilting his head back enough to whisper in her ear, Artearis said, "Some things are best left for later."

Silky laughed softly.

When the player who had scooped up the dice did the same to Silky, Artearis gave the man a good natured grin. Picking up the dice placed in front of him as a signal it was his turn to throw, Artearis told the man, "She is a gifted enchantress."

The men at the table laughed. One said, "There're few better in this place."

Artearis placed his bet and rolled: a two and a three. He passed the dice on to his distracted companion. The man waved them on to the next shooter. Artearis stayed for two more throws before excusing himself. He used the passage of a large group of men to mask him exiting the inn.

Even thinking about it now as he sat at his perch, Artearis caught his breath, and his heart nearly stopped beating. Silky had caused him to lose sight of his objective, unlike Katie's casual flirting and silly stories of lurid behavior that had merely amused him. He hadn't even cared about Jake's request to Bill or even the jibes from the other players, but that warm hand gliding over his chest and abdomen seriously unbalanced him. He wasn't prepared for this. He wasn't in control.

The voice of Marte sounded in his head. "Experience

is the only teacher who tests pass/fail for every kind of encounter. Until you pass her tests, you aren't in control."

Thinking about the events since that last day at Guild headquarters, Artearis realized just how not in control of himself he was. He had been mortally afraid when his brother had gotten the upper hand in their battle, disgusted with Jekan Geylas's task, and agitated at the memories that still haunted him from his first Guild assignment. Not being able to save Marte, the one person who understood him, had nearly broken Artearis. Only the child Geylas wanted dead stopped Artearis from letting the last snake end his life. The child shouldn't have to die because he wanted out of this misery.

If Artearis was going to survive long enough to save the boy, he needed to pass those lessons of experience and quickly because not only his brother wanted his life but also some unknown opponent — the person he was sure was responsible for Marte's death and the appearance of the assassin on the road. What plans could Artearis possibly have disrupted to draw that kind of attention? For that matter, how was Artearis going to disrupt Norland and Garad's assassination plans if he couldn't determine who they were hired to kill?

Artearis glanced at the moon. Daylight was only a few hours off. It looked like he'd have to chance going in while the inn was still conducting business. Again, he stretched the muscles of each leg. He didn't want them cramping up when he shifted off his perch. He reached up to grab the edge of the roof to swing himself back to the open window. Before he could move, light flooded the right doorway of the inn. The voices of men — some happy and some angry — spilled into the alley.

The voice of the bartender growled, "Keep it down."

Artearis let go of the roof and crouched down to watch. He could hear someone counting as the men exited. The person counting said something to the bartender that Artearis couldn't make out.

The bartender turned back into the room. "One short, boss. I'd check with Silky."

The bartender went back inside. About five minutes later a man was dumped outside. His belongings followed. Once the fellow had scrambled into his clothes and headed down the alley, women emerged from the doorway. Again, Artearis could hear the sound of counting.

This time Artearis heard the voice tell the bartender, "Everyone but Silky and Yasmine."

The bartender laughed.

"All clear, boss," he called inside then said to the other, "Okay, time to lock up."

The two stepped outside. The bartender shut and locked the door then both disappeared up the alley.

A few minutes later, a woman holding her cheek

extinguished the light in the second room from the end. Artearis was sure it was the same woman whose warm hand had caused him so much confusion earlier tonight. His pulse quickened. She had looked very ... how had Katie put it ... yummy? The light in the far room went out. Voices drifted out of the window across from Artearis. He heard the stinging sound of a slap followed by the tearing of cloth.

Norland's distinctive voice said, "You know the rules. No free time and certainly NOT in my bed." Another loud slap.

Damn! Silky was Norland's, and he'd let the opportunity slip. Amateur.

More voices entered the room as the light was lowered.

In the time it took Artearis to swing up through the window and move out of hearing distance, his face was burning. What a loathsome pair. Artearis shook his head to clear it. Develop a thicker skin he told himself.

Artearis looked around the empty warehouse. He needed a hiding place for later, so he could follow the two men. A few fairly large crates were stacked near the cargo door, but they didn't provide much cover. The loading platforms had been cleared. That left the ceiling. Artearis scurried along the rafters toward two cargo winches mounted to the rafters. Both winches had been retracted from the loading platform. The winch in front of the cargo door hung suspended midway. The second was retracted fully, resting against the rafter parallel to his location. As long as there's no activity later today, that one should provide sufficient cover. Satisfied, Artearis used his small grappling hook and rope to rappel to the ground. He still needed to find the tunnel to the inn.

Contrary to normal expectations, the tunnel entrance probably wasn't straight across from the inn's underground doorway. Most guild tunnels had at least one angle. Artearis decided to start his search at about the same lateral area where the staircase he saw Norland descend was located. About five feet from his starting point, he noticed the flooring change from stone to wood. A few feet into the wood, a ramp had been built to reach one of the platforms. Artearis studied the ramp. Parallel lines were faintly distinguishable. Artearis checked for traps and found a latch instead. The door opened easily, without sound, as he expected. He descended the steps, scanning for traps along the way. Part way down, he found a tripwire, easily avoided.

At the foot of the stairs Artearis figured it was safe enough to make a light. He pulled out one of his guild torches. The torch gave off an odor different from the smells in the tunnel. He couldn't take the chance that the smell might give him away. He went back up the stairs in search of a local light source. A box of candles was stacked on top of the large crates he'd spotted earlier. He removed a few then headed back down. It didn't take him long to disarm all the traps in the tunnel and reach the door to Norland and Garad's private storage room. He picked the lock and entered.

Artearis studied the room thoroughly before stepping into it. The walls and floor were hard packed dirt. The ceiling was the wooden floor from the room above. A tall cabinet stood against the right wall about three feet from the tunnel entrance. A smaller bookshelf, containing several stacks of papers and four books, stood along the side wall near the inn doorway. A single table was pushed against the wall opposite the tunnel with three chairs around it and a kerosene lamp on top. The floor was covered in footprints leading to each door, the table, the cabinet, and the bookshelf.

Artearis started his search with the shelf. He reached for a stack of papers and stopped. Time was slipping away. He needed to know who the target was. Assassins were taught to log assignments into ledgers. Four books were interspersed among the shelves. The first he picked up contained entries for the Cold Comfort Inn. Artearis scanned the numbers column. These two were quite the entrepreneurs. They'd turned the inn into a highly profitable business. He closed the book and laid it on the shelf as he'd found it.

The second ledger listed names, occupations, amounts, and, occasionally, a notation. Artearis could only assume this was the protection racket scheme. Two names with red stars stood out. One had Mayor in the occupation column. The other had Chief Constable listed. Next to the mayor's name was the word "liaison." Both had negative amounts posted in the amounts column. Bribes? The third book seemed to be random notes, like a journal. Between the pages someone had stashed letters. He set that one aside.

Picking up the last book, Artearis read the first page. It had a list of assassination targets, the probable locations of those targets, any specific habits, protection, date assignment acquired, amount of assignment, date completed, money collected, and from whom. The earliest date was over fifty years ago. He thumbed through the pages. This was one busy sector. All the entries appeared sanctioned until he reached the last dozen completed pages. Artearis grew angrier the longer he read. For more than six months, Norland and Garad had taken on unsanctioned hits. At least seven were extremely lucrative even by the inflated prices Artearis had been demanding. The last entry listed the target as Tanis Fedoral. Under payment, two amounts were already posted — both exceedingly large amounts. Next to the first amount, Artearis read the mayor's name. Next to the second amount was written anonymous benefactor. Penned in the margin was a note: see letters.

Even more angry, Artearis replaced the book. This anonymous business had the feel of outside forces. The Assassins Guild might be a lot of things, but they weren't traitors to the kingdom. Upon this one thing Artearis agreed with his father, even if for different reasons.

Artearis turned his attention to the letters stuffed between the pages. He guessed any pertaining to this assassination would be located toward the latter written entries. He found what he was looking for in the second letter. Clearly, the mayor, the chief constable, and several council members strongly objected to the increased military presence near Hisanth and were willing to REBATE a portion of their bribes if Norland and Garad could remove the immediate problem. "A third party has offered to finish the task once Captain Justinius Fedoral's protégé has been disposed of," it said. The letter included instructions on how to contact this third party using the gnolls camped near Sharp Reef Point.

Artearis carefully replaced the letters, closed the book, and returned it to the shelf. Norland and Garad were finished. The whole operation in Hisanth was finished. Even if Artearis hadn't wanted the Guild to fall, the assassination of a military person with such influential connections would bring too much unwanted attention to the Guild to let this pass without punishment.

At the tunnel entrance, Artearis verified the room was

in the same state as when he entered. Then he did the same for the tunnel, resetting every trap on his way out. In the warehouse, he checked the closed door to be certain it had sealed properly before he used his grappling hook to reach the rafter above, headed out the window, up to the roof, and across it to the wall where he'd hidden another coil of rope in a niche. Once back on the street, Artearis walked casually to the dock sector, hoping his presence at this time of the morning wouldn't be seen as out of place.

# Chapter Twelve
## New Terms

Artearis's followers had fought hard to make their escape. Revlin used the distraction to make his own exit, and for the better part of a day and a half, he had ridden hard to get to Sitar. Revlin knew the kind of news the Duke paid handsomely for, and he wanted to make damn sure he was the one getting paid for this. By the time he reached the ducal estate, false dawn lit the sky. He rode straight to the front entrance. Within minutes of dismounting, he shoved his way into the house to the Duke's empty study and smacked his forehead for being an idiot.

"Sir, please, the Duke is indisposed."

Revlin pushed the servant aside. Taking the stairs to the second floor two at a time, he burst into the Duke's bedroom. The servant followed behind, wringing his hands.

The ruckus caused the blonde-haired woman above Jekan Geylas to lose her rhythm. She attempted to slide out of the way, but Geylas clamped her to him as he shouted for his guards. The brunette at his side continued her own ministrations.

As the servant tried to steer Revlin out of the room, he planted himself firmly to the floor. "Sir, I have news that can't wait."

Geylas, again, shouted for his guards.

"Sir ...." Before Revlin could finish, the first guard appeared.

An angry Jekan Geylas roared, "Remove his head!"

Revlin tried again. "Sir, Zotearis rules!"

A slow smile spread across the Duke's face. "You are certain?"

Revlin nodded.

"Who else knows?"

Revlin began to relax. "No one outside the Guild. Not even Artearis Berain."

Geylas waved the first guard to him. With hesitant steps, the guard moved to the side of the bed. Geylas motioned for him to come closer. Quietly, Jekan Geylas said, "Take him outside and grill him hard. Then get rid of him permanently."

"How?" the guard whispered.

Geylas laughed softly. "He's an assassin."

The guard nodded and returned to the doorway.

In a louder voice, the Duke said, "Go with him and tell your tale in full. Once he's satisfied, he will give you your reward."

To his servant, Geylas said, "Send for Korvin."

Nodding, the servant bowed before backing out of the room after the others and shutting the door. As the latch clicked, he heard the Duke say "Now where were we?"

The blonde shifted herself onto the bed as a knock sounded.

The door opened and closed. "You wanted me?" The rough-looking man suppressed a smile as he observed the brunette worm her way under the covers.

An unsatisfied Jekan Geylas propped himself higher on his pillows and glared at the blonde. "That uppity Berain is no longer in charge. It's time to finally remove that obstacle. He's headed for Gessin to rid me of that brat. Or he's supposed to be. I don't trust him. Take your men and whoever else you need and make sure he does it. If he fails, kill the boy — PERSONALLY. Either way it plays, make sure the boy doesn't leave Gessin alive."

Geylas's private security chief paused before asking,

"What if the boy isn't there?"

The Duke snapped, "Well, do your job and find him; then get rid of the brat. My cousin always spends harvest time among his peasants. Where he goes, the boy goes."

Again the man paused. "Not true."

Jekan Geylas frowned.

"Your cousin has shipped the boy off with the Folk the past few summers. Sources can't reliably say if he did it this year."

"It doesn't matter, Korvin. Handle it. It's what I pay you for!"

"The usual terms?"

The Duke's frown deepened. "You get rid of Berain there'll be a bonus." He wrapped his meaty hand around the upper arm of the blonde woman and shoved her at Korvin. "Take her as down payment on the bonus."

Korvin reached out to grab the woman by the back of the neck. "What's our time frame?"

"He left Ionen eight days ago. Unless he's backed out, he should be in Gessin."

Korvin grunted. "His guild is thorough. He'll spend time doing recon. Give us a chance to get there." The muscular leader tightened his hold on the woman's neck, forcing her upon her toes. With the other hand, he opened the door.

"Korvin."

The man turned.

"It wouldn't be a tragedy if Berain removed my cousin as well."

Korvin nodded and guided the down payment out the door.

# Chapter Thirteen
## Unexpected Complications

False dawn filled the sky before Artearis reached the docks. When he finally saw the Gusty Wind, smoke poured from the chimney. Natty was already at work. He doubted he'd be able to sneak directly into his room unnoticed now. Just one more day. He needed his luck to hold just one more day — long enough for Norland and Garad to be neutralized — then he'd be gone from here. He grabbed the doorknob and turned. Quietly, he opened the door, entered the inn, and closed the door.

From the kitchen, Natty said, "I told ya he was up ta no good."

In front of Artearis a wooden beam crashed down into the metal mount bracket on the door frame above the knob.

From the left and right, tanned, well-muscled arms grabbed him.

A hand yanked back his head and held a sharp blade to his throat. Another hand flipped back his cloak to reveal the grappling hook and thin coil of rope, as well as the dirk. After one of the assailants removed the dirk and hook, his rear attacker moved the blade away from his throat far enough so Artearis could be dragged to a chair by the fire. In the fire, Artearis could see the crimson ends of iron pokers. Looking down, he saw the fire reflected off the weapon held at his chest — Darethan's dagger. The clang of metal thudding against wood drew his eyes to the shorter common room table. Darethan's sword lay upon it.

"Old Gregory an' the cap'n ain't the only ones fed up with these killer games." The voice of the man behind him belonged to the sailor from the docks. "An', thanks to Lemm here, we know yore one o' them."

Lemm said, "No wonder he was all eager to have me dirk 'stead of the cash." Lemm waved his hand back and forth between Darethan's blades. "These things stick out better 'en a whore in a madam's house." Several of the men laughed.

"Like you'd know," came from one, a sailor pinning his arms.

"Yeah, Lemm," the sailor said, "good thing you remembered this bloke when we heard news o' that dead assassin on the road. We figure you must o' come snoopin' to see why they ain't done it yet. Old Gregory warned us someone might come checkin' up on those two."

"Well, Ol' Greg'ry told us that them's in charge might not be too happy with the doings at the inn up there last he was in the yard."

"Oh, Lemm, pipe down. Killers are killers. I'd as soon be rid of the lot an' be done with it. I'm tired of gettin' bled dry."

Artearis risked speaking. "You'll lose more than men and cargo if Norland and Garad aren't stopped."

The other hand pitched Artearis forward and slammed him back against the chair. "Shut up."

Artearis winced but dared to continue. "They've been hired to kill the lieutenant in charge of the fort."

"Just how do you know that?" Lemm asked.

Artearis angled his head toward the grappling hook. "I've been ... investigating."

"Keep talkin'," Natty said from the kitchen doorway.

Artearis briefly sketched out the contents of the final ledger entry and the part of the letter concerning the city officials. "The Assassins Guild would never risk endangering Corellith. It would be ... um ... bad for business."

Natty said, "Well, it's a safe bet if we know about the dead man that those two up there do. They'll be a lookin' for trouble, young'un."

Artearis frowned. It was a good thing he hadn't wagered on that conversation.

The innkeeper came huffing and puffing through the back door and into the main room. Dropping the basket that he carried at his feet, he leaned over to catch his breath. "The merchants," he wheezed, "the merchants are riled up. One o' those mili'try riders came through 'bout sun up. Guess he let slip the soldiers ain't supposed to come to town an' they's mad about it." The innkeeper shook his head. "Don't know why. Ain't no way that rider could git to that there fort a'fore those men head out this mornin'.'"

Artearis said, "Then Norland and Garad will have to strike today. They can't risk waiting until the next leave."

"What would Greg'ry do?" Lemm asked.

The room filled with chatter.

"Old Gregory would cut this one's throat then string him up next to that other corpse. Then he'd do the same to those other two blokes."

Artearis couldn't help chuckling at the words. "Sounds the way that wharf rat would handle it, too."

Natty walked over to the chair holding Artearis. "How'd ya know that, young'un?"

Artearis regretted looking up into Natty's face. Her piercing stare made him feel like a fly he once saw pinned to a merchant's counter. The fly had died.

Natty looked at the sailor and asked again, "How'd ya

know Gregory was a dock hand? No one on the docks woulda told ya."

The sailor shook his head "no."

Artearis thought about lying to the woman for as long as it took for her penetrating eyes to capture his again. He thought back to the first time he and Gregory met, before Artearis had begun his initiation. He had seen the golden earring Gregory wore and jokingly called him a pirate. "Let's just say calling Gregory a wharf rat is much safer than calling him a pirate, even if he looks like one with that golden earring."

Natty turned her thoughtful gaze to the sword on the table. "What makes ya think ya can stop those two ruffians, young'un? They got a good decade more of life each than ya."

Artearis swore silently. Natty was right again.

"An' they got plenty o' help in town," Lemm said.

In town but not at the fort. If Artearis could get to the fort ... what and ask the lieutenant for help? Why would Fedoral help? Artearis let his mind race through the events of last night. The Inn. The warehouse. The tunnel. The room. The ledgers. Yes, the fourth ledger. Artearis could use the ledger to convince Fedoral. He would just have to eliminate the sanctioned guild activity first.

"I'll get Fedoral to help. I'll even help you get rid of the whole operation IF you do something for me."

Natty looked skeptical.

"What kind o' something?" asked the sailor.

"A diversion ... in front of the Cold Comfort Inn at about the time the soldiers would be leaving Hisanth. Something that would empty the place."

Lemm said, "We could do a bit o' disturbin' the peace."

Natty said, "Let him go." She paused, thinking. The sailor held out Artearis's dagger. Then Natty said, "But keep his sword. If he brings us proof o' what he said, we'll give it back."

Artearis froze in the middle of stretching his arms and legs to get feeling back. Without his blades, his odds dropped tremendously.

"We'll be waiting at the side o' the inn fer ya." Natty looked hard at Artearis. "Now, come into the kitchen, so I kin feed ya."

The innkeeper yanked the wooden beam off the door. "The rest o' you varmints clear out. I got an inn to open."


Artearis sank down onto a kitchen chair next to the eating table and studied the room as Natty bustled around the kitchen. It was surprisingly well kept. Artearis wouldn't have thought the Gusty Wind took in enough coin to keep the place so well. Then again, Natty was full of surprises. He wouldn't have thought those men would listen to her like they did.

"How do ...." Artearis began.

"Gregory and I have spent quality time together."

"The innkeeper doesn't ...."

"My partner not my husband. My man, bless his lost soul, left me his share o' this," she waved her hand around the kitchen "and that ship out there with the pretty decoration." She actually smiled as she said the last.

Artearis looked out the window to see the skeleton swaying in the brisk wind — the skeleton that Gregory had strung up.

"Gregory's been good ta me." The smile faded. "We knew it couldna last."

She set a plate in front of Artearis. On it was a light but tasty meal of cheese, eggs, and fruit Artearis had never seen before. A smile returned to her face as she set a second plate of fruit onto the table and sat down. "He'd bring me these in the late fall. They keep surprisingly well, better than apples or 'tatoes."

Artearis took a bite. The taste was sweet and rich and mellow. He started to ask where the fruit came from, but Natty was ahead of him.

"I never heard o' the place — not even from me man. Seresh, Gregory called it." She pointed at the only picture in the kitchen.

Artearis followed the path of her finger. For the second time in as many days, Artearis's heart nearly stopped beating. Upon the wall was a smaller version of the tapestry that hung in his office.

"He brought me that, so I'd know where."

Natty frowned at his changed expression. "Ya know the place?"

Artearis shook his head. "I wish I did …." He yawned.

"Ya need sleep. I'll fetch ya afore the sun goes down."

As Artearis got up to leave, Natty grabbed his arm. "Don' disappoint me, young'un."


Natty made sure Artearis awoke well before sunset. He dressed. The dirk and Darethan's dagger lay on the rumpled bed. Artearis searched around for a cloth. Using the one from the wash stand, he sat on the edge of the bed and picked up his dagger. With carefully controlled rage, he dug out the last of the muck he had smeared on it the day before. He had been so certain he'd played his part perfectly, both in the Cold Comfort Inn and at the docks. Yeah. He'd done such a swell job it had cost him Darethan's sword.

He ran his thumb along the edge of the dagger. Although sharp, guild protocol dictated he hone it further. As he applied the whetstone to it, he berated himself for being careless when entering the Gusty Wind this morning. Artearis drew the blade across the stone in a long, slow, grating motion. Thinking the threat was contained in the warehouse district was a mistake Morgan would have cut a trainee's throat for making.

He ran his finger over the edge again. Artearis had sat there while that damn sailor held his own blade against his throat. Darethan would have given his life rather than let his blades be taken.

*Darethan isn't trying to save the life of a boy and a lieutenant and his country. You can't do that dead.*

Artearis set the dagger aside. What other careless mistakes had he made? He raked the edge of the dirk over the whetstone. And what of Gregory?

His strokes grew longer, harder. Artearis had trusted the man, yet it was now clear Gregory had his own agenda as surely as Norland and Garad.

Artearis set the other side of the edge to the stone and pulled. That's right. He's an assassin. He's not supposed to care for anyone. He's not supposed to want to keep them from harm.

*You're an assassin. You wouldn't grieve over Marte's death. You wouldn't want revenge or \*gasp\* justice. That would show you had emotions and a conscience.*

Artearis threw the dirk onto the bed. He picked up his saddlebags. These people were using him: just like Geylas, just like the Guild, just like his father. His mind saw Marte pulling him up from the ground. "You're a Berain, boy. You've been trained well, but you aren't perfect. The sooner you figure that out, the sooner you'll learn how to stay alive."

He stuffed the clothes he'd worn yesterday into the bags. He was the head of the Assassins Guild. People didn't use him, and they damn well didn't take his most prized possessions away.

He sheathed his dagger and tucked the dirk into his belt. He slung the saddlebags over his shoulder, his hand brushing the stone at his throat. The chain filled the void left by the loss of his mother's scarf — the one he had yanked from his neck to use as a tourniquet on a young woman's knife wound. His father had grabbed the scarf and tossed it into the gutter. "You're a Berain, an assassin. You're in the killing business, not the saving one."

Artearis yanked the door open. *Mind your own business, Father.* He slammed the door shut.

In the kitchen, Natty turned toward the door at his approach. She waved him to a chair and went to the stove to dish up some fish stew. Passing the cutting table, she also picked up a small plate of fruit, carrying both to the table.

"Ya got a temper, doncha, young'un? I think that's not a good thing fer that work o' yours." She trapped his eyes with hers. "What's eatin' ya more? Gettin' got by us or losin' tha sword?" She looked toward the door. "All o' us here feel the same."

The innkeeper put the broom he'd been using in the corner. "What Natty ain't sayin' is we been fightin' to survive fer a long spell. Least the other un's afore those killer blokes broke fingers or arms or legs. Old Gregory caught that bloke swinging out there trying to cut Natty's throat."

"He picked wrong. Who'd want me dead?"

Artearis didn't want excuses. He wanted his sword. He wanted to kill Norland and Garad. He wanted to sacrifice his life to save a child, so he could be done with all of this. "Assassins don't 'pick' wrong."

"See," the innkeeper told Natty. He fished around in his apron pocket. When he pulled out his hand, he was holding a piece of hide. He sat it on the table next to the bowl of soup.

Artearis flattened it out. A crude map showed Hisanth, the fort to the north, a road between the two, the coast line to the west, and a river to the east. Beside the road was written 5.3. Artearis looked up.

"Ya said ya'd hafta do it at tha fort. I figured it would help." The innkeeper shuffled back into the common room.

"Ya can get proof, right, young'un?" Natty turned and went back to her stove.

Artearis crumpled the map under his fingers. He picked up the spoon in his other hand and ate the soup. Once he had eaten, he collected his saddlebags from the floor and his horse from the lean-to. Standing outside the inn, he spread the map out on the saddle. The coast wouldn't be safe to travel at night. The soldiers would be patrolling the road.

He could shadow the river. It appeared to flow north before curving to the northwest behind the fort. But could he trust the map? He still had a few hours before sunset.

Artearis led the horse toward the eastern gate.

# Chapter Fourteen
## The Cold Comfort Inn

The map was surprisingly accurate. Artearis estimated that to go from the eastern gate to the back gate of the fort would take more than an hour in darkness. That didn't leave him much time for getting Natty's proof or convincing the lieutenant. He decided he could increase his lead time by a quarter of an hour by leaving his horse near the western bend of the river. He'd have to move his rope to the northeastern wall, but finding a spot there shouldn't be too difficult.

Artearis carefully inspected the horse as he rubbed it down, checking for swelling in the legs and that the horse had not picked up any unwanted debris in its hooves. He'd have to be alert traveling by the waning moon. The ground had been fairly even, but sections of hazardous ground had forced him to ride around patches during his reconnaissance.

With the horse settled, Artearis chose to spend the last half hour before sunset going through the conditioning exercises from his training. The riding and hiding had left him stiffer than expected. He concentrated on each move, coaxing his muscles to flow with the sound of the river. The rhythm quieted his mind. He lost himself in the movement until the sun flared in his eyes before sinking below the horizon.

He sighed. He hadn't felt this kind of stillness since before Geylas had come to the Guild.

Artearis used the north gate to re-enter Hisanth. The mass of soldiers milling around the square made it easy to slip inside. Getting out wouldn't be so easy. Scanning the crowd, Artearis noticed spotters in the shadows scrutinizing people waiting to leave the city. One spotter tracked a lone traveler dressed in a dark cloak held against his body to keep the wind from whipping it about. The spotter used a reflective surface to send a flash of light toward the gate using the illumination from the roaring fire in the center of the square. The signal was too obvious for Artearis's taste. He edged his way around the crowd toward the eastern part of Hisanth.

Before he had a chance to slip past the clumps of people blocking access to the merchant stalls, he saw two men angling through the crowd in his direction. He shifted his route toward a cart displaying melons but was cut off by a group of sailors carrying mugs and singing off key. One of the louder singers raised his mug as if saluting the cart and yelled, "To G!" Artearis followed the outstretched arm with his eyes. Next to a stall ten feet behind the cart, Lemm and that cursed sailor from the dock stood outlined in the firelight. The seadog inclined his head slightly.

Artearis felt his hand grip the dirk at his waist. Still, he headed to the same food stall. As he approached, Lemm greeted him with a loud "Well hello, mate" and a slap on the back. The sailor moved to Artearis's other side. The man handed him a stick with meat and vegetables skewered on it. To take the food, Artearis had to turn toward the direction he had just come. The maneuver allowed him to see the two men who had been trying to intercept him. They had stopped. One said something to the other as they headed back into the crowd.

Lemm looked at the sailor but spoke to Artearis. "There may not be safety in numbers, but them two are figurin' we'd sooner cut an assassin's throat then be friendly ta one."

The sailor grunted.

Artearis's hand refused to loosen his grip on the dirk.

Lemm studied the stick he held. "We been watchin' ta see if anyone's tryin' ta lure soldiers away. If they are, they ain't doin' it here."

"Don't bother," Artearis told them. "There's too many to track. It's Norland and Garad you needed to find. They've already picked their targets. Maybe even snatched them. Possibly from the Cold Comfort Inn."

The sailor nodded.

Lemm said, "There won' be many soldiers goin' ta that inn. Word is the lieutenant punishes hard them caught for misbehavin' because of goin' there."

Artearis had already guessed as much. *That's why clients leave assassinations to professionals. We don't take forever to figure things out.* He finally felt the ache in his right hand from gripping the dirk. He let go and turned to leave.

The sailor grabbed Artearis's sore hand as if to shake it. He leaned into the gap between them. "It's a good thing Natty's still hale and hearty, or you'd 'ave never seen that pretty sword o' yours again. She's the only reason we didn't slit your throat this mornin'."

Artearis froze. He had wanted to kill Natty. He had wanted to kill them all. He would have if he had been certain he could find his sword in time to deal with Norland and Garad tonight.

"She believes you can help, boy."

Lemm nodded. "Natty just knows things about people. She's steered us through messes here in Hisanth better than that fancy rudder on the cap'n's prized ship."

"Do you still want a diversion tonight?"

A diversion would be useful. Artearis frowned.

"I seen that place got three ways out: two in the back and the one out front," Lemm said. "We can get one o' the girls ta pick a fight with her man if'n they use the back. Maybe start a fight out front if'n they go that way."

That would solve Artearis's problem of dealing with anything unexpected Norland and Garad might come up with and get these clowns out of the way. He nodded.

The sailor dropped Artearis's hand. "Meet Natty at the side street across from the front o' the inn afore midnight."

It hadn't taken Artearis long to find a good spot to climb down the eastern wall and to stash his gear atop it. Even so, it was well after the ninth hour of dark before he settled himself behind the winch of the dimly lit warehouse. He'd spent the time in between scanning the alley and neighboring streets for spotters. It must have been after the tenth hour of dark before he heard the small entrance door creak open. Two dark figures, each dragging something heavy, headed to the loading ramp. One let his burden go long enough to move the panel covering the tunnel. After the second figure lit a lamp and dragged the man shape down the stairs, the other hefted up his man and followed. The light only affected Artearis's sight for a few moments.

His training had steered him right. Norland and Garad chose stealth over deception, but they were sloppy. Neither had bothered to close the panel. Artearis suddenly realized he had been just as inattentive when he had investigated the tunnel.

Maybe a quarter of an hour passed when the two men reappeared unencumbered. They headed for the same door, pausing to whisper to each other before opening it. A gust of wind entered through the door carrying the strong scent of alcohol to Artearis. The two assassins staggered outside. Artearis heard the discordant voices singing until the sound of the door closing cut them off. Moments later, he heard a woman's angry voice drift through the window.

Artearis used his small grappling hook to lower himself to the floor. He snatched a couple more candles from the supply box and headed down into the tunnel opening Norland and Garad hadn't bothered to close.

He checked for the traps he disarmed on the previous visit. None were reset. In the storage room, Artearis found two men in military clothes tied and gagged, unconscious but still breathing. They must be the scapegoats. Artearis didn't waste any more time on the men. He needed to get proof: for Natty — and for the lieutenant.

He took the books and papers from the shelf to the

table. Fortunately, a candle holder sat upon it. He put his candle into the holder to free both his hands and began flipping through the last ten pages of the Assassination Ledger. On the second to last page, fourth entry from the bottom were the details of a contract to kill Gregory, Natty, the ship's captain, and someone named Everlan. The entry below contained the details for another contract with three targets. Natty's name and a notation stating the second and third targets "tbd" were written into the name column. The mayor was listed as the point of contact. The client, although wishing to remain anonymous, was listed as located in Psarkoth. Artearis found Natty's proof, but he couldn't give it to her. He needed the entry on the other side for Fedoral.

He exchanged the ledger for the journal. When he opened it, a letter fell out. Artearis quickly scanned it and realized more was going on in Hisanth than two rogue assassins setting up their own shop. Some kind of underground organization was using Norland and Garad to remove obstacles to its expansion plan — without Guild sanction. He dropped the letter onto the table. The next few letters confirmed it. He fingered the jewel at his throat. If he wasn't so determined to remove himself from the Guild, he'd go to Psarkoth personally and teach these upstarts the penalties that come from cheating the Assassins Guild. He added them to the pile.

Artearis dug through the collection of letters for the

one with information about the gnolls. He dropped it onto the stack. The rest of the letters in the journal were collected into their own pile and placed inside his bag of holding. He looked at the stack on the table. He shoved the letters inside his shirt. Finally, he picked up the Assassination Ledger and began ripping pages from the front and holding them over the candle flame to set them on fire. The paper was slow to catch and burn. This was taking too long. He turned to the last ten pages and ripped them out, stuffing them inside his vest this time.

Dropping the ledger onto the table, Artearis grabbed the edge and shoved the table across the ground to the floor-length wooden cabinet. He pushed the Assassination Ledger to the middle of the table. Picking up the journal and the Inn's accounting ledger, he balanced each against the ledger. He looked around the room for something to use as a fuse. His eyes passed over the candle. The candle had burned down a quarter of its length. He was running out of time. He stared at the candle for a moment. Of course, he had put the spare candle into his pocket. He pulled it out and pared away the wax from the bottom, exposing the wick, he positioned it across the two book ends.

He still needed to make sure no one could put out the fire before it destroyed any evidence incriminating the Assassins Guild. As he expected, the door to the inn had a bar brace. He dropped the bar. For good measure, he grabbed one of the chairs to wedge against the knob. His shoulder struck a metal object hanging from a hook. Perfect. He took the lantern to the table and emptied the oil over the books and papers. The liquid spread to the edge of the table where it spilled over onto the cabinet. The oil ran down the cabinet and started flowing toward the tunnel door and the two men lying on the ground.

Artearis dragged one scapegoat through the tunnel and up the stairs, dumping his body behind the two large crates near the delivery door. He hurried back to the storage room and lit both ends of the horizontal candle before seizing the second man's collar and pulling him out to lie next to his comrade.

# Chapter Fifteen
## Miscalculation

Door or window? The length of his candle warned Artearis he needed to hurry. He snuffed it out before quietly opening the door enough to slip outside. Now he could clearly hear the sound of fighting and yelling coming from the square in front of the Cold Comfort Inn. The diversion should have drawn any spotters to it, but he scanned the shadows to be certain. Once satisfied, Artearis hurried past the kitchen entrance and crossed the side road to the shadows of the alley. It was going to be easy to circle around to the meeting place with Natty. Even so, he studied the alley carefully before continuing.

He hadn't moved fifteen feet when an explosion from behind rocked the ground. He looked back to see flames coming from the back of the inn near the high stakes room exit. Moments later, a second explosion tossed him to the ground as a pillar of flame engulfed the kitchen area. Artearis could see the pillar bend toward the front of the inn as the wind picked up. This was not what he had expected. He had wanted to destroy evidence, not kill people. He hustled around to the street across from the inn.

The area in front of the inn was packed with people yelling, screaming, and crying. Many were trying to escape the heat and flames by fleeing down the streets away from the square. Some fell then staggered to their feet. Others fell and never got back up. Several soldiers were helping townsmen try to douse the fire, but the wind kept gusting, fighting their efforts.

Why wasn't anyone organizing these people? Artearis scanned the open area. Near the flames, he could only make out dark silhouettes against the brightness of the fire. Closer to the street he looked out from, he could tell some were covered in black streaks. He kept looking. In the center of the square was what he sought. Artearis headed toward the well. They needed to start a bucket brigade: standard Guild emergency procedure for fires.

Artearis quickly surveyed the people hustling to the well. The towners scurried back and forth frantically. The soldiers collected their buckets in an orderly fashion.

Artearis grabbed the arm of the next soldier to reach the well.

"Hey!" The soldier tried to shake off Artearis's hand.

Artearis snapped, "Who's your leader?"

"Huh?"

"Who gives the orders?"

The soldier tugged his arm. "The lieutenant."

"Get him!"

The man stopped struggling. "He's at the fort."

Artearis growled out, "Well who do you answer to in town?"

"Sergeant Ingram"

"Find him. Tell him to gather his men and organize a fire brigade. Do it fast."

The man snapped to attention then ran toward the north gate.

Artearis turned his attention to the well. One man was hoisting the rope with a crank. Another was waiting for the bucket. When the bucket emerged from the well, Artearis noticed it hung from a hook instead of being tied to the rope. The man grabbed the bucket and ran toward the inn while another put his bucket on the hook. Artearis counted eleven, twelve buckets.

A boy sprinting past the well came to an abrupt halt as Artearis latched onto his shoulder.

"Let go 'a me!"

Artearis ignored the demand. "Buckets. Where can we get more?"

The boy struggled to get free.

"Kid, we need more buckets. Where can we get some?"

"Warehouses a' course. If'n they don't catch fire."

The man hauling on the crank puffed, "Wind's goin' ta change."

Artearis frowned. "We need to get that fire out."

The boy's face showed shock. "Save that there inn? You're daft."

The man grunted, "Boy's right. Too many barrels."

"Too many barrels?"

The boy nodded. "Inn got a double ship a' oil day afore yester' morn. Twenty barrels down in the hole."

The man said, "Kitchen barrels have already blown. Won't be much longer an' the other's 'll go. Then the warehouses. Then the town."

"We'll have to contain the fire then. Where did you say the buckets were?"

The boy hitched his head toward the inn. "Warehouse behind. Got a crate in a few days back."

Artearis turned the boy to face him. "Find some friends and bring me those buckets. Understand?"

The boy nodded and disappeared into the crowd.

*What kind of mess had he created?*

The rhythmic sound of boots striking earth drew his

attention. Soldiers marched to a stop near the well.

An authoritative man detached himself. "Who's in charge here?"

Artearis started to say he was but changed his mind. "No one. That's the problem." He relayed the information given to him by the boy and the man still working the crank handle.

Sergeant Ingram listened. "Ok, we have this." Ingram pointed at the men in the first row. "Find buckets. The rest of squad one split into brigade duty and head to the well at the east gate. Squad two ... same drill ... docks well. Squad three ... man this well. Mo...."

The boy tugged at Artearis's sleeve. "We got tha buckets."

The sergeant nodded approval. "You know what to do, men."

Before Sergeant Ingram could take more interest in him, Artearis faded into the crowd on the far side of the square. He watched the sergeant begin to organize those towners wielding buckets. Instead of trying to put out the fire, the sergeant concentrated on confining it and letting the inn burn itself out. Those who stumbled into the process were either conscripted or politely but firmly redirected to the area from where Artearis watched. When a pair of refugees stumbled into the bucket line, Artearis could see one soldier detach himself and escort the two in his direction.

A blast of air blew through the square, spreading a curtain of long, silky hair before them — long and — Silky. As the two came closer, he could see half of her hair was gone.

The soldier left the two women at the edge of the crowd. They tried to push their way through without success. Artearis shuddered at the sight of the injured woman's right eye looking out from scorched muscle. The fire had burned away most of the clothing on her right side, exposing a mangled arm and skinless breast.

He weaved his way toward them, sidestepping a couple of drunks cheering the fire and calling for toasted dogs and ale. One actually grabbed at the burned woman's good breast. Artearis neatly stepped between the two and scooped the poor thing into his arms.

Natty's voice was loud and strained as she worked to be heard above the noise. "Poor thing got caught on the second floor. She jumped, or she wouldna be alive at all now."

The smell of burning flesh made Artearis nauseous. "Where to?" he asked Natty to distract himself.

Natty gestured at the second entrance to the left.

Artearis looked down at the human carnage he carried and shuddered. This was his handiwork.

Natty pushed her way through the people blocking the

entrance.

Artearis followed.

Natty grabbed the arm of a healer passing by. The expensively dressed young man tried to shrug off her grip, but Natty held on.

*Natty was one determined woman.*

"We don't do charity," he snapped at Natty.

Natty snapped back, "Yore supposed ta be a healer, so heal!"

The young man snarled, told Natty to go sit on a sideways wagon without the wheel, and turned to address a man wearing a silk shirt.

Artearis looked down at Silky. What clothing that remained was as provocative as the one she wore when she had unsettled him so badly the night before. He looked closer at the left side of her face. It was still exquisite, evoking the memory of her hand sliding down his chest. The ache in the pit of his stomach returned to compete with the nausea from the smell of her burned flesh. She had been so beautiful and vibrant.

Artearis pushed past Natty and the man in the silk shirt and shoved Silky into the healer's chest. The healer's arms automatically came up to catch his burden.

As soon as Artearis felt the weight gone from his arms, he pulled the dirk out of his belt. Sliding beside the man, he raised it to the healer's throat and whispered, "You'll take special care of this patient. If you do the job to Natty's satisfaction, it might even prove profitable. Otherwise, it might prove fatal. Understand?"

The healer nodded as best he could without cutting himself. Artearis purposefully pushed up the sleeve of his arm enough to show the assassin's mark on his hand. He could feel the healer's prominent swallow against the side of the hand holding the dirk.

In a low voice, Natty said, "That temper makes ya rash, young'un, but I think Silky will appreciate it. Lemm's in the alley behind this building. Tell him 'Gregory's satisfied.' He'll give ya back your sword."

Artearis raised his eyebrow.

"Yore runnin' out o' time if'n ya want ta save that lieutenant."

Artearis nodded. He let go of the healer and replaced the dirk at his waist. He removed the bag of holding from his belt. Searching inside, his hand found the small sack containing the jewels from his desk. He pulled it out, removed two gems, and exchanged the sack for the stack of letters. Artearis handed the lot to Natty. "Only if YOU are satisfied."

Natty looked at the letters.

"Your proof. You'll know what to do with it."

Natty smiled. "Git!"

The healer shifted Silky into a more comfortable position at the sight of the ruby and emerald Natty held. "This way, please."

Artearis followed them as far as the stairs to the infirmary. Natty was right. Time was getting away. He walked through the building to the alley and found Lemm leaning against the back wall, for all the world looking as if he was just enjoying the night sky, despite the destruction and death only a few buildings away. A horse was waiting there as well, saddled and ready to go. He made no effort to hide himself.

Like it or not, these people, despite what they had done to him personally, were only doing what they felt was right. Artearis realized he would have to get over his bitterness. Hadn't he made enough mistakes of his own this evening?

Lemm spotted him as he outlined himself in the alley. "Eh? What'r you about?"

Artearis walked toward the man, staying far enough away not to be perceived a threat until he gave his message. "Gregory's satisfied."

Lemm grinned as he stepped off the wall, "Guess you'll be wantin' this," he said as he reached down and into a large crack in the building's stone base, carefully pulling out a long, flat box.

Artearis took a step forward.

Lemm pulled back. "What happened o'er yonder?"

"A couple of killers left their paperwork in the wrong place, and it caught fire." Artearis frowned. "And, so will all those barrels."

"Barrels?"

"The twenty barrels of oil they had shipped in two days ago."

Lemm snorted. "In that inn? Fat chance. Been down in that hole. No room for a score o' barrels AND the inn's supplies."

Artearis's frown deepened.

"That there inn'd be lucky to use half that in a month anywho. Asides. Oil is shipped about in firefern barrels to keep 'em from burning down the ships carryin' 'em. They ain't goin' boom unless they been cracked open."

Artearis dug inside his vest for the ledger pages. He strained to reread the entries in the dim alley. *Gregory. Natty. The ship's captain. Everlan. Firefern barrels are used because they don't explode until breached. Norland and Garad were planning to take out all of them tonight! Those four were to be a ...* "distraction!"

Lemm shoved the box toward Artearis. "I be thinkin' the same. I'm a let the boss know. You take care o' the fort an' the boss will take care o' the town, and killer," Artearis looked up from the box, "make sure you don't screw this up eh. I kinda like safe passage."

Artearis nodded.

"And don' you worry 'bout getting out. There be someun' waitin' for you at the north gate."

Artearis nodded again. He retrieved the sword, and after giving it a quick inspection, sheathed it, buckled it on, mounted, and kicked the horse into a cantor.

# Chapter Sixteen
## Letters of Incrimination

Lemm pawed against the dock wood with his foot. "That killer thinks the same. Those other ones, the ones runnin' the whore and gamblin' racket, are plannin' somethin' sneaky. He knew more than he said, though. You could see it the way his face tightened up and his trap snapped shut before he finally spit it out."

The captain nodded his head. "That one knows more about a lot of things that he's not saying."

Lemm frowned. "He don't trust them. You don't trust him."

"Aye." The captain paused. "But I don't trust them more." The captain rubbed his hand across his chin.

"What you think Ol' Greg'ry would do?"

The captain's hand stopped. "Hum?"

"Greg'ry. About them ... about him ... this ...."

The captain's dark eyes narrowed. "Them ... string them up. Him?" The captain shrugged his shoulders. "Depends on his gut. This?" The captain pointed at his ship, "not take chances." The captain put his thumb and forefinger to his mouth and blew.

The shrill sound made Lemm cover his ears.

Within minutes, the first mate skidded to a stop at the foot of the dock plank. "Yes, Cap'n?"

"Ship search. From stem to stern. From bilge to crow's nest."

"Yes, Cap'n."

The captain grabbed his first mate's shoulder and leaned in. In a quiet voice he said, "Make it a three search. Two old. One new. And watch the new."

"Cap'n?"

"Traitors."

The first mate nodded. "Deck inspection," he yelled on his way back up the plank.

The captain turned back to Lemm. "Natty?"

"Nothin' since the square."

"Make sure she's safe."

"Aye aye, Sir."

Natty followed the healer up the stairs and to the back of a long room with narrow beds jutting out into the middle. She watched him drop Silky onto the one at the far end. Silky screamed when she landed. The healer's head jerked upward, scanning the room for Natty. Her deep frown caused his mouth to blabber out platitudes and apologies. The frown remained fixed on Natty's face.

She didn't particularly care for the room. It was plain with nothing to stare at but dark wooden boards and patients. Only the foot of each bed was well lit from a light fixed onto the wall in front. The smell of the oil wasn't so much unpleasant as it was incompatible with the other smells in the room.

Natty settled herself in the corner, just on the edge of the circle of light, and watched the healer direct two apprentices to strip Silky. The plump young man in the fine robes leaned over Silky and began to peel back the ruined blouse. The more he revealed, the stronger the smell of burned flesh filled the room. He dropped the cloth and tucked his arm across his stomach. Before he could turn away, he vomited on Silky's chest. A heart-wrenching scream burst from Silky when the acid touched her blistering wounds.

Natty's hand spasmed around the two gems Artearis had put there. The strength of her reaction caused pain to shoot up her arm. Natty opened her clenched fist. Light refracted from the gems. The colors painted the bed red and green. The healer, seeing the display, jerked the apprentice upright and shoved him into the walk space at the foot of the bed. Natty traced a thin line of blood with her forefinger before folding her fingers over the gems and putting them away in an apron pocket where her hand brushed against the envelopes she had stuffed there before leaving Artearis.

She ran a finger along the edge of the stack of envelopes. More letters were bundled in the stack than Natty had expected. She drew it from her pocket and slid her forefinger between the first letter and the rest. Her mind began to turn as she rubbed the letter between thumb and forefinger.

A time existed when letters were commonplace in her life. In Allisar — in Pristas — before she had left the Royal Rose Inn. Natty had always been good at reading people. Her parents had hoped it was a sign of mage potential. They sent her off to the Mage Academy, but Natty was not mage material. Her man, before he was her man, had shown more potential: as a water mage. He passed his apprenticeship, struggled through his journeyman work, but failed to master his artisan skills. Sometimes, Natty thought it was her fault. He had met her at the celebration the Academy held for those students who successfully completed journeyman status. After that, he had spent as much time trying to get her into his bed as he had studying, but Natty would have none of it.

Silky coughed and cried out.

Natty looked up. Silky's life could have been hers. Natty looked down at her plain, work worn figure. No, Natty would never have been able to live as well as Silky. Thankfully, Moratam had blessed Natty with the gift of understanding food, and the kitchen master at the Royal Rose Inn decided her talent was enough to take her on as an apprentice. Natty honestly believed all those patron propositions were made because they wanted to get her fired so she would be forced to come and cook for them, but Natty refused to jeopardize her position.

On the day Natty had achieved her own artisan status, her man had asked her to marry him. Natty's hand grew still. Of course, he hadn't said a word about being offered a position on a ship that called Hisanth its home port until after they were married. Natty grimaced. She had been furious with her man — so much so that she nearly spilled the dinner of one of her favorite patrons.

After downing his third helping of her venison stew, and narrowly avoiding being decorated with a fourth, that trouble-making barbarian priest of the All God flat out told her to grow up. Life was filled with desires and the choices they bring. Now was her time to choose what she desired the most: love or her work. Natty did love her man, so she reluctantly gave up her position in the kitchen of the Royal Rose Inn and went with him to Hisanth to make what life they could together by the sea.

Natty made up her mind again. She slid her finger under the flap of that first envelope and retrieved the letter. With a snap of her wrist she shook it open. The handwriting was large, well-formed, strong, and in script. Her husband's letters had been in a spidery, hurried scrawl. It was dated two weeks ago.

"Why is the boy still alive?! I paid you up front for a speedy removal of my problem. Don't make me regret my decision to hire independent contractors."

Natty folded the angry letter and put it back in its envelope. She pulled the next letter free. The date was five days ago. The script was cramped and small and barely legible in the dregs of light.

"Word has come the fort will be locked down within a fortnight. We aren't taking any chances of a setback. Orchestrate the diversions. Get inside that fort and get rid of that lieutenant before another week passes. We'll be ready to do our part when the signal goes up."

Natty set the envelope and letter on the floor in front of her. She dropped the first letter to the side of it. She pulled the third free of its container. It, too, was out of order — dated nine days ago. The writing was small and precise.

"Good job of convincing them to "rebate" part of their

money. The idiots have no clue. Make sure it stays that way until the operation is solidified."

Natty mulled over the letter in her hand. She shifted her focus to the ones on the floor. Finally, her eyes fell on the pile still in her lap. She sat the third letter down on the other side of the first before picking up the stack. She thumbed through the pile: four ... five ... six .... Natty counted ten more letters. She opened each and tried to match the handwriting to those already on the floor. When she had opened all of them and placed each different writer into a pile, she had six stacks in front of her. None of them were signed, but Natty was sure the two on the far right were written by the mayor. The flamboyant style was like his signature on the special permit the Inn had acquired from the town council. Another dated nearly three months ago was in the cramped, small, hard to read script of the second letter.

One, in plain script, didn't match the others. It simply requested a status update be sent to HQ. Two were printed: the first wanting to hire a problem solver and the second rescinding the request. Four more, in that small, precise writing, ranged in date from about the time of the first cramped letter to the day before yesterday. Natty willed her hand not to shake.

"Twice you failed. Now, one is out of reach. Get rid of that captain and his partner. Blow up the ship if you have to. And get rid of that idiot mayor and his greedy constable. The bloody cop is starting to flap his yap. If it's reported that kitchen wench survives a third time, you'd better be dead or you'll wish you were."

Silky started coughing. Natty looked up to see the healer coaxing Silky to drink from a small glass bottle. The smell was strong but pleasant.

Natty carefully placed each letter in its correct envelope, stacked the envelopes in an ordered pile, and placed them in the small pocket of her apron before leveraging herself off of the floor. She stumbled more than walked to the healer's side, her legs grown stiff from sitting. It had taken her as long to examine the envelopes as it had for the healer to have Silky properly cleaned and bandaged. Her friend looked horrifying, but the face that looked up at the healer showed no sign of pain. Natty reached into her large pocket and fished out one of the two gems Artearis had given her. She handed the green stone to the healer.

"I be bringing the other 'un back with me, so take good care o' her," Natty told the healer. She reached down and gently patted Silky on her good shoulder. "Heal up well, me girl." Natty walked past the beds, down the stairs, and out the front door.

# Chapter Seventeen
## Enemies with Benefits

The sword at Tanis Fedoral's throat may have stopped any physical action, but it didn't halt his racing thoughts. The sallow-faced man in front of him was dressed in the standard garrison uniform, but he wasn't one of Fedoral's men. He reeked of smoke, yet his clothes were clean. His features were too pale, too refined for a common soldier. They reminded him of someone .... Tanis mentally shook himself. The man was obviously a professional — mercenary? Spy?

Tanis felt the pressure leave his throat almost at the same instant a white bundle was tossed at him. He let it land in his lap. His inaction sparked a violent outburst from his captor.

"For the love of Moratam, read them!"

Tanis took his time picking up the papers. The hand flexing and unflexing upon the sword hilt warned him that his slowness was unsettling the man. Tanis deliberately took his time reading through the pages. This was a hit list — a very exclusive hit list — with his name as the last entry. Apparently, he had done his job well. His uncle would be proud. Tanis kept his features composed. His sergeant was due to report soon. He needed to get the two of them out of the foyer — to give Maven a head's up.

"So they think an assassin can solve their problems, and you are the best they could come up with?"

The man's eyes narrowed. His jaw tightened. The knuckles gripping the sword turned white. "If I wanted you dead, you'd BE dead."

Tanis let skepticism show on his face.

"Look, my guild did NOT sanction these assassinations."

"And I'm supposed to believe you because?"

The intruder's blue eyes turned to ice. "I was sent to rid the Guild of two renegades. I thought to do you the courtesy of warning you. Take it as you like. Without me, you won't survive."

Tanis chewed over the man's words. He hadn't considered the Assassins Guild's involvement. All evidence pointed to the syndicate and foreign operatives. The man might be right about being in over his head, but the man was also on the verge of an emotional break. Tanis had seen the signs before. If he pushed too far, would the man really snap?

"And why do you think you can provide me more help than the company of soldiers outside."

His captor snorted. "Those ill-trained, unobservant bumblers marching around like painted puppets without a puppet master qualified to manipulate them who run around an unfriendly town like they are on holiday? I'm surprised there's still a kingdom standing. And this place!" The man waved his free hand around. "What kind of security do you call this? Blind spots everywhere. Windows located in walls that give easy access to the dangers on the other side." The man jerked his hand toward Tanis's planning room. "Like in that room you call a study."

Tanis quickly straightened the smile that turned up his lips. Some windows held their own secrets — and surprises — surprises he needed to be nearer to activate.

"If not you," Tanis said, "then who?"

The stranger remained agitated.

Tanis toyed for a moment with the idea of trying to disarm the man. He could then pry the information out of his captor — and risk one or both men dying. No, he couldn't afford to lose this chance. He needed to know the specifics of this plot and who was behind it. He'd have to let this little drama continue in order to ferret out who was really behind the attacks along the coast. He pressed the man harder.

"You come here, tossing this," Tanis flapped the pages, "at me like you expect me to do something." Tanis's voice began to rise. "Yet you waste breath and time criticizing my men instead of providing information to defuse the situation."

"Defuse?!" The man's voice rose to compete with his. "What kind of imbecile are you? There is no diffusing this. It's too far along. The only help you and your men can be is to clean up the mess after!"

*Arrogant upstart!* Tanis clenched his own fingers tightly around the pages he still held, crushing the sides into the palms of his hands. The volume of his voice increased even more. "I'm surprised you even bothered to show me this!" His left hand released the crumpled sheets as his right fist arced upward to hold them inches in front of his captor's chest. His abrupt action nearly sliced off the side of his forefinger and thumb on the sword still between the two men.

This was getting him nowhere. Tanis dropped his voice to a more reasonable level. "What do you think you can offer me?"

Artearis could feel he had lost control of the situation. He needed the lieutenant to trust him. Instead, this exchange was driving a deeper wedge of distrust between them. He considered sharing the letters with Fedoral, yet some level of caution held him back. In frustration he let slip, "Are all military men this dense?"

"An assassin holds me hostage in my own quarters, and he thinks I should be reasonable? Particularly when I will be called to conduct inspection shortly?"

Artearis snapped, "Not as soon as you think. Your men are probably still in town dealing with the fire." Artearis didn't bother to gloat at the surprise on Fedoral's face. He had to get this man to safety, so he could go back and undo what Norland and Garad initiated.

"Look," Artearis exploded, "I burned down my own inn, so I could get here and save your life. What more proof do you want? Time is running out. Garad and Norland are almost here."

A soft spoken voice with a force Artearis had only felt when Marte lost his patience said, "Enough." He turned his head toward the sound. A very old man stood in the doorway to Fedoral's office. He wore a white robe and a frown more potent than even Marte's.

The old man shifted his grip on his staff and ambled back into the office.

Tanis Fedoral ignored the sword that now hung loosely below his ribcage and pushed himself out of the chair to follow. With great concern, Tanis said, "Elder Serenth, you are supposed to be resting."

The elder waved his hand at the two men, his voice soft but stern. "Rest? While two grown men squabble like rough-neck younglings?"

Tanis hurried to Serenth. He brought up his hand to support the elder's left arm. Serenth let the staff roll into the crook of his right arm. He reached over and gently disengaged the hand. "Enough energies clash this night to disrupt the balance. The two of you do, but should not. One of you would tear the world apart with the conflicts that rage within and without from lack of control. As it was before, it cannot be again. The cycle no longer repeats itself."

Thinking the old one under duress strong enough to cause him to spout nonsense, Tanis reached out again to help the elder. Serenth dismissed the kindly gesture.

With this second dismissal by Serenth, Tanis returned to the desk he had been working at before his disruptive visitor arrived. He sighed. "What would you have me do?"

"Listen."


Artearis flinched at the firmness of that word. Who was this Elder Serenth? Why hadn't he heard of the man before?

Serenth settled his hand around the staff like friends linking arms in companionship, not like an old man requiring the need for support. He neither turned to watch

Tanis move away nor shifted his eyes to study Artearis, but Artearis could feel the old man weighing him: his thoughts, his emotions, his intentions, his very essence.

When Artearis failed to do anything, Serenth said in the same stern yet quiet voice, "Speak, Guild Leader."

The words made Artearis flinch again. The old man certainly had a way about him. "I don't know how ...."

Serenth waved his free hand toward Artearis. "Speak of what is relevant."

Artearis took a moment to consider what to say. "The two men coming here tonight care little for guild or kingdom law. They deliberately used the reputation of the Assassins Guild to fatten their purses, regardless of the consequences." Artearis reached into his shirt and pulled out the letter concerning the gnolls. He tossed it onto the desk.

Once Tanis Fedoral picked it up, Artearis continued, "This has gone beyond a simple contract for hire. These two have broken the sanctity of the Guild. A death sentence they laugh at. Men like these will continue to take until they have nothing left to take or they die, no matter the cost to guild or kingdom. I may be an assassin, but believe me when I say that I am still loyal to my kingdom. Today, I am not the enemy."

Fedoral looked at Serenth.

Serenth contemplated the words spoken, contemplated the man who spoke them. "Your energies assert differently."

Fedoral took a step back toward the window.

Again, Serenth waved him off. "The danger he presents is not to you, my old student, of which I, for one, am grateful. It is to the world."

Artearis didn't notice that Elder Serenth had gradually moved closer to him until the elder reached out and wrapped his fingers around the gem that had freed itself from his tunic — or had Serenth called the gem to him?

Serenth uttered a few sibilant words. The sickly glow fell away to reveal a dim light pulsing deep within the gem. "Being human, I have not the sight of my mentor, yet still things I can perceive." Serenth let his fingers stroke the gem while he considered his words. "Magic is not a toy to be played with by the untrained. Strange things leak into the mix unexpectedly. I wonder what events have their roots in this," he mused.

Tanis beheld the gem with disgust. Even without the identification made by the elder, the green gem hanging around this intruder's neck condemned him. "How can he be trusted?"

Artearis slammed his hand down onto the desk. "I never asked to be trusted. I asked to let me save your life."

Still addressing Artearis, Serenth continued, "The props of a sham are only as useful as the skill of the performer."

Tanis ignored Serenth. "Why? It's not your duty. You don't know me. You have no honor. You ...."

Artearis stared into Tanis's brown eyes. "It is what I must do." Artearis turned his head toward the window. "Horses. They come."

Tanis moved to the window and pressed one palm against the lower frame and one against the right. "Enemy without," he spoke to the glass.

Artearis looked at Serenth.

"It has its own secrets."

Tanis marched to the door. "You two had best hide in the back room." He scooped up his sword by the hilt and retreated to his desk after closing the door. Wordlessly, he pointed past the long table to the other door.

Serenth allowed Artearis to take his arm.

Sergeant Maven's "trouble's coming" sense had nagged him since early morning when the carrier delivered the new orders. "The fort is on lock down. All activity is canceled until further notice. Troop rotations will commence immediately upon the arrival of the replacements." The message hadn't arrived until after the first third left on its day pass. The lieutenant had written out a hasty report on the deviation from orders, pinned it to the top of his other reports, and sent the carrier on his way.

The dust from the carrier's horse had hardly cleared the horizon when word came from the landing stage that a dinghy had washed up. The lone survivor reported his ship had been attacked near Sharp Reef Point. A search and rescue operation confirmed the sunken ship but was nearly lost in the process by unknown attackers.

That second report worried the lieutenant to no end. He wanted to recall the troops, but Maven had ignored his "trouble" sense and talked the lieutenant out of it. The sergeant began to regret his actions after a town informant reported unusual activity down at the docks last night and early this morning but nothing in particular the stable hand could put a finger on.

Now it was just past midnight, and maybe two-fifths of the men had returned to the fort by the midnight deadline. Among the missing was Sergeant Ingram. That straight-laced, fourth generation military man would never break a regulation without proper cause. The grizzled, old veteran's "trouble" sense rolled over into high alert status when two men were dragged before him on drunk and disorderly charges. Besides reeking of alcohol, one sported a very dark, and real, black eye. Maven had examined the damage himself. The other kept jingling his purse and boasting of his new lay at the Cold Comfort Inn. What soldier did that in front of his superior, especially when every soldier here knew violation of THAT order got him a transfer to the prison facilities at Wild Wood Fort?

Sergeant Maven made a point of carefully examining all the soldiers from that group, but nothing seemed amiss. Everything down to the military issue uniforms and weapons was spot on. Against his better judgment, Maven called for a mounted escort. But he wasn't letting those two disgraces for soldiers sully the back of a horse. They could weave their way to the lieutenant's quarters and maybe sober up a bit along the march, and Maven marched them hard the entire way, covering the ten-minute walk in six. Both men were out of breath by the time they reached the lieutenant's quarters.

The sergeant was just about to tack on two weeks of heavy labor duty in addition to any punishment meted out by the lieutenant when Maven caught sight of the window of the lieutenant's study. Through it he could see the lieutenant sitting at his desk, bent over as if writing. A fire roared deep red in the fireplace. The rest of the room appeared empty. Maven noticed the two men look at each other, one cracking a smile briefly, all pretense of drunkenness vanished in that look. Maven was about ready to accost the men when his eye caught a trail of spiders roving around the perimeter of the window. The trail began at the lower right corner and grew in a clockwise direction. Another quick glance at the men showed they appeared nearly as intoxicated as when the group left the front gate. Instead of approaching the two, Sergeant Maven walked past them to the front door. He raised his hand and knocked.

"Report."

"Two soldiers hauled in for drunk and disorderly conduct, Sir," the sergeant replied. "They have been at the thieves' inn."

Sergeant Maven could feel the two men he was escorting tense up at the silence that followed. A barely audible sigh of relief escaped both when they heard the words "bring them in."

Before ushering the two men inside, Maven told his escort to tighten up the perimeter for the night. "And have someone find me when the rest of the men arrive." He reached out, turned the knob, shoved open the door, and said, "March." When the two were well into the hallway, Maven pulled the door shut. As his hand dropped toward his side, it casually slid up to loosen the blade strapped to his waist. When the two men hesitated in front of the closed door, Maven barked, "Well, what are you two trouble makers waiting for. Move it!"

From their hiding place behind the door of the sleeping quarters, the assassin and the priest tensed at the sound of approaching boots. Artearis edged Serenth behind the door jamb before he sidestepped the crack to peer into the room. "When I draw my blades, open the door wide."

Serenth placed his gnarled hand on the knob.

As soon as Garad cleared the doorway, Artearis drew his blades. Serenth pulled on the handle, swinging the door inward. "Keep your head on your shoulders, Berain."

The curse Artearis bit out troubled Serenth. He moved to the doorway. Although Artearis had cleared the door quickly, he was too far to intercept the man with light hair pivoting toward the opening to the left of the desk. The man's advance forced Fedoral to retreat behind it. Artearis vaulted across the floor space past the table in the middle just as Garad reached the window.

*Thunk.*

The sound of something hitting the door frame warned the room occupants of the other assassin's entrance. Artearis, glancing left, changed direction enough to slam his left shoulder into the second man, putting the man off balance enough to allow Fedoral's sergeant to shoulder his way into the study. The forceful blow from Maven drove the second man into the middle of the room with Maven between the man and his quarry. Blocked from his original target, Norland drew his blade and squared off against this new one.

Seeing Maven engage the second attacker, Artearis continued after the first man. "Garad!" he snapped. The name hung in the frozen stillness that enveloped the room from the word. The brief disruption gave Artearis enough time to cross the room and vault the desk to land beside Fedoral, his weapons at the ready.

Serenth, hands wrapped around his staff, moved into the corner of the room beside the fireplace. The new view brought Norland's face into sight. Norland's widened eyes told Serenth that the man knew he had risked everything on this gambit and lost. When they narrowed sharply, it was clear the man had every intention of taking out anyone in his way. Norland lunged at Sergeant Maven.

Garad tossed his sword into his left hand so he could pull a hidden dagger from his tunic. He used the dagger to take a backhanded slash at Fedoral while he tried to trap Artearis's sword against the desk with his own. Although neither were life threatening, Garad managed a cut to Fedoral's face and neck faster than the lieutenant could block. A second back-swipe strike to Fedoral's thigh missed as Garad twisted around to prevent Artearis's dagger from connecting, leaving Garad with his back pinned against the wall.

Fedoral used the opening provided by Artearis to drive his knee up into Garad's groin. As Garad doubled over, Artearis drove his dagger into the man's stomach and yanked upward.

Norland slashed out with his sword. The battle-hardened sergeant blocked the move, but the assassin wasn't done. Norland had his own hidden dagger. He whipped it out, and with a quick flash, sliced the sergeant across his right forearm, but he overextended himself. Maven picked up on the mistake. Pressing forward, his blade snaked out to stab Norland in the kidney area. The assassin pivoted out of the way.

Norland leaped forward, his sword leveled in a horizontal sweep at the waist. The tip ripped the front of Maven's uniform.

Serenth began his sleep spell.

Hearing the sibilant sound from behind, Norland twisted his head up and around. His eyes met Serenth's. Norland flipped his dagger in his hand and threw it at the priest. The wild throw clanged off the fireplace mantle, missing Serenth but interrupting his spell. Norland charged Maven.

Behind the desk, Fedoral let Garad slide to the floor. When Artearis, reacting to the sound of the dagger hitting the fireplace, dove over the desk to intercept Norland, his shoulder hit the edge of the table, but the momentum was enough for him to roll over the top and land on his knees on the opposite side. Fedoral's eyes followed Artearis's movements.

Garad made one last attempt at his target. He used the wall to pull himself upright. Gripping his dagger tightly, Garad lunged and missed, slamming his weapon into the desk, the tip lodging into the wood. Before Garad could pull it out, Fedoral ran him through.

Norland dropped to his knees and thrust up with his sword. Maven jumped back but Norland's blade slashed Maven across the lower ribs. The sergeant collapsed to his knees.

Serenth watched as Artearis jumped forward, bringing his sword down to catch the hilt of Norland's blade on its upward swing. In one fluid sequence, Norland twisted into a side roll, gained his feet, and stepped forward to engage Artearis.

Artearis sidestepped the sergeant to catch Norland's next swing with both blades as it sliced in high from the left side. The desperate move had counted on brute force to remove Artearis's head. Instead, Artearis used the momentum of the attack to guide the cut in an arc away from himself and down to the floor. With sword pressing down on sword, Artearis brought his dagger up and around, slicing a gash in Norland's right shoulder.

Norland twisted to his left; while crouched, he darted between Maven and Artearis and once past them tossed his sword to his left hand as he straightened. The maneuver turned him around and put him within striking distance of an unprotected Fedoral. Pulling a second dagger from his tunic with his left hand, Norland simultaneously stepped back with his left foot and pumped his arm back.

Artearis slid into the void Norland's backward step had created, sword hand sweeping out and down, slicing through flesh at Norland's wrist. Too late, the dagger arced across the desk. Artearis used his own dagger to cut Norland's throat.

Artearis watched Norland's body drop to the floor. From behind the desk, Artearis thought he heard a quiet hiss. He looked up to see Fedoral leaning upon the desk. Turning around, he saw the sergeant on his knees and the priest leaning over the man.

Artearis helped Fedoral carry Maven to the padded seat by the door. The distance wasn't far, a handful of feet at best, but it was enough to set the old sergeant groaning as they put him down.

"Damn, that hurts," Maven grunted after catching his breath from the move. "It's a good thing your men have not been minding their sword work; otherwise, I would have been skewered instead of pinpricked, boy."

A scowl immediately settled onto Artearis's face. "They were traitors — to everyone. They deserved death."

Sergeant Maven took a little more time to size up the stranger who had fought with the lieutenant and him. His eyes roved over the man's clothing. Uniform or not, this man was no soldier — would never be able to pass as one like the two dead men — an officer maybe but not a common soldier.

Maven took in the blades the stranger held. He knew bladespinner weapons when he saw them. His eyes passed over the hilt of the sword pointing in his direction. Just as he knew the crest worked into the pommel of that sword. "I can think of other things that warrant a death sentence," Maven said, but the words lacked force.

Serenth moved toward the three men. "I can think of things that bring death whether the person is entitled or not. Now please stand away." The amount of blood pooling at the feet of the men worried Serenth. With surprising strength for an old man, he gripped Maven's tunic and ripped it apart at the left seam. He motioned for someone to help him turn the sergeant to the side. The wound was deep, and probably painful, but not life threatening. There should not be so much blood. Serenth transferred his staff to Fedoral and placed one hand over the entrance wound and one over the damaged rib area. He prayed to the All God, asking for renewed health for Sergeant Maven to right the imbalance of tonight's struggle.

Finally, Maven sighed in relief. Serenth collected his staff from Tanis and moved to the first man lying on the floor. He knelt down and felt for a pulse. When he couldn't find one, Serenth offered a prayer to the All God to let the man's soul find its place in the other life. Serenth leaned into his staff to help him stand so that he might tend to the needs of the second man on the ground and saw a swatch of blood along the side of the staff. He heaved himself to his feet.

Holding the staff firmly, Serenth shifted around to look at the three men still breathing. The sergeant was resting, even if not that comfortably. Artearis, clutching and unclutching the still pulsing gem hanging from his throat, otherwise seemed fine. When Serenth raised his eyes to study Tanis, standing behind the other two, he saw a face drained of all color. Serenth examined the lieutenant's body. His arms and chest showed minor cuts. The right leg muscles bulged as if they were holding the weight of his entire body. Blood soaked the left leg. Serenth shrugged his way past Artearis and began to kneel beside the wounded leg when Tanis began to sway.

"Berain, please put your hands to better use. Move Tanis to the table."

Artearis quickly dropped the gem as he took two strides to bring him to Fedoral's right side. Tanis sagged into him. Artearis gasped, "Sergeant?"

Maven winced as he shoved himself out of the chair. The pain didn't slow his advance toward the lieutenant. Snatching up the man's left arm, the sergeant wrapped it around his own neck. The two men walked Tanis to the table. While Maven took Tanis's weight, Artearis scooped up his legs and hoisted them over the top of the table. Together, they laid the lieutenant down so his injured leg was parallel to the edge.

Without asking permission from Serenth, Artearis ripped away the cloth covering the leg. "Can you heal him?"

Serenth allowed the sorrow to show on his face even though a shrug was the only reply he gave Artearis before asking the sergeant to fetch bandages and a first aid kit. The sergeant went into the back room.

Artearis clenched his jaw. "You are a priest. Heal him!"

Again Serenth shrugged. "I am a very old priest who has already asked for all of his blessings this night."

"So ask again. You can't let him die."

The stern look that always appeared on Marte's face when Artearis pushed too far was now showing on the elder's.

Artearis's voice dropped to whisper. "He was my responsibility to save."

Serenth took the first aid kit from Sergeant Maven. He hunted through the kit for a needle and length of thread sufficient to close the wound. "Sergeant, would you sterilize this in the fire? And when you are done, find me some soap and a basin of water?" Maven answered with a grunt as he moved toward the fireplace.

"Young Berain," Serenth finally answered, "losing people we care about, that we are responsible for, is part of the order of things. Their loss sets before us the new task of honoring their memories. Their pain provides the lesson for our own transformation. Some sacrifice so others may succeed, as one Berain did for another Berain in an age past."

Serenth's hands remained steady as he stitched at the artery inside the wound. When he was satisfied, he asked Artearis to bring him a lighted candle. Serenth used the candle to break the thread and examine the wound. Certain that it was closed properly, he began stitching the flesh closed.

"Sergeant, would you fetch a glass, a pitcher of water, and something stronger to drink, please?"

Once the last stitch was tied off and thread severed with the flame of the candle, the elder carefully cleaned the wound, then taking the warm, soft wax that ran down the side, he used it to seal the wound closed. With that final step done, he placed his hands over the seal and prayed.

The sergeant finally returned. "Wine was the strongest drink I could find, Elder."

Serenth took the glass and filled it with water. He held the glass to the lieutenant's lips. "Give him water. Wait. Give him wine. Wait. Give him more water."

Maven nodded.

He opened his mouth to speak, but again the elder intervened. "The wax will not stay long before it will flake away — a few hours, maybe. Watch the wound for signs of blood pooling under the surface."

"Yes ...."

Even Elder Serenth jumped when a fist started pounding on the door. Both Artearis and Serenth looked at Sergeant Maven.

"I have no clue." The sergeant headed into the hallway.

When Artearis started to follow, Serenth placed his staff across Artearis's path. The elder ambled forward, inserting himself between Artearis and the door. This time when he leaned on his staff, Artearis could tell it was because Serenth needed it for support. Fatigue did not stop the elder from taking hold of the green gem and speaking more sibilant phrases. The deep, pulsing aura faded. The sickly green light reappeared.

Serenth used the staff to assist him to the doorway into the back room. "Good intentions are only as 'good' as the desire to see them through." The elder crossed the threshold. "Following them may mean trapping oneself in a place of one's own fears. When the choice is in doubt, there is the light."

Artearis stood irresolute.

A pale shadow of the voice that had argued with him earlier said, "Stairs ... over the wall ... now," then fell silent.

Left with no choice, Artearis watched for his chance,

slipped out the door and up the stairs.

# Chapter Eighteen
## Oil and Water

Natty took several determined strides toward the soldiers near the well before a hand clamped down on her shoulder. Natty spun around to confront her detainer.

"Relax, Natty, it's just me," Lemm said. "The Cap'n was worried 'bout you."

Natty pulled the letters out of her pocket. "Good reason," she said, waving the letters in front of Lemm. She stuffed them back into her pocket just as the sky flashed midnight.

*KABOOM! KABOOOM!*

Natty felt the ground shake as it had when the Cold Comfort Inn had exploded.

Lemm growled, "What the ...."

Both of them turned toward the northwest, toward the rich homes in town, where the noise came from. A bright light blossomed in the distance, holding steady against the now dark sky. From their position of higher ground, they could see the fire was at the edge of town, maybe near the water, but nothing more.

*KABOOM! KABOOOM!*

The ground shook again. This time the sky brightened to the northeast.

"Squad three, attention. You and you. Check out the northwest. You two the northeast. Double time it. I need six two-man teams for a sweep search. Team one sweep the warehouse district. Team two the rich quarter. Team three the east gate section. Team four the docks. Team five what's left of this square. Team six you have the Market Square. Break down the doors if you have to but be thorough. Team three inform squad one to relocate half the men to Market Square. Team four same message to squad two. You two are on fire watch. The rest of squad three, follow me to Market Square."

Natty watched in amazement as the sergeant clipped out the order to move; suddenly the middle of the square was empty. Her hand clutched the edge of her apron. The weight of the letters pressed down on her hand. She followed the sergeant toward Market Square.

Lemm grabbed Natty by the arm. "What're you

doin'?"

Not stopping, Natty said, "Figuring."

Natty's determination to tail the sergeant forced Lemm to follow after her. "But the Cap'n ...."

"Will want ta know what's going on same as me. This ain't the young'un's doing, Lemm."

Merchant Square might have emptied of the gawkers at the inn fire, but another crowd had gathered around the source of the latest explosion. As the two moved up the road toward Market Square, the crowd that had parted for the soldiers flowed back into place. Natty and Lemm were forced to weave their way among the crowd. When Natty's gentle prodding finally met with a wall of resistance, Lemm took the lead.

"Where to?"

Natty stood on her tiptoes. She still couldn't see over the heads in front of her. "Where's the man shouting orders?"

"Over to the well. Givin' more orders."

Natty nodded. "We gotta go there, Lemm."

Lemm pushed people out of the way until he and Natty were standing with their backs against the melon seller's stall. Constables kept the crowd from pressing into the cleared area around the burning jail. The heat was intense, but the flames were nothing like those of the Inn.

The flickering light of the fire poked through the door and windows and the hole in the stone wall. The city wall behind the jail now had a jagged rip along the top part. Some of the stone must have exploded up and outward.

Two soldiers broke through the crowd on the west side and muscled their way past the constables to report to their sergeant. Natty was thankful Lemm had found them the spot behind the stall. Only a few other folks took refuge there, and they were more intent on staring, not talking. Natty was able to hear the two men tell their sergeant that the other explosion came from the mayor's house. The force leveled the building and killed those inside. Because it was built on a small promontory by the water, what still burned wasn't a threat to the rest of the town. From what they could tell, the cause was a trail of mage fire leading to some barrels. Two were definitely made of firefern wood. Small projectiles of the containers littered the surrounding area. The others were of undetermined type.

The remains of the fire cast the sergeant's frown in a hellish glow. He said something to the two men that Natty couldn't hear. They moved off as another group of men approached from the eastern gate way. Two soldiers and two other men marched three manacled prisoners past the destroyed jail to the sergeant. His frown deepened.

One of the uniformed soldiers halted the group in front of the sergeant. "We found those two," he pointed toward the two half-dressed men, "tied up in the supply warehouse behind the inn. Those three," he waved his hand at the prisoners, "were igniting a mage powder trail that led to an opened firefern barrel containing explosive oil."

"Where?"

"Some fancy house off the Merchant Square tucked up against the inner wall of the east quarter."

A stocky constable holding back the crowd to Natty's left yelled, "Hey, that's my house."

The sergeant ignored the man. "Threat level?"

"We extinguished the flame, sealed the barrel, and tasked squad one to secure it." The soldier pointed at the three men. "We couldn't have them tagging along for the rest of the search, so we figured it'd be best to hand them over to you."

Sergeant Ingram nodded. "Best leave them to the lieutenant. You men, secure the prisoners then march them to the fort. You two," Ingram addressed the two freed men, "go with them. Sergeant Maven will expect a full accounting. You both continue your sweep," Ingram told his search team.

*KABOOM!*

Everyone jerked their attention in the direction of the eastern gate.

*KABOOM!*

"What the ...."

Natty clamped her hands to her ears, cutting off the

rest of the sergeant's words.

*KABOOOM!*

The series of explosions nearly knocked Natty off her feet. Lemm braced himself against the stall and grabbed Natty's shoulders to steady her.

Sergeant Ingram started shouting out orders to lock down the town — seal off each section — send for reinforcements from the fort. Natty took that as their cue to get back to the docks. She told Lemm to find them a way out of the square. Lemm shook his head in confusion. Natty raised her voice. Lemm cupped his hand to his ear. Natty pointed toward Merchant's Way. Lemm nodded. He plowed a path to the Market Square exit.

The captain stared thoughtfully at the four recovered barrels of explosive oil sitting on the dock. Next to them, his men had dumped the traitor. The unrepentant man scowled up at the captain.

The sailor who had threatened Artearis earlier that evening tossed a small bag onto one of the barrels. "What new crew mate has fifty gold to stash in his berth?"

The first mate said, "None that's ever sailed with us, 'cept maybe Greg'ry."

"Old Gregory is, well ... Old Gregory, an' this here

bloke ain't."

"Pardon his look, Cap'n," said the first mate. "We thought softening him up a bit would speed things along."

"And?"

The sailor laughed. "He sang like a pretty keekii bird."

The first mate glared at the sailor. "You were right. Bought and paid for by the same ones that went after Natty before. 'Cept this time you and the ship were on the list. After we found these, I sent a few of the crew to have a look see at the Inn."

The captain said, "Natty?"

Both the first mate and the sailor shrugged.

"Nothin' from Lemm, either, Cap'n," both men said in unison.

The first mate punched the sailor in the arm.

The captain growled, "Take your feud elsewhere. We've got work." Before either could respond, he headed with all speed toward the Gusty Wind Inn. The two shipmates hurried to catch up. They had put the dock behind them and were approaching the cutoff to the delivery entrance of the inn before they sighted one of the crew hovering around the kitchen stairs.

The first mate snapped, "Report!"

One of the dock hands scuttled out the kitchen door. "Someone's lookin' to have some fireworks here tonight."

The sound of an explosion ripped through the air,

lighting up the sky in the north. The blast shook the ground hard.

"You mean more fireworks," said the crew mate, picking himself up off the ground in the kitchen yard.

The first mate steadied himself. "What'd you find?"

The dock hand slapped the side of the barrel by the door. "Two of them barrels untopped out here. Nothing inside yet."

The innkeeper, huffing and puffing, pushed through the door. "Nothin' inside. Don't know how the varmits would git anythin' in there anywho. Been busier than Natty's stove tonight, even with her gone. Where be the ole girl?"

The first mate and the sailor shrugged their shoulders again.

The captain finally spoke. "Well, I'm not fond of my favorite watering hole turning into fireworks. It's time we took care of the matter. Innkeeper, do you have a couple of empty barrels around about the size of these?"

When the innkeeper nodded, the captain ordered the sailor and some of the men to collect them, take them down to the dock and fill them with water, and bring them back and put them just the way the two barrels were positioned. He then ordered his first mate to haul the oil barrels to where the other four were being watched. When the innkeeper asked what he could do, the captain told him to take a head count of the patrons not from the docks or ship and report back.

Not long after, Natty and Lemm stumbled along the path to the kitchen. While bent over trying to catch his breath, Lemm panted out, "Soldiers ... orders ... seal ... town." Nodding in agreement, Natty, clutching her side, took several deep breaths before saying, "Them's well thought of targets: the mayor's place, the jail ...."

"Mister high 'n mighty constable." Lemm added, "Sir," after seeing the first mate standing on the steps.

"And, we heard tell on the way here the town hall."

"One 'o them sergeants from the fort's a shutting down each part o' the town and doing a hard search o' each," Lemm told the first mate. "We just beat 'em here."

"They're barrin' the road now." Unfamiliar noise coming from the kitchen caught Natty's attention. She tried to peer past the man standing in the door. "What're they doin' in there?"

The innkeeper bustled out to where the sailors waited. "There's three of them parked inside. Two at the bar and one near the fireplace. Where're you needin' me to be now?"

Carrying an ale barrel each, two of the captain's men halted behind the innkeeper. One grumbled. The other ordered the innkeeper out of the way. He shuffled to the side long enough for the two to pass just to be pushed aside by Natty as she went to check on her kitchen. Natty, in turn, barely missed running into the captain emerging from the cellar.

The captain took Natty by the arm and led her outside, signaling the rest to follow. "Here's what we're going to do." He laid out the plan. Some of his men would replace the barrels and hide nearby. A few needed to go inside and stir up enough worry over the news the innkeeper would quietly spread about the soldiers to get the three to act. "Make sure you stay on them when they leave," he told them. Turning to Natty, he asked, "How do you feel about being bait?"

Working under the captain's orders, the sailors made a great deal of grumbling over the highhandedness of the military. One dock worker ordered a round for the house, giving a drunken speech about how no one was going to chase him away from his off duty pursuits. Another leaned over to whisper into one of the mark's ear, "Them blokes need to mind their own business or we'll give 'em what for, if'n they try to make us leave."

The mood in the Gusty Wind was turning black. The two infiltrators at the bar grew nervous. They couldn't afford military intervention. If they didn't act soon, the plan would fail. One lifted his drink to his lips and took a long pull to steady his courage. The other took out a coin and flipped it into the air twice before tossing it on the bar. Upon seeing the coin toss, the man near the fireplace eased his way to the front door and slipped out. When they were sure he was alone, the two at the bar waited for the innkeeper to return to the kitchen. Following after, each pulled a weighted slug from his pocket, ready to knock him out. Oblivious to his danger, the innkeeper headed into the cellar. One slipped down the stairs after him and threw the door shut, locking it. The other stuffed his weapon back into his pocket and scanned the room for Natty. All he saw was a kitchen in the middle of being scrubbed down and an open door to the outside. He headed for the door, followed by his partner.

Natty hauled the bucket of garbage outside, only to find a man laying out a trail of powder that stretched from the barrels beside the door to somewhere around the corner of the inn toward the road. Before Natty had a chance to call for help, the stranger dropped the bag containing the powder and made a grab for her. She took a step backward, colliding with the two from inside. One clamped a hand around her mouth and his free arm around her waist. The intruder outside caught up her legs. With Natty in hand, the three maneuvered her down the back stairs to the place where the mage fire trail began. As soon as they turned the corner, the captain's men sprang the trap.

The first mate pulled Natty from their grasp while Lemm relieved the last one of the bag of mage fire powder he had picked up. The captain let his men pound out some of their frustration before he used the hilt of his dagger to knock two of them unconscious. With orders to bind the three and drag them down to the dock for questioning, the captain guided Natty away from the inn.

Natty worked hard to maintain her composure, but she couldn't prevent her hand from creeping into the pocket of her apron. She didn't understand why, but the letters Artearis gave her had become a private lifeline for her, one she clung to tightly, so when the first mate approached and asked her if he could have her apron, Natty's face went white. Giving up the apron meant exposing the letters and all the questionable content inside. When he repeated his request, she couldn't think of any reason not to hand it over. With one hand still holding tightly to the letters, she used the other to untie the apron and pass it to the first mate who carried it away.

Her reluctance did not go unnoticed by the captain, nor did the letters she still held. He waited for her to explain, but when she remained silent, he led her down to the docks where the first mate prepared to question the man the captain had left conscious. Tossing the apron to one of the men kneeling beside the prisoner, the first mate nodded. The sailor folded the apron into a large square big enough to cover the mouth and nose of their prisoner before dipping it into the water. The sailor looked at the first mate who turned to the captain. At the captain's nod, the first mate gave the signal. The sailor slapped the cloth over their prisoner's face.

Watching in horror as the man struggled to breathe, Natty counted to ten before the sailor removed the cloth and looked at the first mate for instructions. A knot curled around her stomach at the sound of the prisoner gasping for air. Still, she kept quiet.

In a firm voice, the captain said, "Again."

The sailor dipped the folded cloth into the water, saturating it more before slapping it across the prisoner's mouth and nose.

Natty could almost feel the water run down his throat and into his lungs the way he twisted and turned in the hold of the captain's men.

The captain lightly touched her arm. Natty tried to tear her eyes away from the man but couldn't.

"Natty, three times they tried to kill you."

"I know."

"It wasn't a mistake."

Natty's grip tightened on the letters. "I know."

The captain tried the direct approach. "What is so

important in the bundle you are mangling with your fingers that you won't share with us?"

A sharp twist by the prisoner made Natty wince.

The captain nodded to the sailor.

Natty cringed as the man sucked in air.

"Wasn't just me they was after." Natty remembered all the different handwritings. "I can't get the straight of who wants ta kill who. I just know they want us dead."

"Who wants who dead, Natty."

She stared hard at the captain. "Me and Gregory and you and our ship. Why'd ya want ta kill a ship? And some boy and that lieutenant up there at that fort."

Lemm growled, "I knew I shoulda skewered that assassin instead o' givin' him back his sword."

Natty shook her head. "He's the only one I know isn't trying ta do us in."

"What do you mean," the captain asked her.

"He said I'd know what ta do with these, but I don't. I can't wrap my head around 'em 'cept ta know there's more goin' on then killin' us."

Lemm kicked the leg of their prisoner. "Maybe he can tell us."

"Maybe he can." The captain ordered the sailor to continue the interrogation.

As the cloth descended, the prisoner's eyeballs nearly popped out of his head. Natty averted her gaze.

This time when the cloth was removed the captain had questions. The prisoner didn't know as much as they'd hoped. All they could get from him was someone from the Capitol wanted independent ships gone, and they were willing to work with gnolls to get rid of them. For their services, the gnolls demanded they disrupt the town so the soldiers would leave the fort unprotected. When his people were sure the soldiers were occupied, they were to blow up the Gusty Wind Inn followed by the captain's ship, detonating the barrel to starboard, then the one to aft, and finally, the two in the hold.

Armed with that information, the captain ordered his men to secure three boats, load two with an unconscious man and one barrel of oil and a third with the interrogated prisoner and the other two barrels they had unearthed in their sweep. When the first mate asked about the traitor they had ferreted out earlier, the captain ordered him to be put in one of the boats. He sent four others to haul the barrels they'd found outside the inn up to the point behind it.

"Be mindful of them soldiers," Natty added. "They'd like as not be on us soon."

Her words gave the captain pause. "Natty, do you think you can distract them with those letters long enough for us to send the signal?"

She looked at the letters in her hand and nodded. The

lieutenant at the fort would know what to do with them.

Waiting in a longboat behind the natural jetty that separated the harbor from the bay before Sharp Reef Point were two gnoll scouts. They began to quarrel as the time for the signal passed. One wanted to turn back. The other insisted on waiting. They had just squared off when an explosion ripped through the night air. Shortly after, another smaller one went off then a second. The two shouted in excitement when a final explosion as loud as the first detonated. Each plopped down on a rowing bench and bent his back to the oars.

# Chapter Nineteen
## Allies in the Dark

Artearis had been lucky to get to his horse and get away before the back gates opened and troops poured out. He thanked the Winds of Fortune they headed toward the coast and not the river. He cursed softly when he realized they weren't the only ones canvassing in the dark. His honed senses warned him of the shadowy figures doing crisscross sweeps perhaps half a mile from the fort.

Some were spiraling outward and some inward, creating a net around the fort. He gauged the timing of the arc in their sweeps and slipped through, making it another half mile or so when he heard more sounds in the dark. Off to his right, coming up behind him, the snarls and snuffles from earlier drifted on the wind. Ahead and to his left, the creak of wheels mixed with the whiffle of horses. Someone was riding straight into the sweep area.

He looked up at the stars marking the descent of night. He didn't have time for this. Heading his horse midway between the two groups, he tensed as the snarls grew louder behind him. His heels urged the horse to a faster pace. From the right, a child's shriek stopped him. *Damn!* He changed direction.

Moving as quickly as the light and ground allowed, Artearis approached. He slowed down when he realized what was ahead. Even without their colors flying, he'd recognize a Folk caravan.

These people were no match for the armed intruders willing to take on the kingdom's military. They also weren't going to let him just ride in, and the intruders weren't going to stop and ask questions.

Artearis rode up alongside the caravan and kept pace with it while keeping the light from the caravan to the side. As he waited, he ran through the things Marte had taught him about the Folk. Wrapping the reins loosely around the pommel of his saddle, Artearis crossed his arms, resting his hands on his elbows. It didn't take long for him to be noticed.

Big, burly men spread out in a circle around Artearis. Keeping his face expressionless and arms crossed, he used his legs to tell his horse to stop. When one larger than the others approached him alone, Artearis said, "This is not the place for a traveler to carve a path alone without a strong purpose or close fellowship." The man pulled a large club from his belt and stood silently between Artearis and the wagons.

Judging from the number of shadows moving his way, his words carried farther than he'd have liked in the darkness. He prayed they hadn't carried as far as the intruders. Intently studying those who approached, Artearis singled out a thin man a few inches shorter than he striding confidently toward him with a light in hand. Although Artearis didn't like the idea of losing what little night vision he still had, he nudged his horse in the man's direction. Once in the light, he could see the Folk features clearly: black hair, dark eyes, weathered skin, and athletic build much as Marte had been. This man was wary but not hostile.

"Well met, Gaujo," the man said. "What brings you to our vardo?"

Artearis quietly repeated his words.

The man studied him for a few moments before waving over the owner of the huge club. He leaned closer to whisper into the burly man's ear. The burly man nodded. Before he headed into the heart of the caravan, he signaled to the others surrounding Artearis.

The newcomer remained cautious but polite. "Armon will inform the elders of your arrival. You will do us the courtesy of waiting for their answer."

The distant sounds behind Artearis made it hard for him to keep from scowling. While not getting noticeably closer, the number of sounds had increased. Whatever was out there was gathering in strength. "You'd better hope they answer quickly."

The newcomer frowned.

The intensity of the night's events had worn away Artearis's desire for courtesy. He dropped his arms and grabbed up the reins. Just as he was ready to send his horse into the encampment, the guards tightened their circle around him. His sword hand itched to draw his weapon, but he knew these people weren't the enemy, and showing steel would lose him any cooperation that might be coming. He took a deep breath and counted to five. He needed to convince this man his people were courting danger out here. "Have you been sending out scouts to make sure the way is safe?"

"What?"

"Have you been doing reconnaissance?"

"Why?"

Artearis counted to five again. "Because," he jabbed his thumb at the darkness behind him, "there's nasty things out there trying to keep people from leaving Hisanth and the fort."

The man stood there.

"They're sending patrols out to isolate this place."

The man simply stared at Arteais.

"Do you understand what that means?" When the group of men stayed silent, in a voice soft and deadly, he said, "That means they'll kill anyone who tries to get out. Anyone. Everyone."

A voice with the weight of age said from behind him, "Timerus, listen."

Arteais tensed enough to cause his horse to sidle back and forth. Why hadn't he heard the old one approach? He wanted to curse at all of the gods for his carelessness these last few days.

The dark-haired man in front of Arteais signaled to his men.

The others backed away a few steps, each giving the flicker of respect to the Folk elder standing just outside the light.

"Where is the threat?" The old one's voice was strong if a bit rough.

Arteais swung around enough to take in the balding, bent stick apparently in charge. "Behind me. Or more accurately, between us and the fort. There is more than one group out there. The ones still within hearing are sweeping the land between the road and the river."

"Timerus, send someone to check. Quietly."

"Yes, Corsanth."

While Timerus obeyed the Folk elder, both Arteais

and Corsanth stared off into the darkness. This time, unlike with the Folk elder, Artearis heard the scout long before he saw her. She was good, but he knew what to listen for. When she confirmed the news, Corsanth silently withdrew to the elder's wagon.

One of the guards asked Timerus what they should do with Artearis. When Timerus didn't answer, another tapped him on the shoulder. Timerus had the same kind of scowl on his face that Artearis had suppressed earlier.

"Do with him?" Timerus shook his head. "We don't. That's for the elders to decide. Our task is to figure out how to get this news to the kingdom heads."

When one of the guards disappeared only to return on a barrel pony, the scowl Artearis had suppressed earlier appeared. "You've got to be kidding."

He spent what he counted as more precious minutes arguing with Timerus while keeping an ear to the darkness. The intruders were slowly drawing closer. Swearing softly, Artearis dismounted. "Who's your smartest rider?" he asked as he yanked his gear off his horse. Timerus waved another of the burly guards over. Artearis wanted to strangle someone. Trying to keep his voice civil, he said, "Who is your most conscientious rider?"

The scout stepped forward. "I am."

Artearis scrutinized her carefully. She had shown herself a competent scout, and she was light enough to get good mileage out of his mount without breaking its wind. "Bring him back to me hale, or you'll not ride anything again." He wanted to smile at the shiver that went through her. Instead, he handed over the reins. "They are sweeping in an arc. You should be able to ride past when they move close to the road."

"So why didn't you?" Timerus asked as he watched the scout ride off.

Slinging his gear over his shoulder, Artearis ignored the question. He calculated it would take him maybe three days to get to Banton's Folly on foot.

"Gaujo, you can't wander around in the dark, alone, with enemies about. You've done us a good turn. For mine, I can offer you sanctuary until we reach a town."

Artearis considered the offer. He traveled fast enough on foot — at least as fast as a traveling caravan — but with them he would be more rested, and it would give him a good reason for being there, as long as they got out of here in one piece. He extended his hand in acceptance as Marte had taught him.

Weaving his way behind Timerus through the throng of people, animals, and wagons, Artearis grew impressed. The Folk might travel in a caravan, but they did it efficiently. By the time Timerus had found him a seat on a laden supply wagon, the caravan had altered its direction to the northeast where a scattering of hills could mask their retreat, and if he remembered correctly from his early canvas of the river, there was a decent crossing there.

He had just settled his belongings at his feet when an elderly woman hopped up onto the driver's side of the seat, grabbed the reins, and with a sharp crack, set the wagon in motion. The horses stepped into their paces without so much as flinching.

"You aren't quite what I expected," she told him.

Artearis tensed.

"Thinner ... more refined ... like your mother ... though tall ... like your father."

The steel in his eyes stabbed at the woman beside him who continued smoothly, "And his eyes. Do you have his black disposition?"

His hands clenched around the edge of the seat.

"Are you the monster your father was?"

He tried to loosen his grip.

"There are stories that suggest as much."

The knuckles turned white with the pressure he exerted on the wood.

"They say you have no compunction in killing children. Your father ...."

"My father was a brutal sadist who enjoyed hurting anyone in his way." Artearis's voice was low and controlled.

"Your father's legacy to you was to kill the child whisked from his grasp."

He flinched at her sharp tone. The *clop clop* of hooves striking the hard ground filled the silence between the two for quite some time. How did this old Folk know who he was, know so much about his family? She wandered around the kingdom in a wagon, so where did she get her information? She sat there so calmly, maneuvering the wagon through the rough terrain. What did she want from him?

She took her eyes from the uneven ground long enough to assess his reaction. "Did he tell you the story of the massacre? Did he tell you how he thrust his dagger into Remora's stomach and yanked it upward? Or, how he beheaded Farin while the man was on his knees begging for the life of his wife and child? Or, how he sent a throwing knife at the child in a desperate attempt to kill her but missed?"

Her words stunned Artearis.

"By the way, the knife didn't miss. It struck the abdomen of the child's maid. Marion gave up her chance to ever have a child of her own."

*Marion?* The woman who cared for him after his mother died was named Marion.

Another long silence stretched between them.

Timerus rode up to them on a barrel pony to inform the Folk elder they were reaching the river crossing.

"Bring me two weir lights for the rails."

"Yes, Elder."

By the time the lights arrived, they had reached the river. Once they were attached, she cracked the reins. The draft horses picked up their feet. The wagon headed into the water. The water didn't reach the axle, but the riverbed wasn't smooth. The wagon wobbled slowly across it.

The light and the slow progress of the caravan worried Artearis. Whatever was out there could still be expanding. Even the river might not be a protective barrier. A splash to his left alerted him that others were crossing as well. The wagon lurched. She urged the horses onward. The horses strained in their harnesses. The front wheels rocked: one working its way over the rocks, one sliding around the rocks, angling the wheel.

The cracking of wood blended with her next words. "Another rumor is being whispered about. The Head of the Assassins Guild has left his sanctuary to kill another child."

Artearis groaned. Why was he doomed to be labeled the monster that slays children?

# Chapter Twenty
## Adversary or Ally

As the eldest of this vardo, Lucia took the responsibility for her people's safety and well-being very seriously. Her sight had warned her the Gaujo was a threat. She could feel the anger and turmoil raging inside him which surprised her considering all Berains purge themselves of emotion. Her son had verified the truth of that. But a threat to whom?

His willingness to warn the Folk when it would have been easier to leave them to fate suggested some understanding of moral responsibility that didn't align with the reputation he had for brutality. Still, he was his father's son, and Cresten Berain had been a master of cloaking his intentions, and Lathan Morden's son was here. Lucia greatly wished to know the game the assassin played.

She signaled to a nearby Folk.

"Yes, Elder?"

"Find me Ronin."

"Yes, Elder."

Lucia spent the time waiting by inspecting the status of the vardo. A broken wheel on a prop cart confirmed her fear; two river crossings were more than the wagons could take without maintenance.

When Ronin finally caught up with her, Lucia took his massive arm and steered him toward her wagon. Her small frame easily cleared the entrance to her living quarters; Ronin, on the other hand, was forced not only to duck but to turn sideways to get his muscled bulk through. Lucia waved him to a seat as she closed the door. Ronin chose to sit on the floor.

"What's up?"

"The carts and wagons."

The dark-haired blacksmith nodded. "They've taken a beating. We should have had them tended to before we headed south."

"What do you suggest?"

Ronin pondered her question. "We had planned to refit at Banton's Folly."

"And, now?"

"I'd have to inspect the damage."

Lucia said, "Do so."

Ronin lifted a knowing eyebrow.

Lucia chuckled. "You know me much too well."

"Why drag me into your wagon to discuss the damage to our transportation? You're worried about the Gaujo."

It was her turn to show surprise.

"Who is he, Lucia?"

"You don't know?"

Ronin shook his head.

"So why would you think I'd be worried about him?"

Ronin frowned. "You've kept him under your eye since he arrived."

Lucia straightened the cushions of her seat. "Keep him close, Ronin."

"And Alandran?"

She hissed, "Don't leave the Gaujo alone with him — ever!"

Ronin's response was interrupted by a knock on the door.

A stare worthy of Artearis punctuated her last words as she passed him and swung the door open.

"Pardon, Elder, the boy ...."

For a big man, Ronin was quick to spring to his feet and edge past Lucia before she could step outside and ask, "What about the boy?"

"He's missing, Master Blacksmith."

Ronin and Lucia looked at each other. Ronin's arm snaked out to assist the elder to the ground. Lucia said quietly, "Find him. Find them both."

Still perched on the wagon seat, Artearis studied the activity playing out in the predawn light. A small boy with black hair wandered among the adults checking animals and equipment. If Artearis had to guess, he'd say the boy was nine or ten — dark of skin but not the deep dark of those always in the sun like the Folk but more like the rich golden dark of one from Psartas. As the boy wandered near the edge of the camp, Artearis left his seat to follow. They were still too near the threat from last night for Artearis to feel comfortable letting the boy roam alone.

A feeling of wistfulness crept up on Artearis. He had done his own wandering at that age in the city of Ionen. It was one of the few times in his life when he felt, well, normal. Somehow Artearis didn't think normal was what the boy was feeling as he ran his hand along the leaves of the bushes shielding the river bank. The shoulders hunched a little too far forward for someone reveling in freedom. A good twenty minutes later, the boy found a place free of bushes. He slid down the bank and sat with his toes just out of reach of the water.

Artearis approached only close enough to let his shadow fall upon the boy. "You do know it isn't safe out here?"

The boy sighed.

"Won't someone be worried that you are gone?"

"I was in the way."

Artearis stood lost in thought. He knew what it felt like to be "in the way." His father's men cursed him for being in the way in the main guild halls which was why he would slip out into the city.

"Someone must care that you've disappeared."

The boy nodded. "Ronin will worry ... and Lucia. Lucia always worries ... about everything."

"Who is Lucia?"

The boy looked at him funny.

"Lucia is THE elder. She doesn't really like you, does she?"

Artearis frowned.

"She had that tone when she talked with you during the night."

That tiny old woman who set Artearis on edge during their ride last night was the leader of this Folk caravan?

"Are you all right?"

Artearis worked to keep his voice steady. "All right?"

"Your face. It changed color like Papa's does when he hears bad news."

The boy was remarkably perceptive for his age. "How do you know what ...."

An impish grin spread across the boy's face. "I stole a ride in the back of the wagon. It was better than being cooped up inside." The grin disappeared. "Please don't tell her."

Artearis gave him a conspiratorial smile. "I won't ... IF you come back to the camp."

The boy sighed. "Fine." He stood up and dusted himself off.

Artearis extended his hand. The boy grabbed it to help him scramble up the bank.

"Thank you ... um," The boy's face tightened as if he were puzzling out something. "Gaujo? That's a funny name."

"I don't think it's a proper name, but it will do. And yours?"

Wrinkling his brow hard, the boy finally said, "Lucia says to tell people Aland, but that's not my proper name either."

Artearis shook the hand he still held. "Nice to meet you, Aland."

Alandran grinned. "Nice to meet you, too."

Alandran's hand crept into Artearis's when the two

saw the uproar at the camp. Artearis couldn't help but look down at the boy's head and wonder. The sight of the two of them together captured more than one Folk's attention. Within minutes, Ronin and Lucia appeared. Alandran squeezed his hand harder. At the look in Lucia's eyes, a coldness touched Artearis's spine much like that from his father's displeasure. His free hand slid up to the stone under his tunic. He desperately wanted to pull it out and rub it between his fingers, but something stopped him. He settled for letting his hand rest against it.

For a small woman, Lucia covered ground fast. She was in front of the two of them before they drew even with the perimeter. A bear of a man arrived on her heels. At the sight of the man, Alandran's head dropped. Artearis patted the boy's hand.

Alandran squeaked out, "I'm sorry, Ronin."

Artearis expected angry words, so it surprised him when the huge man simply held out his hand. Giving Artearis's hand a heartfelt squeeze, Alandran released it and gravely walked to the man.

Lucia regarded Artearis thoughtfully. Even so, he could still read distrust in her stance.

"Ronin, I need that report sooner than immediately. Get the Gaujo to help you," she said as she turned on her heel and headed back to her home.

Alandran tugged on Ronin's hand. "May I help?"

Ronin patted the boy on the shoulder. "Fetch my journal." Alandran's face lit up. He scooted off in the direction of the craftsman's circle. "And a pen," Ronin called after him.

Artearis expected the man to question him, but again, he surprised Artearis with his silence.

The entire morning and part of the afternoon was spent crawling under and around everything in the caravan that had wheels. At first, Ronin let Alandran keep the tally of problems, but the boy's studious determination to be helpful couldn't compete with the long night and the tediousness of an inspection. Three vehicles later, Ronin took the journal and pen from the sleeping boy, handed both to Artearis, and gently carried Alandran to Lucia's wagon.

The thoroughness of Ronin's inspection astonished Artearis. He'd always considered himself meticulous, particularly with stockpiles and mounts, but this went well beyond. Artearis flipped through the pages containing his handwriting. Every vehicle had at least some wear that needed addressing. Ronin assured him the damage to brackets and metal workings would be dealt with when they made a proper camp near a good supply of fuel. The crack in the back axle of the main supply wagon, the splintered spokes on a second supply wagon, and the damaged linchpins of a sleeping wagon required a wheelwright, however. Lucia wouldn't be happy.

Artearis shifted in his blankets. The open space in front of Lucia's wagon left him feeling exposed. The new view brought him face to face with the fire where Ronin had reported his findings to Lucia, Corsanth, and Timerus. The debate that ensued burned hotter than the stoked wood. The old man thought it best to continue to Banton's Folly where they could barter entertainment for a wheelwright and supplies. Artearis silently agreed with the destination if not the reasoning.

Lucia wasn't sure the vardo could make it that far. She felt Hisanth was the better choice. Timerus threw in his lot with Lucia. The three tossed reasons back and forth for some time before realizing that the blacksmith hadn't weighed in on a choice. When Ronin remained silent, Artearis quietly reminded them that an unknown enemy lay between the caravan and Hisanth. This started a new round of debates, but Artearis was more interested in the thoughts of their quiet companion than heated voices repeating old arguments.

He could almost see the wheels spinning inside Ronin's head as the man weighed the information presented to him. When the heated voices finally quieted, the blacksmith's deep voice filled the void. There was a small farming town to the north, Ghans, that had a wheelwright. It was closer than Banton's Folly and didn't require crossing the river again as it would to continue to Hisanth. The vardo would not survive another river crossing without the repairs. If they traveled a bit north and east, they should come upon the road to Ghans. It should be well kept as the town supplied food to the fort nearby.

Artearis inspected each face. Like him, Corsanth chaffed at the additional delay. Timerus appeared to want to argue further, but Lucia had that thoughtful look that said she respected the thoughts of the blacksmith. When she ruled in favor of Ghans, no one opposed her. Timerus stalked away, presumably to his own wagon. Ronin offered Artearis a place at his lodging, but Lucia would have none of it. The old woman wanted Artearis close, and he thought he knew why.

When the others had gone, Lucia and Corsanth retired to the large wagon Artearis had come to associate with Lucia. He hadn't realized she shared it with the other elder. His mind began to consider what kind of relationship the two had when their voices grew loud enough for him to distinguish their words.

The old man spoke slowly as if he was weighing each word. "I know you have profound reasons for not wanting him here."

"He complicates things."

THE CRYSTAL BLADES

Artearis could almost see the old man nod.

"It goes beyond that, Lucia, and you know it. I know his family has caused you much grief. And that you have exercised much forbearance in withholding your hand these long years."

"It was necessary."

"She loved him, too. Never forget that. She chose the hard path ... to protect him and to protect her family."

"I know that."

"But you still can't forgive her."

"She nearly broke him."

There was a long silence before Corsanth spoke again.

"No, Lucia, she didn't. That monster nearly did. Just as he nearly broke her."

"Just as he took my grandchildren away from me." The bitterness of her words sent chills down Artearis's spine. "Marion ...."

"Marion knew the danger. In truth, she was fortunate to survive."

"And yet, we welcome that bastard's spawn into our vardo."

"He is her son, too, and she willingly used her death to strengthen your son's place in that hell."

Artearis thought he heard Lucia sigh.

"She did not run from the foretelling. She embraced it." A sorrowful kindness overlaid Lucia's words.

"At the cost of her own life, she gave us hope."

"Did she?"

"Your son thought so."

"Yes, he did."

"Do we trust him?"

This time it was Lucia who spoke as if she weighed each word. "No. We don't trust him. We trust my son."

If there was more spoken between the two elders, it was said too quietly for Artearis to hear. What they had said deeply disturbed him. The monster had to be his father. Cresten Berain was worse than a monster.

Staring at the flames flickering against the darkness, Artearis could see the tyrant who had abused his mother. Oh, he hadn't beat her precisely. At least, she never revealed any marks that told the tale. But on those rare times she had come to him, she would take care not to flinch when he wrapped his arms around her waist and squeezed with his child's strength or crawled up in her lap and lay his head on her chest and listened to his mother read to him.

When she was carrying his brother, she came to see Artearis more often, and she smiled and hugged him as she never had before or after. And it was only after Zotearis was born that she visited hardly at all.

That was when Marion came — Marion who taught him to read and to write, to be curious, and to ask questions, although Artearis found out early that there were people you didn't ask questions of unless you didn't mind the pain. His father was one of those people. Marte was not.

If there was anyone in the world Artearis was grateful for besides his mother, it was Marte. Even before his mother was gone, Marte spoke kindly to him whenever chance brought him around, which, Artearis just realized, happened more often shortly before his mother died.

Maybe that was why when he had sneaked away from the funeral rites, he found himself in the Guild training halls — not that he knew they were assassin training arenas then. To Artearis, they were curiosities that he needed to explore. In one of them, he had found Marte. The man had been leaning against a vault mount, staring into space. Artearis had not yet learned to walk silently, and his child-sized steps announced his entry into Marte's domain.

That day was the one and only time that Marte picked him up and held Artearis in his arms. It was also the first and last time Artearis cried for his mother. Artearis turned his back on the fire and prayed for sleep.

Sleep evaded Lucia as her mind replayed her conversation with Corsanth. He was right to be concerned.

When the web of fate being spun for her son was kept

at a distance, Lucia had been able to leave it be and keep her focus on her people. Now that the strands had stretched this far, she found it hard to separate personal feelings from her responsibilities.

It wasn't enough to tell Corsanth to trust her son. Lucia needed to believe in that trust with unshakable conviction — conviction she knew eluded her. She needed to see more clearly.

Shifting her old bones from their comfortable position, she climbed from her bed, and quietly, so as not to disturb Corsanth, she slipped behind the covering that separated the sleeping quarters from the living area.

For this, she would need a focus. Shifting the bottles of medicine and the tins of powders to the side, she reached to the back of the shelf that contained her unconventional supplies and lifted out a misshapen crystal. Misshapen to the untrained eye, that is. For those who knew how to look, a web pattern anchored by not three but five points curved up from the lower lip to the upper rim.

Lucia carefully put it down on her scrying table. She kept her voice soft as she began her chant, drawing a small amount of energy from the world around her to send through the strands of her focus. With great care, she shaped the essence of that which haunted her.

The image seared into her mind. A reflection that was more than a reflection sucked in the life being carried on the threads of a powerful web. Behind the reflection stood a thin, slightly bent shadow weaving words the world had not heard for hundreds of years — words she had only seen in the book Corsanth protected but had never heard. The words enticed her to join the stream of power, to become one with the source.

The lure was an old one — one Lucia had made peace with many decades ago. She let go of the threads binding her focus. Instead of finding clarity, she found more uncertainty. With a troubled sigh, she woke her companion.

# Chapter Twenty-One
## New Game in Town

"Damn, Lathan Morden!" Korvin crushed the note in his hand and threw it.

"Damn, Artearis Berain!" He backhanded the blonde bitch given to him by Jekan Geylas, sending her across the room to join the note.

How can two men fall so completely off the grid when one is as close to royalty as you can get without being royalty and the other is being hunted by nearly every political group in the kingdom since his brother let slip his departure from Guild headquarters?

Korvin paced the length of the private room and back twice before stopping to take a swig from his mug. Well, they couldn't stay here much longer without drawing too much attention. Bribes only kept people quiet for so long.

He paced to the window. Nestled against the edge of town was a high-walled manor with plenty of room for men, gear, and horses, and since the Duke wasn't home to enjoy it .... Korvin smiled that nasty smile that warned the blonde she was in for a rough afternoon. Poking his head out the door, he yelled to his men to meet him in his room at the sixth hour of evening, "and bring plenty of food and drink." The smile grew crueler, "and entertainment!" His foot kicked the door shut.

Justen pulled off his cap and scratched his head, his fingers barely disturbing the close-cropped hair. "The town doesn't really have guards," said the small, wiry man. "Local enforcement is done by a poorly paid citizen's brigade. When anything serious comes up, they petition the Duke for use of his arms men."

Korvin nodded at his most reliable recon man. "And the manor?"

Justen stared uncomfortably at the fortyish, balding man making one last stab downward before he pulled himself to his feet. With a flourish, Zeke waved his hand at the brunette on her back. "Feel free."

Korvin chortled at the daggers leaving Justen's eyes.

"Well?"

Zeke took a moment to arrange himself. "There's still a decent sized force at the manor: two pairs of roving sentries at all times, two perimeter guards for the front and side entrance, an old man who tends the stable, two old crones that appear to be the cook and a maid, and," he grinned sadistically, "three younger women, a girl of about ten, and a boy," Korvin stiffened with excitement. Zeke finished, "Naw, not that one. This one's maybe thirteen and fine looking but country stock for certain."

Korvin grunted. He turned to his second-in-command, who was fondling another of the whores sent over by the madam in town. "So what do you think, Frisk?"

Frisk studied the rounded mound under his heavy hand. He squeezed and laughed as his ride tried to buck him off. Once she calmed down, he said, "Has to be a one-nighter. Two groups. First, take out the rovers when they hit a blind spot."

"What blind spot?" Korvin's trap specialist cradled a cup of very strong ale in his hands.

Zeke laughed. "There're always blind spots: odd corners, deep shadows, obstacles. And there's at least three along each route."

Frisk continued, "Like I said, take out the rovers then hit the guards. The place is ours."

Korvin pulled his blonde onto his lap. "Pour me a

drink, sweetie," he growled into her ear. "Sounds like a plan. What's the catch?"

The youngest member of the group roused himself from the view out the window. Yorn collected his thoughts. "The general grocer let slip reinforcements are expected in less than a fortnight. Too many for us to handle if we're stuck here that long."

Justen added, "Not to mention, the people of Gessin are loyal to their Duke. We could take over the place, but once the town figures out what we done, it'll be us against all of them."

Frisk stretched. Picking himself off the floor, he sauntered up to Justen. In a low voice, he said, "That one's a touch better than Zeke's. You should give her a try." To Korvin, he said, "Best if we hire ourselves a bit of muscle, first."

Korvin grabbed his blonde around her neck and pulled her up with him. He walked her to the door and held her tightly while he took stock of the room. He hadn't thought of keeping chains around their necks — strong enough to hold 'em in place, thin enough not to get in the way. He ran the toe of his boot along the side of the redhead not in service at the moment. A threesome might not be a bad idea. Then Zeke dropped down beside her. Oh, well.

To his men, he said, "Have your fun now. We hit the place tonight. It goes well, you can move your toys in with your gear. All of you except Frisk and Yorn. As soon as it's done, you head to Banton's Folly and recruit us some muscle. I'll let you know when I'm ready." Korvin didn't bother to shut the door on his way out.

# Chapter Twenty-Two
## Ghans

Rhealle stood at the door of her father's house, staring at the rain. Eight days ago a stranger had come to Ghans carrying a large satchel. The late morning was hot and bright. The quiet man politely asked where he could get some refreshment.

Rhealle opened her mouth to speak. Her sister Lilleth was quicker. She directed the man to the cafe in the main town square. Rhealle followed the stranger down the dusty road to the cool shade of their father's business. She slipped inside after him and waited for the server to return with his drink. Her hands shook as she took the tray and carried it to his table.

Instead of choosing one of the square tables pushed

against the walls like most of their patrons, the stranger chose a round one in front of the unlit fireplace. Leaning over to set the drink down, she caught her breathe.

On the table was a mirror that would fit across both of her hands put together. Silver etching lined the oval edge. Rhealle couldn't tell what the shapes were, but they glistened even in the darkened room, and the glass ... the glass pulsed with a sparkling light. When the stranger noticed her staring at the mirror, he smiled kindly and put it away. Rhealle lowered her head to hide her sigh.

When she looked up, he was watching her intently. His silver eyes looked into her brown ones as if waiting for an answer to a question. She stepped back a pace. His lips formed the words, "What is your name?" Rhealle hesitated.

The vibration of footsteps on the wooden floor made Rhealle look behind her. The serving woman opened her mouth and spoke words slowly. "Rhealle. Her name is Rhealle. She doesn't usually speak."

Rhealle turned back to the stranger. His eyes were warm, his mouth soft as he slowly spoke her name. How could silver feel so warm? Rhealle smiled.

The stranger asked the serving woman for another drink before turning his attention to a piece of parchment stretched across a thin board. For a few more moments, Rhealle stood beside the table watching him. He looked up and gave her another kind smile. Before he could do anything else, she edged her way to the front entrance.

Outside, Rhealle sat on the edge of the landing. The mirror was so bright, so beautiful. Where could he have gotten it? Would the stranger let her hold it?

The feel of the wooden planks giving in beside her, caused Rhealle look up. The stranger stood above her. He gave her another of those smiles that made her feel warm inside. She shyly smiled back. Settling the satchel he carried under his arm, he shifted his gaze to the roads leading out of the town square. With a glance at the sun, he headed down the steps and toward the road that led to the town's fields. A curious Rhealle decided to follow him.

For the rest of the scorching day, the stranger wandered the fertile land around the town. He walked the western edge of the crop fields to the river where he pulled out his parchment and added marks to it. Then he crossed the shallow river to walk the perimeter of the golden hay fields, again making marks on his parchment every so often. Once in a while, he would stand in the hay field and adjust his hand to the height of the hay. After this, too, he would mark on the parchment.

Rhealle followed as the stranger continued his puzzling behavior at the crop fields and finally among the garden plots, and she was sure that every so often he would look nearly in her direction and smile. By the time the stranger walked back into town, a tired and dusty Rhealle wanted nothing more than to go home and sleep.

That did not stop her from waking early so she could see the stranger again. After walking every road in town twice, she settled herself on the veranda of her father's cafe. With legs drawn up and head resting on her knees, Rhealle stared across the square at nothing. The feel of a hand upon her shoulder startled her. She looked up into the face of the stranger.

"Good morning," his lips formed.

She smiled and nodded.

He reached down to help her up. "Join me?"

The stranger didn't wait for Rhealle to reply. He simply guided her through the door and to a table away from other customers. Once seated, he said something to someone behind Rhealle that she couldn't read in the darkened corner. Soon a steaming cup of tea was placed in front of her.

Rhealle started to form the words "thank you." At the sight of the beautiful mirror she had seen yesterday, all thought of responding went away. The stranger laid it carefully on the table.

Gently lifting her hand, he unfolded her clenched fingers and lightly brushed the tips of them across the silver tracing. Rhealle sucked in her breath. Very carefully, she used her forefinger to trace the silver carving. As her finger rubbed along the surface, a light began to glow from inside the glass.

She withdrew her finger from the mirror, and the light faded. Before her hand moved more than a few inches from the frame, the stranger captured it in his and settled it upon the silver tracings again. This time he kept his hand cupped over hers as he brushed her fingertips along the edge. The glass began to pulse. When he was sure she wouldn't take her fingers away, he rested his hands around his cup.

Rhealle stroked the mirror, watching the light pulses change rhythm as her movements changed. When the stranger's hand folded itself around her fingers and drew them away from the mirror, and the light died within, Rhealle sighed. She watched the hand place hers on the table and release it, as if it didn't belong to her. His long fingers curled around into a loose fist as the hand slowly moved up to her face, lifting her chin so that he could look into her eyes.

"Would you like to be my guide today?" he said slowly.

Rhealle's hand shook as it rested on the table. She swallowed hard. He dropped his hand away, but she couldn't move her eyes. She swallowed again. He waited. Finally, she nodded.

"Good." He held her gaze while he put the mirror inside his satchel. Once the satchel was secured, he pushed away his chair. Coming around to hers, he pulled it back for her to stand. Rhealle froze. She was no guide. He turned her around to face him. His eyes told her he could see she was having second thoughts. She imagined the softness of his voice as he said, "You don't need to talk. I will name a place, and you bring me there. Good enough?"

She could do that. She nodded.

To her surprise, Rhealle enjoyed herself. He asked to see places like the smithy and other places to eat in town and the different stores. When she didn't understand what he said, which happened often as he had a strange way of forming words, he patiently repeated himself until she did. At mid-day, the two of them ate sticks of spiced pork cubes, tomatoes, and onions in front of the meat vendor in the western quarter of the town.

After they had eaten, he asked to see where the town kept its crops. The big storage silo always frightened her. Still, she took him there. He paced around the hexagonal building, pulled out his parchment, and marked on it. He asked Rhealle if the town stored food in other places. She nodded.

"Will you show me?"

So Rhealle took him to the smaller silo out on the far side of the fields and the grain bins built on the small hill overlooking the river and the place where they put extra produce from the gardens. At each location, he walked around the perimeter before making those strange marks on his parchment.

As the sun began to set, he asked Rhealle if she would show him one more place. She muffled a yawn as she nodded.

"Where is the hay kept?"

Rhealle sighed with relief. The hay barn was just on the southern edge of town, not far from the main square. She and Lilleth used to play there as girls. Rhealle still went there on occasion when she felt lonely. No one ever bothered her in the hay loft.

She waited for him to walk around the barn and to record his marks on the parchment. When he was done, she turned to go home. He placed his hand on her arm and carefully turned her to face him.

"Take me inside, please."

Rhealle's stomach contracted. She knew why some of the other girls in Ghans came to the hay barn, and it wasn't to daydream.

The stranger's face grew serious. "Don't worry. I wish to see how the hay is stored. Nothing more."

She studied his face. He seemed sincere, and he had been thoughtful the entire day. Rhealle spoke for the first time. "Come." She didn't know what to think when his eyes filled with surprise, so she simply walked past him to the door and lifted the latch.

Inside was dark and growing darker as the sun met

the horizon. The stranger pulled the mirror out of his satchel and stroked the frame. A light filled the barn. After examining the stalls filled with hay and the huge mound resting against the back wall, he climbed the ladder to the loft and lit the wooden boards with light from the glass.

When he climbed back down, instead of marking on his parchment, he propped the mirror on a shelf on the wall behind the ladder. Rhealle could not see his lips move, but she could see the mirror pulse with light. Then the mirror flared brightly, and she could see the stranger's reflection in it. His lips moved as if he were speaking, but the movement made the surface of the glass waver, and when the glass grew still, Rhealle couldn't understand the words his lips formed.

The stars were bright in the sky before they returned to her house along the town square. The stranger kissed the back of her hand. "Thank you," he spoke clearly. His parting smile left her feeling warm inside.

A sigh escaped Rhealle as she leaned her forehead against the glass of the door. A thin film of moisture dampened her brow. She sighed again. Ghans hadn't seen the sun since ... since the day the stranger had left. It wasn't normal. Ghans always had plenty of rain. Sometimes it would rain all afternoon, or a storm would roll in during the night, but it never rained all day and all night for days at a time. Since the stranger left, every day it rained a little harder.

Rhealle wondered why he had been so interested in the town. On the second day after he left, she began to walk the path he had taken as he explored the fields and the town. The crops were missing the sun, and the soil was having a hard time taking in the water. She followed his path to the gardens. Some plants were beginning to droop. Even her father's prized tomato plants were struggling under the excess water.

Approaching Ghans from the south, Rhealle passed the hay barn. It struck her how insistent he had been to go inside. Rhealle entered.

Without the light from the mirror, she had to find a lantern, and it took several tries to light the one she finally found because she couldn't stop shivering from her wet clothing. Rhealle raised the lantern high. Everything looked as she expected. Slowly, she turned in a circle. Nothing looked wrong. Then the light fell on the ladder. She carried the lantern to the wall where the stranger had propped up the mirror behind the ladder and talked to it. Nothing.

Rhealle frowned. Something had changed in the barn. She could feel it, but what? As Rhealle pulled the lantern back, her hand smacked into the ladder. He had gone up to the loft before talking to the mirror. She shifted the lantern to her other hand and climbed up. Holding the lantern high, she looked around. In the center of the loft, light reflected back at her. Rhealle stepped onto the wooden support. The lantern light reflected back from the stranger's mirror. Rhealle set the lantern beside it.

It was a beautiful piece of craftsmanship, so elegant, so delicate. She stroked the mirror as she had done that day in the cafe. A bright light flared from inside the glass. She gasped and pulled her hand away. The surface of the glass shimmered like a soft ripple in the water then grew still. The light dimmed, yet remained. Rhealle gently ran her forefinger along part of the silver tracing. The light within brightened; the surface rippled more intently. Rhealle's finger stilled.

As the light faded, the ripples smoothed away. Rhealle couldn't help herself. She ran her fingertips around the entire circumference of the mirror. The flare of light was so bright it nearly blinded her. When her vision finally cleared enough to look at the glass, Rhealle saw a face staring at her. The face spoke, but the words were unfamiliar and came too fast for her to read them. She sat back on her heels and waited for the face to repeat itself.

The mouth in the mirror remained still. The deep brown eyes, however, were vibrantly alive, watching her intently for long minutes before finally disappearing from view.

Rhealle could see light in the mirror like the kind that shines in a very large room, bright near the source and growing dimmer until the edges of the room were in shadow. Some of the brightest light surrounded a stone table — no not a table, there weren't any legs, more like a flat stone sitting on top of a stone box carved with markings similar to the silver tracing along the mirror's frame.

Before she could figure out any details, another much sterner face filled the glass. Eyes almost colorless yet compelling in their intensity captured hers. Rhealle couldn't help herself. Without taking her eyes from the surface of the mirror, she leaned over and placed both of her hands upon the silver frame.

Those ancient eyes stared into hers. They asked her a question. Rhealle tried to look at his lips to see what he asked, but she couldn't tear herself away from the colorless pools. The eyes asked her again. This time, pain nearly split her head apart as the words stabbed at her mind. "Who ... you .... Why ... mirror ...." Rhealle began to pass out.

The word "NO" jerked her back to attention. The pressure inside her skull lessened. The stabbing pain softened to discomfort so that she was able to understand the voice, his voice, speaking inside her head. The voice was cold, insistent, annoyed. It wanted to know who she was. Before Rhealle had a chance to do more than form the thought of her name, the voice in her head said, "Greetings, Rhealle. Why do you play with my mirror?"

Rhealle tried to pull her hands away from the frame.

They refused to move.

"You don't like my mirror anymore?"

Rhealle tried to answer, but no words formed. Instead, her mind grew quiet and fuzzy.

"Yes, it is a beautiful piece of craftsmanship. Would you like to keep it?"

Again, Rhealle tried to answer, but before a thought was formed, he answered for her. "Of course, you would."

Rhealle's head felt like something was poking at it: first by her eyes, then at the base of her skull, and finally in the middle of her brain. The sensation made her stomach heave.

The cold voice spoke again inside her head. "I see there is something you desire more than my mirror."

Inside her head, Rhealle could see herself singing as she walked along the path to the family garden as she had before the sickness took away her hearing. Every little while, the vision of herself would cock her head to one side and listen to the sound of birds or wind and water or her father's voice.

Brittle laughter bounced around her head. She wanted to close her eyes, wanted the sound to go away. The ancient eyes clung to hers, drew her deeper into their depths.

"I can give that to you. I can let you hear again. If ... you will do something for me."

This time the voice let her form her thoughts. "What

would I need to do?"

"Care for my mirror. Protect it from harm. If you do this, I will give you the mirror and your hearing back."

Rhealle couldn't help thinking "For how long?"

"Until I release you from your task."

Rhealle thought hard about what he asked. How could keeping the mirror safe hurt anything? She could take it home and hide it away ....

The voice said sharply, "No, the mirror must stay here. Every day you must come here alone and make sure it is safe."

What harm could the mirror do inside the barn?

"No harm. Will you do this?"

Rhealle nodded.

The voice said "By the pain of Ashlemar you must swear your soul to keep the mirror safe."

Rhealle nodded.

"No, you must SPEAK the words."

Rhealle frowned.

"It matters not if they sound proper. You MUST speak them."

Rhealle nodded. Opening her mouth, she formed the words. As each syllable tumbled out, her mind felt a pinch. When she had finished, a sharp pain stabbed her in the heart, bringing tears to her eyes.

"It is done. You and the mirror are one."

Every day since then, about this time, Rhealle felt drawn to stand at the door and watch the rain. Every day since she became bound to the mirror, she felt compelled to go to the barn and climb into the loft to stare into the mirror. Every day since the pain erupted in her heart, the rain came down a little harder. Rhealle pushed her hand against the door to open it.

# Chapter Twenty-Three
## An Uncooperative Town

Still gripping the edge of the door frame, Rhealle stepped onto the veranda of the house. Part of her felt compelled to go to the mirror. Part of her refused to move.

Rhealle looked out. The main square was empty: no dogs barking, no young ones playing, no customers coming and going from the shops lining the square. The rain had turned the road into mud and the tips of the grass in the square swayed in the pools of water covering it.

Stepping onto the first riser, Rhealle lost her grip on the door. It snapped back from her hand — the force causing the stairs to shake. She hoped the rain prevented the sound from drawing attention.

Rhealle realized the rain had let her down when she

saw three men slogging through the muddy road change direction. Even though the rain itself wasn't heavy, the mist from the heat and moisture made it hard for Rhealle to make out who approached. She descended another riser.

The three drew closer. More strangers. Rhealle nervously descended the last riser. The man on the left wore his black hair tied against the back of his neck. Her eyes followed the curve of his face to a pair of agitated brown ones.

Before Rhealle could properly study this attractive stranger, the thin man next to him gestured sharply, catching her attention. With the rain soaking him from head to toe, Rhealle couldn't tell the color of the second stranger's hair. It may have been a light brown or a dirty blond. The second man was several inches taller with steel blue eyes that sent shivers along Rhealle's spine. Although less imposing physically than either of the other two, he radiated a strength and unpredictability more potent than even the stranger from eight days ago. This was no man to cross.

Looking behind him at the one who towered over both of the others, Rhealle felt the dark-haired one was also not a man to cross, but unlike the thin one, this man had a quiet strength about him that did not speak so much of force as protection.

This solid giant tapped the dangerous one on the shoulder, his callused forefinger extended in Rhealle's direction. "Gaujo."

The light-headed one nodded. The three men quickly closed the distance between them and her. Rhealle gave up the idea to visit the mirror. She headed for the strangers instead. Soon, she was close enough to properly read what they said.

She wasn't the only one paying attention to details. Artearis scoured the square with his eyes. "There's someone else standing at the door of that building across the square," he said to his companions.

He turned his attention back to Rhealle. She could see how tight he was strung: his jaw clenched and his knuckles white from gripping the hilts of his weapons. If he were a bow, he would snap if someone used him or send the arrow completely through his target if he didn't. Bending to whisper something in his ear that Rhealle couldn't read, the giant placed a hand firmly on his shoulder and squeezed briefly. If Rhealle didn't know better, she would swear the big man was a metalworker with those thick arms and strong hands.

The three men had nearly reached Rhealle when the compulsion to return to the mirror struck her hard. Rhealle pivoted sharply toward the hay barn. Turning too fast on the wet grass, Rhealle's feet slid out from under her. The black-haired stranger was quick. Before she knew it, he had locked his arms around her to keep her upright. Rhealle shifted her feet to regain her footing, but she couldn't stop the rapid beat of her heart. Even though the staccato rhythm interfered with the vibrations of his voice, Rhealle could not look up, not until he tilted her chin upward.

"Are you all right?"

Rhealle watched the firm mouth as it formed words that sent flutters through her stomach. She wasn't sure if it was his unfamiliar accent or his pleasant way of speaking that made it hard for her to understand him. When he repeated himself, Rhealle swallowed hard as she nodded.

He held her while he assured himself she could stand without falling. Then all of a sudden she was free. Rhealle took a step back to keep her balance only to feel someone grab her arm and pull her away from him. The sudden shift almost sent her to the ground a second time. Her savior reached out to catch her again. He stopped. Rhealle turned around.

"... that is my daughter!" Her father had that disapproving "how dare you cross the line" stare.

Her father tensed. "What do the Folk want here in Ghans?"

This was definitely one of those times Rhealle was glad she couldn't hear. His voice was going to get angrier every time he said something just like when she was a child.

"Mayor Durnin is who. You want something, you negotiate with me."

Rhealle tried not to roll her eyes.

Durnin appeared exasperated. "Ghans has no use for more strangers. Nothing but bad has happened since the last one left."

Rhealle forced herself not to look down. Her father was right. Nothing but rain had come since the first stranger left. She watched the anger grow in her father's face. It's what happened when he couldn't fix the town's problems himself.

Durnin said, "Not going to happen. We need Illen to keep the carts and wagons working through this damn rain."

The mayor frowned. "Bad enough. If we lose the crops now, we won't have time to plant more to pay the town's tithe."

Her father's expression shifted from a frown to annoyance. "The people you need to talk to are in the fields. They don't have any more time to deal with you than I have."

"If it will get me rid of you. Jojo!" Rhealle could feel the vibrations in the air from her father shouting for the boy.

She turned back toward the strangers. The Gaujo and his giant friend followed Jojo. Her black-haired savior stood still.

"Rhealle, come!" Durnin headed toward the cafe but stopped when he realized the troublesome man still stood next to Rhealle. "What do you want?"

"Timerus." Timerus worked his jaw back and forth.

"Something hot to drink would be welcome."

The mayor grudgingly led him to the cafe. As Rhealle followed the two men inside, she formed the word "Timerus" over and over.

When Durnin abandoned him to find the kitchen, Timerus surveyed the inside of the cafe. Off to the right of the door midway down the wall was a lit fireplace. Timerus edged his way to the crackling fire. Instead of taking a seat, he chose to lean his back against the stone hearth, giving himself a view of the entire room.

Shortly after Timerus had settled himself, Rhealle came to tend the fire. As she fought to roll the two bands of grating to the side, Timerus struggled to keep himself from helping her. He watched her carefully retrieve pieces of wood from the neatly stacked pile beside the hearth and even more carefully arrange them within the fire.

All of a sudden a large pop exploded into the air, startling Timerus but not the woman. He wondered why. He knelt to assist her that he might study her better. To his surprise, she was softly humming the Night Bird song, a lullaby Folk mothers sang to put their children to sleep. When his offer to help didn't bring a response, he reached for the thick log she struggled to place. His touch made her jump. Timerus gently but firmly pulled her hands away, shifted the log into place, and rearranged the other pieces of wood into a more efficient configuration for burning before helping her replace the grating. This time, he paid particular attention not to touch her.

She smiled her thanks before retreating to the kitchen. Timerus regained his spot by the hearth in time to see an angry Durnin approach. "My daughter can handle her tasks without help."

Timerus began to explain that "the log wasn't split to the proper size for her to handle" but thought better of it. Townspeople would suspect Folk actions until the world ended. That was just the way it was, and Lucia was counting on him negotiate for a wheelwright.

Durnin lowered himself into a chair by the round table in front of the fire. As the mayor stretched his legs, he yelled for a hot drink and pastries.

As with the stranger before, Rhealle took the filled tray from their serving woman. With very precise movements she placed her father's cup, cream, and plate exactly as he required. She returned the tray to the kitchen but soon after returned with a mug that she brought to Timerus. He wanted to smile and thank her. The thunderous look on her father's face limited Timerus to a solemn nod of his head.

In an angry voice, the mayor asked him, "Why are you

still here? I've already told you we are in no position to lend you our wheelwright."

Timerus took a slow sip of the mug he held before saying, "Ronin will know if there is anything the Folk can do to aid the town. I am here to negotiate a price should the wheelwright's services become available." Timerus took another sip of the hot beverage.

The drink had a soft bite like some kind of non-fermented, non-spicy fruit cider that took the chill from his bones even if it was rather bland. His mind raced as he took a third sip. Raising the mug in the direction of the mayor, Timerus asked, "Local?"

"Banton's Folly. Ghans doesn't have its own drink."

"What other drinks do you serve?"

Timerus watched expressions of exasperation, then annoyance, then pride, and finally interest cross Durnin's face. "We have a mild spiced milk we mix from supplies brought in from Hisanth. There is the fruit juice imported from Kellia. And my personal favorite, Camden Tea, straight from the Capitol itself."

"Nothing more exotic?"

Durnin clenched his hand around the cup he had been savoring.

"No offense." Finishing his drink, Timerus put the cup down. "I was ... your pardon." Easing himself out of the chair, Timerus offered a polite bow then took a step toward the door. At the same time, Rhealle came around the table to retrieve his cup. Timerus unbalanced Rhealle. He reached out to steady her. "Excuse me," he said.

Durnin scowled. He rapped the floor three times with his foot to get Rhealle's attention. "To the kitchen with you girl and stay there."

Rhealle picked up the empty cup and the plate with her father's half-eaten pastry. Straightening, she turned toward the kitchen, giving Timerus a grateful smile as she passed him. Again, Timerus gave her a solemn nod of his head. Without bothering to see what the mayor's reaction was to their little exchange, he walked out.

Worn out from fighting the compulsion to look into the mirror, Rhealle slipped away to the hay barn. The heat and humidity inside competed with the rain and dropping temperature outside to saturate the air. She tried to ignore the moisture that was making it hard for her to breathe as she climbed the ladder. It was even hotter in the loft. She considered abandoning the mirror for today, but her presence had already drawn its attention. The mirror began to glow without her touch. Rhealle couldn't resist its pull.

Every step she took strengthened the light radiating from the glass. Kneeling, she gasped at the intensity of the angry, colorless eyes searching for her from the other side. Her head nearly exploded from the pain of those eyes snaring hers — from the cold voice inside her head demanding to know why she had not come sooner. The voice that probed her mind burned like ice. It ripped the images of the three men from her thoughts, examining every detail she could remember.

The voice grew soft, edgy. "So, the Folk have come to Ghans. For what purpose?" The voice mulled over the words her father spoke to the three strangers. "And why would they care about the crops in such an insignificant town such as Ghans?"

Rhealle's mind wandered back to Timerus. Her straying thoughts seemed to irritate the voice. It continued to poke at her mind, looking for anything that would answer his questions. Time and again he came back to the thin stranger, the one Rhealle feared. It was almost as if this unknown person worried him. The voice probed harder, making Rhealle want to scream, but she had been too caught up in her encounter with Timerus to provide the voice more information.

Finally, it stopped probing. "Well, if the Folk wish to interfere, let them deal with something more potent."

The voice compelled Rhealle to run her hands along the silver tracing. Pain, unlike any before, exploded inside her head. Releasing the mirror, she doubled over. Her mind

271

went black.

Rhealle had no idea how long she was lost in the dark. She only knew she needed to get back before her father missed her.

Timerus vaulted up the cafe steps. The extended roof sheltered him enough to shake off some of the rain. He stood in front of the door for a moment, watching water pool at his feet. He prayed this idea of his would work. The rain certainly wasn't cooperating, coming down harder than when he had left. *Please let up so that the mayor will be more tractable.* Patting his chest to reassure himself his prize was still there, Timerus took a deep breath and opened the door.

Two steps into the building brought Timerus up short, nearly knocking a tray full of hot drinks out of the serving woman's hands. He quickly apologized and stepped aside to let her pass. Touching the small bulge in his tunic, Timerus searched the room. His target paced back and forth from the kitchen to the counter.

Before Timerus could move to intercept him, the front door opened, blocking his way. Timerus scowled. His patience with this whole negotiation process was wearing thin. Why didn't Corsanth just send a rider to Banton's Folly and .... The sight of a drenched Rhealle stumbling through the opened door stopped his thoughts.

For the third time, Timerus reached out to stop Rhealle from falling. With his arm wrapped around her, he drew Rhealle away from the entrance and toward the fireplace where he had stood earlier. While they waited for three patrons to push their way past, Timerus took a good look at Rhealle.

The woman was nearly white and shaking badly. The only free tables were around the fire. Once their path to an empty one was clear, he guided Rhealle to a chair. His concern grew as she collapsed onto it. Taking the chair opposite her, Timerus asked, "What happened?" When Rhealle didn't respond, he reached across the table to tilt her chin upward so she could see him speak. "What happened?"

During his last visit, Timerus suspected the woman was deaf. Now he was sure. *So how had she known the song?* The rhythm and pitch were nearly perfect. He felt her shaking increase. His thumb gently stroked her cheek as his father used to do for his mother when she was terrified from the attacks on the caravan. "How can I help?"

A strong hand crashed down on his shoulder. "What are you doing back here ... and with my daughter?"

Timerus let his hand drop to the table. "I came to bargain." He noticed the serving woman pass by. Timerus motioned to her. "I need two cups of very hot water and a spoon." As the serving woman walked away, Timerus reached inside his vest. He withdrew a small, dark colored jar sealed with wax and placed it on the table.

In a harsh voice, Durnin said, "Rhealle, to the kitchen with you, girl!"

Durnin plopped down in the chair emptied by his daughter and grabbed the jar, holding it to the firelight as he tried to determine the contents. Timerus deftly snatched the jar away and placed it on the table halfway between them.

"This," Timerus said, "is my bargaining chip. It comes from the mountains southeast of Novus."

Durnin grew interested. "What is it?"

Timerus said nothing. He simply waited. As he settled into his chair, his eyes scanned the room for Rhealle. His disappointment at not finding her translated itself into a deep sigh he had to stifle when Durnin looked at him suspiciously. To take his mind off the woman who kept invading his thoughts, Timerus quietly hummed the same tune he had heard earlier. The melody conjured an image of Rhealle tending the fire. *Damn!* Timerus plucked the jar from the table. Slowly, he rolled the container between his palms.

Durnin's interest turned to impatience. "What are you waiting for?"

"Two cups of very hot water and a spoon."

Durnin barked orders for the items to be brought immediately. Once the requested items were delivered,

Timerus ran his thumbnail around the edge of the lid, breaking the seal on the jar.

While the mayor fidgeted with impatience, he picked up the spoon and carefully measured one allotment of the contents. With deliberate slowness, he carried the contents to the cup closest to him and let the contents flow smoothly into it. The aroma of the tea wafted upward. Just as slowly, he repeated the steps for the second cup.

When Durnin reached for one, Timerus placed his hand over the top of the cup. "The tea must soak in the water for at least five minutes."

"Tea?" Durnin looked disappointed. "I have tea. What do I need more for?"

Timerus mentally relaxed. The mayor reacted as many of the Folk's potential customers react in the beginning: dismissive. As the alluring aroma drifted out of the cups, Timerus watched Durnin. The mayor's nose began to twitch from the tantalizing smell. Timerus wanted to smile but knew better.

There was a precise order that must be maintained. The potential customer had to be shown he needed the specialty goods that only the Folk could provide in Torenium. Timerus studied Durnin's face; the level of anticipation grew.

Then the customer had to desire the goods for

himself. Timerus removed his hand from the mayor's cup. Durnin grabbed for it, wincing as the hot surface burned his fingertips. Durnin sipped the liquid. A pleased expression crossed his face.

Next, the customer would act as though it would be a burden to stock such specialty items. Durnin sat back in his chair, cradling the cup of steaming liquid. Timerus watched him savor the taste of the green tea. Timerus pocketed the jar of Salfon tea before picking up his own cup. As the eyes of the mayor rested on the lump in his vest, Timerus chuckled inwardly. The man already coveted the rare blend.

Durnin cleared his throat. "Fine flavor it has certainly. Too fine for a town like Ghans. We rarely entertain people who would appreciate it. The demand wouldn't be worth the cost."

Finally, the customer would pretend that he was doing the Folk a favor by hosting their wares. Pushing his chair back, Timerus stood. "I see I've wasted my time."

Putting down his cup, Durnin, too, rose to his feet. "Of course, if you did leave a sample here and discerning travelers stopped in, I could let them try your tea. Should they enjoy it, they might wish to buy it from you. I would actually be providing you a service by offering it to prospective customers."

Once all of those steps were taken, negotiations would finally begin.

# Chapter Twenty-Four
## No Solution at Hand

By the time Artearis, Ronin, and the townspeople returned from the crop fields, the rain was coming down hard enough to wash away a good amount of the mud coating their legs if not their feet. Artearis was at a loss what to do. Once at the main square in town, most of the people wandered off to shops and homes. A fairly large group headed for the building where the town's mayor had come from earlier.

The stocky man with short, dark brown hair who had identified himself as Farel, the crop manager, walked off in a huff toward another large building on the opposite side of the square. Standing a short distance from Ronin were Lilleth, the hay foreman Weiz, and the wheelwright Illen.

Artearis was still amazed that such a slim man for six feet worked as a wheelwright.

"Where is Timerus?" Ronin whispered.

Artearis shook his head to clear his eyes. Water sprayed around him. By the blessing of Kaylei, Artearis was grateful it was a hot August. Even so, the cold rain chilled him through. Like Ronin, he scanned the square for clues to where the Folk's knife thrower had gone.

In the same low voice, Ronin said, "These people can't see this is a lost cause. Water is standing several inches in the fields, and the river separating them is slowly rising from the runoff. Without levees, the river is going to wash away any crops that have managed to survive."

"Any chance of raising some before that happens?"

Ronin shook his head.

Artearis muttered, "And still they won't lend us the services of their wheelwright."

Ronin shrugged.

"Then our time is better spent riding to Banton's Folly to hire one. Let's find Timerus."

Artearis had not noticed that his voice had grown loud enough for Lilleth to hear him until she tapped him on the arm.

"Before you go, you should come inside for something warm to drink. My father's cafe is just in front of us."

Both Weiz and Illen followed Lilleth. Artearis looked to Ronin to see what the blacksmith thought. Ronin simply shrugged. Artearis trailed after the small group.

Rarely had he been grateful for a roaring fire in summer. Even though it was tempting to warm himself at the fireplace, Artearis followed the three to a long counter. Lilleth disappeared into the kitchen.

Illen leaned against the counter. "I'm sorry I can't help you. All my time has been taken up repairing the broken wheels and axles of our farm carts because of mud."

"For all the good it does us," complained Weiz. "I'm going to lose this round of hay for certain. I'm just glad the hay barn is full enough to keep the stock fed for a couple growing seasons. Too bad Farel didn't plan that far ahead."

Illen replied, "In his defense, he hasn't held the position long enough for that. And Gereld wasn't ... well ...."

"Gereld was an idiot," Lilleth said, "which is why the town council removed him." She set a tray filled with steaming mugs on the counter.

Illen took a sip from one of the mugs. "Besides, it never rains this much in August. Who could have planned for something that doesn't happen?"

Weiz muttered, "Someone who leaves nothing to chance."

"Well, I don't have the luxury of that kind of planning. Even with canning and drying, the town needs a steady supply of fresh vegetables. We can't afford to haul in produce from other farm towns for the year. I've got to do something."

Neither townsman said a word.

Illen finally broke the silence. "You know, Lilleth, if you pursue this, Farel is going to stir up trouble. He was quite adamant out in the field when he said saving the crops will come first."

Lilleth nodded. "I don't care. He doesn't have to feed the town ... only its coffers."

She turned her attention to Artearis. "Back in the fields, you said there were ways to control water damage to the land."

Artearis frowned. He wished he had never remembered that old treatise on land management. The topic hadn't really interested him, so he had only skimmed the material. Now, this woman wanted him to come up with a miracle from the bits and pieces he could recall? A glance at Ronin warned Artearis pursuing this topic was a bad idea.

"Please," Lilleth said. "I've got thirty-two other townspeople as concerned as I am. I'm sure they'd be willing to try anything that had even a slim chance of working."

Ronin asked, "how much land are we talking?"

"A little more than six acres," Illen said. "We need more, but with the cash crops and the hay fields, the town barely manages to keep that much going."

"I'm not sure I can help. Most of what I remember is for large tracts of land."

Ronin cut in. "How far is this land from here?"

Artearis gave Ronin a questioning look.

Lilleth said, "Maybe a ten-minute walk from the edge of town."

Ronin motioned for Lilleth to show them.

The rain had settled to a steady but persistent pour that had Artearis, Ronin, and Lilleth soaked to the skin before they reached the first plantings. Ronin insisted on walking the entire perimeter before he would give his thoughts.

"The Folk travel through many lands. To the south, in Allisar, their land has many river branches and streams, making water a serious problem to overcome in order to raise food even though the soil is rich. Some places are too poorly located for dams and such, so they use mounds and man-made channels. For a layout like this, they would build drainage ditches. Within the enclosed land, they would carve drainage furrows to intersect the ditches." Ronin picked up a stick to draw the configuration in the mud.

"There is an oldster that has experience with this sort of thing." Ronin tossed the stick to the ground.

Artearis picked it up and stabbed the earth with it.

The stick sank easily into the wet ground. "Mud is a bad condition to work with under normal circumstances. This with rain still falling ... I don't know."

Ronin shrugged. "It can't hurt to ask him."

Lilleth asked the two what equipment they would need. "Digging tools and ...."

"And string at the least," Ronin answered.

"String?"

"To mark the paths for digging," Ronin said.

"So they'll need a supply of poles to tie the string to," Artearis added.

Ronin nodded.

Lilleth said, "I'd like to start tonight if possible."

This time Ronin was the one to frown. "That should be the decision of the oldster."

"Tell us what to do, and my people will do it — darkness or no."

Ronin nodded. "Go with her back to town. I will see him."

Artearis reluctantly followed Lilleth to the cafe. Inside, the place was packed with people except around the center of the counter. There, he could hear Farel's angry voice complaining about the lack of support for his efforts. When Farel saw Artearis trailing behind Lilleth, his voice grew louder and more belligerent. Artearis could smell trouble brewing.

# Chapter Twenty-Five
## Tensions Rise

Durnin shoved himself out of his chair. "I'd sooner bargain my defective daughter than the services of our wheelwright to the likes of the Folk and that won't EVER happen."

Before Timerus could respond, a crash and a sound like hail falling silenced both men. Durnin nearly sent his chair onto its side in his attempt to get a better view. "By the mighty axe of Moratam, what are you doing to my cafe?"

Shattered glass littered the floor in front of the counter. More pieces lay on top of it. Holding the jagged neck of a bottle was a stocky man with dark brown hair cut short and straight. Timerus didn't like the look of him.

Durnin's voice rose an octave. "Farel, you are going to

pay for that and anything else you break in here or else I'll bring sanctions against you."

"Cork it, Durnin. These two fools think an answer to our problem will just sprout from the ground." Farel waved his empty hand at Weiz and Lilleth. "And them ... these Folk," this time his curled fist beat the air in the direction of Artearis standing behind Lilleth, "encouraging the two instead of helping me save the town."

Timerus glared at Artearis. All the Folk needed was one more town distrusting them. He edged toward the assassin, winding his way through the crowd until he was just behind and to the right of Farel. From his new position, Timerus had a better view of Lilleth. The woman seemed familiar, although Timerus couldn't believe he would forget that burnished auburn hair.

Lilleth drew herself up to her full five feet seven inches. "When are you going to get it, Farel? The crops are gone. There's too many acres to save."

"Lilleth, shut up. We need the crops more than we need your pathetic vegetables. The crops pay the crown. The vegetables don't."

Even though Lilleth refused to raise her voice to a shout, it was firm and strong. "The vegetables feed us. We don't have the reserves to survive the next growing season as Weiz does with his hay."

"Damn it woman. SHUT UP!"

When Lilleth opened her mouth to speak again, Farel backhanded her across her right cheek, his ring leaving a thin line of blood from cheekbone to nose. Once his arm had reached its arc, he opened his hand and sent it back to strike her across her left cheek.

Timerus caught his arm, yanking Farel around to face him. Before Farel had a chance to react, Timerus slammed his own fist into the crop manager's face.

Farel shook off the blow. Still wielding the broken bottle in his left hand, Farel used it to force Timerus to back up.

Artearis slid between Lilleth and Farel's back. He had his dagger halfway out of its scabbard before Artearis saw the murderous look Timerus threw him. The Folk knife thrower wanted no help from an assassin. As more people gathered around the brawl, Artearis realized his own danger. He turned his head enough to see Lilleth's face. Quietly, he said, "Get your people and get out before no one can leave."

Lilleth compressed her lips together. She turned around to whisper something to Illen.

Artearis waited long enough to see her back away from the counter before weaving his way through the press to the door and left, hoping his trust in someone else fixing this situation wasn't misplaced.

Using his knuckles as a battering ram, Timerus struck at the back of Farel's hand, jarring the broken bottle loose and sending it onto a nearby table newly vacated by two patrons. Farel winced from the blow, but it didn't stop him. He brought his hand around to backhand Timerus across the face. Ignoring the blood at the corner of his mouth, Timerus sent his own fist flying at Farel's jaw.

Several more patrons hurriedly backed away from the two men, as Farel blocked the punch and tried to grapple Timerus to the ground. Timerus bent his knees and dropped his weight to keep from being taken down. The two men remained locked in stasis for several heartbeats before Timerus broke free. Pushing Farel off balance, Timerus followed with his right fist, but the towner caught himself mid-step and was able to lean back enough to avoid the blow. Farel charged forward, aiming his shoulder at his opponent's stomach.

By this time, the towners had put at least one table between them and the brawlers. They watched as Timerus dropped down to the floor, barely missing a table. When he kicked Farel up onto the table across from him, two of the townspeople backed up even farther.

Gaining his feet, Timerus closed the gap between the two men, but a gleam in Farel's eye said he had other plans. Farel edged his way left. When he reached the next table, he felt behind him. Not finding what he wanted, Farel quickly looked back. Seeing the broken bottle, he snatched it up. Now armed, Farel swung his arm wildly in Timerus's direction. The broken end connected with Timerus's right forearm, opening a jagged gash across the top. Blood sprayed across the table and onto the blouse of the woman standing behind it. More dripped down his arm and onto the floor before Timerus could clamp his hand around the wound.

The sight of blood broke the spell on the room. Men surged around the table to grab hold of Farel, clearing a path to the door. Standing at the entrance studying Timerus was Lucia. Her face had THAT look on it. Timerus took a step toward her only to have his knees buckle. He reached out his good arm to catch himself. Instead of falling, a pair of arms wrapped themselves around him and guided him away from the door.

While the others were fighting to get Farel under control, Rhealle helped Timerus into the kitchen. She had enough time to prop the man on a stool and use a cloth to slow the bleeding before she felt the stomp of her father's foot. Rhealle took Timerus's good hand and placed it over the cloth she was pressing. Timerus looked up at her.

"Stay."

His eyes widened in surprise. Rhealle patted him on the shoulder as she went past him. Her father was going to be in a very bad mood.

Blood was spilling onto Durnin's prized hardwood floor before he was able to push himself through the wall of people. "Sanctions," he yelled. "I call sanctions ... against Farel and ... and this here Folk. Ruined my beautiful floor they have ... that and lost me business. I demand the council impose sanctions!"

The call for sanctions scattered the onlookers. Those who couldn't find a chair headed out the door.

When the room had finally returned to some semblance of Durnin's orderly cafe, the mayor surveyed the damage. Fortunately, no furniture was broken, but the dark red stain would probably require replacing the damaged planks, or at least, the section refinished. Durnin stomped his foot three times. When Rhealle hadn't appeared after a mental count of ten, he raised his leg to stomp again. Before he could finish the signal, she appeared. He pointed at the mess on the floor. "Fix this ... then bring me my tea."

Durnin huffed back to his favorite table. He waved Gereld out of his chair and sank his bulk down gratefully. Muttering to himself, Durnin said, "What am I going to do with them Folk? I've got to get rid of them before my reputation's ruined."

"Perhaps I can help you with that."

Durnin looked into the face of the oldest person he had ever seen.

The old woman graciously asked, "May I sit?"

Remembering his manners, Durnin waved away the patron in the chair across from him. "Of course. Excuse my manners."

"Lucia."

"Excuse my manners, Lucia."

The woman might be old, but her smile set Durnin's heart aflutter. He hadn't felt such warmth since his dear wife passed. Durnin couldn't help but notice the grace with which she moved.

"You have a problem with the Folk?" The last two words were said with subtle irony.

Durnin tensed. "Pardon me, madam, but it was a Folk caused the ruckus in here just moments ago."

"Slapping a woman is common practice in this town then."

"My daughter knew the risk when she agitated Farel," he said defensively.

Lucia's eyebrow arched upward.

"I have already declared sanctions against him. The council will pass judgment at the next meeting."

"You have declared sanctions against the Folk as well."

Durnin grumbled "I had to. They were both involved. Can't show favoritism ... not and make Farel pay."

Lucia tapped each of the fingers of her left hand on the table in a rhythmic fashion. After several repetitions, she said, "And the Folk? What does sanctions mean for them?"

Durnin sighed. "The Folk could be banned from Ghans for a year minimum."

Lucia tapped out the rhythm twice more. "Alternatives?"

"Some form of restitution."

"Nothing was damaged."

Durnin snapped, "My beautiful floor was damaged."

"Why should the Folk care about returning here?"

Before Durnin could reply, a disturbance at the door drew their attention.

As the minutes ticked away, Rhealle chafed at the length of time it took to clear the blood from the floor to her father's liking. Timerus's wound needed immediate tending in order to heal properly. The floor could have waited. Dumping out the pan of bloody water, Rhealle stacked the basin with the rest of the dirty dishes before retrieving a clean one and filling it. Why was her father so obsessed with this place? What happened to the papa who cared about people?

She had already carried the basin to her patient before she realized she had no place but the floor to set it. Rhealle set it down so she could push a small cutting table beside Timerus. Ghans had always been a hospitable town — that is until the stranger came — until the rain started.

Adding some thread, a needle, and bandages to the basin she placed on the table, Rhealle picked up a spare cloth and dipped it into the water before rubbing soap into it. She had Timerus lay his arm on the table. As gently as she could, Rhealle wiped away the drying blood, exposing bits of glass in the wound. When she pulled out a piece, Timerus jerked his arm back hard enough for it to cause another cut. Tears filled her eyes. Rhealle looked up. He tried to smile to mask his pain.

There was nothing Rhealle could do for him. Her father did not permit alcohol inside the cafe. Rhealle dropped her eyes.

Timerus used his good hand to lift her chin so she could see him speak. "Hot water, please, and a spoon."

Rhealle nodded. Setting the cloth down, she collected a cup and filled it from the kettle. Carrying it carefully to the table, she put it down next to him. Timerus reached inside his vest to pull out a sealed packet of tea leaves. He tried to open the packet with his good hand but dropped it onto the table. Rhealle scooped up the packet. Holding it open so he could insert the spoon, she watched him precisely measure leaves into the cup and stir the contents.

Timerus locked his eyes with hers. "Elim tea. Once it steeps, it will help the pain." He sat the aromatic cup on the table and extended his arm. "Go ahead and clean it while the tea strengthens."

Rhealle picked up the soft cloth. Blood had dried around the remaining pieces of glass. She squeezed a bit of water on those spots. While the water loosened the glass, Rhealle stroked his palm. His hand was nearly as big as the mirror. Her fingers traced the lines of his palm. They were long and strong. A light scrape across the top of the table snapped her thoughts back to the task at hand. She finished removing the glass and drying the area.

While Rhealle tore strips from the roll of bandages, she watched Timerus drink his tea. It only took a few minutes to see it have an effect. The muscles around his mouth and chin relaxed. By the time she had sterilized the needle, he was leaning back against the wall with his eyes closed — the cup resting on the table.

Her hands shook as she threaded the needle. Why was this so hard for her? Timerus wasn't the first person she had stitched up or even the most badly injured. Her hand slipped when she snapped the thread, knocking over the empty cup.

The noise roused Timerus. With his good hand, he righted the cup, moving it farther from the workspace. He frowned when he saw the way her hands were shaking.

She was being an idiot. Rhealle took a deep breath and slowly let it out. Her hands still shook. She took another breath. Still, her hands shook. Just as she began to inhale again, her breath caught in her throat as she felt his good hand alongside her face. His thumb stroked her cheek the way it had by the fire. The gesture comforted Rhealle. Soon her hands stopped trembling, and when they did, his hand went away. She laid a clean cloth beside the wound and inserted the needle.

Once the last stitch was in place, Rhealle cleaned away the additional blood and applied a neat bandage. Then she gathered up the bloody cloth. She straightened up. Before she could run away, Timerus caught hold of her arm. Rhealle gave him a questioning look.

"Thank you, Rhealle."

The question turned into a shy smile.

Timerus held onto her arm for several more moments. It seemed to Rhealle those moments would stretch for an eternity — until a tap on her arm broke the spell.

Once the kitchen boy had her attention, he said, "Your father has been signaling for you. He is getting very impatient."

Rhealle sighed. Dropping the bandages onto the table

for the boy to clear away, she took a step toward the common room then stopped. She didn't want to leave. The injured arm hung between her and Timerus. She gathered it up and ran her fingers carefully along the entire bandage. Everything felt secure. With regret, she released his arm. She took one more deep breath, squared her shoulders, and left the kitchen.

# Chapter Twenty-Six
## More Guests

Barring the entrance were two well-built guards, six feet in height, with military haircuts and the royal insignia. Their hard set features warned anyone who approached to find another way out. The two dwarfed the man standing halfway between them, who was lucky to weigh 120 pounds soaked as he was with rainwater, by a good seven inches. The room was too dark to distinguish the color of his hair, unlike the woman with hair so blonde it appeared nearly white when light from the kitchen struck it. Although not as tall as the guards, the stocky man next to her was quite a few inches taller than their traveling companion behind them. The five newcomers waited for someone to acknowledge them.

When the group still blocked the entrance ten minutes

later, the woman became impatient. As the serving woman passed by again, the woman grabbed her arm. "Who runs this place?"

The serving woman bobbed her head in the direction of the mayor.

The woman released her grip and marched over. Seeing no empty chair, she grabbed one from a different table and parked herself between Durnin and Lucia across from the fire. "Waitress, bring me something hot," she commanded the serving woman before turning her attention to the two occupants. "And you are?"

"Mayor Durnin."

Nethandia looked the rotund man up and down before waving the rest of the group over. "Nethandia Warden, Head of the Farmers' Guild and my traveling companions who are tired and thirsty. What's it going to take to get them settled?"

For the first time in a very long time, Durnin was speechless.

"Well?"

After stomping his foot three times, he ordered the party occupying the square table across from him to vacate it. The men grumbled but moved.

The arrangement only partly satisfied Nethandia. Waving her short companion to her table, she left her chair to grab one from another table and pulled it up across from her old one. While taking her seat, she said, "This is Winshill Kalverian. The Kings have tasked him with discovering why crop towns are having issues this growing season. I'm here to make sure he has your full cooperation."

Winshill nodded.

Nethandia rested her folded hands on the table. "Does this place actually serve people, or is it just a gossip center?"

An uncomfortable Durnin stomped his foot three more times.

"What in blazes is that nonsense for?"

"Pardon me. My daughter is deaf. The vibrations signal her," he said apologetically.

Nethandia didn't look appeased.

Lucia finally spoke. "You must excuse the girl. There was a … misunderstanding earlier. She is still tending to the casualties."

Durnin grumbled, "Casualty, you mean. That Folk should have minded his own business!" Durnin stomped for his daughter a third time. "Blasted girl!"

At the mention of the Folk, both Nethandia and Winshill sharpened their attention.

Lucia, seeing their interest sparked, told Durnin, "You have more important matters to attend to. We can discuss our … little matter another time."

Faced with these new, unwanted visitors, Durnin simply nodded.

Without introducing herself, Lucia bid them all a good night. Before the two newcomers thought to question her, Lucia was gone, and Rhealle was making her way to her father.

"About time. Bring our guests my best tea and be quick about it!"

Nethandia added, "And don't forget the others." She realized her error when Durnin repeated the reminder. The girl needed to see someone speak to read what was said. Nethandia watched her disappear into the kitchen.

When Rhealle had gone to her father, Timerus propped himself against the wall and let the Elim tea quiet his mind and ease the pain in his arm. He wanted to doze, but despite the kitchen serving only drinks and pastries, it bustled with activity.

Hot drinks appeared to be the favorite tonight, he thought, as he watched a serving boy change kettles on the hook a fourth time. He was wondering how these patrons could drink so much of the second rate beverages served here when Rhealle returned.

Her face was pinched, her hands clasped tightly together. Timerus reached his good hand out to her. She turned toward him. "What's wrong?"

Hearing his question as she entered the kitchen, the serving woman said, "Her father has important guests, and they be getting impatient for hot drink."

"How important?" Timerus asked the serving woman.

"The woman's from the Farmers' Guild. Don't know 'bout the others," she said.

The serving boy chimed in, "Not a good thing to get on the bad side of the Farmers' Guild."

Rhealle tried to move past Timerus, but he held onto her. "Wait." When he was sure she wouldn't go anywhere, he reached inside his vest and pulled out the jar of Salfon tea. "How many guests?"

Rhealle held up five fingers.

Timerus handed her the jar. "Use one level spoonful per cup. It should be enough for six."

Rhealle attempted a weak smile.

Timerus sank back against the wall and watched her carry the jar to one of the kitchen tables. He really should be getting back to the vardo, but his arm throbbed when he moved too much. He adjusted the stool so he could lean his back into the corner and sank down on it, closing his eyes against the light.

By the time their drinks arrived, Nethandia had

described the drought conditions the group found in Grand Tothen and King's Fields.

At first, Winshill believed the unusual weather was some kind of anomaly since rain patterns appeared to be normal in neighboring areas. Then, the group learned River's Run suffered from an excess of rain. Investigation of the rain revealed it fell only within the boundaries of the town and its crop fields. The uncultivated lands around the town were dry, as expected for this time of year.

Durnin tried to maintain an interest in the conversation, but he didn't see what all this talk about weather patterns and anomalies had to do with Ghans. When his boredom got the better of him, Durnin took a drink from his mug to mask his desire to yawn. The delicious flavor startled him.

Nethandia caught the look of surprise before Durnin's usual placid expression reasserted itself. Should they be worried? Gingerly, she sipped her own mug. For the first time since they had arrived in Ghans, Nethandia smiled. "I could almost forgive our un-welcome," she said. After taking another sip, she set the mug down.

Winshill nodded his agreement. "If I may ask, where did you manage to find Salfon tea this far north?"

Durnin smiled. "Ghans may be small, but we do our best to accommodate our distinguished guests."

Nethandia studied Durnin. A town this small didn't

have that kind of connections, unless someone was being paid off.

Durnin's composure began to crack under her scrutiny. In desperation, he asked, "How did you learn of our predicament?"

When Nethandia remained silent, Winshill said, "Word came from Banton's Folly that it started raining in Ghans six days ago, and the rain hasn't stopped. In River's Run by the sixth day, the rain had nearly dissipated. The weather finally cleared after intermittent showers for another two days."

"Still," Nethandia cut in, "their entire crop was lost."

"Here the rain not only continues to fall, but," Winshill cocked his head to one side, "it's raining harder than when we arrived."

Nethandia frowned. "Can you determine why?"

Winshill shook his head. "Not yet. Something is driving it. Something unnatural. I'll need to look for the source come daylight."

"I don't suppose this place has sleeping rooms."

An unhappy Durnin said, "No. Inn across the square is the best we've got." Under his breath, Durnin mumbled, "Damn you to the shades, Farel." Still, it was loud enough for Nethandia to hear and to wonder about.

As if his words had been a signal, the door opened to

admit an angry Farel. Durnin cursed. Of course Farel would storm in now, complaining about the crops and wanting to know where those two Folk were. "Somewhere with that ignorant daughter of yours wasting precious time, hey Durnin?"

A puzzled Nethandia caught and held Durnin's gaze. "Explain!"

Durnin told her that the town divided up the growing among three appointed keepers. Farel was in charge of the crops for tithes and bartering. Weiz guaranteed the town had hay for their livestock, and if there's a surplus, it was sold to buy more livestock. His daughter Lilleth, was tasked with overseeing the vegetable acreage. "With last year's yield not providing enough to cover two growing seasons, she's been desperate to save what she can of this season's produce."

Nethandia nodded her understanding. "I want to speak to all three."

Durnin said, "Weiz went home to avoid getting involved with the ruckus earlier. I'm not sure of Lilleth."

Passing the table on her way to serve customers, the serving woman said, "Lilleth left with those other two Folk after Farel here backhanded her, and that other Folk took a swing at him. I'm thinking they said something 'bout the garden."

Nethandia looked at Winshill. "Feel like getting wet again?"

Winshill chuckled. "What's a little rain to an air mage?"

# Chapter Twenty-Seven
## Questionable Flood Control

The tall, thin Gaujo keeping company with the Folk scared Alandran. At the same time, he intrigued the boy. He was like Alandran's papa, serious yet polite, but fiercer than Papa. His stare chilled Alandran, and when the Gaujo walked, he moved with strength like Croc, his papa's personal protector, so the boy didn't think the Gaujo would need all the guards Papa kept nearby. Alandran watched everyone working. People listened to him, even Ronin.

Alandran peered through the rain at the people digging in the mud. They already had a big ditch almost as long as the length of the plants along one side. Some were even starting on the other. The boy wanted to help, but he was afraid he would be in the way. Still, being here was better than sitting around doing nothing. He picked up a rock and threw it into the ditch. The rock made a loud "*plop.*" Alandran crept to the edge. Water streamed down the sides, pooling up at the bottom. Tossing another rock into the ditch, the boy felt water spray upward where the rock hit. He looked around to see if anyone heard the splash. Ronin wouldn't be happy to find him so near the edge.

Alandran sighed. Ronin, Lucia, even Armon, had not had much time for him lately — what with the monsters and the broken wagons and the Gaujo.

Staring at the rings on the water from raindrops hitting it almost as hard as his rock, the boy wondered what his papa was doing right now. Was he still in Gessin, or had he gone to Saron to visit Mama? Papa had promised him he could see Mama this time. The water on Alandran's face stung his eyes. He needed to see her, to know she was kept safe. Papa had not permitted him to attend that part of the rites.

He leaned to pick up another rock; lights bobbing in the dark caught the boy's attention. Please, please, don't be Armon or Lucia come to look for him. He released one of those long wistful sighs that saddened Ronin. He had better tell them that people are coming.

Something nagged at the back of Artearis's mind, something he read that had made him question why anyone would risk digging ditches in the first place, at least not without proper planning, and here he was, digging ditches, in the rain no less, with two groups of people more interested in how this solved other problems rather than how this could turn out to be a problem in itself.

His hands involuntarily felt for the pommels of his weapons. When they found only cloth, fear boiled up in the pit of his stomach before he remembered he had left them in Ronin's lodgings. The blacksmith had been kind enough to stash his things after warning Artearis that digging in the mud might not be a good time to wear such noticeable weapons. Standing here, covered in the stuff, Ronin's wisdom didn't reduce the feeling of loss.

"Gaujo."

Alandran's voice shook him out of his reverie. What was the boy doing out here?

"Gaujo, lights are coming."

Artearis almost felt relieved. Maybe the rest of the town had come to its senses, or decided to partake in this madness, depending how one looked at it, and came to help get this done. Then the worry in the boy's voice struck Artearis. Aland thought the people coming were Folk, and if he wasn't supposed to be here ....

Once Alandran was close enough that Artearis needn't

shout, he told the boy to find Ronin. The blacksmith supervised the work at the end of the ditch. "Tell him I want to talk to the old one again." Playing messenger would at least give the boy a cover should the newcomers be Folk.

Alandran nodded as he scooted past Artearis.

"And keep away from the edge of the ditch. The ground is getting unsafe."

That nagging sensation wouldn't leave. To satisfy the inner voice, weir light in hand, he walked from the beginning of the trench along the inner ridge, inspecting the rim and sides of the channel. The ground was wet but stable where the trench started.

He pulled up one of the pole markers set out to mark the cross furrows and measured the water level. The farther along the ditch he walked, the softer the bank and the higher the water level gradually became. Every fifty paces or so a shallow furrow drained into the trench. It reminded him of something, something he had read in a tactics manual — in inclement weather, position yourself to use the flow to your advantage to flood out your opponent.

The trench and the furrows replicated a small river system, but one that remained narrow along its length, not widening to relieve the pressure from tributaries flowing in, and this thrice blasted rain kept falling!

Tossing the pole to one side, Artearis abandoned his investigation in favor of finding Ronin and the old one from the south. Even without a thorough examination, he could feel the ground becoming more unstable as he rapidly covered the distance to the other end of the field.

It didn't take long for him to reach the diggers. Their desperation to save this field became even more clear as he saw men and women shoveling mud onto the bank while standing in water reaching their thighs. They had abandoned the original plan to dig a three-foot-wide and five-foot-deep continuous stretch when the water began pooling at the end point. Now, the diggers were completing sections and not connecting them until the width and depth matched the specifications.

By the time Artearis reached the main work force, another section was about to be added to the main trench. All that separated it from the trench was a two foot thick wall of earth.

Ahead of him, voices shouted for people to clear out of the completed area. Artearis picked up speed and nearly fell face first as his foot caught a pile of rocks. Catching himself, he noticed large chunks littering the edge of the trench and realized this end of the field was considerably rockier than the beginning. His hand reached up to rest against the amulet under his shirt as that nagging feeling descended with a vengeance.

A booming voice calling for fresh diggers told Artearis he found one of the two people he sought. A group of mud-stained people approached the earthen barrier lit by his weir light. Among them was the boy.

Ronin asked Artearis to bring the light closer. Two diggers in the trench and two up top on the sides should do the trick he decided. The weight of the water would do the rest. The old one warned them not to break through below until above the water line was cleared and the diggers in the trench had moved out.

"Top or bottom?" the woman beside him asked.

Artearis didn't know what possessed him to say, "Middle to the middle ... then down. Hand me a shovel." He jumped into the new section. The woman joined him.

People along the bank backed up as mud flew out of the ditch. Ronin grunted his approval at the evenness of the excavation. It didn't stop the knot in Artearis's stomach from constricting even more.

He cursed as his shovel struck something hard. Propping the shovel against the side of the trench, he carefully worked loose a sizable stone. Fortunately, it was small enough not to weaken the earthen barrier. He handed it up to waiting hands and retrieved his shovel. At least removing the rocks cut down on digging. The woman beside him followed his lead in extricating her own stumbling block.

The two cleared almost all they could without piercing the wall. Artearis tossed up his shovel and turned to assist the woman out of the trench when he heard a sucking sound come from the top of the earthen work. There was a grunt from above and to the side followed by a pop and a squeal.

Water poured through a large semi-circular gap that appeared from the displacement of another sizable rock. Artearis braced himself. The woman hadn't thought that quickly. More water poured through the opening, making it wider and deeper, allowing even more water to enter. The pressure was just enough in their slick surroundings to sweep the woman's legs out from under her.

Artearis made a grab for her hand. She grasped his tightly and tried to regain her footing. Thinking he could lift her out, he pulled her to him and grabbed her waist. With a heave, he lifted up.

He thought faster than the spectators along the muddy bank. No hands reached down to pull the woman up. He shouted for someone to take her, but by the time anyone reacted, another sizable rock had dislodged from the dirt wall and banged into his leg. He lost his hold, and the woman fell into the water. Artearis helped her stand.

From the darkness in front of him, he heard someone yell for rope. Soon hands appeared to try to help them, but the rain and the mud decided that anyone close enough to pull them out could join them. Another body landed in the water with a splash. The two helped the newcomer to his feet.

"Where's that rope?!"

Artearis thought he heard Aland's voice answer. *By Moratam's axe, please keep the boy away from here.*

The water finally settled, allowing Artearis and the townsman to help the woman onto the bank. Once she was safely away, ropes splashed into the water. Artearis looped one around his waist and tied it securely. After the second rope was secured, he helped the unfortunate rescuer out and followed. Thankfully, that only left one section to complete.

He removed the rope and coiled it up as he stood there dripping muddy water, waiting to see what Ronin planned next. The blacksmith strode off to inspect the final section. Here, the land sloped downward a bit, giving their man-made river system a runoff point littered with large, jagged rocks.

Someone had tasked diggers with the difficult chore of lowering this end more than a hand span for overflow control. Another fifteen minutes and this section would be ready to join with the rest of the ditch. Artearis took up a position at the earthen wall between them. If anyone was going down in the channel to dig away this barrier it was him, and he wasn't allowing another woman down there this time. He just wished the knots in his stomach would loosen up or the rain would quit so the ground would stop turning into a slick, muddy soup.

At the signal to clear the channel, Artearis took a shovel from an exiting worker and slid down the muddy slope. He sighed. Even if the mud did come out, the stains wouldn't.

The four workers repeated the same tactics they used to remove the previous earthwork. This time, they paid particular attention to the rocks embedded in the soil — for all the good it did — the pressure from the increased rain and water flow eroded the center of the wall quicker than before.

People above tossed ropes down as soon as the dam broke. The second man in the ditch grabbed an end. The side of dirt nearest him broke loose. The force of the water was enough to propel embedded rocks into him, causing the townsman to lose his balance. Another wave of rocks slammed into his head.

Seeing the man go down from the break, Artearis flattened himself against the side wall and dug his fingers into the mud. It didn't stop rocks on his side of the ditch from pounding into him, but it kept them from dragging him under. He held tight to keep himself upright.

From above something smacked into his head. Someone had tossed another rope. This one he snagged up and pulled on. Instead of the line tightening as he expected, it gave. A small shape disrupted the water, splashing him. *Damn, not again!* Artearis twisted around to get a grip on the unlucky helper. The cursing increased when he saw Aland try to keep his head above the water. Artearis made a grab for him at the same time another, neater, splash cleaved the water.

A blonde head surfaced next to Alandran. She wrapped one arm around the boy's chest and tugged on the rope tied around her waist. Within a couple of heartbeats, both were lifted clear. When a third rope smacked Artearis on the head, he snatched it up and tied himself off, so his rescuers could drag him out of this mess.

Nethandia set the boy down beside Ronin. "What in the bloody hell were you people thinking?" She wiped the water from her face, leaving a smear of mud along her cheek. "Excavating a drainage ditch at night in the rain on saturated ground? Of all the stupid, irresponsible ...."

When Artearis's hands clenched into fists, Ronin rested his mighty paw on the Gaujo's shoulder. His fists remained closed, but Artearis held his tongue.

Nethandia yanked the rope from her waist. "Do any of you amateurs have any experience with water works?"

The old one who had explained the construct to Ronin stepped around to speak. Artearis raised his hand, palm outward, to stop him. When the man persisted, Ronin shook his head.

Crossing her arms in front of her chest and shifting her weight to one leg, Nethandia eyed the group of men in front of her. "Well?" When no one answered, her voice rose in volume. "Doesn't anyone have a tongue here, either, or are you all as deaf as that woman back in town?" Winshill copied Ronin's gesture and laid his hand on her shoulder. Nethandia shrugged it off.

Artearis, seeing the woman wasn't going to let up, answered. "Desperate people do desperate things when they run out of options."

As Nethandia eyed the body someone had fished out of the water, her look hardened. "Desperation doesn't give people a license to get others killed."

As much as Artearis wanted to agree with the woman, he would not condone her "holier than thou" attitude. He hadn't liked the plan, either, but when the townspeople determined to employ it anyway, he felt someone needed to provide some sort of organization to keep things from seriously spiraling out of control. Since he stepped willingly into that role, he was going to take responsibility for the outcome, including the unfortunate death of the worker. "The drainage ditch was the best solution," Artearis started to say 'we' but what came out was "I ... could manage."

"You're lucky I don't haul you before the Guild board to demand sanctions against you!"

Artearis had no idea what 'sanctions' meant, but judging by the sudden inhalation of breath from nearby townspeople and the loss of color in the mayor's face, it meant something serious to these people. He tried to refocus the woman's attention. "None of this would have happened without this ungodly rain."

Winshill tapped Nethandia on the arm. "The man speaks the truth. It shouldn't be raining. Some force keeps it here."

From the look in her eyes, the woman wanted to press the issue. Artearis chose to ignore her and concentrate on her companion. "What would make rain stay in one place?"

Winshill frowned. "Water magic," he said, "or perhaps air magic. This would take a powerful mage, but even he couldn't keep it here for … how long?"

"Going on seven days now," the mayor put in. "Who could do this to us, Mage? We've not got any magic workers among us."

Someone from the crowd of people gathered around them said, "I'll bet them there Folk do."

Again, the old one wanted to say something, but Artearis stopped him with a gesture. To the mage, Artearis said, "Seven days ago, the Folk were far from here. We only came to this town to barter for the assistance of their wheelwright."

An angry townsman yelled, "Since when do Folk speak the truth?"

Artearis could feel his hand reach for his absent

sword. If Artearis learned one thing about the Folk from Marte, it was that Folk revile liars.

Before Artearis could do anything rash, Winshill addressed Nethandia. "This deserves a proper investigation ... in the light of day. I suggest everyone retire until then." Like Artearis, Nethandia wasn't ready to let it go, so Winshill circumvented her wrath by taking her arm and steering her toward town.

# Chapter Twenty-Eight
## Search for a Traitor

Winshill settled himself into a chair next to the cold fireplace and ordered tea. The serving woman took the order, but it was the deaf one, Rhealle, who brought it to him.

Fatigue and worry nearly masked the wisps of was it magic that dusted her like a fine mist from an ocean breeze? The strange sensation had him curious and, strangely, made him a little homesick for Corath.

Closing his eyes as he rolled the mug between his hands, his mind envisioned the roll of a ship's deck under his feet, the fine spray from the wake refreshing as it covered his skin, the sun trying to burn it away before it drenched him. He had been content to work the trade routes of his city — until he boarded the ship to Seresh. A shiver colder than the ones from this unnatural rain stilled his hands. He took a long drink from the mug.

The clank of a plate drew his attention upward. The tired woman gave him a kind smile over the plate of pastries he hadn't ordered. If not for the immediate problem at hand, he'd have tried to discover the mystery surrounding Rhealle. As it was, the unnatural feel to this weather required his attention, and he hoped this place would provide him clues. Places of gossip often did.

Unlike Nethandia, he preferred freely given information. He picked up a pastry and began to nibble the end, letting his eyes close as if enjoying the taste and allowing his ears to roam around the room and eavesdrop on the increasing number of conversations.

The animosity toward the Folk didn't surprise him. The harsh words directed at the deaf woman did. Anger rolled from more than one tongue, accusing Rhealle of conspiring with the odd stranger who wandered into town nine days past. Who was this stranger who took such an interest in Ghans that he spent two days sizing up the place?

"Bah. Like any of them gave the man a second thought."

Winshill opened his eyes.

Glad to have someone to vent to, the serving woman said, "The stranger sat in that very chair and listened to the chatter in this here room for a good part of the morning before he laid eyes on Rhealle. Sort of like you ...."

The serving woman gave him a queer look and snapped her mouth shut. She hustled to the kitchen as if Ashlemar herself had come to take her home.

Patrons at nearby tables heard the serving woman's words. Friendly faces tightened in distrust as their voices dropped or grew silent. Others began to notice the frost in the air, caught the wave of distrust and toward whom it was directed. They, too, stopped talking. The infectious silence grew until Winshill could not coax an intelligible word from the air.

Waves of distrust broke against him, ruining any chance to glean information here. Setting the half-eaten pastry on its plate and the mug in the center of the table, he brushed the crumbs from his hands and prepared to leave.

Without warning, the door to the cafe swung open, admitting a soaked Nethandia. Every patron in the cafe turned to see who entered. Recognizing the Head of the Farmers' Guild, it seemed the entire cafe held its breath. Apparently oblivious to the tension inside, Nethandia called out for a cup of their best tea and sauntered over to his table where she dropped down into the chair across from him and asked how his research was going.

The waves settled to a gentle rocking. Winshill couldn't believe the change. It was as if the squall about to engulf him magically broke apart. Now he understood why the Kings insisted a member of the Farmers' Guild accompany him. Reaching for his half full cup of tea, he pondered whether to give her the satisfaction of telling her "nowhere" when his hand touched the cup, and he froze.

Something powerful had been where his cup was, something containing such strong magic that traces of it lingered on the table, and now that Winshill had the scent of the magic, he felt its tendrils lingering in the air. He moved the cup and flattened his hand against the wooden surface, hunting for the shape of its essence. Once he determined that essence, he sought the air for a matching pattern. The object had come and gone from this place more than a few times. Standing up, he followed the trail outside.

Still sitting slouched in her chair, Nethandia called after him, "Wait! My tea!" She grabbed the cup from the serving woman without so much as a "thank you" and took herself off after the air mage.

Artearis sat by the Folk fire, brooding over his depleted gear. His sword lay across his lap, a polishing cloth held in a hand that refused to move. Instead of the weapon he intended to clean he saw the battered face of the man Nethandia had accused him of killing with his recklessness.

His instinct had warned him, but he hadn't listened,

or rather, he had listened but had failed to act on it. Her biting remark that it didn't take much common sense to tie a rope around a waist as a safety precaution hit home with precisely the gut punch she intended, and once he made the decision to take responsibility, he couldn't even refute it.

A shadow passed across the sword.

"Lucia said you'd take this to heart."

Artearis peered up into the wizened, brown eyes of the second elder of the Folk. Then, they weren't the old man's eyes; they were Marte's — Marte who had taken his measure and saw potential, who had treated him like a son as much as a pupil, who died because Artearis couldn't come to grips with who he was, a killer. "What would an old woman know?" he muttered.

Corsanth studied him thoughtfully. There was still a richness to the tenor of his aged voice as he spoke. "If you don't like the outcome, learn to take control ... not stand and do nothing."

Artearis dropped his eyes. He had just stood there, clinging to the mud wall. He hadn't even tried to help the man in the water.

The old man's voice sharpened. "Loss is a part of life. Get over it."

Involuntarily Artearis's hand reached up to the green stone under his shirt; he said quietly, "Not three, not four, but five times my gut warned me of trouble waiting to happen ...."

"And you did nothing."

Artearis nodded.

Corsanth refused to let up. "Would it have changed anything?"

Artearis shrugged.

"When you are sure you could have, then you can wallow in despair over the loss."

The old man's shadow disappeared only to be replaced by a larger one.

Ronin crossed to the door of Lucia's wagon and poked his head inside. "The boy's run off again."

Lucia nearly flew out the door.

Artearis shoved his weapons into their sheathes. "I think I know where to look." Not waiting for a response, he stalked past her wagon and down the road to Ghans. Lucia started to follow, only to find the blacksmith's hand come down onto her shoulder and stop her. Eyes full of fury, she spun around on her heel to tear into Ronin.

"Let him go, Lucia. If he wanted to hurt the boy, he'd have tried something last night. Lord knows he had enough opportunities to make it look like an accident. Besides, the boy trusts him." Anyone watching the two could see the distrust settle on her face.

From the doorway, Corsanth said, "Trust in Marte."

Nethandia didn't trust anyone associated with this accursed town: not the Folk, not that sap of a mayor, not that overbearing crop manager, and certainly not the people of Ghans who only wanted a way to wriggle out of their obligation. If it were up to her, she'd rule in favor of a localized disaster, as she had in the other towns, and leave it to Ghans to figure out a way to settle up with the kingdom accountants.

She brushed the rain out of her eyes. Well, it wasn't up to her, and while Winshill Kalverian was an easy going travel companion, he was also a stickler for thoroughness, although what was left to investigate in this hell hole eluded her.

For several hours, the air mage wandered around town — studying air currents he told her. Nethandia couldn't see him do anything but stare into air. Just when she thought he'd given up, he trudged along the northwest road out of town. Nethandia took a deep breath to control her frustration and marched after.

About the only thing of even remote interest out here was a boy sitting on the riverbank tossing rocks into the water. From the far side of the bridge, a man with blond hair … no it couldn't be that idiot from last night.

Nethandia took two steps in his direction with every intention of laying out for him every bit of stupidity his thoughtless actions had caused. Her foot was poised for a third when Winshill gasped and darted off toward the crop field nearby, calling for her to follow. She sucked in another lungful of air and very slowly let it out. Oh, please, someone, get her out of this irritating town!

A worried Winshill called for her again. Nethandia had to hurry to catch up with the mage. He ran his hand along the air about waist high as if it were following a fence line. Every so often, his fingers would bend and straighten like they had slid around a thin pole. Not knowing what to think, Nethandia trudged after, praying for an end to this madness.

If the boy kept to the same pattern of behavior, he'd head for a river, but most of the waterways around Ghans were within the deluge of rain. Then he remembered the bridge near town. He picked up his pace. Before long the bridge came into sight. Just beyond it, on the other side of the water, sat Alandran.

The boy picked up something and threw it into the water. *Plop.* His eyes focused on the location of the sound. Artearis slowed his pace.

"Aland." Artearis kept his tone neutral.

When the boy didn't answer, Artearis repeated his

name a bit louder.

Alandran looked up. "They want me back."

"They never wanted you to leave," Artearis said, approaching the boy.

"They worry about me. Everyone worries about me."

"One person in particular."

"What do you mean?"

"You know what I mean. The old woman."

"Lucia?"

"Lucia. She looks calm, but every time you go missing, her eyes flare in panic and the entire caravan gets tense. Are you her grandson or something?"

The boy started to nod his head. Then his gray eyes met blue ones. Artearis's eyes hadn't darkened to the steel blue they colored when he was filled with intense emotion, but they had enough intensity to cause the boy to stop his attempt to answer yes.

"I don't know what she is to me. Last year Papa sent me with the Folk ... and the year before ... and finally decided this year ... but after the wagons went away. I think he wasn't going to send me this year, but riders came ... one in late spring ... two in the summer. Papa was really worried."

Artearis watched the boy grow agitated. Alandran picked up a rock and threw it at the water.

"Papa packed everyone up to go to Gessin. We never go to Gessin until harvest time." The boy picked up another rock and began to bounce it up and down in his hand.

"When the Folk came to Gessin, Papa screwed up his face all funny and went to talk with Lucia. When he came back, he went to my room and packed my things back up and took me to the wagons. Papa said to Lucia to be vigilant. She had a screwed up look on her face, too, and nodded in a solemn way I hadn't seen her do before."

"What do you mean?"

"She nodded the way the rest of the Folk nod to her when she speaks importantly."

"Why would they do that to an old woman?"

The boy wrinkled his nose and flattened his voice to one of whispered respect. "Because Lucia is the mistress of the Folk. What she says is to the Folk what it's like Papa saying to his people. Not even Corsanth argues with her when she uses her tone. You'd best not either, Gaujo. Strange things happen to people who cross the Folk."

"So why do you keep disappearing if she doesn't like it?"

"She never said I couldn't. I'm a whole ten summers old. I can look after myself!"

"That doesn't answer my question."

The boy shrugged his shoulders and turned his gaze to the frog sunning itself on a wide, flat stone. He let out what sounded to Artearis like a sob. "I don't want them to know I miss my mama."

Artearis knelt beside the boy. He started to say something then changed his mind. He shifted to a sitting position and sat quietly, watching the boy with solemn eyes.

Not taking his eyes off the frog, the boy sighed. "I miss my mama. So does Papa."

"Papa?"

The boy nodded his head. "Papa tries not to show it, so the people won't worry."

Artearis arched an eyebrow. He waited for the boy to say something else, but the silence stretched out. "Why would people worry?"

"Papa takes care of the people here."

"You mean the Folk?"

The boy shook his head. "Lucia takes care of the Folk. Papa looks after the people here and at home."

"What happened to your mama?"

The boy's voice trembled when he said, "She went away."

Artearis said in a gentle voice, "She could come back."

The boy shook his head. "No ... Papa said she couldn't come back. She would want to but ...."

"... but she couldn't," Artearis finished for the boy, his mind seeing another boy of seven summers asking the same kind of question to Marian. "Sometimes mamas go away because bad people don't want them around. Do you think a bad person made your mama leave?"

The boy thought hard. "I don't think so. Mama didn't feel good for a long time. Then she just went away." The tears he had been holding back slid down his small face.

Artearis picked up a rock and side-armed it into the water. The rock skipped three times before it dropped below the surface, creating strong ripples that lapped at the stone and made the frog hop away.

The boy wiped the tears on his face. "Was your mama nice?"

"She was very nice, but she went away, too."

"Does your papa miss her as much as my papa misses Mama?"

Artearis thought about lying to the boy. Looking at the tears still rolling down his cheeks, he really wanted to lie. He didn't think it would hurt anything. Then he thought back to his own mother: how people had lied to him about what had happened to her. "No, my papa didn't miss my mama much. He had too many people to worry about to miss her."

The boy looked at Artearis intently. Something the boy saw made him reach out his arm and pat Artearis on his clenched shoulder. "Maybe our mamas went to the same place and made friends."

# Chapter Twenty-Nine
## Coming Undone

It was probably a mistake coming back into the rain, especially with his injured arm, but Timerus felt he owed Rhealle. He checked the inside of his vest to make sure the contents remained dry. Damn this unnatural rain — turned the roads to soup and caused tempers to flare. By mid-afternoon towns like this are usually bustling. Not Ghans. The main square was as empty as yesterday — well, almost empty. That looked like Rhealle hurrying along the road south. Timerus followed.

When Rhealle reached the edge of town, she stopped in front of a large barn. Despite the rain pouring down, she stood at the door. Timerus thought he saw her hesitate with her hand on the knob. He slowed his steps. One. Two. Three.

Four. Five. He feared to take the next step. He didn't want to scare her with his approach. Perhaps, it would be better to leave the package at the cafe. He was half tempted to turn around when she opened the door and went inside.

Once Timerus reached the entrance, he found the door not quite shut. He debated the wisdom of going inside. If he was found in an isolated place like the barn with a woman of the town, the Folk would suffer. Lucia had already dressed him down for the incident yesterday.

Still, he couldn't afford to stay in the rain much longer, and he needed to give Rhealle his gift. Just like the woman, Timerus stood at the door for several long breaths before he could bring himself to pull on the handle. The door resisted his attempt. He pulled harder. How had Rhealle opened it so easily?

Timerus rested his palm on the wood. He shivered at the sight of the hairs on the back of his arm standing up.

Something wasn't right. The air quivered something like it did when Lucia performed the ritual of seeing.

He made the sign of warding. The air still vibrated, but the hairs on his arm went limp. This time, instead of reaching for the handle, Timerus grabbed the edge of the door and pulled. Still resisting the intrusion, the door moved barely enough for him to enter.

Once inside, he found it hard to breathe; the air was so hot and humid. Taking a breath was like sucking in a fine mist. By the time his breathing had adapted enough so he didn't feel like he was drowning, his eyes had adjusted to the dimness. Rhealle stood in front of a ladder off to his right. As before, her hand was poised to do something, climb the ladder, but the action was frozen.

Timerus softly called her name. Rhealle didn't respond. Timerus tried again. Still nothing. It was as if she were in a trance.

Unsure if it was wise, Timerus approached. Rhealle ignored him. He placed his hand on her shoulder. She didn't move. Timerus placed his other hand atop the one clutching the ladder. When she didn't pull away, he gently pried her hand loose. It was cold.

He turned her around so that he could see her face. Her eyes had a faraway look to them. Timerus frowned. He needed to get her out of this cursed place. Draping his arm protectively around her, he turned toward the entrance.

Rhealle cried out.

"What are you doing to my sister?"

Timerus turned toward the new voice. Standing just inside the door was the woman that oaf had backhanded last night. No wonder she had seemed familiar but wasn't.

As gently as he could, Timerus tried to move Rhealle away from the ladder. With each slow step they put between themselves and it, Rhealle cried. After the third step,

Timerus stopped.

"What's wrong with her? What did you try to do?" Lilleth didn't wait for him to answer. She marched across the floor to the barn's hanging lantern. Taking down the box of matches from the shelf, Lilleth lit it. "Now, let's see what you've done."

Concern for Rhealle constricted his throat. Timerus barely managed to get out "Nothing, there's some ...." before Lilleth yanked her sister out of his embrace.

The motion brought another cry from Rhealle as it took her farther from the ladder. Ignoring the cry, Lilleth inspected her sister for any sign of molestation. "Good. I arrived in time."

Dragging Rhealle toward the door, Lilleth said to Timerus, "The Council will know what to do with someone like you," and to Rhealle, "Father will certainly cut off your wandering, now. I warned him after your escapade around town with that stranger that ...."

Rhealle let out a piercing scream and dropped to her knees in front of the open door. Lilleth's normally composed face showed shock.

Rushing to Rhealle's side, Timerus knelt beside her. "I tried to tell you. There's some kind of curse at work here."

Lilleth's shock turned to disbelief.

"I felt it when I tried to follow her inside." Timerus draped his arm around Rhealle's shaking form.

Lilleth's distrust returned.

His anxiety over the Folk's reputation compelled Timerus to take the time to try and explain. "It's nothing like that. I brought her a gift for fixing me up last night." He reached inside his vest and pulled out the container of Elim tea.

"So why didn't you take ...."

"I was. Then I saw her leaving."

"And so you followed her to ...."

Timerus sighed. It was always the same. A Folk can only have bad intentions. "To give her this. That's all."

Lilleth knelt next to them. "What's wrong with her?"

Following Nethandia inside the barn, Winshill said, "A compulsion from the look of it."

Catching the surprise on their faces, Nethandia said, "We heard the scream on our way back from the vegetable fields."

Winshill studied Rhealle's white features. "How long has she been like this?"

Timerus said, "Since we took her away from the ladder." At the same time, Lilleth said, "She's been obsessed with this barn ever since she made herself a nuisance to that stranger a week ago."

At the word, ladder, Winshill turned his attention in its direction until Lilleth mentioned a stranger. His gaze shot back to her. "The stranger?"

"Some traveler who stopped for supplies. Had a strange accent and excellent manners. Not many passersby are polite enough to show interest in our town. He was even considerate enough to let Rhealle be his guide instead of disrupting our pre-harvest work."

Winshill looked puzzled.

Both Lilleth and Timerus said, "Rhealle is deaf."

"Ah, yes, that" was all Winshill replied. The air mage turned his thoughts inward.

Nethandia had her own questions. "Your father is?"

"Durnin, the mayor."

"And you are?"

"His older daughter." Nethandia's stern expression prodded Lilleth to add, "and overseer of the produce fields."

"Yes, now I place you. You encouraged that lunacy last night."

Lilleth's face tightened.

"Reckless but gutsy. I hope it works all things considered."

Lilleth frowned. "Unless this rain stops, nothing will help."

The air mage turned his attention back to the occupants of the hay barn. "None of the other towns mentioned a stranger. What did this stranger do?"

Lilleth shrugged. "Rhealle is the only one who paid

the man any mind. I think she only did so because she liked his fancy mirror."

Both Winshill and Nethandia silently demanded her to continue.

"Some mirror he carried around with him — that and that board he kept checking."

"What did the mirror look like?"

Again, Lilleth shrugged. "I don't have time for foolish things." She looked at Rhealle. Her sister had curled up in the protection of the Folk's arms, letting him rock her as she sobbed quietly. "Good luck getting her to tell you."

Bending over to get a clearer view of Rhealle's predicament, Winshill asked Lilleth if her father carried any other specialty teas.

"Father doesn't really have specialty teas. The best he's got is Camden tea he imports from the Capitol."

"Where'd the Salfon tea come from last night?" Nethandia demanded.

"From me," Timerus answered. "I gave it to Rhealle to give to you."

Winshill looked thoughtfully at Timerus. "What other kinds of tea do you carry around with you?"

"Pretty much any kind of tea you could want."

"How long to bring me some Elim tea?"

Timerus snorted, "Elim tea is what's got me smack in the middle of this."

That startled Winshill.

Timerus drew out the packet he'd replaced in his vest. "I was bringing her this as a gift for patching me up last night."

Winshill nodded. To Lilleth, "Can you fetch some hot water and a cup?"

"And a spoon," Timerus added.

Rising from the floor, Lilleth brushed strands of hay from her skirt. "Five maybe ten minutes."

Winshill watched her leave before speaking. "She won't admit bad magic has had a hand here."

Timerus muttered, "Very bad."

Winshill stared hard at Timerus, as Nethandia said, "Spill it."

"Touch the handle of the door."

Winshill did.

"Can't you feel it? The vibrations? The entrance is cursed!"

With eyes closed, Winshill probed at the door with his mage sight. "The same energies as those surrounding the fields. The focal point has to be around here somewhere."

"And I'm wagering she knows where," Nethandia said.

Timerus tightened his hold on Rhealle.

# Chapter Thirty
## A Rival Power

For twenty minutes, the two investigators waited patiently for Lilleth to return. Nethandia watched the road from the doorway, while Winshill used his mage sight to follow the lines of power cutting through the air currents.

The rain made it difficult to trace back the currents using traditional methods because the raindrops intermittently broke the stream, derailing the flow of power. Even so, Winshill was sure the lines radiated out like the anchor points of a web from a central point nearby. He couldn't keep a pulse long enough to gauge if other strands bound the threads together like a spider's web. That the source was here, inside this barn, he was absolutely certain.

"When will that wretched woman return?" Nethandia

complained to no one in particular.

"Hum ... oh ... soon, I hope. We need answers."

Winshill checked on the two young people. The girl remained curled up in the young man's arms. He stroked her hair while humming a melody Winshill didn't know. Since the girl was deaf, he didn't understand why the Folk would go to the trouble, but his actions seemed to keep her calm, so Winshill let them be. He wasn't sure he could get any useful information out of her anyway since she was deaf.

The sound of Nethandia's boot slamming into the door frame shifted his attention. "Incompetents ... this town deserves what it gets."

Winshill wanted to disagree — no one deserved this — but to argue with her when she was losing her patience never ended well. They both needed to get back to work. If the source was in the barn, maybe the two of them could ferret it out without the help of the girl. He pulled a clear, crystal sphere about the size of his palm from one of the pouches strapped to his waist.

Nethandia saw him. "Now, what are you up to?"

"Investigating."

With all the energy flying around from the rain, Winshill easily coaxed some of it into the crystal, creating a cloudy light, bright enough to outshine the hanging lantern. "Think you can tear yourself away from your post to help me search?"

Nethandia gave him a nasty look. "You look. It's cooler by the door."

Winshill shrugged. He moved the light around the stalls of hay. From the fragmentation of the lines there, he doubted he'd find anything, but he had to be thorough. No telling what traps were laid on the lines to prevent tampering.

He inspected all the nooks. Nothing. Winshill turned his attention to the main area in front of the door. Some kind of locking spell discouraged entry not by preventing a person from opening the door but by preventing the mechanism that operated the door from working.

Closer inspection revealed the moving parts had frozen. Examining the spell more carefully, he determined that the state of the mechanism changed with the person trying to enter, a subtle and difficult twist to weave into any spell.

Learning all he could from that part of the barn, Winshill finally approached the area around the ladder. Disconnected threads floated around a shelf on the wall behind it. Something powerful had rested on that shelf, but the owner cleverly obscured the source.

That left the loft above. Winshill grabbed the highest rung he could reach. Leveraging the elbow of the hand holding the light, he balanced himself on the rung his feet rested on and prepared to pull himself farther up. When his head came level with the loft floor, Winshill froze. The lines of power nearly overwhelmed his mage sight. He backed down the ladder by one rung.

"What did you find?"

"A headache."

Nethandia gave him a strange look.

"All the lines we've followed thus far are only tethers. The lines that fuel the spell radiate from up high. That's why we couldn't make sense of the readings. All the lines down low are there to hold the perimeter in check. The ones up here ...."

"Power the spell. And since no one does readings high in the air ...."

"No one would think to check above." Winshill retreated down the ladder. "The focus is up there."

"So, go get rid of it," Nethandia snapped.

Wiping his hands on his trousers as he came back to Nethandia, Winshill said, "It won't be that simple. The energy flowing up there nearly blinds my mage sight. I haven't seen that kind of power before, so I don't know what will happen once the focus is destroyed, and ...."

"And, what?"

Winshill turned his head toward the couple.

Nethandia said impatiently, "Well?"

"I don't know what it would do to her."

"Kill her probably. Save us the trouble of an

execution."

Nethandia's callousness troubled Winshill. Council mages did not indiscriminately kill people.

Nethandia left her perch at the door and reached down to grab Rhealle's arm. Timerus stopped her.

"We can't wait any longer. Get her on her feet."

Timerus glared at the woman.

"Now!"

Sobs broke from Rhealle's throat.

Cradling her tighter, Timerus stroked her cheek and whispered, "Shhh. It's okay."

Resting his hand on Timerus' shoulder, Winshill asked the Folk if he could help Rhealle into the loft. A skeptical Timerus tilted his head enough to study Winshill's expression.

The mage kept his voice soft. "Going up there is more likely to hurt you, boy, than her. It's where she's compelled to go."

Doubt clearly showed on Timerus's face.

Nethandia began to speak, but this time Winshill made a swift gesture to stop her.

"I need to see how she is connected to the focus. I can't do that from down here."

Timerus nodded. Shifting to a crouching position, he helped Rhealle gain her feet, straightening himself as she stood. To his relief, moving toward the ladder eased some of the tension in her body. Guiding her to the ladder, he placed her hand on it and used his leverage behind her to help her ascend. Once Rhealle reached the loft, she broke free of his grasp.

"Don't let her touch the focus."

"The what?"

"The mirror!"

Timerus darted up the last of the rungs, and before she could take more than a few steps toward the mirror, he caught her up in his arms again. At first, Rhealle struggled, until she felt the vibrations against her ear. The soothing rhythm coaxed her into relaxing against him.

Winshill cleared the floor of the loft in time to witness the brief struggle. He had never seen the victim of a compulsion forsake it in favor of a person, and he had seen a fair number of them as a council mage.

Holding his light aloft, he swept his eyes across the floor in the direction where the power was strongest. Upon the wooden boards rested a round mirror in a silver frame, round except for the four cardinal points worked into the elaborate design. The design vaguely reminded him of a type of script he had seen in his travels to the south.

"Bring her closer, but don't let her ...."

"Touch it," Timerus finished for him. "I got it, mage." He and Rhealle advanced toward the mirror. Before Timerus could stop her, she knelt down beside it. Seeing the hair stand up on his arms again, he caught up her hands. "Do you feel it? Do you feel the vibrations?"

"I feel the power. Nethandia?"

"I think I'll remain down here and wait for that useless woman."

Winshill positioned himself on the other side of the mirror, so he could watch the effect the mirror had on Rhealle.

The compulsion struggled against Timerus's intervention.

Pulling one hand free, Winshill barely had time to snatch it away from the frame before she touched it. He could feel her pulling against his hold, as if she were trying to stroke the edge. The girl wasn't a conduit for the magic, but something linked the two.

Doing his best to shield his mage sight from the radiance of the spell, Winshill worked through the interconnecting lines. Each strong thread he followed was created by magic — each one a part of the intricate spell — until his sight passed over a thin thread of a different consistency.

Because it was so thin and nearly transparent, he almost missed it. This wasn't magic. This thread was created from an oath to a god. It bound the girl to the mirror and the spell with the strength of a mithril chain. Even if they could break the mirror, the girl would be bound to the remains — if she lived.

"Can you get her to move away from the mirror, boy?"

For an answer, Timerus scooped her up in his arms and carried her toward the ladder. Her sobs arrested his movement before he descended with her to the ground. Timerus looked to Winshill.

The mage stood indecisively.

"What's going on up there? Is it done?"

Winshill's eyes met Timerus's.

"Breaking it really will kill her, won't it?"

"I don't know. This magic requires more than a single mage to break. The more power involved, the greater the risk."

From the base of the ladder, Nethandia said, "We don't have time to petition for more mages. Just find something heavy and smash the damn thing."

Timerus lowered the two of them to the ground, so he could comfort Rhealle better. "Does it have to be a mage?"

"What did you have in mind?"

"Lucia might ...."

"That's why that old woman seemed familiar," Nethandia nearly shouted.

Winshill was lost. When he didn't say anything, Nethandia added, "She's the old Folk witch. The one all the whispers are about."

"She's not a witch. Lucia is a seer."

"Witch, seer, same difference."

Timerus shrugged. "Ghans hasn't exactly been friendly to the Folk."

"Nethandia, get someone to fetch her."

A few colorful words rose up the ladder before the Head of the Farmers' Guild moved out of hearing.

Nethandia chafed at the slowness of the Folk. One mention of magic mirrors and the witch went white while the old goat nearly burst a blood vessel.

What was the big deal? Climb the ladder, smash the mirror, clean up the mess, and move on to the next affected town. Instead, an hour had slipped by waiting for the old man to interpret a book. Nethandia finally told the man to "bring it with. Winshill can figure it out."

Lucia's agreement startled her but didn't unsettle Nethandia as much as her ominous words. "The window is closing." There wasn't any window to close. Then the witch not only insisted on bringing the crazy, old man but also the Gaujo. Who or what was a Gaujo? Another old crony? Nethandia almost drew blood from her lip, she bit down on it so hard. The Gaujo was the tall, arrogant stranger from last night. Could this day get any worse?

Seeing the throng of people hovering around the buildings near the barn, Nethandia began to think, yes. The party of Folk cautiously approached the entrance.

Before she would permit any of them to pass, Lucia laid her hand on the door. The hand remained still for only a moment before it began to quiver violently. Lucia muttered strange sounds that made Nethandia uncomfortable. The shaking stopped, and she removed her hand.

"Corsanth, the book cannot pass this way. Gaujo, I fear your … um … talismans … will not be able to either."

Nethandia couldn't prevent the string of curses that burst from her in frustration. "Just figure it out and get this done!"

Her patience wasn't the only thing coming to an end. The steel hardened eyes of the Gaujo let Nethandia know his patience was almost done with her.

His voice was just as hard. "Give me a few minutes."

She tried to contain her impatience as he disappeared around the side of the building. When he returned in short order, Nethandia whispered a silent "Thanks," to Kaylei. "Well?"

"If someone lowers the winch, we can climb up."

Corsanth looked dubious.

"Don't worry, Elder. You just need to hold on."

When Nethandia demanded to know more, the Gaujo gripped her shoulder and shoved her around to the west side.

Before she could squirm out of his grip, he pointed up at an opening. A winch extended out over a loading platform.

He hissed, "This ... is what I do. Go inside. Find the way up to the staging area, and get the damn hook down here." In a much louder voice, he said, "Someone find me a pair of thick gloves and a sturdy belt."

Lucia and Corsanth watched the battle of wills without comment. Realizing that no one would come to her aid, Nethandia took a step back toward the front. The gesture — signaling her defeat — prompted Lucia to approach. The old woman laid her hand upon the wall under the opening. Again, she muttered those strange words that set Nethandia's stomach in knots. The hands began to quiver, then stilled.

Lucia nodded. "This is the way."

Corsanth remained behind with that hateful Gaujo while Lucia followed her inside. Behind the two women, Lilleth came, carrying a steaming kettle and a basket.

"Winshill," Nethandia shouted. When he didn't answer, she screeched, "Winnsshhill!" The light sphere appeared at the top of the ladder. "Hey!" The mage's head appeared in the light. Sweat streamed from his temples to his jawline. "Did you see a pulley system up there earlier?"

The light shifted and faded. Scattered remnants of light poked through the wooden boards above, leaving a faint trail to the southwest. A few minutes later, the thud of wood striking wood was followed by the sound of a squeaky crank turning. Indistinguishable voices mixed with the noise; then silence followed by a fresh squealing of the crank. While the noise continued, Winshill appeared above the ladder without his light.

"Did that woman ever make it back?" he asked while negotiating the rungs.

Lilleth held out the kettle and basket.

"Nethandia, fill the cup and bring it and the spoon to me."

Winshill opened one of his small pouches and carefully measured a blue powder into the water. "Take the cup up to the boy. Tell him to double the strength. You, woman, please leave."

Both women were ready to voice objections until they saw the firmness of his jaw. Lilleth backed all the way outside. Nethandia began to climb. She was halfway up when a hand on her lower back made her look down.

Lucia stood at the bottom with her own stern expression. "Do not touch the mirror. Not unless you are prepared for a different life." Her hand dropped away.

Nethandia scooted up the rest of the ladder. The two young people had become so entwined in each other that they looked like lovers. Nethandia sat the cup down before her shaking hands spilled the contents.

In the light radiating from near the center of the loft,

the two appeared drained of color — the girl lying limp in his arms. Nethandia passed on the message. Listlessly, the boy complied, carefully setting the drink on the ground when done. Before Nethandia had a chance to object, he told her the tea must steep.

A bead of sweat rolled down her cheek. Nethandia took that as her cue to get back to the ground, but before her foot touched the first rung, Winshill was there blocking the way.

"Help the couple down the ladder after she has drunk the tea," Winshill told her. "When you are done with that, go help those two. They will need your hands."

"Mage," Corsanth said, "a word, if you will."

Winshill shuffled toward the two men bent over a strange looking book.

"Your companion said you might be able to decipher this."

Nethandia gnashed her teeth together as the three men hovered around the ancient tome. Why were they dragging this out? How difficult was it to break a mirror?

Nethandia counted the number of times her finger tapped against the wooden frame of the ladder opening. She could just feel the cooler air from below. After the fiftieth tap, she decided it was better to go down and wait than sit here and steam. She hooked her foot on the first rung.

"Sure you want to go down first?" The male voice from

behind startled her. "Let me take the weight. Just keep her steady."

"Don't think I can handle it, boy?"

The insult sparked a wave of energy strong enough for him to spout his own string of insults at her. "Get it straight. Timerus or Trade Warden. You can take your boy and ...."

From below, Lucia said, "Enough, Timerus. Bring her down."

For only being a slight young woman, the two found it a challenge to get her to the ground. Besides being unable to hold onto anything, every step downward was a fight. Lucia, finally had to step in to help. The three maneuvered her directly under the mirror before allowing her to collapse once again into Timerus's arms.

Lucia then sent Nethandia to join the men. "Remember my warning." Had the old woman really said the words, or had she only heard them in her head? This heat was definitely getting to her.

Winshill warned the two men to give him enough time to set the shielding. As he passed Nethandia on the way to the ladder, he gave her shoulder an encouraging pat. "Soon, it will be done."

"Blessed be to Kaylei."

Corsanth heard the words and smiled. "Come. Hold the book for me."

"Why can't he do it?"

"Because he has his own part to do. Sit here."

Nethandia knelt where he indicated.

Corsanth raised an eyebrow. "Are you certain?"

Nethandia had no clue what the old man was fussing about.

When she remained kneeling, he rested the book against her knees. To keep it upright, she was forced to support the upper corners with her hands. In only a few minutes, her knees ached from the weight of it, and her hands wanted to drop to the ground. Nethandia tilted the book forward.

Keeping the weight of it against her palms, she tried to shift into a cross-legged position. The book tilted forward. As Nethandia grabbed for it with one hand, two things happened. Winshill yelled that he was ready, and Nethandia lost her balance. Her other hand reached back to stop her from falling, only it didn't land on wood. The hand pressed into a metal surface with raised etchings.

The shrill chime stopped the heart of the seer. Someone not attuned to one of the mirrors had opened the way. The seer stared into the magical space to try to determine which mirror had been violated. He never found out. A blast from behind sent him flying through the cavern, smashing his body hard enough against the rock wall to shatter his bones.

Impatient with the unexpected interruption but not concerned, Serastus peered into the magical space. His fingers ran nimbly along the black edge, adjusting the focus, sharpening the image. The loft in Ghans solidified. It was brighter than when he last looked upon it. Serastus methodically checked each line of power. All resonated at the proper harmony.

He was growing tired of the nuisance called Ghans. All he needed was a few adjustments to the weave to turn the rain into a storm strong enough to rid himself of that particular inconvenience.

Running his hand along the edge until it encountered the symbol for destruction, Serastus tapped it three times. A small thread of magic appeared. He used his other hand to gather up the thread and pull it to the anchor point for the mirror in the loft. He tapped the symbol three more times. Gathering up the second thread, he studied the pattern on the other side.

Yes, the channeling thread would do nicely. Holding the end of the thread securely he began the incantation to alter the spell.

The first syllables rolled off his tongue, activating the symbol. The second round bound the anchor point to that symbol. The third part of the spell would open the way and allow him to bind the thread he held to the line that channeled the original spell. He spoke those final syllables.

With the thread grasped tightly, he shoved his hand into the magical space. Instead of passing freely, the hand met a wall of resistance. Withdrawing his hand, Serastus peered more intently into the space. The mirror reflected exactly what he expected until he realized what it hadn't shown him: the person who had opened the way.

Serastus negated the spell of change and released the thread. He uttered the words to allow him to hear what passed on the other side.

Someone spoke in a sing-song voice. He amplified the spell to increase its sensitivity to sound. Words from the old language chilled his spine — words lost in the time before this time.

As the words grew stronger, a shadow passed over the focus of the mirror. A round shape hovered in the air. In the center was etched a sigil. At its heart was the symbol for the path of honor. Hovering in the air was the ancient symbol for the house of Berain — the one relinquished when they became assassins. The one etched into the blades used by Darethan Berain.

No! Enough was enough. Time to destroy Ghans for good.

Unholy sounds rolled from his mouth that struck so much fear into the ceremonial cavern that even the spiders high in the crevices above cowered into a ball. He formed his left hand into a claw as he called to the lines of energy that poured into the magical space from this side.

Slowly, he began to close the claw, calling the energy from the other side to the magical space. When enough energy passed through from his side, he changed the pitch and rhythm of the spell. With his right hand, he severed the anchor as his left closed into a fist. A satisfied smile crossed his lips at the light that flared intensely before the opening went black. Good riddance to Ghans and to whoever held that accursed weapon.

# Chapter Thirty-One
## Fallout

The arm holding the dagger remained steady as Artearis waited for Corsanth to give the signal to strike, but his free hand ached from the pressure of him squeezing the amulet around his neck.

As he loosened his grip on the green stone, Nethandia fell backward. Artearis made a grab for her and missed. Her hand flew back to catch herself, and in doing so, her palm landed atop the mirror's frame.

Energy shot upward, flowing into the point of his dagger and up his arm. In his mind, Artearis saw an old man peer into empty space. All of a sudden, the man flew backward to disappear from sight.

He tightened his hand around the amulet and tried to

still his mind. A cowled figure came into his consciousness. A figure that made his skin burn as if from cold. Then the words began, chilling his mind.

Drawing on the warmth radiating from the hand holding the stone, he fought the numbness, mentally calling to mind the mantra of quiet. The steady rhythm shut out those dark words — and almost shut out Corsanth.

"... Artearis, reverse the blade, and smash the frame."

The weight of the power and the dark words fought with his ability to think. He concentrated harder on the stone in his hand, gripping it tighter. A light of life and blood blazed from his fist, clearing his mind enough to register Corsanth's command. He flipped his dagger point up and started to bring the pommel down before realizing Nethandia's hand was underneath it. Shifting his arm to the other side, he brought it down hard enough to break part of the frame away. The world exploded around him.

When Artearis came to, a cold, wet wind chilled him after the intense heat in the barn. He wondered how they had gotten him outside, but then he saw Winshill helping Corsanth to his feet and Nethandia huddled in a heap beside a broken ring of blackened metal.

Despite a splitting headache, Artearis retrieved his weapon and went to aid her. The woman's hand was blistered where it had touched the mirror's frame; otherwise, physically, she was undamaged. Artearis wasn't so sure about mentally. Her eyes, filled with fear, stared off into the distance as if waiting for something horrifying to find her.

After Winshill assisted Corsanth down the ladder, Artearis tried to get Nethandia to follow. The woman remained lost in the vision that had snared her. Swearing softly, Artearis scooped her up and wrestled her listless body down to the floor below where he propped her against the wall bracing the ladder. "How's Lucia?"

Timerus groaned. "How do you think she is?"

Artearis focused his attention on the area under the loft. Timerus and his latest cause stood quietly beside Lucia. The Folk elder stared off into space.

Corsanth still clutched the ancient text. "Lucia, the tome. Whatever it was, heard."

"Yes."

For a handful of heartbeats, Lucia stood there shivering. "And saw."

Fear unlike any Artearis had known wrapped itself around his heart. The moment passed but not the memory.

Lucia was her unshakable self when she told them they needed to leave now. She arranged for Artearis and Nethandia to take Corsanth out the front way, asking them to draw as much attention to their exit as they could. She and Winshill would quietly escort the others to the cafe.

Between the storm and Corsanth's weakened

condition, it took Artearis and Nethandia longer than expected to escort him to the caravan. Artearis actually thought he would have carry the elder Folk. On their return to town, he thought he'd have to carry Nethandia back as she started weaving as she walked and would slow down nearly to a stop before shrugging her shoulders and picking up her pace again.

Artearis took hold of her arm. "What's eating you?"

Eyes glowering, Nethandia stared at his hand on her arm.

"Seriously, what's wrong? You've been … quiet … since the explosion."

Nethandia dropped her eyes.

Artearis steered her to a pile of large rocks beside the road. Thankfully, the storm didn't reach this far out of town. He helped her take a seat. Putting his foot on a rock beside her, Artearis leaned down, resting his arm on his thigh. "You saw into the mirror?"

Nethandia didn't answer.

"You felt the pull?"

"I don't believe in magic."

"You travel around with a mage of the Council, and you don't believe in magic?"

Nethandia nodded.

Artearis couldn't keep the disbelief from his face. "Next, you'll be saying you don't believe in assassins or evil or the gods."

"Assassins, yes. They are just men. Evil?" She shrugged. "Evil is just men abusing their power or position."

Shaking his head, Artearis said, "You don't think what we experienced was evil?"

Nethandia hesitated. The blue eyes intently studying her made her too nervous to answer without swallowing a few times to clear her throat. "I don't know. I'm not even sure whether it was human. Certainly not dwarf. Maybe elven?"

"Not elven," Artearis said emphatically. "Not any kind of elf I've heard of anyway."

Nethandia dared to meet his eyes. "What do you think it was?"

Taking the question seriously, Artearis frowned. Was this how Marte felt all those times Artearis had come to him? Knowing the answer and knowing Artearis wasn't ready to understand it? He carefully chose his words. "Something more than evil. Something out of control. It's no wonder that deaf woman was ensnared."

Nethandia turned away.

"What?"

Her color went from deep red to gray. Her voice shaking, she said, "In the barn, I told Winshill she deserved to die for her part in this."

"And now?"

"I don't know."

Again, Artearis took his time answering, wishing Marte was here to handle it. How would he handle this? "What happened in the barn hasn't given you a new perspective?"

"I don't know?"

"Well you don't believe in magic, so you won't find an answer there. So what do you believe in?"

When Nethandia opened her mouth to answer, Artearis did what Marte would have done. He interrupted her, saying "It's not for me to know but for you to consider. Everything changes." With that statement, he straightened himself and headed into Ghans — alone.

The storm raged outside the cafe. An exhausted Winshill slouched against the chair, hand clasped around a mug of Salfon tea. *May Kaylei always be generous to you, Timerus.*

None of them had been prepared for the spell caster to destroy his own creation. Even positioned in the eye of the power web, he and Lucia struggled to hold the protection shield in place. Without the warning light from above, the two wouldn't have had time to strengthen their work. That Lucia sat so calmly across from him after their ordeal amazed the air mage.

At least, now they knew how these weather anomalies occur and why no magical trace exists for the investigators to find. The real question was how many towns have been infiltrated.

"Welcome, Gaujo." Even Lucia's voice was calm.

Winshill finally realized the man had blond hair not brown and that his features were too aristocratic for a Folk. "What kind of name is Gaujo. I can't place it."

Lucia replied, "Gaujo is not a name — rather a description."

The Folk elder left it at that. It didn't matter. Winshill had his suspicions of what the man was by his manners and his weapons, if not who he was. What worried Winshill was what kind of assassin practiced magic?

Artearis settled himself into the chair next to the fire. "The crowd outside is growing."

Winshill nodded. "Not surprising. I'd want answers, too, if an explosion blew out the western wall of my town's hay barn."

"They don't want answers. They want blood."

Lucia frowned. "I thought we removed them quietly."

Artearis studied Lucia thoughtfully. What had she

known? "The sister, Lilleth. When she went on your little errand, she told her father and the serving woman who was in the barn with her. That agitator from last night overheard. Farel is stirring up trouble for the mayor by blaming the catastrophe on his daughters. Since Lilleth was outside in the sight of witnesses, the blame's falling on the deaf one, Rhealle."

"By Moratam's double-bladed axe," Winshill swore, "that man is a public nuisance."

"That's what happens when long running feuds get fresh fuel." The bitterness dripped from Artearis's words.

Lucia said, "Remember that, Gaujo."

Nethandia flopped into the empty chair. "It won't be long before some of them break in to drag her out."

Artearis fingered the stone at his throat. "Isn't there anything you two can do? You are kingdom agents."

Winshill shook his head. "The Council's concern is the caster and his intentions."

At the mention of the caster, Nethandia's face paled, and her fingers nervously drummed upon the table. "The weather caused the crop failure. The best I can do is rule on disaster relief."

At her words, a flustered Durnin stopped his agitated wandering around the cafe to listen. "Please say it's good news, or else I'm ruined ... ruined. Farel's calling for my removal." Durnin wrung his hands together.

"Where is she?" Lucia asked.

Durnin's hands started their flapping again. "Ruined."

Artearis grabbed for the nearest waving arm. "Where is your daughter?"

"Lilleth's with Weiz, assessing the damage. Poor girl ... has to shoulder all this ...." Durnin continued pacing about.

Artearis jerked him back to the group before he could wander away.

Lucia's voice remained calm as she rephrased her question. "Where is Rhealle?"

"Huh ... oh her. That defective, troublesome daughter of mine is hiding out in the kitchen with that troublesome Folk boy of yours. Can't even get a decent day's work out of her now." Durnin tried to pull away from Artearis, who looked to Lucia for instruction.

"Someone please bring them here." Artearis took those words to mean hang on to Durnin. When the portly man kept trying to pull free, Artearis vacated his chair and shoved it into Durnin, unbalancing the man, so he fell into it.

He was about to release his grip and head to the kitchen when Nethandia beat him to it. While she retrieved Rhealle and Timerus, Artearis reached out to a nearby table. Using his foot to move the chairs between him and the table, he pulled the second table up against the first. He swung one of the extra chairs around, so he could straddle it, resting his free arm across the back. Winshill shuffled the rest of the chairs so that everyone would have a seat.

The two from the kitchen appeared worn but undamaged. Timerus seated Rhealle next to Winshill before dragging a chair up behind her for himself. Nethandia seated herself in the only chair left, across from Lucia. The old Folk's scrutiny of Nethandia sent its own set of chills along Artearis's spine, and it was clear Nethandia felt something similar.

When Lucia continued to dissect her, Nethandia cleared her throat. Her first words could barely be heard, "As Head of the Farmers' Guild," but her voice grew stronger as she continued, "it falls to me to decide the financial fate of Ghans if the town fails to meet its obligation to the crown. Which, the way it stands, Ghans won't be able to do."

Moaning louder, Durnin broke in, "The town's ruined. I'm ruined. What are we to do?"

Not removing her eyes from Nethandia, Lucia finally spoke. "What if Ghans could provide some of the tithe?"

Nethandia's drumming picked up its tempo. The sound made Durnin fidget. "How much?"

Durnin moaned, "None, we can't. Just enough seed for next year's crops. That's it. That's all the seed we've got."

Artearis had to admire Lucia. Even though her face was beginning to show the strain of today's events, she remained composed.

"Say half."

Burying his head in his hands, Durnin said, "We don't have it. We don't, I tell you."

Artearis grasped the man by the shoulder and gave him a good shaking. "Hold it together, man."

"Summon the crop manager."

Few people had the will to resist Lucia when she used that voice. When Artearis moved to comply, Lucia's eyes told him no. Winshill made their request to the serving woman. Artearis hooked another chair with his foot and slid it toward Durnin. Spoons clattering against cups and furtive whisperings from patrons filled the silence until Farel arrived.

Lucia broke the silence. "Nethandia, as the representative of the Farmers' Guild, if Ghans can provide half their tithe this year, would that honor their obligation?"

Nethandia nodded.

Farel frowned. "We don't have it and no time to grow it."

Lucia's game became clear to Artearis. "What would a solution be worth to Ghans?" His question brought the hint of a smile to Lucia's face.

For more than an hour, the people sitting around the tables bartered back and forth, or rather everyone but Rhealle, who had trouble following the negotiations, and

Artearis, who acted as physical moderator between Farel and Timerus.

Timerus insisted on the deaf girl accompanying the Folk. Farel shook his fist at Timerus and demanded she be held accountable for Ghans' plight. Winshill reminded Farel that the entire town paid the stranger no mind, thinking him harmless. How would the town pay?

Lucia stood. "Ghans welcomed the hand of ruin, yet it continues to push away the means of salvation. Perhaps the Gaujo had the sense of it. Our efforts are better spent negotiating with Banton's Folly."

Durnin begged Farel to reconsider.

An unhappy Farel grudgingly gave in to Lucia's final proposal. The Folk would provide enough seed of a hybrid rice to grow the town's allotment of crops in exchange for exclusive access to the wheelwright until their wagons were mended and a limited supply of Salfon tea for Durnin in exchange for Rhealle. To guarantee the girl's safety, she would leave through the kitchen with Timerus and Artearis as escorts.

Nethandia warned them the agreement wasn't official until it was signed and witnessed.

Durnin said, "Then let's get this done."

# Chapter Thirty-Two
## Recruitment Troubles

Yorn rubbed at the sweat clinging to his brown hair above the base of his neck. Swearing softly, he pulled out a cloth and wiped his forehead and the nape of his neck. Lord but the temperature shot up overnight. He shifted in his chair, attempting to catch a breeze across his narrow shoulders.

After a frustrating morning trying to find a place to recruit from, Frisk finally used threats to convince this innkeeper to move a table and two chairs to this shaded veranda outside, but without so much as an intermittent breeze, even this location made it miserable to conduct their business.

Already an hour past noon and only half their quota

met. Korvin, adamant they find twelve bullies, wanted them crude and nasty, just the way Frisk liked, in case he needed to turn them out in the town. The half dozen ruffians lounging at the other end of the veranda filled that bill.

They made Yorn's skin crawl. Not mercs, or even thugs, they were out of control adolescents with raging hormones in adult bodies. One had the nerve to ask Frisk how often he was going to get to bed the snippety wenches in Gessin which sparked another to ask how often they were going to raid the local goods. The ruffian preferred fresh meat each time, not leftovers. A third man poked that one in the ribs, saying, "Which is why you're stuck looking for work in this backward town."

Frisk let out a raucous howl and slapped the man on the back. "We'll see what we can do."

The more they yammered, the more Yorn worried. A job like this required disciplined men who put the objective first, not these crazed fiends.

He mopped his forehead again. After his first inquiries about town, Yorn had gotten knots in his stomach accompanied by the feeling that Banton's Folly was the wrong place to be. Over the course of those first two hours he'd dropped word of their interest at two other inns in town, a tavern already serving at mid-morning, a meat stand, and a tinker station; he had even felt out the town law for news of troublemakers that Frisk might find promising. Each time, his feelers came back sketchy.

In fact, the only good lead he had was a pair of mercs that headed up north retired from the military, and their companion, who were supposed to come back through town that evening. Yorn just hoped it was before they packed up or filled their quota.

Qualified men found homes in the Duke of Saron's guard, not off the street side work. Apparently, he was a loyal master who paid fair wages — if not the lucrative pay handed out by the Duke of Sitar.

Then again, Jekan Geylas required his ... um ... employees to resolve their assigned contracts using ... well ... unorthodox methods. Yorn almost wished he'd run into Lathan Morden's recruiter before Tebbin pleaded with him to take his current position.

Quiet except for the new hirelings squabbling over their dice game, Yorn opted to find something to quench his thirst if not cool him off. Easing himself out of the chair, he headed for the door.

"Bring me back something wet ... with a kick."

Yorn scrutinized Frisk. Guess it made sense the man didn't hire professionals; he wasn't much of one himself. Yorn gave Frisk a curt nod.

Ambling up to the bar, Yorn asked, "Innkeeper, have you got something cold that will take the edge off this heat and something with a decent kick to satisfy him?" Yorn cocked his head in the direction of the door.

The tough old man gave him an appraising look. "If ye be askin', aye."

He went into the kitchen and returned shortly with a tall mug beaded with moisture, set it on the bar next to Yorn. Grabbing up a short glass from a shelf behind the bar, he poured a two-finger measure of some foul smelling concoction.

"One silver for that and three for this," he said, setting the glass in front of Yorn. Against Frisk's orders, he dug the four silver out of his pouch and put them into the gnarled hand in front of him. The man gave him another measuring look before pocketing the coins. "YER business is welcome here."

While Frisk's business wasn't, Yorn read in the man's expression. He inclined his head to show understanding.

The old innkeeper leaned closer. "Yer partner's just askin' for trouble takin' on those layabouts and trustin' they'll behave when they finally get bored of waitin'."

Yorn tried to suppress a grimace. The old man's face warned Yorn that he wasn't successful. "We're waiting on a pair of mercs supposed to be coming through tonight," he said as a way of explanation.

"Aye. I know the ones. Solid choice those two. Companion's supposed to be even better 'cept no one's seen him. Not so much their travelin' man."

That puzzled Yorn.

"Ye be welcome to stay out front long as ye don't cause trouble, and ye pay yer tab."

Picking up the drinks, Yorn turned to go.

"And thank ye for the rent."

Yorn prayed the innkeeper's voice didn't reach the veranda.

Frisk only looked pleased when Yorn set the glass in front of him.

Two new men lounged against the railing watching the dice fall. Loud curses from the outcome of the roll drew the attention of passersby; Yorn prayed they'd still be here when those men came through. The woman scowled at the ruffians spouting their foul language. She took her son's hand and led him across the street. Yorn wanted to smack himself upside the head. "The boy."

Frisk frowned. "What about 'im? He'll learn to curse eventually."

Yorn shook his head. "Korvin said to find out what we could about Lathan Morden's son. Why ...?"

Frisk got angry. "Korvin says do something ... do it. Don't ask why. And, hop to it. I want to be gone soon as we pick up the last four."

Three hours of trudging around in this heat on a fruitless task that had lightened his purse considerably tested even Yorn's self-control. He weighed the pouch hanging on his belt and gauged there was probably enough to buy more cooperation and a drink, if he could get past Frisk lounging in his chair with his eyes closed.

"What did you find?"

So much for the drink. "Morden had the boy with him when he came around in early summer. No one's seen either since then. I tried to feel out whether the boy might be with the Folk, but no one's sure. The Folk came through shortly after, but nobody saw the boy."

Frisk stretched in his chair, nearly sending it crashing to the floor. "Figures. Same song as Gessin."

"I thought we could find out for ourselves since word's been going around about them coming through for their fall performance. Odd thing is the Folk haven't been seen either since the spring. Got more than a few townspeople curious. Apparently, the Folk keep a firm schedule."

With a grunt, Frisk adjusted his chair; he sighed as he settled back into it, closing his eyes. Yorn slid past him to the door.

Frisk's voice was casual as he said, "The innkeeper's had enough of our money."

Yorn pulled the door open.

The innkeeper looked up from his task. Seeing Yorn,

he waved the man over. "Word is ye been askin' around about his lordship and the boy. That's not smart. Duke's been good to Banton's Folly. Real good, if ye know what I mean."

Yorn did.

"Hallan's on peace duty this evenin' hour. He don't take kindly to strangers wantin' to know about his lordship. Best ye and yer crew be gone afore Hallan takes it into his head ye mean his lordship harm."

Yorn did an about-face. Before he could take a step, the old innkeeper tugged on his sleeve. "Ye did right by me, today. I'll not forget. If'n ye get in over yer head ...."

That tight feeling in Yorn's stomach appeared again.

"No drink this time?" Frisk asked in a lazy drawl. "Why I stick with intimidation. They give me what I want or else."

Considering that the eight, no nine, men did little more than curse loudly at each other, Yorn began to wonder if he'd been wrong about Frisk.

The last hire, made while he was inside, appeared to possess the right detached attitude for this kind of job. Then Yorn saw the woman at his side. When she bent down to pick up the pack he deliberately dropped at her feet, her blouse slid up, revealing an intricate pattern carved into her lower back and even lower still if the pattern was complete. The man's face turned to ice at the sight of her exposed flesh.

Seeing his glare, the woman shrunk into herself even as she straightened her clothing. Maybe not the right temperament.

Yorn settled into the seat he vacated earlier. At least it was starting to cool off.

From across the table Frisk tunelessly whistled a popular ditty at local inns these days. "If'n your intel holds true and those three show up soon, we'll make it back to base in plenty of time to enjoy ourselves before we get down to serious work."

The evening crowd forced them to relocate to the same end of the veranda as the dice players. Yorn would have preferred the street to being this close to their new recruits. The only thing going in his favor was Frisk's determination to head back at sun down whether they filled the quota or not. Yorn slapped at the gnats crawling around his sweat-stained shirt. A grating laugh at the top of the stairs to the veranda distracted Yorn from the bugs.

"So you're the bloke scooping up local talent, Frisk? Looks like we wasted our time."

Frisk didn't bother straightening in his chair. "Hiring you is the real waste of time, Dalton."

The man had seen better days. His dark hair and

beard showed signs of being well kept previously but were a shaggy imitation now. As he reached the top of the stairs, Yorn could see he was tall and slim, probably just shy of six feet, and his watery, blue eyes were hard and angry, unlike the calm, brown eyes of his two companions.

One stood slightly taller than Dalton, the other half a hand shorter. It was difficult to tell their physical condition wrapped as they were in long, dark cloaks, but they were obviously strangers to Torenium with those flowing black locks interspersed with four equally long braids on each side their heads interwoven with some kind of feathers.

Yorn peered at the feathers. The ones from the taller man came from a different bird than the shorter man. These definitely weren't ex-military men. He could tell both men knew he was scrutinizing them, yet they maintained a casualness that implied it was of no consequence.

Strapped across each back, Yorn noted a hefty staff with strange carvings and no other weapons visible upon their persons, but he felt more than knew that it was a deception. They may not be military trained, but he'd bet money they were warriors — the real deal, not those shifty pieces of refuse Frisk had already hired.

Yorn had been so intent on sizing up the two strangers he missed the escalation of tension between Frisk and Dalton, but the strangers hadn't. Yorn could see their eyes flit back and forth between the two men ready to come to blows. For being his partner, it was strange that neither reacted; they simply watched.

When Frisk said, "We don't need you or any vermin you think to drag along. Be gone with you,"

Yorn slid out of his chair to stand before the two strange men. "How much?"

The shorter man said, "Pardon?" in the strangest accent Yorn had ever heard.

"How much to hire you and your friend?"

"We are three." The taller man possessed a much quieter voice than Yorn had imagined.

Frisk raged, "Hell no! There's no way I'm hiring him," pointing at Dalton.

The shorter man said, "He is not our third. He is our ...." He consulted with his companion before adding, "traveling partner."

Dalton barked out an almost hysterical laugh. "I don't even come close to their other companion ... and I wouldn't even want to," he said slyly.

Yorn began to wonder if he was making a mistake with the offer.

"Room, board, and one gold, twenty silver each per week and fifty silver for me as a finder's fee."

"Like hell I'm paying you a finder's fee, and if they want the job, it's one gold each," Frisk shouted loud enough that Yorn almost missed the tall man's words, "And a traveling partner."

Puzzled, Yorn started to ask what he meant when Dalton said, "A guide. They require a guide."

Yorn dropped his depleted bag of coins on the ground in front of Dalton.

"No," Frisk screamed. "I'm not hiring muscle I've not seen."

"Oh, their companion's got muscle alright and in all the right places," Dalton smirked.

"I'm not taking your bloody word for it."

Yorn might have had doubts, but his stomach didn't. "We can make the hire contingent on Korvin's approval. It fills our quota."

Frisk glared at him but said nothing.

The shorter man reached out his hand to shake Yorn's. "This is how it is done, yes?"

Yorn gripped the man's hand and shook it firmly. "Where's your companion?"

"Back at camp," Dalton said. "We didn't want any … uh … mishaps. I'll see to it they get where they need to be. Just say where."

Still angry, Frisk shook his head. "No way!"

Yorn said, "Just take the road east. Someone will meet you in the morning."

When Dalton opened his mouth to try and pry more information out of them, Frisk doubled up his fist. "Take it or leave it."

Dalton laughed. "Come along, you two. Let's go collect your friend." As he walked away, Yorn heard him say under his breath, "I'd sure like to be there when Korvin meets that one."

Frisk muttered, "You'd better be right about them." He barked orders to the rest of the men to collect up their gear and move out.

# Chapter Thirty-Three
## New Recruits

When the sun breached the horizon, Yorn considered breaking camp and riding back along the road to Banton's Folly. In the dead of night, when Frisk had ordered him to stay behind for the three strangers, he had gratefully accepted. A night without sleep was preferable to the company of the new hires.

As the sun rose, he began to have second thoughts. Had the man Dalton duped them? Yorn sent a heartfelt thank you to the Winds of Fortune that Frisk hadn't actually paid the two for their services, so the only coin they were out was what was left of the funds Korvin gave him to buy information.

He led his horse to the watering stream that ran

alongside the road. While his horse drank, Yorn checked him over. He prized his mount, a gift from his older sister, above about everything he owned. She had spared no expense for her half-brother.

Yorn sighed. He'd better have a damned good explanation for his rash decision, he thought, as he saddled the horse, mounted, and pointed his horse in the direction of Gessin. It came as a shock when a half mile up the road Dalton and three cloaked figures waited along the stream side.

"Thought you'd never get here," Dalton sneered.

Yorn frowned.

The older man said, "Light brightened the dark, so we went around."

Dalton laughed. "Yeah, probably his light. I told you it wasn't necessary."

A higher pitched voice said, "Caution is never unnecessary."

Yorn nearly curled up in his boots. Korvin was going to kill him.

Dalton nearly laughed himself off his horse. "I hope you've made peace with your gods."

Frisk's account of the strangers peaked Korvin's

interest. He insisted on inspecting each of them as if they were horse flesh, and he didn't care if it offended the three standing in front of him. When none of the strangers complied, he ordered his men to surround them and relieve them of their belongings.

Yorn had never seen weapons appear in the hands of fighters as quickly as the staves and knives appeared in their hands. The tallest one uttered angry words to his companions in a language Yorn didn't understand.

The one standing just in front of the other two replied in a quieter but firm tone before slowly undoing the clasp of his cloak and carefully removing it. Within seconds a heavy looking pack rested at his feet with the cloak draped over it, and the staff he had taken from his back a moment before was loosely held in his hand. He took several steps forward. "I am Kiel Trelfang-senchanshi of the hawk aerie."

From behind the trio, a sharp whistle split the air. Across the man's back and the back of his arms was tattooed the back of a hawk. Across his chest and the front of his arms were the head, neck, chest, and wings of the bird. He wore a leather vest and leggings made of some kind of tanned animal skin and closed by thin laces of similar leather. His boots, if one could call them boots, had talons protruding from them. On his forearms where there was no tattooing, he wore leather bracers.

Korvin grinned. "I'd keep that cloak wrapped around

me, too, if I were covered in those."

Kiel replaced his cloak, shouldered his belongings, and stepped to the side of the shortest companion, the one cloaked head to toe. Taking his place, the tall one said, "I am Glor Trelfang-senchan of the eagle aerie." He was less willing to remove his cloak and pack to reveal tattooing of an eagle covering his chest and back. His muscles rippled as he snatched up his belongings and took his place along the other side of their companion.

"Well," Korvin said when the third one stood still.

With a sick feeling, Yorn watched the lack of exchange between Korvin and the mystery recruit. Korvin's grin melted into a scowl. The stranger's eyes looked like they would cut Korvin down where they stood, and by the tightening of his jaw, Korvin knew it, too.

The man named Kiel whispered something into the cloaked companion's ear. Hissing something hateful back, the cloaked stranger sheathed a pair of knives. Not bothering to step forward, the last one dropped a heavy pack to the ground BEFORE removing the cloak. More than one whistle broke the silence. Before them stood a well-muscled, well-proportioned woman with a falcon tattooed across her chest and back. She, too, wore the same leather vest, leggings, armbands, and boots as her companions. From the grunts and whispers, Yorn could tell there was more than one of Korvin's crew who wondered just how much of her chest those tattoos covered.

"I am Jezra Trelfang of the falcon aerie," she said in a cold voice that Frisk's heated "We don't hire women" couldn't melt.

The scowl on Korvin's face turned back into a grin. "I'll give you a try ... just make yourself comfortable right here." He pointed at the ground in front of his feet. "I'm sure you wouldn't mind an unbiased audience."

Again more whispers among the three. The appraisal she finally gave Korvin made Yorn's blood chill even more. "To take me, you have to beat me. You are too soft to win."

Raucous laughter broke out from the men.

The scowl reappeared on Korvin's face. "You're mine, woman."

The vicious smile that appeared as she unlaced her vest and tossed it to Glor silenced the men. A sharp whistle of appreciation from Yorn's right was cut off by Frisk's, "I've seen better."

The whistler's voice held disbelief. "Where? I've never seen work that good, ever!"

Yorn fought to keep a smile from his face at Frisk's scowl. He failed miserably when Korvin's sly comment about her undress was countered by a biting, "This is less than practice."

A pair of knives appeared in her hands. Like these

people, they were nothing like the men had seen before, blades as long as her hand from wrist to middle finger with curved notches along their length and a hilt that was part of the blade and wrapped with strips of white.

Jezra whispered something in that strange language of hers and charged straight at Korvin, knives held wide like the expanse of a pair of wings. Korvin yanked free his own blades, stepping back and to the side barely quick enough to avoid being gutted by her swooping strike. He squared himself around in time to parry the one-two thrusts aimed at his face and throat.

As she stepped back for her next attack, Korvin, seeing a chance to confuse the savage, rushed forward, bringing his short sword across in an angled arch. Jezra fluttered backward, like a bird beating back its wings, allowing Korvin's blade to slash downward at empty air.

Before he could fully recover for his next attack, Jezra swooped down between his legs, slicing each just above the knee hard enough to cut through cloth and skin but not permanently injure the man. Leaning into her momentum, she arched upward and twisted around, only to find Korvin's short sword waiting for her. The intensity on her face didn't flicker as the blade slashed her side. She brought up a knife to hook his blade and wrench it from his grasp before backing up to stand between her companions, blood drops splattering on the ground.

Korvin's men clapped and whistled their appreciation at her unusual technique. When Korvin didn't engage her again, the knot of men broke apart, some muttering among themselves as they left by the western gate to town, others heading for the main house. One stopped long enough to give Jezra a long, appraising look before moving on. Yorn guessed the man preferred to find easier game.

To Yorn's relief, although Korvin didn't share their sentiment, he was practical enough to know these three would be useful. In exchange for protecting the place, Korvin offered each a gold coin for the week, and if the job took longer, a gold coin each per week until it was over. The three conferred among themselves before adding, "and a ...." They whispered among themselves again. "A guide as he agreed," said Kiel, pointing at Yorn.

Korvin snorted. "I don't provide guides." As he sauntered toward the main house, he said, "Take that up with him. You three," he took in Yorn, "make that four, get this watch." Not long after he entered, the silence that had settled with everyone's departure was broken.

Not one of the strangers reacted to the noise coming from the manor that turned Yorn's insides out. At seeing his discomfort, Kiel said, "If they don't want a man inside, they should learn to keep him out."

Clutching her wound, Jezra nodded to Yorn. "The

aerie's stance when women beg to make it stop. So I ... learned." The two men with her nodded. She ran her hand along the path of the wicked scar on her abdomen. "The old warrior refused to teach me when I was with child. When the deceiver's spawn stood in my way, I cut it out with my own hand." What she didn't tell Yorn was that killing a child meant death.

Yorn's face drained of color.

"And when I was made warrior, I found him, and I," her voice dripped venom, "made it so he would find it ...." She searched for the word. "Difficult ... to be inside again."

Slapping her on the back, Glor said, "Our cousin took back her honor. She did the line proud that day." Kiel nodded. Glor signaled for Kiel to take the west wall. He mounted the north one.

Jezra picked up her gear. To Yorn, she said, "Does Kaylei not exist in this land?"

Yorn tried to understand the meaning behind her words.

"Have you no growing things?"

He asked, "Like a garden?"

It was Jezra's turn to look puzzled.

Yorn extended his hand to take her arm with the intent of guiding her but dropped it when he saw the distrust on her face. "This way," he said instead.

In a walled off partition behind the stables was a once

verdant garden with marble benches and a fountain shaped like a stallion pawing the air — all now gone wild. Word came to Yorn in town that it belonged to the late Duchess of Saron. Her husband could not bring himself to remove it, but it brought too many painful memories to keep it as she had.

Jezra dropped her gear and knelt upon the unkempt grass. Taking both hands and smearing them with blood from her wound, she rested her head and hands upon the ground and began to recite strange words.

Yorn watched in amazement as the wound slowly closed. He knew priests of the All God possessed the power to heal, but he would swear by that same god this woman was not one of his priests.

When the words stopped, she kissed the ground, raised up on her knees, and spread her arms wide. The shrill sounds she uttered loudly, this time, resembled bird noise.

He wasn't sure, but Yorn thought her noises were reciprocated. As she settled into a sitting position, she picked up the leather vest and replaced it, casually lacing the thin but sturdy strings in place. Here was the warrior he could never be. "You said your father told you that you should learn to keep them out. What does that mean?"

She gave him a hard stare. Instead of answering Yorn, Jezra stared across the greenery to the barren, brown wall behind. In her mind's eye, she saw her father's eagle aerie brother approach him with the look of one who wishes to present a petition. As with all aerie business, her father dismissed her.

Yorn waited, hoping she would say something.

Almost as if she were teaching lore to a child, she finally said, "The fertility ritual of spring fell on the night before I reached my status as breeder. I did not know what that meant. My father kept me away from that part of aerie life. I knew the closer that day drew the more unhappy he became. That as one of the great council, it was his duty to pass judgment on petitions presented to him without bias."

Yorn studied the strong-willed woman who reminded him so much of his older sister in spirit if not in looks. As hard as she tried, she could not banish the tears that welled up in her eyes — just as Laeith tried to dismiss her tears the day he rode away on the horse she bought him.

"The petition was to allow me to join the ritual that season, since it was but a matter of moon rays before it was my time anyway. The signatures on the petition came from men of power and rank. Any one of them he would gladly see me mated with should the ritual bear strong fruit. It is an honor to be chosen as wife after only one ritual come to term. If he denied the petition, he feared he would ruin my chances to secure myself a place of honor. He placed his mark of approval on the petition."

A muscle along her jawline began to twitch. Yorn wondered what would happen to him if he tried to smooth it away.

"There were many names attached."

Puzzled, Yorn asked, "Wouldn't that be a good thing? It would mean the petition was a popular one."

Jezra couldn't mask the horror on her face when she turned to look him full in the face. "Every name on that petition entered my hut that ritual night."

The color drained from Yorn's face as comprehension set in.

She waved her hand in the direction of the main house. "The women in that hut are fortunate. There are few to enter."

Yorn tried to settle his insides as he asked, "So you're married."

She understood that term. A wicked smile flickered across her lips. "No. I bring my father honor in a different way." Her hand rubbed her belly where the wicked scar was. "The first, he was powerful, but he was cruel, and he deceived the aerie. He drank something to make him more potent, and when he was done and the seer declared to him I had caught, he bribed her to remain silent until the last name had left. He didn't care if it put a question of the child's father. A child born from ritual to a pair not mated cannot carry the ancestor's line. It didn't matter whose child I carried — except to him."

"So why did he bribe her if it didn't matter?"

"The more that lay with me, the more who would envy this pairing, who would admire his," she struggled to find the right word, "ability?" Fresh anger made her words come hard in her throat. "He had done his aerie and his line well that night, catching eight others whose ... admirers ... did not. To sire so many during the ritual brings special honor and the favor of the council. They granted his request to ...." Her anger stopped her.

Yorn shook his head in disbelief. "But that would mean each woman is ...." A vision of his sisters forced to endure such barbarity made his shudder.

"It is our way. The ritual cannot be declared complete until the seer announces to the council the making of a fledgling — the survival of the aeries depends on it — which she did after his return."

"How do you know of his deception?"

Jezra frowned. "The old one told me. Many entered to form a fledgling and left to silence. The council fretted. How could my father have an empty daughter? And the deceiver made much noise of it. Boasting of the nine strong warriors his drink had given the aeries. Listening ears passed the tale to the old one. He ...," Jezra hesitated, "approved my petition to be a warrior."

"And your father?"

"The seer told the truth after I earned my place as warrior and took her bribe from her. Father granted the deceiver's petition to make me his mate in gratitude of saving my honor. IF he could win me. Against custom, he stole a kiss, so I drew blood from his lip. He laughed as he wiped the blood away."

Yorn shifted his legs to ease the cramping from sitting so long. "And you?"

Her smile was even more cruel. "I tasted his blood. I offered it to Kaylei in trade for revenge." She stared hard at Yorn. "No one goes inside," she hissed, "that I do not permit." Then her look softened slightly and her voice had less of an angry edge. "You are ... um ... different ... gentler on the inside I think. You know when you are unwelcome." The stillness of inactivity allowed the sound of crying to reach them. She looked at the faint line of a new scar, and her eyes hardened. "Not like that one. Him, I will have to kill."

Yorn swallowed hard.

# Chapter Thirty-Four
## Banton's Folly

"I can't just go waltzing into Banton's Folly," Artearis said in frustration.

Ronin agreed. He may not know who the Gaujo was, but he knew two things beyond doubt: The man worked hard, harder than many Folk — and that was saying something — and the weapons he carried were heirlooms crafted by one of the finest metalworkers that ever existed if Ronin's inspection of the blades ran true. Even in the Capitol he hadn't seen their like except hanging on the walls of the palace. If the Gaujo hadn't stolen the blades, his line held high rank and dated back to at least the ancient war. Only one exorcised from such a house would hide such fine blades.

As if reading his thoughts, Lucia whispered near his ear, "Two houses of high rank. One high enough to sit on the throne his ancestors spurned generations ago." By the tone of her words, Lucia seemed sad and angry.

Ronin stored this new information away. With arms crossed, he stood, tapping his forefinger against his elbow. His eyes took in the stained clothing and the practical sheathes belted around the Gaujo's waist. Those coverings weren't made for the weapons they protected.

From out of nowhere, Ronin asked, "Fighter by trade?"

"You could say that," said Artearis.

Lucia's laugh was harsh. "Better than any fighter you'll meet Ronin ... unless you meet another of his kind."

His kind? That remark unsettled Ronin.

"Are you only good with that thing," Ronin's hand gestured to the dagger Artearis had strapped to his side, "as a blade or can ...."

Before Ronin could finish his question, Artearis slipped free a knife from inside his sleeve and sent it into the center of the practice target resting against the prop cart.

"He'll do," Lucia said loud enough for everyone present to hear. To Ronin, she said more quietly, "Pray you never meet another of his kind." The elder disappeared into her wagon.

Ronin asked him if he could do that every time.

"Why?"

Timerus shuffled into Artearis's view. "Because I can't perform yet," he said bitterly. "They're trying to replace me." He waited for the backlash of words about his rash behavior, but none came.

Ronin frowned. "If you mean find a stand-in until you heal, yes." To Artearis, he asked, "How are you at throwing at live targets?"

"Standing still or moving?"

"Standing still."

His face was deadly serious when Artearis answered, "center mass every time."

Ronin ignored the angry mutterings from Timerus. "We don't ...."

Artearis let out an exasperated sigh. "I know what you want. I've had it described to me in detail and seen the performance twice many summers ago. How do you train a new knife thrower? Surely, you don't just stand someone in front of him and tell him to throw?"

Timerus snorted. "Of course, not. We use practice dummies."

Artearis all but ordered the two to show him. For the best part of the morning, he practiced putting Folk knives around the outline of a straw stuffed figure. On a whim, he made a double throw, sinking each knife a hand's width from where each ear would be. Vigorous clapping came from behind him. Sitting on a wagon seat was Alandran.

The boy cried excitedly, "You're as good as Timerus."

Artearis gave the boy a solemn bow.

Alandran jumped down from the wagon and ran up to Artearis, throwing his arms around the Gaujo's waist. "Really good. Too bad Lucia won't let you do a double throw in the show. She banned it. Said it was bad for business whatever that means."

Artearis ruffled the head of black hair in front of him. "It means, it's too easy for something to go wrong and frighten the customers away."

Alandran looked up at him. "Really?"

"Lucia cares about her people. She puts their safety first."

The boy nodded. "Just like Papa."

Artearis frowned. *Just who was this boy's family?*

Alandran tugged on his sleeve. "Can you teach me how to throw knives?"

It was a question Artearis could see himself asking at that age. He looked around the caravan. Rhealle had Timerus cornered next to the wagon assigned to her, and Ronin had been conscripted to help set up for the afternoon performance. The straw dummy waited for him to collect the knives. He walked to the practice target to retrieve them. Pulling the last one free, he flipped it over and over in his hand while he debated Alandran's request.

To the boy's credit, he waited patiently for Artearis to make up his mind. *Such an enigma, this boy. Much too young to act this grown up.* Then Artearis saw Lucia standing in the doorway of her wagon, watching the knife launch into the air and come down, as if she knew his thoughts, and her expression said she didn't like them. Artearis averted his eyes.

The knives were fairly well balanced but were heavy enough to require strength he doubted the boy possessed to make them fly true for any real distance, and knives weren't toys. Perching himself on a wooden stump left next to the practice ring, Artearis ran his thumb lightly along the edge of the blade, feeling for imperfections, while he tried to determine what to say.

"Aland."

Tears misted in the boy's eyes. "You won't teach me."

"I would if your papa AND Lucia gave consent, but I don't ...."

"No, they won't. Timerus started to last summer until Lucia found out."

"You knew this, and still you asked me?"

"You aren't like Timerus. You aren't ...."

"Rash?" Artearis provided for the boy.

Alandran nodded. "And people listen to you not like ...."

"Not like Timerus," Artearis finished.

The boy shook his head then nodded before growing still.

"Aland, why did your papa send you with the Folk?"

"This summer?" Alandran shrugged his thin shoulders.

Artearis caught the boy in his piercing stare. "This summer ... last summer ... the summer before?"

Alandran started to shrug his shoulders again, but the penetrating stare made his face burn red. He tumbled out, "I think because of the bad men."

Artearis cocked his head to one side as he eased up on the stare.

"Papa didn't say so, but he got real nervous after the riders came last spring. He even asked Granpapa for help. Papa doesn't ask Granpapa for anything. Not since Granpapa almost dis ... uh ...."

"Disinherited him?"

"Yeah that ... for marrying Mama ... so Croc said."

"Why didn't your Granpapa like your mama?"

"Oh, Granpapa loved Mama as much as he loved anyone. Everyone loved Mama. Granpapa didn't like the family Mama's sister married into. Said it tain ... um ...."

"Tainted?"

"Yes, tainted the line. Bad people that do bad things."

Artearis began to feel like he was walking along a dark

corridor to an execution chamber. In front of him was the door, and only not knowing would keep the door closed, but something inside him had to ask, "Aland do you know your Grandpa's family name?"

"Granpapa Morden or Grandpa Olney?"

In his mind, Artearis saw the door swing open. In the middle of the chamber was a chopping block. Beside the block was a hooded man with a long-handled axe.

Artearis took in every detail of the boy: his features, his build, his clothes, the way he stood quietly. "Aland, your Papa is the Duke of Saron."

Alandran's eyes grew wide. He put his finger to his lips, "Shhh. Lucia said never to say it here — ever."

"Lucia is a very wise woman." Artearis glanced around. Rhealle had vanished. Timerus struggled to lend Ronin a hand with some props, and Lucia had disappeared. He leaned close to the boy. "I won't teach you how to throw knives, but I will teach you a few ways to use one. But," he hissed, "you must keep it secret from everyone just like who your papa is."

"Everyone? Even Lucia?"

"Even Lucia. Even Ronin."

Alandran sucked in his breath.

"If you don't, I can't teach you."

Alandran shifted from one foot to the other.

"If I teach you, you must do exactly what I say with it.

A knife isn't a toy."

The thought of learning a grown up thing must have decided the boy. He straightened up tall. "I swear by Mama's soul not to tell."

Artearis studied the boy. "And to only use what I teach how I tell you to."

Alandran bobbed his head up and down. "Yes, I swear that, too, by Mama's soul."

Artearis nodded.

Alandran whispered, "Now?"

Glancing at the position of the sun, Artearis shook his head. "It will have to be after the evening performance if at all tonight. Meet me behind the little tent used for changing, and we'll find a quiet place."

Shaking his head, the boy said, "I can't. I'm not allowed to go to the performances. Lucia says it isn't safe."

Artearis wanted to smack himself on the forehead. Of course, it wouldn't be safe! "I'll find you at Ronin's wagon." He looked up to see Ronin and Timerus approaching the practice circle. "I have work."

The boy nodded.

"And Aland ...."

"Yes, Gaujo?"

"Don't wander from the wagons while we're near this town."

"Not you, too!"

Artearis gave him a questioning look.

Alandran let out a deep sigh. "Lucia AND Ronin said the same."

Patting the boy on his head, Artearis left him to his own devices.

It troubled Artearis that he was becoming used to the absence of Darethan's blades. It troubled him even more when his foray into the town proper revealed two men recruiting "help" for a job. One of those men asked a lot of questions about the Folk, and according to one source, a few too many about the Duke of Saron and his son.

After buying the man, Dalton, a few rounds at a local inn, he even gave up the number and descriptions of the help, chuckling to himself when he passed on vague information about the three cloaked strangers.

"Wish I coulda been there when Korvin met them," said Dalton, as he raised a full glass in the air. He downed it in one go and yelled at the innkeeper for another. "On this guy," he said, slapping Artearis across the back. The innkeeper all but slammed the new glass onto the bar. Artearis paid for the drink and added a little extra for the innkeeper's trouble. "Yea, ole Frisssk may jusss be fisssh bait by now." He laughed so hard he knocked over his drink.

"Another one ... better yet a whole bottle. On this nice bloke, of course."

Artearis shook his head at the innkeeper.

"That pretty boy with ole Frisssk ssshould be looking mighty handsssome by now."

The innkeeper's hand clawed into the cloth he was using to wipe up the spilled drink.

In a low voice, Artearis said, "Just one more."

Dalton heard him and yelled, "Make it a double!"

When the innkeeper waited for his approval, Artearis nodded.

Dalton tossed back the drink with a pleased sigh.

Both Artearis and the innkeeper watched as the obnoxious man slumped against the bar. Artearis used his knee to bump the man hard. When he slid to the floor, Artearis laid a few more coins on the bar. "For rent," he said as he turned to leave.

The bartender said, "Strange pairs these days."

Artearis stopped.

"No offense, mister."

"What do you mean?" Artearis said, straightening around to face the innkeeper.

"It's just ye and that pretty fella this one was a yammerin' about are to him and the other one like horses to mules. Ye may look similar, but ye sure don't behave the same. They's just plain mean, and ye two ...." The innkeeper shook his head and walked away.

Artearis leaned against the bar, thinking about the old man's words. A few minutes later, the old man shuffled back. He extended his hand. In it were more coins than what Artearis had given him.

"The boy did me right ... 'spite of his partner. Ye run across him, send him my way if'n he needs patchin' up. Name's Yorn"

Artearis looked at the coin. "What makes you think I'll see him?"

The innkeeper snorted. "Ye be lookin' for them like they was lookin' fer the lord and his boy says all that listenin'."

Artearis nodded. "Keep it. If he's still breathing, I'll pass along your message."

# Chapter Thirty-Five
## Disconcerting Outcomes

Frisk shook his head. "They'd have ta travel the main road with all those wagons. Be slow, easy targets. Too bad, there ain't some place to funnel them, stretch 'em out, make 'em even easier."

Justen frowned. "This is supposed to be recon not a raid. Figure out if the boy's there. If he is, snatch him and get. If he isn't, don't let them know we're around."

"Bah!" Zeke sneered. "Them Folk caravans get hit all the time ... by locals as well as brigands. They'll not put it together with us." He laughed. "At least, not until it don't matter."

Justen glared at Zeke. "They'll figure it out soon enough if we've got to pinch the boy."

Lounging against his latest acquisition, Korvin weighed the arguments of both of his reconnaissance specialists. Running his hand along the supple arm he held against his chest pulled his thoughts in a different direction. He liked this one much better than the blond thrust onto him by Geylas. Once he had broken her, she proved to be most accommodating. Still, there weren't enough diversions to keep his men occupied let alone the new crew. He needed to find some way for them to sate their restless mood.

A strike on a Folk caravan might be just the thing. At worse, he'd lose a hired muscle or two. He grinned. At best, he'd get the boy and booty. Folk women were said to be quite spirited. But who to send? He certainly couldn't send Justen and Zeke this time, not with them at odds. He'd learned that lesson with Frisk and Dalton. He could afford to lose Zeke. Donnie. Donnie had enough sense not to get himself killed.

"Zeke, take eight of the recruits out the back way. Circuit the town and head toward Banton's Folly. When you spot the Folk, hit them from the side not from the road. Donnie, give him a hand."

The trap specialist nodded.

Korvin shifted his position. "Finding the boy is the first priority. If he's there, Donnie, I want you to bring me word."

"And me," Zeke growled.

Korvin laughed. "You and your boys do what you do

best."

Korvin waited for Donnie to ask the question in his eyes.

"You said take eight. We have twelve. Which eight?"

This time Zeke burst out laughing.

Korvin said, "Leave the strangers. They make better guards than the rest."

"And you don't trust 'em," Zeke said.

"Not for this kind of work. If you really want to take that cold-blooded snake, Larosh, go ahead. Make it nine. The choice is yours. I don't really need him around here." He thought, *it might give me an opportunity to get my hands on his woman.* Korvin ran the side of his hand along his latest scar — although that one wasn't the one he most desired to get his hands on.

"Well, what are you waiting for? Go find me that boy!"

Two horses galloping at full speed toward Daric sent her hand to the sword strapped at her side. Assassins might not train for mounted combat, but the military did. She only wished she'd found time for more practice while inside the Guild as the distance between her and the unknown horsemen decreased. She considered angling off in a southwesterly direction but realized they had probably

405

already seen her, too. Then again it was just after dawn, and they were headed east. As the gap closed further, her hand tightened around the hilt.

Tension flowed out of her when the riders kept to their fast pace, passing her without so much as a glance at her or her uniform. She, however, scrutinized them. Both were male. She could see as they passed that one had a makeshift bandage around his thigh; the other cradled his arm against his chest as if someone or something had seriously injured it.

Perhaps riding around in military dress wasn't such a good idea right now. She couldn't afford to lose time helping people sort out whatever was going on up the road.

Daric reined in her mount and grabbed a set of plain traveler's clothes from the right saddlebag. Sliding off the horse, she used it as a shield between her and the road in case any more refugees came her way.

To help sell the new her, she led her horse to the stream running parallel to the northern edge of the road and liberally smeared mud on his chest and legs. She walked the horse alongside the stream, waiting for the mud to dry enough to flake off the thicker areas so it didn't look like she'd been riding in the stream but enough to make a passing look miss the quality of her mount.

It might even be a good idea to cross the stream and follow the north bank until she either came to a safe town or had to cross the river separating her and Hisanth. Daric didn't like the idea of riding into the coastal town nearly blind, but she couldn't risk someone identifying her as either military or assassin out here. This was territory stacked with supporters loyal to Zotearis, and Jekan Geylas had shown way too much interest in Gessin for her to feel safe trading for information there. Perhaps Banton's Folly. A day's ride at most for her horse.

She patted his nose and mounted. Zellen had done her proud. They'd made good time until they got to Sitar. If not for the tension in that city, Daric would have ridden through without a thought, but Geylas had been plotting something when he came to Guild headquarters, and from the look of the mutilated, and headless, corpse swinging by its arms under the gallows, he'd started his campaign against the Guild. Then she'd caught rumors that he'd sent an armed force to the west, but a day trying to discover why proved fruitless.

Daric added that tidbit to the rest of the intel she needed to pass on in Saron, tucked herself into the hidey hole of the rundown stable yard Arteris kept for emergencies that night, and headed toward Saron as early as she could safely get out of Sitar.

The shock she'd gotten at the Guild's inn in Saron rattled her so much she nearly got arrested barging into the protector's office dressed in her assassin's garb.

Fortunately, Uncle Hereticus was within easy reach and could verify her identity. She spewed out her report so fast she wasn't sure anyone had made sense of it and darted out before her uncle could assign her new duties or start asking involved questions.

That's when she literally bumped into the last person she expected to find in Saron. Gregory Barnes pulled her to a quiet alley and sketched her in on his meeting with Artearis in Ionen and the Guild Leader's impromptu trip to Hisanth, so Hisanth was where Daric headed.

As three more riders sped past on the road, Daric was grateful she still traveled alongside the stream. She picked up the horse's pace, keeping a wary eye on the road in front and a trained ear on the road behind.

No more riders passed her by the time the sun reached mid-morning. She angled her mount toward the road and pulled to a halt when she saw the camp stretched out in front of her. She'd either have to cross the stream and travel over unknown ground or circle wide to the south if she wanted to avoid notice.

Running her hand along Zellen's neck, she decided it wasn't fair to put him through either choice. She'd just have to take her chances riding past it and hope for the best.

Her luck failed her this time. No sooner had she come within easy range of the camp than half a dozen armed men spread out around her to stop her progress. The meaty one in front swinging a huge club was presumably the leader.

Daric knew she could take him alone but with five more to back him up? She could risk a wide arc on the south side, but there again she would be taking a chance with her already stressed horse.

She could always pull her military card, even though she preferred not to. While thinking, she stroked Zellen's neck until the stallion whinnied in irritation at his master's unusual behavior.

When Daric finally decided she'd try the diplomatic approach, she realized there weren't six men closing around her but seven. The seventh was tall, thin, and blonde with a sword in one hand and a dagger in the other. She sighed in relief.

"Boss."

The familiar voice startled Artearis. After conducting a more thorough appraisal to be sure, he strode through the front line to meet his blood guard. Keeping his voice low, he said, "You aren't supposed to be here."

Daric leaned forward. "I have news that can't wait."

Artearis held up his hand. Retracing his steps to Armon, he asked the Folk's security man to give him time to find Lucia.

Armon nodded but said, "That one comes no nearer."

Artearis agreed and headed back to the main

gathering area where Ronin and Timerus waited to see what this new intruder foretold. Artearis didn't bother to explain as he marched past them to Lucia's door.

Corsanth answered the knock. Seeing who it was and that Artearis did not grip his weapons as he did when he was agitated, the elder permitted him entry. For nearly a quarter of an hour, Artearis contended with Lucia to gain Daric entry into the camp.

Rubbing his temples, he finally exclaimed, "I need to know what's going on." Lucia and Corsanth exchanged looks.

Corsanth asked her, "Does the one who is bound to him pose a threat to us?"

When Lucia said no, Corsanth replied, "Then I will grant her sanctuary until we reach a town."

Lucia didn't look happy. "One is bad. Two is ...." She tensed and turned away.

Corsanth accompanied Artearis to Armon where he informed the protector of the visitor's new status. Armon offered his assistance. Daric, collecting the reins of her horse, thanked the man but politely declined and led her horse to the stream to wash the mud away. Artearis followed.

He kept his voice low when he demanded to know why his blood guard had left the compound. Seeing Daric's shoulders bunch under her worn shirt, he knew he wasn't going to like the answer.

"Zotearis staged a takeover after he completed the

ritual of the fifth circle."

Artearis clenched his hand around his sword hilt.

"Jastis is dead and Ronin and Kera. Leyana got three trainees out, but no one knows where they went. Lorr made it out, too. He was last seen in Saron. Artearis," she said in her soft, deep voice, "Zotearis has a kill order out on you. He's labeled you a traitor to the Guild."

His other hand wrapped itself around his dagger and squeezed.

Daric continued. "To make it worse, the Duke of Sitar has men looking for you ... men sent in this direction."

Artearis frowned. Now the activity in Banton's Folly made sense. Twelve thugs to kill one boy was overkill. Twelve thugs to kill the Head of the Assassins Guild was prudent but poor judgment.

He waited for Daric to finish tending her horse before leading both toward his niche by the fire. They had just circled around Lucia's wagon when a dark-headed mass ran into his legs and hugged them.

Daric looked from Artearis to the boy. Artearis watched her struggle to keep a composed face. Somehow, she knew who the boy was. Not far behind Alandran came a giant of a man who introduced himself as Ronin. Again, Daric lost her composure for the briefest of moments, but long enough for Artearis to register it. The second time didn't come as a surprise, for Artearis had gotten a similar shock when

Timerus finally introduced the blacksmith to him. Daric took the outstretched hand and gave it a firm shake.

"A blacksmith's grip, or it should be," he said, giving Daric one of his rare smiles.

Daric returned the compliment with a polite bow.

Donnie fought through the pain in his arm to break the news to Korvin that a sweep of the Folk camp didn't turn up any sign of the boy. Korvin received a similar report from each of the thugs as they returned. Donnie took himself off to have his arm looked at by a healer in town when the trap specialist saw the signs that said Korvin had lost his patience with this lot.

When the answers to his questions came too slowly, Korvin unsheathed the long knife he carried in his waistband, slammed the hand of the man in front of him onto the table, and hacked the pinkie off it. "Where is Zeke?!"

One of the others muttered, "He didn't make it."

Another said, "We're lucky to get back. Them Folk fight like demons."

"And you're sure there weren't no boy?" Frisk barked.

All three nodded their heads vigorously.

Korvin shoved the sniveling fool in front of him out of his way. He didn't mind the loss of the five crew fodder, but

Zeke! And, he was still clueless about the boy. The only answer could be Morden hauled the boy with him when he ran off to Saron.

"Justen pack up. You and Donnie are headed to Saron."

# Chapter Thirty-Six
## A Touchy Situation

As much as Daric detested people who abused their mounts, she rode Zellen hard when Gessin appeared on the horizon. Artearis had given a brief but detailed sketch of the plots boiling over in Hisanth and the attack on the fort. Daric figured she could use that as her in, but that would mean looking the part, and a fresh horse wouldn't do. She pounded past a rundown tavern on her left to finally slow her pace as a stable appeared on her right.

She tossed her reins to the stable hand who emerged from inside. "Where do I find the Lord of this town?"

The lanky man snorted. "Heck if anyone in town knows. Some says at his manor. Some says Saron. Some says the cemetery."

That set Daric back on her heels. So much for playing messenger.

"Last word from the Gallows is he's retired ... or soon will be. Don't really matter to me."

Daric scowled. "Does taking care of my horse matter to you?"

The man shrugged. "What I gets paid to do."

Sliding off Zellen, she pulled three coppers from her purse and tossed them at his feet. When he bent to pick them up, she brought her dagger blade up against his throat.

He swallowed hard.

She gave him a callous smile. When it was clear they understood each other, she asked, "Where is this Gallows?"

"The long way or the short?"

"Short."

"Not much for seeing the town, huh?" At her severe stare, he shrugged and said, "Cross the field behind the stables. Take you to Sandling road. You walk straight enough, be in front of you."

Daric tossed another copper on the ground. This time the stable hand was more cautious in leaning down to pick it up.

The man's directions were surprisingly accurate, considering his manner. It was still a trek, and Daric's stomach reminded her she hadn't eaten since last night. The smells coming from inside the Gallows didn't inspire her to find food here and neither did the outside.

It was big for an inn — two stories for most of it except the front room, but Daric wouldn't want to take a room on the second floor, not if the frames falling apart around the windows and the warped and cracked boards of the entryway were any indication of the soundness of the place.

From the loud grunts and squeals coming from above, others weren't so particular. A half-naked woman darted down the stairs, laughing, as a stocky, bald man tumbled down after while trying to pull up his trousers.

"Hey, keep it in your room. This ain't no brothel!"

Stopping in front of the innkeeper, she pursed her lips into a pout. Pecking his cheek, she turned around and scooped up her companion's arm, leading him up the stairs.

The innkeeper eyed Daric coldly. "If you be thinking of bunking here, boy, you'd best remember what I said. I don't repeat myself."

Daric weighed the heavy-built man carefully. The shifty eyes warned Daric staying here would cost quite a bit more than the price of a room. In her best harried traveler voice, she said, "Right now I'd prefer a more relaxing pastime."

"Well, we don't do relaxing here. If you aren't eating or needing a room or ...." He did his own sizing up of Daric, "wanting to test your luck, find someone else's time to waste."

More squeals drifted from upstairs. She hitched her pack higher on her shoulder and walked out but not before letting him see his last words had peaked her interest.

"We run 'em all day and most of the night, boy."

And collect a tidy sum from those gullible enough to play, she thought.

After another two hours of traversing the circular Sandling road, Daric wanted to smack herself for not bothering to ask directions to a better part of town. By the standards of the other places she passed, the Gallows was actually above par.

The people here matched the buildings: worn, rundown, and not much for talking. They didn't particularly hate the Duke; they simply had too many worries to care about him.

She finally reached a major intersection. The tantalizing smell of pastries convinced her to keep to her current route. The raspberry turnover she purchased set her stomach to complaining for more. The baker knew appreciation when she saw it; she offered Daric another at half price and a loaf of good bread for a reasonable one.

"Just up the road is a quality meat vendor. Tell him Mindy sent you, and he'll make sure you get fresh."

Daric gave her a grateful smile. "Got a suggestion for a place to put my head?"

"If you want fleeced, take a room at the Gallows. Lonnie will treat you better at the Winds of Fortune. He's fair, and he minds his own business."

Daric started to offer her thanks when two men shoved open the door of the shop and pushed her off to the side.

"Korvin says to cut the bread delivery in half." When the woman started to protest, the ruffian backhanded her, leaving a sizable bruise on her cheek.

Daric itched to return the favor.

"What do you think about her, Tully?"

The ruffian shook his head. "Naw, too porky for us. Besides, there'd go Korvin's pastries, and that wouldn't make it pleasant."

The other one pouted. "I want fresh meat. Them others been pounded on way too much."

"Wag, old buddy, wouldn't you want fresh, sweet meat?"

As they left, Daric heard the one called Wag say, "What'd ya have in mind?"

Tully laughed. "Two delectable dishes ...." The door and distance cut off the rest.

The baker shook her head. "The first ones set up shop here were bad enough. The ones they dragged in after are real terrors. I'll be lucky to break even while they're still here. Demanding goods ... changing orders ... putting off paying," she muttered more to herself than Daric.

Daric patted her arm in sympathy. "I'll take one of those loaves they don't want."

The baker patted her on the shoulder. "That's mighty kind of you, son, but it'll be fine. Now get on to Renfry's before he runs out of fresh meat. Then again ...." She turned back to her counter.

Daric's stomach agreed. She continued up the street. Renfry's meat shop sat a bit back from the road. In front were some tables where people could stop and eat what they purchased from him.

She stopped into the general store next door long enough to buy something to drink and spread her purchases upon one of the tables. Her brothers would be proud of her the way she wolfed her food down — just like one of them. Her father always said she made a better son than either of them.

As she sat there letting her food settle, Daric wondered if it wasn't time for the daughter to make an appearance. People tell women different things than they do men.

She remembered seeing an old clothing shop on the road that wound around to here. Retracing her steps, she went inside, pretending she was looking for something to bring to a sweetheart back home. The scruffy girl lounging on a stool didn't seem to care one way or the other. She took

Daric's coin without really looking at it and tossed it in a box on a shelf beside her. Daric rolled up the blouse, skirt, and scarf she bought and shoved the lot into her pack.

When she exited the darkened shop, she realized the day was getting on, and she still didn't have a place for the night. Back along the road she went toward the baker's. This time she headed right at the fork. She followed the new road until she saw the Market Square Mindy told her about. When she drew even with the dairy stall Mindy used as a landmark, she headed north.

Thankfully, this inn had a stable attached to it, too. She peeked inside. The stalls were much cleaner than the one she found on coming into Gessin. She'd collect Zellen once she'd negotiated housing for both of them. Daric was about to leave the stable when a rough-looking man stormed out of the inn. "I don't care a rat's ass where you served old man. You're here now, and until we say otherwise, this is our town."

Daric backed into the nearest stall. Must be another of this Korvin's crew. The man who stalked past looked like he'd be part of some goon squad: close cut hair, bad attitude, impatient stride, hard face. She wasn't sure she'd want to be in the same room with him. Only one of them would be walking out of it. She'd bet he served, too. All the ex-military she'd ever met had an air about them from their time spent serving. He was no different.

If this Lonnie really was an ex, too, he might be sympathetic to another soldier, maybe be a little loose with town gossip. She dug out her uniform.

The innkeeper seemed pretty calm, considering the threats leveled at him a few moments before. At first, Daric thought she'd have to ease her way into friendly banter with the man, but one look at her uniform and he was quick to pour a mug of ale and slap it down on the counter, saying "on the house."

Daric grinned and raised the mug in a salute.

"If you's looking for a room, I still got one available. But you best be taking it quick. What with the harvest celebration starting and all." He gave her a friendly wink.

Daric's grin widened. "Got room for a horse, too?"

Lonnie's face took on a mock frown. "Don't know's if a horse would fit in the bed with you. It's mostly made for one."

She laughed. She liked this large man with kind, brown eyes and salt and pepper hair in a ring around his bald top. Then her eyes fell on his left hand or what was left of it. He saw where her gaze stopped.

"Souvenir of my last campaign. Never seen creatures like on that island. Vicious things. Not sure it's worth the trouble to harvest the trees there. But enough of that. How long you wanting to stay?"

The question caught her off guard. When she and Artearis decided on her going into Gessin first, they hadn't discussed how long they'd be here.

Lonnie must have picked up on her indecision. "Tell you what. You pony up five silver, and I'll keep your room for you until you're ready to leave. We can settle up then."

Daric thanked him.

"Where'd you leave your horse? I didn't hear a beast when you came in."

She told him about leaving Zellen at that questionable stable just inside town until she found a better place.

"Tch. That's no place to leave a nag, let alone a quality beast. I'll send Breesa for it. You go drop your gear off in the room at the end of the hall upstairs and bring yourself back down. I'll tell Darna to fix you up some grub. Double quick, now. Darna doesn't take kindly to people letting her cooking getting cold."

Daric hadn't enjoyed a meal, or the company, this much in a long time. Apparently, Lonnie had quite a colorful career while he served, and he wasn't sheepish about sharing his experiences. As the hour grew late, Daric assured herself Zellen was well tended before turning in for a restful sleep.

She liked Lonnie and his family but not enough to trust him with her secret — not yet. The next morning, she left dressed in her uniform with her pack slung over her shoulder. Stopping to check on Zellen, she changed into the women's clothing she picked up the day before. From snatches of conversation between Lonnie's daughters, Daric chose to hang around the main marketplace she skirted yesterday.

Her decision proved profitable. Two more of Korvin's thugs made trouble for the stall owners at the marketplace. Both complained bitterly about the lock down Korvin was imposing at sundown. "Even if we manage to sneak out before, there's no way we're getting back in undetected with 'them' watching," said one to the other.

The second man said, "Frisk 'll get what we need. He and Tebbin. They got their marks picked out already. Gonna teach that fat snob a lesson he won't forget."

Daric didn't like what she heard, but she was running out of time. Artearis figured the Folk would make it to town sometime today, and by the buzz in the marketplace, they had. She changed back into her traveling garb and headed to the staging area assigned to the Folk.

# Chapter Thirty-Seven
## That Annoying Itch

The display before Daric astonished her. Gone were the drab wagons and plain clothing. The wagons providing the makeshift backdrop of the stage for the performance area were decked out in brightly colored streamers and intricately designed banners of magnificent creatures. A highly detailed rendering of a keekii bird on a dark blue background fluttered next to a side view of a dragon done on a daring shade of green.

Off to the right, some Folk practiced tossing and catching various objects: from plateware to torches to shiny metal rings. In the center, more Folk were tossing each other into the air and coming down doing twists and rolls. On the left, in front of a straw target, Artearis stood deep in conversation with a black-haired Folk of athletic build. Artearis spun around, releasing a knife just before stopping himself in front of the target. The knife struck two inches above and to the left of the straw head.

The black-haired man frowned. "She won't like it," Daric heard him say as she approached.

"Timerus, it's all about the timing. If you give the throw a bit of a lead before you come square with it, the worse that can happen is it will go wide before it reaches the target. Stretch a large piece of canvas in back of the target if you're worried about what's behind."

Timerus didn't look convinced.

"Talk to Ronin. I'm sure he can figure out additional safety measures. Maybe mark the backdrop so you know when to release." When Timerus remained silent, Artearis said, "It's not like you'll be performing that trick tonight."

The frown eased.

Daric gave Artearis a questioning look.

"We're trying to spice up the knife throwing act."

"You mean you're trying to spice it up," Timerus said, reproachfully. "Lucia isn't amenable to my ... um ... deviations."

"Because you don't think them all the way through. Lucia puts safety first. If you miss your mark, instead of releasing late and risk injuring your assistant, you can make another spin an impromptu part of the act like a count of one

... spin ... two ... spin ... three and release. If it really worries you, have a special target made up and use that for this part of the act. Maybe a large plant or a statue or some banners?"

Timerus shrugged. "I'll think about it."

"You'd better rest that arm if you're going to take the evening performance."

Daric found a movable stump to perch upon.

"How did it go?" Artearis asked her after he was sure no one could hear.

"I found out more than I expected." She started with the rumors about the Duke. From there, she filled him in on the crew that had made themselves at home in Gessin during the Duke's absence. The prevailing belief is Morden hired them to counter any unexpected surprises in his absence, but some believe he doesn't know they're here. "They aren't the kind of men he hires."

From what she could determine, seven originally made the Gallows their base but moved to new quarters just before more men joined them. The best guess is they've taken over the Duke's own residence. At least, that's where deliveries of meat and baked goods are made each day even though he's not here." She did note she hadn't had time to verify that intel herself.

"They must have had some kind of setback because they slashed their standing orders in half yesterday."

That bit of news worried Artearis. "The attack on the

Folk the day before yesterday cost the attackers. We counted five bodies, and some that got away weren't in the best of shape."

"Well, this Korvin who's in charge is getting paranoid. He's tightening the reins on his men and increasing security. And, whoever he's putting on the night watch must be pretty damn good because some of the crew are trying to figure out how to get a hold of their 'entertainment' before the lock down tonight."

Artearis didn't look happy. "So, we have an unconfirmed count of nine and most likely more."

Daric nodded.

"I need to get a look at Lathan Morden's manor."

"I've set up camp at a place called the Winds of Fortune. The innkeeper is ex-military. He keeps a watchful eye on the place, but otherwise, he minds his own business. Follow that secondary road," Daric pointed at the slightly rutted road that circled north then east. "It ends at the main road north. The inn is farther south along a narrower street. The manor is east of the intersection. Past what passes for their aristocrats' outdoor market." Daric could see him storing away everything she said. "But like I said, come nightfall getting inside for recon is going to be nearly impossible. The best I can do is check my new connections around town to see if I can put together a layout of the place."

Artearis nodded. "You do that. I'm still going to pay it a visit."

Something still wasn't right. Korvin absently stroked the hair of the woman kneeling before him as his mind turned over the most disturbing problem he faced. Where was Artearis Berain? The boy he could deal with when Korvin's men unearthed him, as they would eventually. Berain? Well, Berain was trained by the best. If the man needed to disappear, he would ... until it was time to come out of hiding to fulfill his contract, and Geylas swore the assassin was headed for Gessin. Had to be here by the Harvest Festival which started today, yet Berain was nowhere to be found. The only other 'in' Korvin could see was the Folk. He cursed himself for not sending a man on the Folk raid who could identify the guild leader by sight.

He yanked the woman to her feet. "Find me Frisk!"

She reached for the cloth beside her.

The sneer on his face warned her that her time was up. "Don't bother. Find him, and do it quick. If you aren't quick enough," he laughed, "there are some men who are dying to get a shine from my latest trophy."

Korvin was too caught up in this frustrating problem to do more than straighten his pants as he began pacing the length of the room.

An irritated Frisk didn't look happy at being disturbed during his raid planning, but Korvin didn't care. "You can spot Artearis Berain if you see him, right?"

Frisk's annoyance turned to interest. "I seen him. When he was a boy. When his bastard of a father gave me my necklace." His finger unconsciously slid under the scarf around his neck near one ear and slid under it to stop at the other ear. "And again when my old crew was hired to pinch him before his old man locked him away in that underground fort. Why?'

"The boy isn't our only target."

Frisk's interest melted into anger. "Berain, really? And you didn't bother to let ME in on this? Why not?"

Korvin snorted. "Because there can't be any mistakes with Berain, and you ... well, you get wild when it gets ... personal."

Frisk's anger didn't lessen. "Well, I can tell you he ain't been seen around town. Those pretty features of his would stick out in a town full of roughnecks. Too noble-looking like that bitch of a mother of his."

That's what Korvin thought. "The Folk."

Frisk's interest reappeared. "Really? You think they'd harbor such a deadly snake? Still ... you'd have thought one of the boy's woulda mentioned him."

"Not if they'd never seen him ... and not if we hadn't

told them to watch for him. Most of 'em you brought back don't get high marks for being bright."

Frisk chuckled. "Yep. Just the way I like 'em. Easy to hire. Easy to control. Easy to turn loose to create havoc."

Korvin laughed. "You find him, you make sure he comes looking for us."

"Can I kill him?"

Korvin's laugh tightened. "If you think you can get away with it. If you can't, be the bait. Cause a distraction to lure him. Whatever. Just get him here."

Frisk nodded as he strode to the hall.

Korvin's laugh became sadistic. "Oh, and Frisk. Make sure you bring me another diversion when you return. I hope the boys enjoy the old one."

Hearty laughter echoed along the hallway marking Frisk's passage. Korvin's grew loud enough to match when he heard Frisk say, "All yours, boys." An evil smile settled on Korvin's lips as the men vied for a turn. *Throw them a bone, and you own their souls.*

Other than changing into his costume, Artearis had nothing left to prepare for the afternoon performance. He used the time to do his own recon. Daric may not have set eyes on the manor, but her intel was too accurate for his liking. It was going to take him most of the night to clear the place once he decided to go in. His stint with the Folk was done after this show, so he needed somewhere to stay while he figured this out.

Daric's directions for finding the Winds of Fortune Inn were just as reliable. Artearis opened the door of the sturdy building. He might not know construction work, but someone took pains to keep this place in shape. The man who greeted him may not have taken the same pains with his own appearance, but he hadn't let himself go either.

The man took his time sizing up Artearis before he extended his hand. "Name's Lonnie. How can I be of service?"

He was friendly enough, all things considered from Daric's report. "I'm in need of a room, and a friend recommended this place." Artearis looked around. The same care was lavished on the inside.

Lonnie frowned. "Not much left with the festival and all."

*Dammit, Daric, why didn't you tell me that part?* "Anything you've got. I'll only be needing it for a few days." Artearis could see Lonnie doing more than sizing him up. "I didn't plan on needing a room." Artearis shrugged. "Plans change."

"I've got a space up in the attic. Charge you two silver up front and the rest when you hie outta here. It's hot and dusty, but you can stretch out in peace."

Artearis was tempted to kick Daric up there and confiscate her room. Well, it was better than the alternatives. He dug two silver out of his purse.

"Anything else I can do for you?" Lonnie sniffed the air. "Darna's got a nice stew on the fire. Smells mighty close to being done."

Artearis accepted. "Keep it light if you would. I'm not fond of a big meal during the day."

Lonnie chuckled. "A wise man takes his meals when and how he can get them." He ambled into the kitchen, returning with a medium sized bowl. While Artearis ate, the innkeeper regaled him with stories from his military days. They weren't the heroic tales Artearis was expecting. They were about the quirky things that happen, sometimes funny and sometimes not. Daric had been right about Lonnie, too. That seemed odd for a merchant's daughter joining the Assassins Guild for revenge. Artearis stowed his gear in the space assigned to him before heading back to the Folk for his final performance.

Korvin was right to think Frisk would go off script where that bastard's son was concerned. "Try to take me out 'cause you think I ain't assassin material, will ya?" he muttered to himself.

"What'd ya say?" Tebbin asked him.

Frisk focused on their supply specialist. *Well, coming up with men was sorta like getting supplies.* "I said, you head over to the Gallows and get that fat lout to pony up a dozen or so thugs. He owes us after all the gold we funneled into his shitty place. When you got 'em, head over to the Winds of Fortune and make yourselves at home outside. Keep those inside in and those outside out. Got it?"

Tebbin didn't look too happy, but right now Frisk didn't give a crap about Tebbin's feelings. He almost wished it was Yorn with him. The snooty boy was too uppity for Frisk's liking, but he kept himself professional.

"Where're you goin'?"

Frisk's jaw clenched. "To take care of Korvin's other orders."

He cut down and around Gessin's seedier part of town to come upon the Folk wagons from the other side. Most of the crowds wandering over that way were making their way to the main road side, and Frisk wanted to scope things out before losing himself in a crowd of people who didn't particularly like him.

His caution paid off. The show was in full swing when Frisk arrived. People packed the northern and eastern sides. Mostly overflow drifted to the southern side of the caravan. Dressed in a gaudy shirt with ribbons flapping in the wind and even gaudier pants covered with reflective sequins was the object of Frisk's hunt throwing knives at a wooden board with a very attractive woman standing in front of it. *Why hadn't those fools brought this treat back with them?*

Frisk weighed his options. He'd never get close enough to stick the assassin in the back. One of his old crew had tried that on a bodyguard the day they tried to pinch the kid. It was like the man had eyes in the back of his head. The poor bloke was dead before he'd figured out his mistake.

No, if Frisk wanted to take Berain out, he'd have to do it from a distance. Frisk scooted his way into the crowd just far enough to draw level with the assassin's back. He pulled a dagger free and flipped it over so the point rested in his palm.

As Artearis released his knife at the woman, Frisk sent his hurling at the assassin, but like the bodyguard, it was as if Berain possessed eyes in the back of his head. He dropped straight down, letting the knife sail over him and strike the wooden backing.

People around Frisk tensed and quieted. Well, his plan to eliminate the assassin didn't work, but Frisk could pretty much guarantee his next move would get Berain's attention AND keep him occupied long enough for Frisk to fade away. He wasn't worried about the assassin tracking him.

As loud as he could, Frisk yelled, "Artearis Berain, you

bloody assassin!"

# Chapter Thirty-Eight
## Alandran

Artearis heard the satin-like *woosh* and dropped. A dagger quivered in the wooden backing about the height of his heart in his body. He snapped himself off the ground and scrutinized the crowd for clues to his attacker, narrowing in on the rough tough with the burning eyes just as the man yelled his name. Artearis didn't need to look around to know that now the crowd was focusing on him.

He backed up to the first wagon of the semi-circle. Standing beside it were three cloaked figures. He took them to be a threat, too, until he realized the easy stance they all had and that curiosity filled the three pair of eyes that followed his actions, like people watching an entertaining play.

One of the banners affixed to his arm slapped him across the face from the wind that finally picked up the pace it had been threatening to acquire all morning. He needed cover. The cloaks gave him an idea.

Without stopping to think, he headed toward the three and made a grab for the cloak nearest the road. His mark was more alert than Artearis at first thought. He grabbed the loose cloth and pulled it back in place but not before Artearis saw the strange artwork underneath. He knew he didn't have time for a second shot. Skirting past the three, he made his way to the rugged area south of the town and bolted into a run.

Alandran stared at the feathers woven into the hair of the strangers lounging by Armon's wagon. He'd never ever heard Papa talk about people wearing feathers like that. He looked hard at them, trying to decide from which birds they came when one of the cloaks flew open. The strange designs on the man's arm sparked Alandran's imagination so that when they quietly agreed to leave, he tagged along after.

In the crowd, the boy had a hard time keeping up with the three. He could duck under and slip between people, but they seemed to flow around obstacles in their way. Still, Alandran was determined to follow.

He was proud of how well he kept them in sight until a hand seized him by the collar of his shirt as he reached the northern road where they turned to follow the main one. Alandran struggled to break free from his captor. He sucked in a lungful of air to let out a scream for help.

Before he had fully inhaled, a hand clamped down hard over his mouth. An arm pinned him against muscled flesh and hauled him off his feet.

"Take him to the inn stables," Tebbin said. "We'll wait for Frisk there."

Disgustingly stinky breath blew on his neck, as the man holding him grunted.

Alandran did his best to worm his way free, but the man only held on tighter.

Frisk didn't look pleased with what he saw. "I thought I told you a dozen or more, not seven."

"It's all that rotten innkeeper could dig up on short notice," Tebbin told him. "But we did fill another order." Tebbin waved the burly captor forward. "Caught him roaming the streets."

Frisk's displeasure vanished. Eyeing the man holding the boy, he said, "Hand him over to those two. I need you inside. You two," he pointed at two other husky men, "you secure both girls. You there," he snapped at a thin, lanky-haired man staring at his toes, "You help them. If they give you too much trouble, knock 'em out, but don't damage their faces. Korvin likes to do that himself. And don't get any ideas about them. Korvin breaks 'em in, and I hand 'em off when we're done with 'em."

At the grumbles and mutterings, Frisk said, "Don't worry. Do your job, and you'll get your share. Just not first."

The hulking thug who turned the boy over asked belligerently, "What ya want o' me?"

The evil grin that appeared on Frisk's face scared the big man straight. "I want you to beat the shit out of that innkeeper. That goes for the rest of you lame excuses for a crew. Let's go!"

The two keeping watch over the boy grew bored after ten minutes had passed and no one reappeared from the inn. One muttered, "Why do the big louts get all the fun? We can kick 'em when they're down just as good as they can."

Alandran perked up when the two started whining to each other. He eased the knife Artearis had given him from his boot. When the one undid his pants to relieve himself, Alandran plunged the blade into the leg of the other man and ran for it.

The wounded one let out an ear-splitting scream. His partner fumbled to get his pants fastened but not fast enough. Frisk barreled out of the inn with the rest in tow. He ordered the two struggling with their squirming baggage to get them back to the manor and the rest to take off after the boy. To the two delivery boys, he hissed, "You don't make it back with them, you'd better be dead."

As hard as he tried, Alandran couldn't run fast enough. Then he saw Timerus ahead of him, calling his name frantically. The boy changed direction, running straight into Timerus's arms.

The band of thugs closed the gap, circling the two. The hateful glare Frisk gave the other townspeople on the street sent them scurrying away. Yanking the boy from Timerus, he ordered his men to take care of the problem. He picked up their prize and headed back to the manor, laughing harder with each thump and crunch.

Ronin and Corsanth had sent Timerus on ahead while they scoured the road between the vardo and the town intersection. Rhealle refused to be left behind. Despite the chaos at the knife throwing act, most of the townspeople remained for the show, leaving the road lightly occupied, as more people headed to see the Folk. By the time the three reached a proper street, even the buildings were shuttered.

Rhealle stopped and grabbed Ronin's arm. When the blacksmith finally determined what had caught her attention, he swore softly, startling Corsanth. Just ahead, lying on the ground was the battered body of their friend. The three rushed forward.

A sigh of relief escaped Ronin when Timerus drew in air to speak. "Alandran."

Rhealle leaned over Timerus to examine the extent of his injuries. Tears welled up in her eyes at the damage.

In a quiet voice, Corsanth said, "There's a decent healer not far from Morden's residence. Can you get him there, Ronin?"

For an answer, Ronin knelt down and scooped the broken man up into his arms.

"This way."

Rhealle followed the two men.

The people of Gessin were either too terrified of assassins to give chase, or they thought the whole thing was part of the act. *Well, they could be bad at hunting down people,* Artearis silently amended. Damn but he really wished he'd had more time to get the lay of this town. Keeping distance between himself and the dilapidated shops, he skirted the edge until the open market came into view.

He'd removed the streamers, but he couldn't do anything about the sequins on his pants except remove the pants, and that would probably cause more of a stir than the sequins. The best he could do was casually stroll along the road between the square and the shops until he came to the narrow road that led to the Winds of Fortune. He ducked inside the front door at the first opportunity only to get a nasty shock.

Stretched out on the floor of his own inn was Lonnie — his left leg bent in an unnatural angle and his half hand shapeless as if someone had smashed the bones still remaining in it. Darkening bruises covered the man's face and arms where his rolled up sleeves exposed flesh.

Arteais leaned over and checked for a pulse. He started to debate where the innkeeper might keep healing supplies when the smell of something burning caught his attention. Lonnie's daughters. He darted into the kitchen. A large pot boiled over, emptying its contents on the fire below, but no women. Arteais tore through the entire inn, shoving open doors to empty guest rooms and searching the cellar and even his space in the attic. Nothing. He hurried back down the stairs to see if he could get anything out of the innkeeper.

From talking with the merchants who made regular deliveries to the Duke's manor, Daric had formed a good idea of the layout of the grounds and the main floor except for a cluster of rooms on the west side. Standing outside of the residence, she kicked aside the bundle of meat lying on the grass under the tree where she took shade. People were coming and going too sporadically for her to slip in to get a firsthand view. Even if they believed she was a delivery person, whoever was guarding the entrance wasn't letting anyone in who wasn't expected.

Daric let out a nasty string of curses that would have done her brothers proud. No one uninvited was getting in and out of there in one piece. She picked up her bundle. Maybe she could trade its contents for some insurance.

Heading back along the road to the town proper, Daric followed it to the road bordering the elites' outdoor shopping area. Turning north, she walked half the distance of the glitzy ground before entering a plain building on her right.

She got something of a shock to see the healer had company. From what she'd learned, the man didn't have much business when the Duke was gone, except for the occasional farming accident. Her surprise increased when she realized the patient was the black-haired man Artearis had been with that morning. *What was his name? Timerus, that was it.* With the man were two other men and an attractive young woman who looked out of place with her companions.

The healer said, "That's the best I can do. He needs a proper priest healer."

The old man frowned even as he nodded. The larger one picked up Timerus and waited. Touching the sleeve of her traveler's garb, the healer asked Daric what he could do for her. Half listening to him and half to the three men, she said in a distracted tone, "How many healing potions can I get for this?" She pushed the bundle of meat at him as she strained to hear the men talk.

She could tell just talking hurt Timerus, but even though the old one tried to keep him quiet, he grabbed the elder's arm and croaked, "They took the boy. They took Alandran. Ronin, find the Gaujo."

Daric couldn't help her swift intake of breath. She turned to ask who the Gaujo was when the healer took hold of her arm, drawing her attention back to him. He spoke to her in a soft voice. "People don't come to me with a request like yours unless they are used to danger. Help them. Help them find my lord's son for these." The healer quickly but carefully loaded a small bag with six bottles from a shelf and shoved it at her.

Watching the exchange between the healer and Daric, Ronin gave her a going over that nearly unnerved her. Ronin said to the old man, "He's the one who came the morning after the raid. Maybe he knows."

Surprise from the healer's request vied with puzzlement from the big man's words. "I don't know a Gau ...."

For an old man, Corsanth's voice was strong and steady when he said, "Artearis Berain. Where can we find Artearis Berain?"

The healer drew in his breath, as Daric edged herself toward the door. Ronin, shifting his burden in his arms, said, "We need him to find the boy."

Daric wasn't sure if she could trust these people. She took another step backward.

Irritated and angry voices from the road outside helped her make up her mind. "Which one's the bloody healer? Korvin said don't come back without him and his potions."

Fear of losing her newly acquired stash overcame her uncertainty too late for any of them to make it out unnoticed, but the healer had been Morden's personal healer in combat. He'd learned long ago how to think on his feet. He took her arm and shoved her through the door to his personal quarters and waved the others after.

"Go through to the back," he whispered. "Take the stairs up. Head toward the front. When you hear the front door close, exit the window to the upper landing outside and take the stairs at the end of the shops."

Corsanth guided Rhealle through the door. Ronin followed carrying Timerus. Daric lead the way. When they reached the window, Rhealle came forward and placed her hand upon the sill. Only when she nodded did Corsanth raise the sash for them to leave. Daric threw a questioning look at Ronin.

He mouthed, "She's deaf." When it was clear Daric didn't understand, he moved closer to her and said, "She gauges vibrations for location." It was enough of an answer for Daric at the moment. The four made their way to the fancy market square before stopping.

Ronin said, "Corsanth, I can't carry him all the way to the vardo. Not alone."

Realizing the inn where she and Artearis were staying was much closer, Daric offered her assistance. "Give me an arm," she said in a quiet voice. "I know a place close by." The two carried Timerus between them as Daric directed the group to the Winds of Fortune Inn.

# Chapter Thirty-Nine
## Making Plans

The recent turn of events confirmed that Jekan Geylas was one of the luckiest bastards Korvin had ever met. Maybe he really was destined to be the power behind the human throne. For all that it mattered. Destroying Berain and removing the obstacle to Geylas's fondest desire was going to secure Korvin's worth to the Duke of Sitar, so he laid his plans carefully.

Frisk locked the boy and the healer upstairs in the only room without a landing, ledge, or trellis to facilitate an escape out the window, and to make doubly sure, his second-in-command removed anything that could be used to construct a rope.

While Frisk was busy upstairs, Korvin dispatched

Tebbin to the gates with orders to seal the northern gate and bar entry at the western to those not part of the crew. He set Yorn the task of determining the status of their supplies. Any possible shortage was to be replenished before sundown, and only crew were allowed to bring thoroughly searched supplies inside. Any man not assigned a task, he ordered to sleep. And Korvin meant SLEEP. Anyone caught engaging in unassigned activity would be permanently removed from duty. He even parted with a small amount of a healing potion to mend the leg of the moron stupid enough to get stabbed by a boy of ten summers.

Once the room cleared except for Frisk, Korvin passed along his last set of instructions. "Berain shows his face tonight, I want those seven you hauled back today to dispose of our barbaric hires ... if they're still alive. If Fortune's wind continues to blow our way, they'll solve our problem for us, or Berain will relieve me of the problem. Knowing his reputation, I'm not putting money down."

"Even if they take the three down, most of those clods won't make it," Frisk said.

Korvin kept his laughter low. "I'm deploying what's left of the crew from Banton's Folly down here. They should prove useful fodder to wear Berain down."

"What about Tebbin?" Frisk scowled, "or Yorn?"

"Tebbin's preparing a surprise at the kitchen door."

"One man?"

Korvin grinned. "Berain likes hacking up women. Let's give him one to play with."

Frisk's disappointment showed clearly. "What about the other one?"

"She's going to be ... um ... tending to the stairs. As for Yorn, he can continue to play host to his recruits. I'm going to hate losing his connections."

Frisk laughed then cursed. "We could sure use Donnie tonight."

Korvin's face tightened at being reminded of his decision to split the team.

"And me?"

"You and me are gonna take the high ground."

Frisk started to speak.

"And, Frisk." Korvin's second snapped his mouth shut. "If I go down, slit the boy's throat then and there. Afterward, you can make it look like the assassin did it."

Yorn might not be a fighter, but he'd had plenty of practice at keeping himself unnoticed. When Tebbin talked him into taking up with this crew, he warned Yorn that Korvin didn't like loose ends that could tell tales. Yorn only just realized that applied to his own crew. Yorn backed through the side door he'd entered, weaving his way around the manor to enter the main room through the other side. He gave his report. Korvin seemed pleased to hear their supplies would last into tomorrow. Yorn excused himself.

His strangers kept themselves apart from the rest of the men, making camp in the ruined garden. They took shifts during the day to sleep. Occasionally, like this afternoon, they wandered around town. When Yorn found them, they were sitting on a patch of faded grass deep in discussion. He hesitated to interrupt.

"Speak, young one," Kiel told him.

Yorn searched his mind for a diplomatic way to tell these people that Korvin planned to betray them. His hesitant manner was enough for Kiel to read the truth.

Kiel laid a friendly hand on his shoulder. "When?"

"When the assassin attacks," Yorn squeezed from his tight throat.

"The man who stole away?" Glor asked.

Yorn was confused.

Kiel saw the confusion and added, "Your mad one attacked without honor. After, he yelled words."

"Assassin," Glor said.

"Bloody assassin," Jezra said.

"The mad one showed he was not to be trusted."

Jezra ran her hand along the new scar visible along her side. "As your lead man cannot be trusted." Turning to Kiel, she said, "I should have killed him."

Glor nodded, but Kiel shook his head. "No, that is dishonor, cousin. Better him."

Glor snorted.

Yorn silently agreed with Glor. Killing Korvin would be doing the world a great service. "What will you do? Korvin has locked the place down. When he kills the assassin, he'll kill the boy." Yorn muttered, "He'll kill the boy regardless."

While Kiel sat thinking, Glor and Jezra wrangled back and forth in that strange language of theirs. Yorn took a seat at the edge of their circle and waited.

Kiel shook himself out of his thoughts. "Glor speaks true. Moving at night is best." Glor looked pleased until Kiel spoke again. "We have no guide."

Jezra hissed, "The boy must not die. It brings more dishonor than killing HIM."

Both men nodded solemnly.

Kiel decided. "We will take him. When their eyes are most heavy."

"What about the assassin?" Yorn asked.

"Will he kill the boy?" Kiel asked.

Yorn shrugged, "It's what he's contracted to do, but Korvin means to betray him. Assassins don't take betrayal well."

Kiel nodded. "He appears ... we will see."

Glor didn't look happy.

"Before the sun touches our feathers, we will be away,

Glor."

Jezra stared hard at Yorn. "What of you? You promised a guide as payment."

A pleased smile appeared on Kiel's face.

Yorn sighed. What did he have to lose now? "I'll be your guide."

"You're already missing half, so the rest won't bother ya much." Frisk had told Lonnie as he slammed his boot down.

Everything after that was a blur until his latest guest arrived.

With the help of Artearis, Lonnie sat up and took stock of his injuries. For the most part, he suffered from cuts and bruises — the exception being his left leg and the fingers of his half hand.

"Where are my girls?"

Artearis couldn't help him. "Where's your healing supplies?"

Lonnie directed him to the kitchen and the shelf by the cellar door. Before Artearis had a chance to retrieve the kit, the sound of footsteps at the entrance attracted their attention. Again, Artearis cursed the need to keep his blades hidden.

Lonnie whispered, "Why'd they come back?"

Artearis made ready to hurl himself at the first one to enter with the intent of knocking the intruder back into the others, giving him time to secure the entrance, so they would have to come at him one at a time instead of having the entire room to surround both of them.

Both men relaxed when they saw Daric assisting Timerus through the door with Ronin right behind. Daric directed Ronin up the stairs to her room. Corsanth and Rhealle followed.

Thirty minutes later, Daric and Ronin descended the stairs to find Artearis busy splinting Lonnie's damaged leg. Daric drew the small bag the healer had given her over her head and fished out a bottle that she handed to Lonnie. In a quiet but hard tone she said, "This town really needs a priest healer."

Lonnie gave her a half smile. "Hadn't been a concern until now." He downed the potion nearly choking at the sight of Daric's reproving look.

Seeing the effect that the bottle had on Lonnie, Artearis regarded Daric sharply.

Daric turned from his appraisal. "I thought they might come in handy."

Corsanth shuffled down the stairs. For the first time since Artearis had met the elder Folk, he looked his age. "Timerus says they took the boy east."

Artearis tensed.

Corsanth asked no one in particular, "What's east along the main road?"

Artearis, Daric, and Lonnie said, "The Duke's manor."

Artearis swore louder than he meant to.

As if reading his mind, Daric said, "Geylas. He didn't trust you to get the job done?"

His answer was the curling of his hands into fists so tight his knuckles turned white.

"What has the Duke of Sitar to do with this?" Lonnie demanded.

Artearis forced his words through clenched teeth. "He wants Lathan Morden's son removed from the line of succession."

Corsanth's tone was neutral when he added, "So he hired the Assassins Guild."

"Not just the Assassins Guild," Artearis ground out. "Me, personally. If I fail, he has his excuse to move against the Guild. If I succeed, ...."

"The Kings will do it for him," Corsanth said.

"Those men are his way of ensuring the boy dies." Artearis slammed his fist into the floor. "I should have put it together when that spectator sent a knife at my back. Morden wouldn't need to be underhanded."

"Men like that ...." Lonnie groaned. "My girls!"

Ronin finally spoke. "The boy is my responsibility. I

go tonight to get him."

Lonnie struggled to his feet. "I'm going with you to get my girls."

Artearis cursed even more loudly. "Geylas only hires the best. At minimum, you'll be facing nine adversaries. Most likely more. They'll tear you two apart. This is best left to professionals."

Lonnie refused to listen. "I've seen my share of action. I'm going!"

"The wounded don't participate in an opening offensive," Daric reminded Lonnie. "You would best serve by providing intel."

Artearis's eyes narrowed at her words.

Daric went to the fireplace and rummaged through the ashes for a couple of charred pieces thick enough to use for drawing. Bringing them back and handing Lonnie one, she sketched on the floor the description of the manor as told to her by her informants. When she was done, Lonnie wiped away several lines before adding his own details to the sketch. By the time he was done, all of them realized the tactical disadvantage facing them.

# Chapter Forty
## Ten Minutes to Midnight

Artearis grunted with satisfaction. In the predictable mindset of most mercs, Korvin blockaded one of the gates but then left it unguarded except for the roving patrol. Daric kept watch. He waited for her to give him the all clear signal. When it came, he threw the grapple over the wall. This time, he'd wrapped the end in cloth to deaden the sound of it hitting the stone archway. Tugging on the rope until the hooks caught, he pulled himself up the closed north gate to lie flat on the arch. Ronin boosted Lonnie up high enough so that Artearis could grab his good hand. Artearis eased Lonnie down onto the barrels stacked on top of the wagon used for the blockade.

When Lonnie made it to the stables just to the east of

the gate, Artearis motioned for Ronin to climb. The huge man looked skeptical, but before he could utter another protest, Daric reappeared and made a cradle of her interlaced fingers to give him a boost. An unhappy Ronin used the momentum to pull himself up the rope far enough for Artearis to give him a hand. As Artearis prepared to lower him down, Ronin waved him off, pointing to the shadowy figure slowly approaching from the west. Artearis shook his head and pointed down. Ronin swallowed his sigh and climbed down.

Daric sidled up alongside Artearis, dislodging the grapple and quickly winding the rope before sliding down onto the wagon with Artearis landing beside her. She let out a soft curse when the shield strapped to her back lightly thumped into a barrel. The footsteps stopped. Both shifted their positions to meld more fully into the shadows cast by the side of the wagon. Neither moved until the footsteps had resumed and finally faded. The two darted toward the stables.

Lonnie pointed almost directly across from their position. He kept his voice low as he said, "Kitchen entrance is almost straight in front of us. Main entrance is midway along the west wall." The hand he'd used to point out the kitchen shifted farther to the right. Artearis tensed at the sight of the open ground. Lonnie understood.

"Best we scoot around the stables and follow the

garden wall to the storage building. On the other side, we keep going until we get to the manor proper. Daric and I can head along the east wall and around the corner to the kitchen. You and Ronin can slip between the south wall and the manor to the private practice grounds and come at the main entrance from the west. Unless we're very unlucky, the rooms 'll be empty back there. You'll just have to get around the window in the front."

Artearis nodded. "Guards?"

"The Duke kept a two-man roving patrol. Now?" Lonnie shrugged.

Daric whispered, "You and Ronin go first. We'll give you a good lead before we start. The midnight flash?"

In answer, Artearis disappeared into the darkness of the stable wall. Ronin adjusted his hammer, so it wouldn't hit the wall and followed."

Lonnie stifled a curse. "What's the signal?"

Daric patted his arm. "You'll figure it out." She counted out the measure under her breath; tugging on Lonnie's arm, she trailed after the others. It surprised her how quickly they covered the ground to the kitchen entrance. She settled down to wait, trusting that Lonnie would be patient.

The flash of midnight came and went. Daric pondered whether they should attempt a breach anyway when the sound of Ronin's hammer smashing into the main door brought a quiet but sharp "about time" from Lonnie.

Daric rested her hand on Lonnie's arm. "Are you sure this entrance won't be well lit?"

"Not normally. Couldn't say for sure anymore."

"Yeah, I know. Just keep me in shadow the best that you can."

Lonnie patted her arm in acknowledgment and stepped through the kitchen door. Daric pinned herself to his bulky frame and nearly sent them both flying forward when he stopped suddenly several paces inside. She peered under his shield arm, taking in as much of the room's details as she could from her position.

Not eight paces ahead of Lonnie a woman sat bound to a chair. Behind the chair, strips of cloth ran across the stone floor to a flat pot. More strips went from the pot to where a man knelt on the ground next to a lighted candle. Looking more closely at the strips leading from the chair, she realized they were part of the woman's dress — ripped from the hem in a spiral fashion that left one end still attached. She sniffed at the air. Kerosene wafted from the direction of the woman.

Before Daric could gauge her best course of action, Tebbin spoke. "Bah! I expected a fighter, and what do I get? A broken papa." His eyes caressed the woman in the chair. "You make a better stud than a fighter." He let out an exaggerated sigh. "It would be a shame to destroy such fine offspring. Toss down that sword and shield, and I'll consider snuffing out the flame."

In a quick, light motion, Daric pulled back on Lonnie's elbow. Loosening the axe strapped to her leg, she gripped it tightly in both hands.

When Lonnie did nothing, Tebbin became impatient. "Fine. Papa wants his daughter to light up the room."

Daric didn't wait for him to grab the candle. She stepped to the side of Lonnie and did a dive and roll the way Marte had taught her, coming up next to the pot. She brought her axe down, severing the cloth strips and pushing them away in the same stroke before she smashed the flat of it into the container on the return swing, sweeping the contents toward her target.

Enough of the liquid splashed onto the candle to ignite it. Tebbin shrieked and began rolling around to put out the places where the kerosene splashed onto his clothing. Daric smashed the flat of her axe into the side of his head before grabbing the bucket of ash by the fireplace to smother the remaining flames.

To Lonnie, she said, "Find some rope to tie him up then get her some place safe."

"What about you?"

Daric headed down the hallway beside the door.

Everything played out exactly as Lonnie said until Artearis and Ronin reached the corner of the manor bordering the practice area. At first Artearis's attention rested on the dark figure patrolling the top of the west wall.

As Kiel headed on his northward sweep, Artearis rounded the corner into the unkempt area without registering another shadowy figure hunched on a bench beside the wall until it was too late to withdraw. He motioned for Ronin to wait. Dropping quietly to the ground, Artearis crawled until he was close enough to attack, dagger ready to slit the man's throat. Only Ronin's deep voice saying stop stilled his hand.

Artearis pulled the surprised Yorn to his feet, the dagger resting lightly against Yorn's sternum. Artearis rotated Yorn to see why Ronin had asked him to stop. He didn't understand until Ronin moved closer, revealing a large lump on his back that didn't resemble his hammer.

A female voice startled Artearis. "I warned you, Yorn. No place belonging to HIM is safe."

Artearis still couldn't perceive how this woman was a threat. Why didn't Ronin toss her off?

Ronin stepped closer to the bench, away from the shadows. A cloaked figure clung to his back — an arm firmly clamped to his chest. The other arm, bent at the elbow, rested on his shoulder. The boots weren't wrapped around Ronin's waist as Artearis expected but were hooked into the belt he wore.

Her voice was low and hard. "We take offense at you damaging our guide."

Her words sounded off, as if they were unfamiliar and in an accent unlike any with which he was familiar.

"Free our guide or lose your ...." She struggled as if searching for the right word.

"Companion," Yorn finished for her. "His companion, Jezra."

Even Ronin's normally stoic expression showed surprise.

Artearis contemplated whether he could eliminate his captive and deal with this new threat before she could harm Ronin. Jezra must have read his thoughts for she tapped a white blade against the back of Ronin's neck. Then another thought struck him. The woman, Jezra, hadn't sounded an alarm.

"This one perceives much given time," she said as if to herself not Yorn.

Yorn spread his hands out in a sign of parlay. "Jezra expects to be betrayed."

"Kiel should have let me kill the one without honor," she muttered angrily.

Artearis used his unoccupied hand to search for any

weapons his captive possessed. The lack of them surprised him. Artearis drew his sword and lowered his dagger. The name Yorn was familiar. Where had he heard it? The innkeeper in Banton's Folly had spoken well of a Yorn. Artearis allowed the man to retake his seat on the bench.

Yorn stared at the weapons of his captor. After careful consideration, he said, "Korvin will kill the boy once he knows you've come."

Jezra spat out words Artearis didn't understand.

Yorn must have had a sense of their meaning. "Will you save him, Assassin?"

The request stunned Artearis. *Why would members of Korvin's crew want Alandran saved?*

When Artearis didn't respond, Yorn frowned. "He's a boy, not a pawn."

"Not a king, you mean," Artearis growled.

Yorn sighed in frustration. "The boy is upstairs. Second from the left. But know that even if Korvin falls, Frisk will cut his throat. Frisk has always been loyal to Korvin."

The sky overhead flashed midnight. Artearis cursed loud enough for Ronin to hear the frustration in his voice. They were out of position. What plan they had was coming apart fast. He calculated if he could tackle Ronin hard enough to dislodge Jezra. Her eyes dared him to try.

The loud *thwump* of wood slamming against stone broke the deadlock. Jezra spat out something in her strange language and slid off Ronin's back to rush toward the western gate. The other three ran to the open area in front of the manor. Men poured from the top of the guard quarters wedged against the intersection of the north and west outer wall.

The first to clear the opening tried to tackle Glor, the sentry who almost discovered the group as they infiltrated the manor. A second jumped onto Glor's back. A third barreled into him nearly knocking him off his feet. Jezra fairly flew up the stairs ascending to the walkway above but not before Kiel passed her on his way to join the fray.

Artearis didn't have time to debate his next move. Ronin, now free of Jezra, rushed to the main entrance, barely remembering to crouch under the window between them and the door. Artearis was scarcely three steps behind. When Ronin stopped long enough to yank his huge hammer from his back and slam it into the door so hard the wood splintered on the first blow, Artearis found he had a shadow of his own. Yorn had followed them not Jezra.

As Ronin took another swing, Yorn leaned close to Artearis. "Korvin is using some innkeeper's daughters as leverage." That was all Yorn had time for before Ronin broke down the door and charged inside.

Jezra let out a piercing screech; Kiel a sharp whistle. From out of the sky a falcon dove toward her. Not finding his accustomed perch, he landed on the back of the closest attacker and dug his beak into the spot below where the neck and skull met.

The attacker dropped his club and tried to dislodge the bird, but he was so intent on getting rid of it, he didn't pay attention to how close his feet were from the outer edge of the wall. With his arms flailing wildly at his avian attacker, he lost his balance and went over the side, breaking his neck when his head struck the stone at an unnatural angle.

Kiel thrust his staff between the legs of the thug in front of him. Swiveling the shaft abruptly to the right, he toppled his opponent to the walkway. He raised the staff and brought it down hard, smashing in the skull beneath. Kiel kicked the body over the wall.

Jezra, seeing the knife arcing through the air as the greatest threat to Glor, ignored the other two attackers to block the knife thrust aimed at Glor's abdomen with her own knife. Her right hand moved up and across his attacker's body.

In one smooth motion, she set the blade to his neck and pulled it across his throat. She kicked the body away in order to reach the attacker clinging to Glor's back who was trying to choke him with the handle of a club.

Using the hunched form of the one stupid enough to

attempt to trip Glor by grabbing the sentry's powerful leg, Jezra launched herself onto her target's back. This time she didn't hesitate to slice through skin, muscle, and vertebrae, severing his spinal cord. She glided to the ground as her opponent collapsed to the stone.

Kiel leveled his staff and thrust at the man trying to beat off Kiel's hawk with a heavy stick. The blow caught the thug squarely in his midsection. Behind Kiel, Glor turned and smashed his own staff down, cracking the thug's skull but leaving himself open to the knife of their last assailant, patiently waiting for the right opening to strike, before Jezra could counter it. The anger that drove her killing blow nearly decapitated the man and snapped the blade from its handle.

Seeing no more attackers, in their tongue, Jezra told Kiel to take Glor to Kaylei's haven. She'd tend to him when she was done. The falcon, seeing the armband available, landed. Jezra stroked his feathers for a moment before uttering a softer screech and sending her arm upward, giving the bird some lift so he could soar away. Frustrated with taking the stairs two at a time, she leaped off the side, propelling herself toward the manor entrance.

The four men waiting in the foyer were expecting one assassin, not an assassin and a very angry blacksmith.

Ronin's first swing sent Larosh skittering across the floor to stop just shy of the entrance to the dining hall. The mighty blow gave Tully and Wagoner time to come at Ronin with clubs raised.

Artearis intercepted the last recruit before he could stick Ronin with his knives.

Ronin did his best to counter the clubs raining blows down on him, but his anger put him at a grave disadvantage.

Korvin's muffled voice coming from a room past the top of the stairs warned Artearis they didn't have time to recover from Ronin's rash entrance. He pushed the knife wielder to make a mistake, but the man was actually better than he expected, and Artearis was running out of time.

From the corner of his eye, Artearis saw his blood guard barrel into one of Ronin's attackers, sending Tully to the floor. Without hesitation she upended her axe and brought it down, severing the arm holding the club. Grabbing the shield off her back, Daric slid in beside him, catching a knife with it.

"I've got this," she told him.

Artearis jumped back. It took seconds to get a sense of his surroundings. His primary target now stood at the top of the stairs half undressed but holding a short sword. Between him and Artearis a girl had been tied to the railing of the staircase, presumably as a barrier.

Korvin should have gathered more intel on assassin

training. Artearis launched himself at the railing, vaulting up and over it and the girl to land on the other side. He raced up the stairs.

A flash of white sailed past his head.

Ahead of him, he watched Korvin yell, "Frisk, do ...." Whatever else Korvin meant to say was cut off by a knife lodged in his throat.

Artearis didn't stop to figure out what happened. He cut left the moment he reached the top.

# Chapter Forty-One
## Vendetta

The door to Alandran's room slamming shut made him jump. The rage of the man that took him scared the boy as much as the ranting.

Frisk rammed the piece of wood he'd brought with him into the crack between the lock and the jamb. He motioned to the four town guards.

The bully, Brody, leaned casually against Alandran's writing desk.

Marlen, not caring that his cleated boots poked holes in the bed cover Alandran's mother spent weeks embroidering, pushed his foot against the bed frame while setting his back to the bed post.

The third town guard, Hanish, hugged the wall just

out of reach of the door's arc.

Will looked uncomfortable as he ran his shaking fingers along the woven wall version of the tree stitched on the covering.

Of the seven people in the room, only Frisk moved restlessly about.

Alandran counted. It took the man ten strides to cross from one end to the other. As he approached the window this time, his foot caught on the brown and green rush rug Papa had brought back from Zenet.

Papa's healer sat quietly in Alandran's guest chair by the window. Alandran liked the healer; he always had a smile for the boy and occasionally slipped Alandran sweet treats imported from Psarkoth. The healer wasn't smiling now. Every time Frisk came close, he pulled away as far as the ropes binding his arms to the chair would let him.

Frisk was on his fourth circuit after slamming the door when a thud made it quiver. The second thud made it shake. Fracture lines appeared in the wood. Frisk stopped next to the window. At the third blow, he pulled his short sword. The healer yanked hard against his ropes, scooting the chair into the wall. Frisk turned.

The grim smile that appeared scared Alandran. He shrank into the corner made by the chair meeting the wall, putting his back to the healer. Facing the door didn't stop the boy from hearing the anguished sigh behind him.

The door to his room flew against the wall. As the Gaujo and Daric burst inside, Frisk grabbed Alandran by the back of the neck and forced the boy in front of him. Setting the blade against the boy's throat, he shouted, "Now!"

The four guards surrounded Alandran's rescuers. Back to back the two waited.

Alandran squirmed in Frisk's grasp as Marlen and Hanish converged on Artearis. A thin stream of blood ran down the boy's chest, but he was too preoccupied with Marlen swinging his sword up and around to pay it any mind.

As Marlen's swing reached its arc, Hanish thrust his short sword at Artearis's side. Alandran wanted to applaud when Artearis blocked Marlen's swing with his dagger; at the same time, he brought his sword down, sticking the point into the floor.

The loud clash of steel made the boy's hands start shaking. They didn't stop even when Artearis sent his left foot crashing into Hanish's knee. The hand holding Alandran's neck tightened.

Artearis darted toward Marlen, leaving Daric's back exposed. Alandran silently cheered as Artearis forced Marlen's sword away, unbalancing the guard enough to thrust his dagger through Marlen's defenses, slicing the jugular open. The sight of blood gushing out nearly made the boy start wretching.

Before Hanish could recover from the blow to his knee, Artearis drove his sword through the guard's chest.

Daric didn't flinch as Brody and Will came at her in a coordinated attack. With hesitant strokes, Will brandished his short sword at the stoic fighter.

Alandran bit down hard on his lip. Poor Will was a fair swordsman, but no real troublemaker. He'd shown the boy how to hold a sword properly and how to slash at a practice dummy, but Brody was the fighter.

Daric leveraged her axe to fend off Brody so she could put her weight into the shield slam she used on Will.

Alandran heard a crack. The lanky guard flew into the dresser.

Brody saw his chance. He went in for the kill.

Alandran screamed, "Look ...." The hand holding the boy's collar let it go to be replaced by an arm pressed tightly against his throat. Alandran scratched at the arm as Daric slammed her shield into Brody's ribs. She turned to finish Will.

In desperation, Alandran kicked his foot back, hoping to damage the leg behind him as Artearis had done to Hanish. The best he could do was cause Frisk to grunt loud enough to attract his rescuers' attention.

Will's face drained of color, seeing Alandran being

strangled by the man who'd hired him to kill the person contracted to murder the boy.

Artearis kicked off of the dying man, sending Marlen crashing to the floor while he used the momentum of the kick to spin himself around.

Frisk slid his arm down to Alandran's chest, pulling the boy against him and waving his sword at Artearis and Daric.

Artearis didn't hesitate. He leaped over Brody's body, bringing his sword between Frisk's and the boy.

Releasing the boy, Frisk squared off against Artearis.

Alandran cried out at the impact of hitting the window sill.

"Get the boy out," Artearis barked.

Daric quickly scanned Will. Even though blood ran down the man's nose, he was too preoccupied with the struggle between Frisk and Artearis to be anything but concerned about the boy.

Daric grabbed Alandran's arm, pulling him away from the two men furiously slashing at each other.

Frisk executed a flurry of sword and knife strikes, forcing Artearis backward.

Artearis miscalculated his step, coming down hard on his right leg.

Gasping at the blood that seeped into the Gaujo's pant

leg, Alandran jerked hard to free himself.

Daric yanked him closer and wrapped her arms around him, lifting him off the ground. "Stay out of it, boy."

Alandran couldn't believe how calm Daric's voice was. Tears rolled down his cheeks. "We've got to help him," he sobbed.

Daric shook her head. "Have faith, boy."

Alandran struggled to get away.


"Damn you to an eternity of walking Silarus as a shade, Artearis Berain!" Frisk said defiantly as the wound in his abdomen poured out black blood.

At Frisk's words, Alandran went still.

After Frisk finally stopped moving, Daric let Alandran go, only to have to catch him as he let his legs collapse.


"Is the Gaujo going to kill me now?" he asked her.

"No, boy. He came a long way to save you."

Alandran raced to Artearis. "Do something, Daric!"

She yanked open dresser drawers until she found something suitable for ripping into strips. Snatching Artearis's dagger, she cut off his pant leg. The wound was deep, barely missing the femoral artery. It needed stitches, but Daric didn't want to chance him bleeding out while she hunted for the first aid supplies.

"Come here, boy. Push this together as hard as you

can." Daric bound the strips tightly around Artearis's leg. By the time she was done, both of their hands were covered in his blood.

"Here." Will tossed each a pillow case from the drawer.

Daric deftly caught one. While she wiped her hands, she told Alandran, "Stay with him until I get back." Then she was gone.

# Chapter Forty-Two
## Loose Ends

As soon as Larosh discovered the capabilities of the men sent against Korvin, he retreated into the dining hall and through it to the sleeping area assigned to the recruits. Valna remained hidden in the corner as instructed, only leaving it when he called. Larosh had to admit Valna was one of his better pets.

He motioned for her to enter the kitchen. Fear shone in her eyes. He didn't care. If any more assailants occupied the back entrance, they would think her a victim and help her or an enemy and slay her. Either way, he'd know it wasn't safe.

Larosh waited long enough to feel certain Valna was alone before stepping into the kitchen himself. Besides his pet, the only body in sight was Tebbin's lifeless corpse staring at the ceiling. Larosh caught up Valna's arm and led her out the door. They hugged the outer wall as he propelled her ahead of him past the storage building and along the garden wall to the stables. There they waited until he could determine the outcome of the struggle.

Even without Daric, Ronin dispatched the last two adversaries, taking only minor cuts and bruises. He pulled out a knife and cut the ropes that bound Breesa to the stairs. The anger that drove him to smash in the front door rekindled when the girl begged him not to hurt her anymore. The blacksmith pulled Breesa to her feet and gave her a push toward the hall where Lonnie waited with Darna.

The innkeeper winced as he pulled his younger daughter into a bear hug. "Everything's gonna be fine, sweetling."

Daric didn't waste time on pleasantries. Someone needed to do a sweep of the manor and grounds. In no time she thoroughly searched the rooms in the master wing and came up empty. As she worked her way along the left corridor, the first yielded nothing. Skipping the second room, she finished her sweep of the upstairs. The other two suites had been ransacked, and the shredded female garments littering the floor of the last bedroom clearly indicated that someone used it for extracurricular pursuits. The corpse confirmed the kind the pursuits.

Back on the ground floor, she gave the dining hall a quick sweep, as well as the room next to it. Some shabby gear, a bunch of makeshift beds, and bits of food scraps were all she turned up, but the room stank of something Daric didn't care to dwell on. Continuing her sweep in the west wing, again, she found it empty of bodies but not of information. Apparently, Korvin could actually read. Among his belongings she found several letters from Jekan Geylas demanding a status report. Daric left them.

Where were Morden's servants and the other women Korvin's men obviously "brought home"?

She exited through the second door in Korvin's room to find herself back in the kitchen. Two things disturbed her. The kitchen door was open, and Lonnie was trying to move Tebbin's dead body. He looked up at her entrance. Her face plainly demanded to know what happened.

Lonnie dropped his head. "Darna smothered him." Raising his eyes to meet hers, he said proudly, "I didn't know she had that kind of toughness in her."

"Did you open the door?"

"Huh?"

"Did you open the door, so you could drag the body outside?"

Lonnie shook his head. "I just wanted to get it out of sight, so Darna wouldn't see her handiwork again."

Daric didn't bother acknowledging him. Pulling free her axe, she strode toward the door. Outside, the cloud cover that had blessed their undertaking was gone. Enough moonlight existed so that now she could see recent dirt mounds among the weeds of what was probably a vegetable garden. Off to the right was the building she and Lonnie had skirted to get to the manor. Daric readied her axe and yanked open the door.

"What did you find?" Lonnie asked when he caught up with her. He thrust the lantern he carried toward the opening. "Where there's kerosene, there's usually lanterns," he said to her unspoken question. Inside were what was left of Lathan Morden's staff and the women Daric had wondered about. She told Lonnie to take them back to the manor and tend to them.

He refused. "Sweeps shouldn't be done alone."

She scowled at him even as she waved them off to the manor.

Only when Daric had assured herself that no one in the building was a threat did she move on to the walled in area Lonnie had referred to as the Lady's private garden when they had drawn the plans on the inn floor.

The moonlight outlined three unusually dressed people. All had long, dark hair and seemed to be wearing a cloak. One stood next to an empty fountain. Not far from it, one lay stretched out on the ground. The third knelt before the supine form. Straining her ears, Daric could just make out the sing-song voice of a woman.

As the woman raised her face to the moonlight, Lonnie said, "That's the one who came bursting through the door and hopped right up onto the stair rail. Then wham. Her knife was sticking out of Korvin's throat. She ran out as fast as she'd come in."

The two edged closer to the trio to get a better view. As they watched, a wicked cut across the man's stomach slowly closed. As Jezra continued her chant, more wounds closed and bruises began to fade.

Lonnie gasped.

The sound caught the attention of the man standing by the fountain. Kiel pulled free his staff and pivoted to stand directly between them and his companions. Daric placed her hand on Lonnie's arm when she felt him reach for his short sword. From the other side of the fountain, Yorn said, "They won't harm you, innkeeper, if you leave them in peace."

The alternating looks of fear and longing on Lonnie's face were potent enough for Kiel to take a step forward.

Daric, guessing at the misunderstanding about to happen and the trouble it could bring, spoke, "Men inside beat him badly and stole his daughters. He's grateful he has them back mostly unharmed, but he still carries his own injuries."

Yorn's regretful, "I know," was almost too quiet for Daric to hear. Was he, they, really part of Korvin's crew?

"What price?" Lonnie asked.

"Pardon?" From his tone, the question caught Yorn off guard.

"What price to heal me?"

From behind Daric, Ronin said, "and Timerus."

"How did you ...," she began to ask only to be interrupted by Ronin's "Artearis sent me to find you." To Yorn, he said, "The Folk have few treasures, but we would find a way to pay."

Daric wanted to say, "and Artearis."

Yorn stood up. "I'm not a broker like Dalton. I'm just a guide. You'll have to bargain with her ... when she finishes."

Facing Lonnie, Daric put her hands on his arms. "You negotiate. I have to finish my sweep."

Gripping her axe firmly, she left Lonnie and Ronin and headed for the stables. The pawing of a horse's hoof warned her of trouble before she saw it. A man wielding a mace and dagger struck out at her from the shadow of the doorway. Daric yanked the shield from her back, sending it up to counter the dagger swipe as she began rotating the axe handle to gain momentum for a blow of her own.

Lorash had hoped for a quick kill. When he saw that wasn't possible, he whistled for Valna and slammed his mace against Daric's shield hard enough to force her back several paces. In the short time it took Daric to recover her stance, Lorash slipped back into the shadows and opened the nearest stalls, spooking the horses to run toward Daric. Without bothering to see if Valna followed, he exited the smaller door near the northern gate and made a beeline for the unguarded western one, the answer to his question apparent.

The disturbance brought Ronin to where Daric tried to corral three horses. Ronin grabbed at the neck of one; using his strength, he wrapped his arm around it and pulled the horse's head to his chest. He spoke soothing words into the horse's ear to calm it, so he could lead it back to a stall.

By using her shield as a sort of movable fence, Daric managed to turn one of the horses back toward the stables. However, she was at a loss for how to get the beast back to its stall with no halter to grab onto and it still in a panic. After confining his own horse, Ronin helped her drive her beast into another empty stall.

Daric offered thanks to whatever god who made the

third horse more interested in food than running. After leaving the stable, it found its way to the vegetable garden and began to eat. Ronin managed to get a halter on it and lead it back to where it belonged. Daric tackled the last building left to search then walked the final quarter of the perimeter not explored before barring the western gate after Larosh and Valna escaped through it and returning to Artearis only to be dispatched to Lonnie's inn to bring Rhealle back.

Jezra consented to heal those wounds of Lonnie's she could only because he helped save the boy. Apparently, letting women be used by men was permissible but killing children was not. Yorn tried his best to explain that, to them, the mating ritual was sacred and complicated and not to be interfered with. They did not understand the concept of casual sex.

Ronin had a more difficult time securing help for Timerus. Only after Jezra inspected his injuries and was made to understand they resulted from trying to protect the boy from Korvin's men did she finally agree but not at the inn. He must come to Kaylei's haven.

Daric helped Artearis to the rundown garden. Jezra knew he was the reason the boy still lived. She dropped to her knees and prayed to Kaylei for the strength to heal his wounds. The goddess refused.

A puzzled Jezra tried to remain calm in the face of the expectant stares.

Glor helped her stand.

"What?" Kiel asked.

"She says it cannot be. Healing him is forbidden." Without saying more, Jezra left the garden.

# Chapter Forty-Three
## Square One

Daric took her time guiding the draft animals over the rough terrain. Taking the road from the start would have been the easier path, but none of the decisions made today had been particularly easy.

Her recon revealed Morden's replacement guards were almost here, but he wasn't, and someone had spent the morning stirring up rumors of an assassination attempt foiled only because the Duke and his son weren't there. The rumor grew as people remembered the words shouted at the show yesterday.

That had everyone looking at the Folk. Corsanth deemed it unsafe for anyone to have Artearis remain with them. Lucia and Artearis agreed it was even less safe for the boy. It was time to return Alandran to his father.

Once Daric reached the road going east, it didn't take long to find Artearis and Alandran. They decided it was better to put some distance between them and Gessin before stopping for the night. Daric let Artearis tie Zellen to the back of the wagon while she settled the boy in the wagon bed.

When Artearis climbed into the driver's seat, she tossed him the reins she'd hooked around the back board. He didn't wait for her to take a seat. He cracked the reins as Lucia had done that first night with the Folk.

Daric snatched up her pack and dropped down into the rocking seat. Rummaging inside the pack, she pulled out some clothing and wedged it under the pack so the wind wouldn't catch hold of it and leaned her pack against the back board. Then without so much as a glance at Artearis, she stripped the traveler's shirt off her back and unwound the binding cloth from her chest. Stuffing both into her pack, she pulled loose a woman's blouse from underneath and put it on. After exchanging her traveler's pants for a skirt and stowing pants and boots away, she wrapped a scarf around her shoulders and neck, shifted herself into a more comfortable position, and settled the pack below.

"What about your feet?"

"There's a pair of shoes wrapped in one of the blankets Lonnie sent with us. I had to pick them up when I bought supplies."

"What else have you got in that pack of yours, Daric?" His tone slid from casual to steel as easily as his dagger slid from sheathe to hand. "If Daric is your real name?"

She kept her voice neutral. "It is, and before you ask, my parents were merchants, and they were killed by one of their competitors, but no one could prove his involvement definitively."

"Where'd the military training come from?"

"My father wanted his sons to follow in his family's tradition. They preferred to be merchants after mother's side, so I joined for him." Daric's eyes retained that studied casualness that served assassins so well. "My father always said I was more of a son than my brothers."

"So he didn't mind his daughter going off to learn to fight."

Artearis saw Daric truly smile for the first time. "The day I received my commission was the day he gifted me with Zellen. He was that proud." The smile fell away. "It was one of the last things he did."

Artearis slowed the animals to a stop and shifted the dagger from his left to his right hand. He tilted the blade to catch the moonlight. The steel in his voice softened a fraction with the note of wistfulness that crept into it. "By rights, as a traitor to the Guild, I should slit your throat."

A slow smile spread across his face at her impassive

stance. "Tell me, Daric, what about you is really what it appears?"

"My loyalty to this land." She turned to face him squarely. "And my loyalty to you."

Artearis studied her for a long while. Loyalty, but not blind loyalty. Daric followed him why? Because she believed in him?

"You will kill me soon enough."

Artearis stared at her.

"If Lathan Morden or Jekan Geylas don't kill you, Zotearis will find a way."

Artearis wasn't following her, and by her look, she knew it.

Her next words sent a feeling of regret through him at his own deception. "When you die ... I die. Guild judgment will be carried out."

The lack of fear in her words or face intrigued and unsettled him.

"Some people are worth dying for."

It amazed him how much conviction her calm tone held.

"If you knew you wouldn't die when I did, would you be as willing to stay with me?"

Daric took the reins from him and started the wagon moving. "Not everyone would trade his life for a child's."

# THE END

Be sure to look for the next book in the series

# The Crystal Blades
# FUGITIVES

Coming Soon!

# ABOUT CHRIS

## Cipriano Christopher Oliva

Chris Oliva is a retired Army sergeant who lives in the Midwest with his family. When he is not working, he enjoys traveling and trying new foods. When at home he is usually busy making his own beer or smoking a brisket on the grill. He immersed himself very early in books and from there it only naturally turned to writing. His first stories and the original idea for the Crystal Blades came about a long time ago while stationed in Korea. He looks forward to a second retirement where he can devote even more time to writing.

# ABOUT LAURA

**Laura Ann Oliva**

At the time this book was finalized, my twitter page had "Please don't ask me if I'm this or that thing. I have no idea what I am. I only know that I will become whatever life needs me to be at the time," as the About Me description. The truth of that statement flows through my entire life. From wife and mother of three incredible sons to loving daughter and sister (yes, and sister-in-law), aunt, cook, seamstress, gardener, marketing coordinator, business owner, perpetual student, tutor, red tape adviser, computer technician, and programmer — there are more but it's already a long, tedious, and pretentious list. The twists and turns of my life have been varied and intriguing — always leaving me guessing what the next twist will be. I hoped one day the turns would come back around to writer. Now that it has, I'm ecstatic to share this new path with our readers. Welcome. Enjoy.